A
WILDERNESS
OF
MIRRORS

A WILDERNESS *of* MIRRORS

MAX FRISCH

TRANSLATED FROM THE GERMAN BY
Michael Bullock

Random House · New York

THOSE WHO WERE present, the last people to talk to him, casual acquaintances, say he was no different that evening from usual, cheerful but not over-exuberant. They dined pleasantly but not luxuriously. Everyone talked a great deal, highbrow small talk; he talked as much as anyone else, at least to begin with. Someone claims to have been struck by the weary expression on his face while he was listening; then he would join in again, to register his presence, witty, in other words no different from usual. Later the whole group went on to a bar, where at first they stood about in their overcoats and later sat down with some other people who didn't know him; perhaps that was why he was quiet. From then on he only ordered coffee. Later, when he came back from the lavatory, they say he was pale, but really they only noticed this when, without sitting down again, he asked them to excuse him, all of a sudden saying he was going home, he didn't feel too good. He made it brief, didn't shake hands, said goodbye casually in order not to interrupt their conversation. Somebody said: Hang on a bit, we shan't stay here all night. But there was no stopping him, and when the cloakroom attendant finally brought his coat he didn't put it on, but took it over his arm as if he were in a hurry. Everyone says he didn't drink much, and they weren't sure whether he really felt off-colour or whether this was an excuse; he was smiling. Perhaps he had another date. The ladies teased him flatteringly; he seemed to confirm the suspicion, but without saying another word. They had to let him go. It wasn't even midnight. When they noticed he had left his pipe on the table, it was too late to run after him. . . He must have died soon after he got into his car; the parking lights were switched on, so was the engine; the blinker was flashing and flashing, as

7

though he were going to drive out into the street at any moment.
When a policeman came to see why the car with the engine running
didn't drive off he found him sitting upright, his head thrown back,
both hands on his collar which he had torn open. It must have
been a quick death, and those who weren't there say an easy death
– I can't imagine it – the sort of death anyone would like to have. . .
I imagine:
That's how Enderlin's end might be.
Or Gantenbein's?
More likely Enderlin's.
Yes, I say too, I knew him. What does that mean! I imagined
him, and now he throws my imaginings back at me like old junk;
he doesn't need stories like clothes any more.

I'm sitting in a bar, afternoon, and hence alone with the barman, who is telling me his life story. Why, actually? He tells
the story and I listen, while I drink or smoke; I'm waiting for
someone, I'm reading a newspaper. That's how it was! he says,
as he rinses the glasses. So it was a true story. I believe you! I say.
I drink – I think: A man has been through an experience, now he
is looking for the story of his experience. . .

He was a man of my age, I followed him from the moment he
left his car, a Citroën, I think it was, slammed the door and put the
bundle of keys in his trouser pocket. He was a figure worth considering. Actually I had been planning to visit a museum, since my
professional business had been dealt with and since I knew nobody
in this town, and it was pure chance that he happened to catch my
attention, I don't know what it was, a movement of the head, as
though it itched; he lit a cigarette. I saw this just as I was about
to light a cigarette myself; I didn't do so. I followed him, still
without having seen his face, turning off to the right, throwing
away my cigarette, without hesitation and without haste. This was
the Sorbonne district, in the morning. As though he had felt something, he went back to his car to make sure he really had locked the

8

doors, looked for his key ring in the wrong pocket. Meanwhile I pretended to be reading a poster and as I did so, as though to distinguish myself from him, I lit a pipe. I was already afraid he might get into the car and drive off while I was pretending to read the poster, a TNP programme. But then I heard the car door slam, turned round and saw him walking away, so that I was able to follow him. I observed his walk, his clothes, his movements. The only striking thing was the way he paddled with his arms. He was evidently in a hurry. I followed him from block to block, in the direction of the Seine, even if it was only because I had nothing else to do in this city. He was now carrying a leather briefcase, after, as I recalled, having originally got out of the car without a briefcase. Pushed aside by people streaming towards me along the pavement, I lost sight of him and was about to give up again; but other people pushed me forward, everyone wanted to get across the street before the light turned red. Without wanting to, I went on. I know for sure that nothing is going to come of it; sooner or later everyone I set my eyes on will disappear into a doorway or suddenly beckon a taxi, and by the time I've spotted a free taxi myself it's always too late; then there's nothing I can do but tell the driver to take me back to my hotel and stretch out on the bed with my clothes and shoes on, exhausted by my senseless walks. . . It's an obsession of mine! . . . Anyhow, no sooner had I given up, actually glad not to have to continue the pursuit, than I recognized him again by the way he paddled with his arms. Although it was morning he was wearing a dark evening suit, as though he had come from the opera. Perhaps this was what linked me with the unknown man, the memory of a morning in a dark evening suit, when I came from a woman. He hadn't felt my pursuit yet, or he felt it no longer. Incidentally, he was hatless like myself. Although he was in a hurry, he didn't get along any faster than I did, even though I couldn't afford to attract attention by the same haste, but had to walk at the same speed as everyone else; for this reason he did get a little ahead of me from block to block, especially as I was ready to give up the fruitless pursuit, but at every red light we

9

landed in the same crowd. I still hadn't seen his face; just as I drew level with him once, taking advantage of a gap in the crush, he looked to the other side. Once he stopped in front of a shop window, so that I could see his face reflected, but I didn't speak to him; his face wasn't worth considering – I went into the next bar to have a belated breakfast. . . The next one I set eyes on had a skin such as only Americans have, milk with freckles, a soapy skin. I followed him nevertheless. I guess his age, from behind, as thirty-five; a fine age. I had just booked my return flight and was actually on the point of spending the remaining few hours wandering around in Central Park. Sorry, he said, because he had bumped into me, and I turned round, but only saw him from the back. He was wearing a slate-grey overcoat; I was eager to find out where he would lead me. At times he seemed not to know himself, he hesitated and seemed to have lost something in this Manhattan. The longer we walked, the more congenial I found him. I wondered what he lived on, what kind of work he did, what sort of place he lived in, what he had already experienced in his life and what he had not, what he was thinking about as he walked along among millions of other people, and how he saw himself. I saw his fair head above the slate-grey overcoat, and we had just crossed 34th Street when he suddenly stopped to light a cigarette; I noticed too late, so that I had accidentally gone past him by the time he drew the first puffs; otherwise I might have taken the opportunity of politely offering him my lighter, in order to get into conversation. When I turned round he had no hair on his head any more, and of course I told myself at once that it couldn't be the same man, I must have lost him and mixed him up with someone else in the crowd, there are plenty of slate-grey overcoats about. Nevertheless, I got a shock when he was suddenly a man of fifty. I hadn't been prepared for that. Can I help you? he asked, and since I didn't need any help he went on his way, a little trail of smoke coming over one shoulder. It was a blue day, sunny, but bitter cold in the shade, windy; the sunlit skyscrapers were reflected in shadowed walls of glass, and it was impossible to stand still in the cold of these gorges. Why shouldn't he be a man of fifty? His face was worth considering. Why not a face with a bald head? I would have liked to have seen him again from in front, but there was no more chance of that; true, he strolled along at a more moderate pace than the younger man before had done but he suddenly disappeared into the door of a building, and although I followed him – I didn't hesitate for more than a couple of seconds – I was only just in time to see him enter a lift whose bronze doors, operated by a Negro in uniform, closed slowly (as in a crematorium), inexorably; to be sure, I took the lift next to it, after also pushing my cigarette into the bucket of sand that is usual in this country, and stood wedged in like all the others who gave the number of a floor on entering and went out when their number was called out; I stood and watched the numbers lighting up one after the other till finally I was alone with the Negro; I shrugged my shoulders when he asked me where I wanted to go; the building had forty-seven floors. . .

A man has been through an experience, now he is looking for the story to go with it – you can't live with an experience that remains without a story, and I often used to imagine that someone else had exactly the story to fit my experience. . .

(It isn't the barman.)

The grey of early morning outside the open window just after six o'clock looked like a wall of rock, grey and unfissured, granite. Out of this granite there suddenly comes like a cry, but soundless, a horse's head with eyes open wide, foam on its teeth, whinnying, but without a sound, a living creature, it has tried to jump out of the granite, which it didn't succeed in doing at the first attempt and, I can see, never will succeed in doing, only the head with the flying mane has emerged from the granite, wild, a head filled with the terror of death, the body remains inside, hopeless, the white eyes, maddened, look at me, begging for mercy –

I switched the light on.

I lay awake.

11

I saw:

– unexpectedly turned rigid, a mane of red terracotta, lifeless, terracotta or wood with chalk-white teeth and shiny black nostrils, all artistically painted, soundlessly the horse's head withdraws into the rock that soundlessly closes, unfissured like the grey of early morning outside the window, grey, granite as on the St Gotthard; in the valley, far down below, a distant road, bends full of brightly-coloured cars all going to Jerusalem (I don't know how I know that!), a convoy of bright-coloured little cars, like toys.

I rang the bell.

Outside it was raining.

I lay with open eyes.

When the nurse came at last and asked me what was the matter, I demanded a bath, which, however, was not possible at this hour without the doctor's permission; instead she gave me a glass of fruit juice and told me to be sensible and go back to sleep, so that I was in good shape when the doctor examined me next day and could be allowed to leave on Saturday; then she put out the light. . .

I imagine:

When the young night nurse finally comes, a Lett (her name was Elke), she finds an empty bed; the patient has run a bath for himself. He has been sweating, and since he is going to have a bath he is standing naked in clouds of steam as he listens to her reproaches, without being able to see her yet, Elke, who is appalled and tells him he doesn't know what he's doing. Only after she has shut the window and as the grey steam, that has also misted the mirror, gradually disappears, does the patient suddenly become aware of his nakedness; he smiles. Go back to bed, she tells him, turn off the tap at once, and as he doesn't do so she tries to do it herself; but he stands naked in her way, and as he has nothing else handy with which to cover himself before the young girl, he tries to cover up with a joke: I'm Adam! She is not amused. He doesn't know why he laughs. Why does he want a bath at this time of night, she asks in a professional tone, and without the doctor's permission? Then she briskly takes a bath towel from the cupboard to put an end to this nonsense; she holds it out to him, so that he shouldn't catch cold, without a word, while he looks at her as though he is seeing Elke for the first time. A girl with water-grey or greenish eyes. He takes her by both shoulders. A girl with dun-coloured hair and big teeth. What's the idea? she says, while he, with his two hands on her two shoulders, hears himself say: I'm Adam and you're Eve! It still sounds like a joke; she daren't call out in the night-time quiet of the hospital and merely presses a bell, while with the other hand she punches the madman, suddenly filled with fear because he has carefully taken off her nurse's cap, the blue one with the red cross. He has known her face for weeks, but her hair is new, her dun-coloured hair that is now loose and springing up. He doesn't want to hurt Elke, only to say: I'm Adam and you're Eve, holding her hair so that she can't move her head. Do you hear? he asks. And she has only to smile, Eve as a night-nurse, a Baltic peasant girl who looks like a student, with green eyes and horse's teeth; only to smile in order to turn everything into a joke again. But she stares at him. He doesn't seem to know that he is naked. She is no longer punching him, he doesn't even feel it; she is only struggling to get her blue cap back, but in vain, although a doctor on night duty has meanwhile appeared in the corridor. He repeats it – naturally the doctor has absolutely no idea what is going on – like a language teacher trying to din something in by repetition: I'm Adam and you're Eve, I'm Adam and you're Eve! – while Elke, as helpless as if dealing with a drunk, shouts not at him but at the doctor and asks why he is standing there and not coming to her assistance. Yet nothing is happening to her. The doctor, both hands in the pockets of his white coat, doesn't move, grinning, not sure if he isn't the one who is behaving shockingly, a *voyeur*, even if involuntarily. What ought he to do? Only when the naked man notices that, although they are Adam and Eve, they are not alone in this corridor, and when he steps towards the doctor, does the latter's grin vanish; but even now he doesn't take his hands out of the pockets of his white coat. Who are you? asks the naked man, as though this doctor on night duty had never existed before. With his hands in the pockets of his white coat, which distinguishes him from the naked man, he does something worse than grinning: he addresses the naked man by his name. In a friendly voice. But from this moment on all is lost. Beyond recall. Elke, released from his threat, bundles up her hair. You're the devil! says the naked man until finally the doctor takes his hands out of his white coat in order to hold on to the banister as he backs away step by step. You're the devil! says the naked man, without shouting, but emphatically, as the man in white stops again and is about to say something. You're the devil, you're the devil! – while Elke, now with her silly cap on her dun-coloured hair again, tries to pacify him, but in vain. He wouldn't dream of going back to his room, the naked man. He wants to go into the lift, but it isn't on this floor, and since he can't wait long, he runs down the stairs – past the doctor – so suddenly that the doctor and Elke can only look at each other. . . Two minutes later, evidently not having been stopped by the bewildered gatekeeper, he actually goes out into the street where he hasn't been for weeks, past people under gleaming umbrellas who are just waiting for the tram and can't believe their eyes: a stark naked man crossing the street at an angle, ignoring the traffic signals and heading in the direction of the University. In the middle of the street, standing still, he adjusts his wrist-watch; a cyclist, a whistling baker's boy, has to stop because of him, skids on the wet tarmac and falls, which makes the naked man jump, so that he suddenly starts running, although no one is pursuing him. On the contrary, people step aside, stand still, only stare after him. Yet he feels pursued. By the University he has to stop for breath; bending forward, his hands resting on his pale knees, then upright again, raising and lowering and raising his arms to the side as in the gym class long ago, he pants. Fortunately it's raining. He doesn't know why it's fortunate, but he feels that it is. He knows he isn't Adam, knows where he is: in Zürich, in his right mind, but naked, so that he has to run again, holding his elbows as loosely as possible. He doesn't know why he is naked, how it happened. Once, without stopping, he makes sure he is wearing his glasses; he notices that he is naked only by the dangling of his member. On then, elbows as loose as possible. If he weren't naked, he would collapse from exhaustion. On then. To save his strength, he trots downhill, although he would rather make for the woods, but he heads towards the town. Once he ran into a diversion, a red light, a column of cars not bound for Jerusalem, and faces behind waving windscreen-wipers, while the stark naked man, with no umbrella, threads his way between gleaming sheet metal: he can't wait, one is more naked when one isn't running. On then, past the traffic policeman, who remains on his dais with outstretched arm, as though he couldn't believe his eyes. Like an animal, he finds what favours him, at one point a building site, NO ENTRY TO UNAUTHORIZED PERSONS, here he gets his breath back behind a wooden hut, but can't stand it for long without running and running. Where to? One time into a public park, where there is no one about at this early hour, especially as it's raining; he could sit down on a wet bench here, unmolested, all the benches are so empty at this time of day; molested solely by his own nakedness, which is not dreamt, oh no, which he sees as soon as he isn't running. There is no waking up as from a dream. He is naked, pale with black pubic hair and member, glasses, wrist-watch. Exhausted and panting, but for a little while happy, earth between his toes, grass between his toes, more slowly, but without coming to a stop, twitching like a man being whipped as he gasps for breath, slowly and ever more slowly, blissful as a skater, his hands on his hips like a skater gliding along relaxed, he runs over the public lawn, now left now right round the next plane tree; and he can't help laughing as he runs: I'm Adam and you're Eve! Only that doesn't mean anything any more, so he runs on and across the street again, his elbows as loose as possible, till he sees the police; they're not coming from in front, but from behind, two motor-cycles, and as he smiles they think he is giving himself up, lean their black vehicles against the nearest kerb, snap the stand down, jerk the cycles back to lift them onto the stand, before striding towards him, two men in black leather jackets and boots and helmets, clad like deep-sea divers, heavy-moving, and by the time they are sitting on their motor-cycles again, by the time they have started the engines, by the time they have turned their motor-cycles round with one foot on the kerb, he has already reached the steps up which motor-cycles can't go. It is only his body that is running now. A front door with brass, which he knows, is locked. Now he trots in the middle of the roadway again, as though to make it easier for them, until the black motor-cycles are there again by a detour, one on the left, one on the right, an escort that amuses him. Their calls to him to stop; they seem to forget that he is stark naked. . .

I remember:

The rest was told to me by somebody to whom it really happened. . . They were kind to him, he says, understanding. He sat on the stage shivering among the scenery from the previous evening. The curtain was up, but the stalls were empty, dark, with the backs of the seats gleaming in the dim daylight that came down over the balcony, the orchestra was also empty. Working light. But rehearsals hadn't started yet; only the stage hands were there. The policeman with his black boots and helmet, diffident, because he was on a stage for the first time in his life, didn't dare sit down, although there was no lack of chairs set around as though in a coronation hall, though shabby-looking when the lighting went out; he stared in amazement into the flies. When doors opened in the auditorium, it was the cleaners, he sent them out. Apart from this, he had nothing to do. He felt shy of walking up and down to make the time pass quicker. Similarly, he felt shy of a dialogue with the naked man, although there was no one in the auditorium, as I have said, not even the cleaners; he leafed through his official notebook, his back to the stalls, which obviously made him uneasy. Because he was shivering a stage hand eventually brought the naked man some costume or other that smelt of camphor, a kind of cloak, wanted to know what was going on; but the policeman, his thumbs in his belt, gestured him away without a word. The naked man

16

thanked the stage-hand, and it sounded like everyday politeness. The cloak was sky-blue with golden tassels, a king's cloak, with a cheap cotton lining. His feet were hurting, they had run through tar, tar strewn with fine gravel. Later a gentleman in civilian clothes appeared, who contrary to expectation did not ask for his particulars; he seemed to know them already. In the car – it wasn't an ambulance, but the driver wore a cap with the city badge – they talked about the weather, a breakdown due to the south wind. In the front of the car: the driver with the cap and the deep-sea diver, who had now taken his helmet on his knee, displaying an improbably small head, both of them mute. In the back of the car: the Inspector (that was how the driver had addressed him) and the man in the king's cloak with gold tassels, but barefoot. Why had he run into the opera house of all places, asked the Inspector casually, but interrupted his own question by offering cigarettes. The man in the king's cloak shook his head. They were not driving towards the canton hospital but in the direction of Balgrist, of course without the destination being mentioned; by the time they reached the Kreuzplatz, at the latest, it was clear that they were treating him as mentally deranged. When they reached Burgweis, after driving in silence since the Kreuzplatz, he enquired calmly whether his mail would be re-directed as from today; he repeated the same question when he was sitting in the ante-room, facing a young intern who was making an effort to show no surprise at the sky-blue cloak with the gold tassels. His clothes would be arriving at any moment, he was told. Once more this kindness which went so far that they avoided uttering his name. The Professor was not in the building yet. To make conversation, he said that nothing of the sort had ever happened to him before, and they believed him, in so far as the intern (once again with his hands in the pockets of his white coat) was entitled to believe anything before the Professor's arrival. He had wanted to scream, he said; yet he sat there perfectly quietly, sensibly, behaving with everyday politeness. When he washed his hands, which were smeared with tar and blood, and when he dried his hands, he saw himself in the mirror; he got a shock when he saw the costume, all he needed now was a crown. His own clothes, he was told again, would be arriving at any moment. Then he said once more that he had wanted to scream. They took note of the fact. To scream? He nodded, yes, in the emphatic manner of a dumb person who feels he has been understood. Why to scream? He didn't know.

It's like falling through a mirror, that's all you know when you wake up, like falling through all the mirrors there are, and afterwards, shortly afterwards, the world is put together again as though nothing had happened. And nothing has happened.

I'm sitting in a flat – my flat. . . It can't be a long time since someone lived here; I see a residue of burgundy in a bottle, little islands of mould on the velvet-red wine, and also remnants of bread, but as hard as a brick. In the refrigerator (I looked, although I didn't feel hungry) ham lies curling up, dried up in the cold and almost black, and there is also some cheese, fissured like the bark of a tree, greenish, and a jar of cream that no longer runs, and in a bowl a melancholy remnant of stewed fruit is still floating, apricot mud. Also a tin of goose liver. Viaticum for a mummy? I don't know why I didn't throw it into the garbage pail. . . I'm sitting in my overcoat and cap, because it's raining outside. I'm sitting on the back of an easy chair playing with a corkscrew. A corkscrew remains a corkscrew, a standard article, a domestic implement in the style of the period. I see: someone has rolled up our carpets, consecrated them with camphor and rolled them up, tying them with string, the shutters are closed against rain and sun and wind, against summer and winter; I don't open them. All the upholstered furniture is covered with white sheets. Funny to look at: as though they were playing at Ku Klux Klan. Or like a funeral in a country with alien customs. Also the ashtrays have been emptied, I see, not merely emptied, but actually washed; all the flower vases have been emptied and washed, so the place shan't stink of rotting vegetation and stagnant water. . . I'm still sitting here in overcoat and cap,

18

hands in trouser pockets. The place smells of dust and floor polish. As to the people who once lived here, it is clear that one was male and one female. I see blouses in the cupboard, some lady's underwear that wouldn't go into the case or is no longer fashionable, ties on the other side, three casual jackets for the gentleman in winter, two for the summer, and down below stand the shoes, lined up as though for roll-call, some of them with shoe-trees in them. Why are empty shoes so horrible? I pick up a lady's shoe, colourful and as light as a flower, I actually smell it. It smells of leather, no more. I hold my breath, as startled as a burglar, and listen. Who could be coming! Still, the doorbell might ring, a hawker perhaps, who can't know that no one lives here any more. I listen, a shoe in my hand; I don't want to be at home. Apart from a tap in the kitchen, which always dripped, there is silence. As at Pompeii. The telephone is silent too. I see she has pulled out the plug. Unfortunately I haven't any matches. How quiet it is, when one doesn't smoke! Outside is the tramway, interspersed with the hooting of horns, but here behind closed shutters, where I'm sitting in overcoat and cap on the back of a white-sheeted armchair, while it rains outside, here it's as at Pompeii: everything still present, only time has gone away. As at Pompeii, you can wander through rooms with your hands in your pockets and imagine how people once lived here, before the hot ashes buried them. And the place echoes (because the carpets have been rolled up) as at Pompeii –

Once the bell really does ring.

I don't open the door –

The gentleman of my name has gone away.

I sit around aimlessly in overcoat and cap, my unlit pipe in my mouth; I can't imagine how people used to live here, even less than at Pompeii, although her blue dressing-gown is still hanging in the bathroom . . . perhaps it's just as well I haven't any matches; it's enough that I should imagine it: how the man who lived here lights a match, how he holds the little flame in the hollow of his hand until it's big enough to hold to the curtain, the first, a second, a third and fourth and fifth, the curtain doesn't burn, not a trace of glow, it merely develops moth-holes, glimmers, stinks, the lampshade doesn't burn properly either, it merely singes and gets a hole with a brown rim, ridiculous, one would need petrol, petrol over the curtains so they really go up in flames, the uphol-stered armchairs, carpets, books, clothes, it can't be done with matches, it would be simply ludicrous.

I shall buy new clothes, but all the time I know it won't help; it's only in the shop-window that they look different. As soon as the salesman brings them into the changing cubicle and then tact-fully disappears so that I can try them on, I know how everything will look in three months. But you can't go about the world naked; so I force myself, turn round in front of the adjustable mirrors to check the cut, which I quite liked in the window. Really I only buy to please the salesman, who is delighted, while I see the back of my head, which can't be altered. I buy in haste and always the same thing. Even the minutes during which the tailor with the pin-cushion on his arm sits down subserviently on the stool and with a professional air marks with chalk how much I deviate from the standard measurements are agony. Whether it is cheap or dear, English or Italian or native makes no odds; the same creases always develop in the same places, I know that.

Another life – ?
I imagine:
A man has an accident, a motoring accident, for example; his face is cut, his life is not in danger, the only danger is that he might lose his sight. He knows that. He lies in hospital with bandaged eyes for a long time. He can speak. He can hear: birds in the park outside the open window, sometimes aeroplanes, then voices in the room, the silence of night, rain at first light. He can smell: stewed apples, flowers, hygiene. He can think what he likes, and he thinks. . . One morning the bandage is removed and he sees that he sees, but he keeps quiet about it; he doesn't tell anyone he can see, doesn't tell anyone ever.

I imagine:

His life henceforth, as he plays the blind man with his tongue in his cheek, his dealings with people who don't know that he can see, his social possibilities, his professional possibilities due to the fact that he never says what he sees, his life as a game, his freedom by virtue of a secret and so on.

I try on stories like clothes!

I'm sitting in a country inn.

I've been lucky, I might now not only be dead but also responsible for the death of eleven children, without having been guilty of dangerous driving – instead I'm sitting in a country inn and ordering a kirsch, while the car (it isn't even my car, but Burri's) is waiting over in the garage for new parts; I daren't picture what might have happened. . .

I've been lucky.

I don't know what I was thinking as I drove into the bend with the cold pipe in my mouth, tranquilly wakeful, not tired, but tranquil and with both hands on the wheel, attentive with my eyes but with my thoughts elsewhere, not thinking of the possibility of sudden black ice. (Perhaps I was thinking of the evening at Burri's.) I wasn't doing more than forty m.p.h., as witnesses confirm, and there hadn't been any black ice on the road till then, not a trace of black ice. (Perhaps I was thinking of my invitation to Harvard –)

Now it has stopped snowing.

I drink my kirsch.

As always when something has happened, I'm astonished that I didn't merely think it, dismayed, as though reality had guessed my hidden intentions or had misconstrued me; suddenly I'm standing in the village square surrounded by eye-witnesses, and by bending down to speak to the man from the garage, who has crawled under the car, I have already admitted that it's me, no one but me, who very nearly killed a dozen Bernese school-

21

children. I look at them, children red with winter cheeks and the banner of their breath waving in the cold air; they're alive. If it had happened, it would seem just as unreal to me; I would be the same person I am now, and not the same, surrounded now by a dozen Bernese schoolchildren, they gawp and chatter and are alive, eye-witnesses of an accident with a date and a place, glad of the excitement, gay, until their school bell rings –

I order a second kirsch.

Ten a.m., Tuesday the such and such...

They've been working for an hour already on the car that isn't mine. The schoolboys guessed right; the axle is twisted, the wheel rim bent, and the ball-bearings will probably have to be replaced too. I don't understand much about these things. The thought of having to spend the night here terrifies me; and yet it is a decent country inn. I still haven't taken off my overcoat, I sit and try to read a newspaper (I could go by train to avoid spending the night here; there's a timetable hanging on the door of the lavatory), sucking my pipe, while in Algeria (I read) people are being tortured –

That's what is going on.

When I read again what is happening in Algeria or elsewhere, and when I am able to picture it to myself for a few moments, nothing else exists, and the picture is almost unbearable. And I am prepared for any action. But I sit here, reading an old newspaper, and bear it. Without taking action . . . I'm waiting for new parts for the car that isn't mine.

It's already a memory:

(while in Algeria people are being tortured)

a cold, dry snow that scarcely lay on the road surface, a light, dusty snow, whirling up behind every moving vehicle, in the centre the road was for the most part free from snow, grey and dry, the whitish veil lay only at the sides, until the next car passed, even the suction of a slow bicycle was enough to whirl it up and gather it in a different way each time like a ruche. I almost never overtook. Even outside built-up areas I barely did more than fifty. It was a built-up area, I saw that, although I was thinking of something else as I looked through the stubborn oscillation of the windscreen wiper, my eyes saw it, and my foot moved away from the accelerator, and my presence of mind, that often borders on the miraculous, did not by any means desert me as I felt the skid first in the wheel, then in my own body. My foot didn't go to the brake, but straight back to the accelerator. As I felt the skid I saw to the left a crowd of schoolchildren, to the right the window of a country dairy with advertisements for cheese and chocolate. For a moment I hoped with complete calm that I could bring the car out of the gentle skid as I had done before; then I knew: this is it! – and I gripped my pipe firmly between my teeth, as though that was the important thing. It lasted, it seemed to me, half an eternity, while the car just spun round, irrespective of how I turned the wheel. There was something derisive about the fact that it didn't spin to the left, but suddenly to the right, like a sledge, right out into the road. I didn't know any more which was right and which was left, nothing was in the proper place any more. Fortunately there was nothing coming towards me at that moment; a lorry with a heavy trailer, that appeared in my memory so to speak, had in reality just gone past. All I saw was the village spinning round. I watched. Powerless and yet fully awake. On the left the window of the dairy, on the right the schoolchildren. Like a merry-go-round. When the crash finally came it was comical, like a delayed echo that didn't surprise me; I had known for a long time that the habitual miracle had deserted me. I had lost my pipe, that was all, and the car was now standing facing in the opposite direction, brought to a stop by a kerbstone; otherwise I should now be in the shop window. The windscreen wipers went on swaying to and fro. Suddenly very much on edge, so that I fiddled about like a learner driver, I tried to drive on, but the car wouldn't go; I was in third gear, the engine stalled, I changed into first gear, pressed the clutch down and started the engine. But even like this the car scarcely moved. It crawled. Finally I got out to have a look at it. No trace of damage to the bodywork. I was relieved; but since I now had the feeling that all the windows of the village were opening on every side, I felt embarrassed, surrounded by the schoolchildren, who were staring at me, I thought – actually they were only staring at the Porsche that had spun round so merrily before their eyes. One boy kept saying: It spun round, it spun round! Now I missed my pipe and had no gesture by which to express my tranquillity; I walked out into the middle of the road and poked about on the ground with the toe of my shoe to show the world that there was black ice. It was only now that the windows opened. I had to wait until the car was towed away, my hands in my trouser pockets, and I enquired, as though I had fallen from the sky, the name of the village.

I'm in Lengnau, in the canton of Bern.

Later in the inn, as I was drinking my kirsch, I learnt from the waitress that all sorts of things had happened on this bend in the road, including fatal accidents.

I don't know why I'm recounting all this.

My accident doesn't interest me.

Let my name be Gantenbein.

The beginning would be easy:

I walk in, it's morning, I simply walk into the shop and stand there. Can I help you? I act as though I didn't understand Swiss German. I look round: spectacles, magnifying glasses, telescopes, spectacles of all kinds, pince-nez, opera glasses, but above all spectacles. What I want has been lying in the window in the Fraumünsterstrasse (front right) for weeks. Actually the white-clad young lady who translates the question, can she help me, from Swiss German first into American, then into High German, isn't free yet, and for the time being my nod as a sign that I have patience, or at least manners, is enough. (I consider it better to embark on my rôle in High German. I always have the feeling I'm acting a part when I speak High German, and hence fewer inhibitions. My English wouldn't be up to it; it's never enough to

24

express more than general agreement. And French is even more out of the question; I feel inferior to every Frenchman, so long as he only knows his own language.) So there I stand, while the young lady serves a lady who stretches out her neck like a bird swallowing water every time a fresh pair of spectacles is put on her face, and I only hope no one will come in who knows me. The lady, an American, is disappointed every time she goes to the mirror with the next pair of glasses; it seems she can't reconcile herself to looking as the mirror shows her, and this can go on for a long time. I have time to reconsider my project, but I remain determined. When the young lady finally serves me, she does so without unfriendliness towards the American lady, by demonstrating all the time that she is only serving the native customer on the side. So I ask – why with a stammer? – for a pair of sun-glasses. Certainly! As she holds out the sun-glasses to me and at the same time chats with the American lady, I see a whole case, an arsenal of sun-glasses, which are equally out of the question. How shall I put it? The young lady in white, a simple salesgirl, but disguised as a scientist, tells me there isn't anything darker; if the glasses were darker you wouldn't see anything at all any more, and what I have seen outside, she tells me, aren't sun-glasses but glasses for the blind. I ask for them. Her surprise – meanwhile the American lady has made up her mind and has to be accompanied to the door with special politeness because she has not found anything to suit her – her surprise at my request has already evaporated when she returns to me, now the only customer; she doesn't refuse to sell me a pair of glasses for the blind in so many words, but she does so by her actions, continuing to show me sun-glasses as though I had only been joking, even pushing some of them onto my face, until I get impatient and ask outright for what I want, nothing else than a pair of black glasses for the blind. Very good, sir! I hope the boss doesn't come out now to serve this special case himself. For all I know one needs a medical certificate! Having at last been served in accordance with my wishes and informed that dark glasses for the blind are only a sham to hide the blind eyes, that's why they're so dark, I enquire

25

the price. Do the glasses sit comfortably? asks the young lady in white – now grey like ashes, lilac-grey, and she reaches for my temples, so that I suddenly see her face at close quarters, her utterly soft lips, now violet like ripe plums, and suddenly it is evening, twilight, an eclipse of the sun. And yet it's morning, I can hear that; voices only sound like this in the brightness of morning. I now see the sun as in my far-off boyhood, when we used to look at it through a sooty piece of glass: dull, much smaller than one would have thought, with no rays of light round it, yellowish to greyish-white, the colour of unripe apricots or something like that, but metallic. The glasses, I tell her, sit perfectly. She tests them again, so that I see her plum-coloured lips again. Close enough to kiss. I shall never kiss again, I think; the stuff of which lips are made is too alien. I smell her perfume and see her close hair, green-black-blue like cock's feathers, and her autumn-crocus skin. I hesitate to see myself in the mirror and take off the glasses; not a trace of dusk, it's morning, outside lies the street, the people, the brightly-coloured metal of the cars, sun, shop windows, the street in the sun, everything as usual, the Fraumünster during the eleven o'clock chimes with gulls. Fortunately another customer comes along; when the young lady in white excuses herself for a moment to serve him, I put the glasses on again. I see my hand, my flesh like marzipan that hasn't been eaten in time, crumbling and grey. In the mirror, yes, I see just in time that it isn't a door leading out, but a mirror, I see a man with my figure, without knowing whether the man in the mirror, whose eyes are not to be seen, also recognizes me. When I step closer, to see his eyes, the other man comes towards me like a blind man who doesn't step aside, as though he were going to walk through me – I have already taken the glasses from my face. Thank you, I say, and pay. . .

The first step has been taken.

What happens next?

Of course I also need a stick –

I imagine:

The first time Gantenbein goes out, not without a beating heart, he doesn't go far; the first person out of whose way Gantenbein, equipped with dark glasses and a black stick, with which he taps the kerb from time to time as blind people do, fails to step, dumbfounds him with the question, has he no eyes in his head, and Gantenbein, instead of being pleased by this first confirmation, stands speechless with anger at the boor and looks round at him. A blind man who looks round! – the first gaffe. His intention not to step out of anyone's way, irrespective of who they are, may be right; but he has gone about it too crudely. Too intentionally. At the beginning one always exaggerates. For a while Gantenbein stands where he is; he must loosen up before walking on, tapping the kerb with his stick. Naturally he has chosen a district he knows. Kreuzplatz, Zeltweg, Heimplatz, once that was the way he went to school every day, he knows it by heart. On the Hohe Promenade, alone in the avenue, he takes off his glasses: Zürich is a blue city, only my glasses make it ash-grey, so that one becomes afraid, ash-grey with a lilac tint. A feeling of saying goodbye, as he puts on the glasses again, cannot be avoided. Forward. The time of day he has chosen may be right too, the midday break, when people are in too much of a hurry to get their lunch to notice things. When later, by the Halmhaus, a gentleman nevertheless comes to his aid and leads him across the street, he feels a fraud. Gantenbein will have to get used to that. Storchengasse, Weinplatz, Rennweg, things are slowly getting better; the tapping with the stick mustn't be exaggerated either, every now and then is enough, I think. The most important thing is that whatever one sees, one should inwardly withhold all judgment. Why don't blind people look sad, but rather conciliatory? Bit by bit, I think, Gantenbein is beginning to enjoy it, until behind him – his glasses don't allow him to see red – suddenly braked tyres squeal, just behind him. Through fright, without having been touched by the car, he has lost his stick; it is lying, Gantenbein sees it at once, between the braked tyres on the tarmac, and already he has committed the second gaffe: the blind man couldn't wait, but bent down to pick up his stick himself. Has he given himself away already? There is no lack of eye-witnesses, the squeal of the braking tyres brought a lot of people to a stop, he sees them, spectres, some of them come up, blue with curiosity or reproach, while in a violet sports car (Karmann) sits a horribly discoloured blonde shaking her head, an Undine with greenish hair, she too with plum-coloured lips. Is he blind? Her fur coat is the colour of rotting seaweed. Is he blind? – He says, yes, he is, for the first time he tells the world he is blind, and looks round to see if people believe him. . . Fortunately there were no police on the spot. The spectres were arguing about who he owed his life to and were in agreement with the excited Karmann lady that he ought to be wearing a yellow armband. Gantenbein hadn't thought of that. He missed his hat, which he saw lying on the nearby tarmac, and apart from the fact that he missed his hat the incident appeared to him to be over, since neither his left calf nor her gleaming bumper showed any visible damage. Why didn't anyone give him his hat? The greenish Undine, still indignant about how lucky he had been, wouldn't drive off without everyone's agreement that she was innocence personified, including the agreement of a housewife who remained rebelliously silent. The issue was no longer Gantenbein, he could see that, but the question of how a woman like that could be driving around in a car like that. He felt sorry for her; suddenly they were all against her. Her eye-sockets looked brownish-black like last year's damp autumn leaves, brownish-black to blackish-blue. On being loudly informed by the housewife, who had taken his arm, that it was a tart who had nearly run over him, definitely a tart, Gantenbein said nothing. A blind man does not sit in judgment. Was he hurt, asked the housewife, as though the discoloured Karmann lady hadn't asked long ago. He was not only unhurt, but suddenly recovered his presence of mind: Gantenbein now asked what had happened. While they were explaining to him that he might very easily be dead, he put on his hat, after picking it up from the tarmac with his own hand in front of all the eye-witnesses. No one doubted his blindness, he could see that. The reproaches of the spectres, who couldn't go back yet to their tedious everyday lives, were now directed

28

against modern traffic as a whole. Someone had already been run over here once. There was general bitterness. Since it wasn't proper for Gantenbein to be the first to move on, he had taken his hat off again to brush off the dust of the street, while the housewife grew coarser and coarser towards the tart. Finally Gantenbein put on his hat again, clean as it now was; it was time; he didn't want to wait till the police came and asked for papers, a driving licence, perhaps also a blind person's licence; he said he owed his life to the Karmann lady and no one else. With her lilac-gloved hand on the sporty-looking gear lever, as she started up the cheap engine, she asked him gratefully where he was going. Home, he said. Where do you live? she asked. Cars were hooting again behind them, and since Gantenbein also saw a tram, which couldn't move forward because of them, he quickly made up his mind and got into her car, barked at by a dog that he really hadn't seen. A poodle with a brush cut. She let the clutch up nervously, a jerk and they were off –

And now, what were they to talk about?

Why wasn't he wearing his yellow armband, she asked, not reproachfully but maternally. To play the blind man, he replied by asking if the dog he had almost squashed was a fox terrier. That was the remark of a dilettante, a beginner. He fell completely silent. The traffic is terrible just here, she reported, to excuse her jerky driving. They were driving towards the town; he saw the lake glittering as though in moonlight, the brightness of night with black trunks and branches, the leaves on them like bronze, no one is wearing a white shirt, the familiar flags on the bridge are flapping, colourful and unfamiliar, the colours of a nation that doesn't exist, that's why they're so funny. Only the familiar silhouette with the towers remained the familiar silhouette. He was happy that no one was wearing a white shirt, relieved, delighted, everywhere he looked. Gulls are lilac. The helmets of the police are lilac too. He was enchanted. Was she pleased with the Karmann, he asked. How did a blind man know she was driving a Karmann? But even that was all right, and he was amazed. To prove he was blind, it was quite enough to miss the ashtray when he tapped the ash from his cigarette, and the only trouble was that they couldn't discuss films. Films bring people together. She too, it seemed, didn't quite know what to talk about to a blind man, and the consequent temptation to talk about intimate matters was great. Was he married? In his dismay at seeing her drive over the whitish-lilac safety line, he couldn't answer, and afterwards both the tram and the question had been left behind; he breathed a sigh of relief. Oh yes, she said, she was pleased with the Karmann. Every now and then she looked at him from the side, curious whose life she had saved. He hoped he wasn't taking her out of her way, he said; he had given her his address, a false one of course, only roughly. With her lilac-gloved hands on the wheel, waiting while another crowd of bluish spectres crossed the street, she asked him again if he hadn't anyone to look after him. Fortunately they had to move on, green light, she had to put the car in gear. He was already getting an inkling of the daily difficulties of his rôle, for example to sit next to a woman who is driving and not to say a word, not to breathe a sigh, not to impart masculine instruction, not even to wince when he sees something she misses, a lorry coming from the right, and to remain friendly when she, not noticing her mistakes, actually gets by once again, friendly, relaxed –

"Thanks," he said. "This is where I live."

"Here?" she said, and stopped, put on the hand-brake and said, "Then we're neighbours."

Gantenbein hadn't reckoned with that.

"Yes," she announced, "we're neighbours!"

They were now sitting in the stationary car, and she also switched off the engine, while Gantenbein, his presence of mind all gone, sat where he was. What now? That a blind man should be able to say from a car in motion, that is to say without tapping the kerb with his stick, that this is where he lives didn't surprise her. She obviously believed in our sixth sense, was evidently glad to have a neighbour who couldn't have seen her gentlemen going in and out, and the thought of appearing a lady to his eyes lent her wings. Would he like some coffee? He would have preferred brandy just now. Or tea? He scarcely dared refuse, he had to treat her as a lady in order to preserve his pose as a blind man, and when she asked him in all innocence what his name was, he couldn't avoid introducing himself.

"Gantenbein?" she asked. "Are you related to –"

"No," he said.

"No," she said. "What a coincidence!"

She said that several more times as she rummaged through her crocodile handbag in order to give her name too, a little card with a deckle edge which he could read very well; but she read it out to him: CAMILLA HUBER. She said nothing about what was written underneath this: manicurist. That wasn't for the blind. Nor the note: by telephone appointment only. He merely repeated what he had heard: CAMILLA HUBER. That was enough. He put the little card in his pocket, while she asked where exactly he, her neighbour, lived.

"There," he said. "In the blue house."

But she couldn't see any blue house.

"H'm," he said. "Where are we then?"

He had to go on lying now.

"Isn't this the Feldeggstrasse?" he asked.

"Of course."

It wasn't the lower end, however, but the upper end of the Feldeggstrasse, which is pretty long, so there was no question of their being neighbours; the fur-coat girl was disappointed, he saw that, and moreover worried, because his sixth sense couldn't be relied upon; she wouldn't be denied, no, under these circumstances certainly not; she started up the engine to take Gantenbein home, if he wouldn't accept her invitation to coffee she couldn't take the responsibility, she would have no peace, etc.

He accepted her invitation.

In the lift, while she is enquiring whether he often loses his way in the town, he closes his eyes, in order to prepare for his first

31

visit as a blind man, in order to stumble in a credible manner (not too much) as he steps out of the lift. Camilla is touching; she relieves him of everything the moment they're in the flat, coat and hat and stick. Camilla doesn't know either whether he needs the little black stick in the flat or not; he is the first blind visitor ever to come here. He definitely needs it, it seems to him, so that it shall remind him of his rôle.

"Sit down!"

She forgets that he can't see any chairs.

"It's nice," he says. "A nice place you've got here."

"Isn't it?" she says, not noticing his gaffe, and adds: "If you could only see my view! You see the whole lake."

Camilla is exaggerating.

"Can you see the mountains?" he asks.

After Camilla, still in her seeweedy fur coat, had surreptitiously opened a window, in order to receive him with fresh air, she enquired again whether he really hadn't hurt himself. He watches as she silently pulls a cover over the couch, silently removes two cognac glasses and a brassière, as though she doubted her guest's blindness, and all that remains, because she obviously overlooks it, is the wrinkled little heap of two stockings, which, when Camilla has her back to him, he takes the opportunity of pushing under the couch with his foot. He is standing just as on any other first visit to a strange flat: a bit embarrassed, under an obligation not to look round, and yet he has received a first impression, which he tries to conceal by immediate small talk. He chats about rents and price increases, while Camilla is now emptying the night's ashtrays, agreeing with everything he says. Then she looks round. It is now, especially as the wrinkled little heap of her stockings has disappeared, a flat that may be seen, the flat of an independent woman. Then he says something about not putting her to any trouble, but in vain; Camilla has already gone into the kitchen to put on water –

Gantenbein alone.

Later, when experience has given him more confidence, Gantenbein will venture into any society; he will stand in a country house, his dark blind man's glasses on his face, and will chat to a Swiss colonel whom he confuses with a notorious racketeer. One can't blame a blind man. He can't distinguish between a lawyer and a forger of signatures who is a cousin of the racketeer. Gantenbein will always allow people to correct him, to prove that he is blind. People will lead him to the dinner table and then tell him in the course of conversation what they wish to be seen and what they do not wish to be seen. They will picture to him a world such as we see in the newspaper, and by pretending to believe them, Gantenbein will make a career for himself. Lack of ability need not bother him; what the world needs is people like Gantenbein, who never say what they see, and his superiors will value him; the economic consequences of the value they set upon him will not fail to follow. Gantenbein will take care not to revoke or even modify his views, just because he sees things that contradict them, so as not to act contrary to his rôle. He will make a political career for himself, not an effective, but an honourable one; he will be present everywhere, supported by his little black stick, so as not to stumble, and since it has been agreed once and for all that Gantenbein can't see what takes place before his eyes, everyone will be glad to ask his opinion. Every now and then, perhaps, it may become embarrassing, for instance when he meets a gentleman who introduces himself as a monsignore and Gantenbein asks blindly who said something about dirty Jews just now; it was the monsignore himself. During this exchange they will be eating caviare. He will meet a gentleman who has just been speaking about cultural freedom and will ask if another gentleman, who played an equally leading rôle under Hitler, is also in the room, and not see that it is the same gentleman. During this exchange they will be smoking cigars, and so on. . . The visit to Camilla Huber, manicurist, is only a first rehearsal, and when she comes back with two little cups Gantenbein is still a beginner.

"What's your doggie's name?" he asks.

"Teddy."

"A splendid little chap."

33

"Isn't he?" she says and doesn't for a moment ask herself how Gantenbein could have found that out. So long as he praises, even a blind man can talk about everything. Gantenbein can't resist testing out the opposite.

"Tell me," he says a little later, "I think these Miller chairs are awful, don't you? Really awful."

She is just pouring out coffee.

"How should you know?" she says curtly, to remind him of his incompetence to judge, then in a friendly tone: "Do you take sugar?"

He nods.

"Cake?"

He hesitates.

"Engadine gâteau," she says. "I'm afraid it has already been cut," she adds frankly, "but it's still quite fresh."

Although he doesn't like cake he asks for it. His first meal as a blind man! Gâteau is simple: you simply feel around the plate with the blind fork until you've got it. (It will be more difficult with trout, which I like to dissect myself; Gantenbein will have to make a showpiece of it: a blind man who dissects his own trout and quicker than any waiter, fabulous, so that the people at the table are simply amazed and ask the blind man to dissect their trout too, delighted by the incredible.)

"Oh God," she says, "the little spoon."

She is posing as gauche.

"It's terrible," she laughs. "I'm no housewife, you know –"

So that seems to be the rôle Camilla wants to play: no housewife. Does she hope that Gantenbein will take her for an intellectual? Anyhow not a housewife; that much is certain. An artist? Gantenbein understands: anyhow a professional woman. Otherwise she wouldn't go there and back for every single spoon, still in her seaweedy fur coat, joyful, as though a new life were beginning for her. This makes her more beautiful than she is, or at least younger. She enjoys not being seen as she sits down on the couch, her legs drawn up under her thighs, after quietly, so that Gantenbein

34

shouldn't notice and misconstrue it, taking off her violet shoes and putting them on the Berber rug within reach.

"It doesn't matter at all," she said.

What doesn't matter at all?

"It's a treat for Teddy."

A piece of his gâteau must have fallen on the floor, but as it wasn't an intentional trick it carries conviction. Only Gantenbein mustn't catch on now, mustn't say thank you now as Camilla pushes another piece of yesterday's Engadine gâteau onto his plate. He sticks his fork into it as though it were the old piece, which meanwhile the dog is eating. Why doesn't he, as a blind man, have a dog? Camilla can imagine the shock it must be suddenly to feel a bumper against your calf. When Gantenbein, to get over the shock, asks for a cognac, she hunts in vain for the bottle, which Gantenbein has been seeing for quite a while. He has to help her by pushing his plate up against the bottle, as though putting it aside. Without interrupting the conversation (why should she?) Camilla goes into the kitchen to wash the two cognac glasses, while Gantenbein, as a cognac connoisseur, cannot help picking up the bottle in question to read the label. As Camilla comes silently back, still in her fur coat but without her shoes, as has been said, and hence without a sound, she finds Gantenbein not merely holding the cognac bottle in his left hand, but also holding his dark glasses in his right hand in order to read better. He couldn't have acted more obviously out of character, but Camilla merely apologizes for not having any other brand of cognac in the flat, and clearly only the shock of having finally been caught out saves him from the gesture that would have aroused Camilla's suspicions: immediately to replace his dark glasses. He doesn't do it. Because of the shock. And when he does put them on again later, after he has already drunk his cognac to get over the shock, it is entirely credible, an act of habit, involuntary, casual, inconspicuous, that doesn't interrupt the conversation for a moment. So they talk about the latest space flight and hence about the future and mankind, that is to say about things no one can see. Incidentally, her fur coat, seen without glasses, is amber-

35

yellow, her hair not of course greenish-blue, but blond, a simple peroxide blond. And her lips are not plum-coloured; Gantenbein has already got used to this and finds the real colour of her lipstick, seen without glasses, equally unnatural. Nevertheless, it was worthwhile having taken off his glasses for a while. Gantenbein now knows that her flat is not violet, but thoroughly tasteful, ordinarily tasteful; it could be the flat of a university woman, in fact, or a graphic artist or something. Only the books are missing. Would he like to listen to a record? This is a bit too cosy for him, so he asks what the time is. Camilla says: just after one. His watch says ten to two. She wants to keep him there, it seems, she is enjoying not being seen. She is enjoying her rôle. As Gantenbein drains his second cognac the clock strikes two. Evidently she doesn't work in an office. A lady? By no means. She seems to take pride in using a vocabulary that excludes any suspicion of her being a middle-class lady, an earthy vocabulary, and as she pulls her feet in under her thighs again Gantenbein is eager to know how Camilla Huber would like to be seen. Rather younger than she is; that in any case. Even when one is as young as she is, she says several times. Gantenbein closes his eyes, in order to comply with her wishes better. Camilla has been married once. Once and never again. Men always think their money entitles them to get away with anything. A professional woman has the same rights as a man, thinks Camilla. To be a man's housekeeper just because you love him, that's the end, she thinks. Absolutely the end. Camilla doesn't sell herself. Those days are over. Of course, she often has a boy friend, young as she is, don't let's be narrow-minded. Who cares what the neighbours think? An independent woman. Self-supporting. Not a lady who always lets her escort pay for her. Very far removed from bourgeois marriage, naturally. Marriage means selling one's independence. Out of the question. Gantenbein understands. A modern woman. A woman with a profession, even if Gantenbein will never see her at work; a woman who stands on her own feet and drives her own car, which, naturally, she has bought with her own earnings. Camilla couldn't imagine her life in any other way, an inde-

36

pendent and self-supporting woman, a woman of today, and there is no need for her to keep saying it over and over again; Gantenbein has already understood the rôle she intends to play in his eyes, and he will accept her in this rôle, if Camilla will let him play the part of a blind man in exchange.

"Certainly," he says, as he is standing on the threshold and after she has given him the little black stick, which he almost forgot, "certainly we shall see each other again, since we're neighbours –"

Camilla nods happily.

A man, an intellectual, has reached the age of forty-one without any special successes, without any special difficulties; only when a special success comes his way is he dismayed by the rôle which he has evidently been playing up to now –

Did he believe in it himself?

It happens while he is at a small, friendly party where he knows himself to be valued, and really nothing happens, nothing at all, an evening like many others. He doesn't know what has dismayed him. He persuades himself he has drunk too much (two glasses! – perhaps he can't take drink any more) and holds back, holds his right hand over his empty glass without a word, in order not to attract attention, but resolutely, even violently, as though the dismay could still be warded off, and at the same time dutifully, preserving the demeanour of an attentive listener, when his friendly host cuts across the conversation with a bottle. What's the matter with him, asks a lady who hasn't been able to take any more part in the conversation for a long time. The host, who has just been scolded by his wife about the empty glasses, also helps to draw attention to him. What's the matter with Enderlin? He only knows that he has nothing to say. Later he allows his glass to be refilled, since it can't be alcohol, on the contrary, he feels horribly sober. Unfortunately it's only eleven, to slip away unnoticed is almost impossible; he drinks. During these last few days a three-line report of Enderlin's invitation to Harvard has been appearing in the Press,

37

not merely in his home town but also abroad (that always creates an entirely different impression, even if the facts are the same), and Enderlin is embarrassed to hear people talking about this report just now, especially when his hostess is seized by an irresistible impulse to drink to this invitation, in order to cheer Enderlin up. In vain he tries to change the subject; Enderlin can't think of anything that will take his own mind off it. Someone in the haze behind the standard lamp, a daughter, doesn't know what Harvard is; this causes a delay, because the host has to explain what Harvard is and what an invitation to Harvard means, before they can drink. Well then, to Harvard! They don't drink solemnly, but with so much friendly seriousness that a silence ensues, a silence round Enderlin. An invitation, oh well, Enderlin tries to make light of it, but nevertheless is rather upset to see that they obviously hadn't considered him capable of it. The wine, burgundy 1947, is passed round, but the silence round Enderlin remains. After all (Enderlin has to say something, in order not to stand there like a monument), even charlatans have been invited to Harvard, and moreover this isn't the first invitation Enderlin has received. So much in passing. To be just, he has to point out that smaller universities, Basel for example, also enjoy a justified esteem. Or Tübingen. But Enderlin really had no reason or wish to talk about that; he merely mentioned it to one other person, while everyone else was fussing round the poodle that had just trotted into the room to show off his well-known capers. A marvellous little fellow! Enderlin thinks so too, glad that for the moment at least everyone's attention is turned to this poodle. When is he going to Harvard, asks a lady, and after this too has been said, unfortunately in such a low voice that the others on the other side of the lampshade ask the same question, and after Enderlin has had to answer again and loud enough for everyone to hear, when Enderlin is probably leaving for Harvard, Enderlin is naturally the centre of attention again, poodle or no poodle. To say something bright now, to tell some anecdote that will set the party going again, seems to him indispensable. But he can't think of one. Everyone is waiting, not too intently, but

38

invitingly. What sort of story can a man tell when faced by his career? Almost all successful men claim to have been expelled from school, everyone knows that, but people like to hear it all over again. But Enderlin can't think of anything, the floor is his, but he knows he hasn't anything to say. Meanwhile the host offers cigars, while his wife thinks it's time to turn the jolly little poodle out again, since it considers itself the centre of the silent company's attention. And it still isn't midnight. . .

"Hermes has entered."

That is all Enderlin can think of to say, a classical proverb which exactly describes the embarrassment of this moment. But that won't do: Hermes is the subject of the book that brought him the invitation to Harvard. . . Finally it is the host who feels responsible for the lull and tries to entertain the company, since it has suddenly ceased to entertain itself, with anecdotes; but they fall flat; everyone is waiting for Enderlin. He can't do anything about it, and the longer he remains silent, his left hand in his trouser pocket, his glass in the other hand, actually the only one in the gathering listening to the host, all the others are listening through him so to speak, they laugh when Enderlin laughs, Enderlin is the centre of attention, the longer he remains silent. It is no help that the host is a brilliant raconteur. The silence when the host goes down into the cellar again begins harmlessly; people change their crossed legs over, tap ash from their cigars, someone opens a window, which everybody welcomes, but the silence grows, someone hands round cakes, people smoke, a pendulum clock strikes twelve, and when the host comes back with fresh bottles he imagines he has missed some utterance by Enderlin, looks round and asks what they are talking about, and uncorks the bottles –

Slowly people begin to chat.

Only for Enderlin, who takes the chance to say goodbye, has something happened, not for the first time incidentally and probably not for the last. Before insight comes to him from this occurrence, a lot of little moments of dismay will be needed. Alone in his car, as he inserts the key rather hesitantly, then with a feeling of relief

39

that at least the engine is working, he no longer thinks about it. An insignificant evening. . .

It was a long and dreary hour – so I imagine it – an agitating hour, as Gantenbein, his blue glasses on his face and his stick between his knees, waited in the anteroom of the Municipal Health Department. Even a blind man, he ought to have seen, is a member of society. Without the yellow armband he had no rights. With his eyes on a painting by a local painter, which has to atone here for having been bought by the municipality, Gantenbein sat all alone in this bare anteroom, perhaps the first person ever to see this picture. What, on the other hand, he could not do was to read the newspaper which he had in his overcoat pocket. At any moment someone might come in. An old woman, tiny, a gnome, her wrinkled shoes and her floppy hat were already far too big for her, so were her false teeth, a citizen fighting for a place in one of the fine old-age homes of the city of Zürich which are rightly extolled in all the newspapers, had been in front of him, and Gantenbein had promised to keep his fingers crossed for her, which he naturally forgot to do as soon as he was alone with the eleven o'clock chimes, worried about his own future, while she was now sitting in front of the well-meaning powerlessness of the Medical Officer, the tiny woman with the big false teeth and hair on her upper lip; she had been there ten minutes already. The eleven o'clock chimes, Zürich's gayest institution, would have been even finer with the window open, more booming, but Gantenbein didn't dare stand up and open the window. With his glasses on his face and the black stick between his knees, as is proper when one wants a yellow armband, he sat patiently. One has to bring documentary evidence, certificates from at least two specialists. The running to and fro (always tapping with his stick against the kerb!), and the talking, before he had been able to deceive two local doctors, who made no extra charge for it, had cost Gantenbein a month, to say nothing of his nerves. But now he had the certificates in his pockets, and all he needed was the rubber stamp of the Health Department, who were said

40

to be very understanding, although they had kept Gantenbein waiting, as though a blind man had nothing more to miss in this world. . . Wouldn't it be more advantageous to be deaf rather than blind, Gantenbein sometimes asks himself; but now it's too late. . . The eleven o'clock chimes have fallen silent; instead he now hears the tapping of a typewriter in the next room, probably to console the old woman by allowing her to give all her particulars over again, date of birth, Christian name of father, whose grave has already been dug, and maiden name of mother, last place of residence, address of a still living son overseas, who could relieve the national health insurance of the burden. Anyhow, something was being typed. Not without a beating heart, Gantenbein thinks over the answers he will give to this typewriter next door. Pangs of conscience? Every now and then Gantenbein closes his eyes, to get the feel of his part. What always opens his eyes again, often after only a few breaths, is not curiosity as to what he can see, not primarily; he knows what the anteroom of a local government office will look like. Perhaps it is already a sign of old age that everything the eyes can see looks like an anteroom. Nevertheless we always open our eyes again. The retina is a protection against the premonition that almost every sound arouses in us, and against time; we see what the clock over on St Peter's is showing, and clocks always show now. A protection against memory and its abysses. Gantenbein is glad he isn't really blind. Incidentally, he has pretty well got used to the discoloration caused by his blue glasses: the milk-glass sun over house-fronts of ashes; the leaves like bronze; clouds that falsely threaten with an inky storm. Strange, and impossible for Gantenbein to get used to, remains the autumn-crocus skin of women.

Once, when Gantenbein just happens to be looking at his watch, an official goes through the anteroom, a black file (only black remains black) in his bluish hand, without a word and without a nod, perhaps he knows already that this is a blind man, anyhow, nobody nods, neither the official nor Gantenbein, and then Gantenbein is sitting alone again, his stick between his knees, and has time to ponder on his project again: advantages, disadvantages –

He sticks to it.

Gradually getting used to the idea that his turn won't come today, municipal offices shut at a quarter to twelve as far as he knows, to relieve traffic congestion, getting used to the idea that he will be asked to come back at two in the afternoon, he fills a pipe, no differently from in the past, an action that can be left to the fingers to perform without looking, blindly. . . The advantages outweigh the disadvantages. . . It is just when he lights the pipe that he looks at the flickering flame, although his tongue already knows that the tobacco is burning. The disadvantage that frightens him most: the intimate revelations to which his blindness lays him open. Now it is drawing. Again and again, Gantenbein is relieved that he isn't really blind; the pipe would taste different if he couldn't see the smoke, bitter, stupefying like a tablet or an injection, but pleasureless. His recent brief meeting with Camilla Huber reinforces his hope of making people freer, free from the fear that one sees their lies. Above all, however, Gantenbein hopes, people won't camouflage themselves much against a blind man, so that one will get to know them better, and a more real relationship will come into being as a result of granting validity to their lies, a more trusting relationship –

At last the doctor sends for him.

Gantenbein, born at such and such a place on such and such a date, it's all in the certificates, which the Medical Officer, after sitting down himself, looks at without curiosity, not superficially but rapidly, because it is almost a quarter to twelve. The certificates seem to be in order, to judge by the Medical Officer's mute indifference. The official blind person's pass, a form occupying two sides of a sheet of paper, is already being put into the typewriter by the secretary; Gantenbein merely has to repeat the truth point by point, which is not easy in so far as every form, as one knows, presupposes a basic case that never exists. For example, Gantenbein has no employer. Capital? An unconstitutional question; it contra-

42

venes the Swiss law of bank secrecy to which this country owes
so much, but Gantenbein, in order not to make difficulties, names a
sum, so that the worried State feels relieved and the young lady
types. In bursts. Her tense concern is not whether it's yes or no,
but not to make a typing mistake. Only that. And on top of that
the face of the Medical Officer; Gantenbein can see that the Medical
Officer distrusts his secretary, not the blind man. That augurs
well, and all that's needed now is for the secretary to have to rub
something out; the Medical Officer, to judge by his appearance,
won't shout at her, but will merely punish her by being friendlier
to the blind man than to her. Preparing to append his signature, as
soon as the yellow card, the real blind person's pass, has at last
been typed, the Medical Officer is already unscrewing his fountain
pen. Everything seems to be in order. What makes Gantenbein
nervous are mostly only his superfluous imaginings; for example,
when he had to swear, to swear by the specialists' certificates. You
see, explains the Medical Officer, a lot of hawkers obtain these
blind persons' cards dishonestly in order to touch the hearts of
housewives. Why does he say that? Incidentally the old woman
seems to have helped him by invoking the views of the blind
gentleman out in the waiting-room. That's easy to say, says the
friendly Medical Officer, refuting Gantenbein's views, but where
are we to put all the old people? He quotes figures, so that he can
then ask: Do you see a solution? A telephone call creates an interruption, so that Gantenbein has time to think things over, until
the question is reiterated: Do you see a solution? Gantenbein con-
fines himself to a growing appreciation of the difficulties with which
a Medical Officer is confronted every day. The blindness of the
views which Gantenbein expressed in the waiting-room, to en-
courage the old woman, come to his aid; it renders his other
blindness credible as well. When the Medical Officer reaches for
matches, in order to dissolve his impatience with his secretary in
smoke, Gantenbein politely clicks his lighter. The Medical Officer
wasn't prepared for that. Now the secretary is rubbing out. For
that the Medical Officer was prepared. Our minds cannot be

43

everywhere at the same instant; he forgets his cigarettes as well as Gantenbein. He looks at the secretary, preoccupied by self-control, until the blind person's card comes at last, mute, while Gantenbein puts away his lighter. Now he signs. The yellow armband will be sent C.O.D., says the secretary. As always when he has obtained what he wants from the authorities, Gantenbein is full of understanding for the latter, in response to which the Medical Officer, on his side grateful for the understanding, perhaps also out of a need to refute his secretary, who thinks him a dreadful man, rises and personally conducts Gantenbein to the lift, not without expressing the hope that in spite of everything Gantenbein will find his way through life. Gantenbein tries to reassure him, sympathy embarrasses him, he assures the doctor that before his blindness he had already seen a great deal of this world: he had not merely been in Greece and Spain, but even in Morocco, which the Medical Officer, for example, has never seen, in Paris, of course, in the Louvre, in Damascus and in his youth once on the Matterhorn, yes indeed, though actually it was misty. Thus, especially as the lift keeps them waiting, they strike up a lively conversation about travel. A medical officer has little opportunity for travel, of course, three or four weeks a year. Gantenbein particularly recommends Havana. Next year, says the Medical Officer, he would like to go to Spain for a change; Gantenbein draws his attention, above all, to the interior of the country, Salamanca, Avila, Segovia, Cordoba. At the present time, Gantenbein assures him, the roads in Turkey, to say nothing of Iraq, are even worse than in Spain – once the lift comes up, but they don't enter, so the doors close again. He has seen enough, says Gantenbein. Only he has never been to Russia, any more than the Medical Officer. They embark upon the first political discussion Gantenbein has ever had as a blind man, and it goes more easily than ever: one simply allows oneself to be informed by the other's views. . . The lift opens for the second time, and there is no time left for the many tips Gantenbein could still give. If Spain, then the caves of Altamira. If Segovia, then eat at the Candido, Hemingway's restaurant, just by the aqueduct. If

Turkey, don't miss the Mosque of Edirne. If Jerusalem, then on a Friday. Gantenbein is already standing in the lift when the Medical Officer asks him not for his hand, but for his finger, which Gantenbein understands at once. For his index finger – in order to place his index finger on the right button on the switch inside the lift, where he is to press as soon as he hears the outside doors of the lift close. Once again Gantenbein has to assure the doctor that there is someone waiting for him down below. The armband, the Medical Officer assures him, will be sent on. . .

So far so good.

Alone in the lift, as relaxed as an actor behind the scenes where he knows no one can see him, Gantenbein immediately reads the official card. It has been legally attested. This at once gives one a different feeling, a different demeanour – even towards the Medical Officer himself when five minutes later, time for the lift to go down and come up again, Gantenbein has to appear before him again; he has left his black stick behind. So you did, says the Medical Officer as he soaps and rinses his hands preparatory to going out to lunch, and since the secretary has already gone, Gantenbein, in order not to trouble the friendly Medical Officer, takes the stick from the back of the chair himself, scared to death by his thoughtlessness, with which he has betrayed not only himself but also two specialists. What now? But the Medical Officer, it seems, thinks nothing of it, so firmly does he believe in his own signature; he merely nods as he now dries his washed hands, for his part slightly embarrassed because he is in shirtsleeves, and a week later, punctually, as is only to be expected from a Swiss government office, the yellow armband arrives, which makes a lot of things easier.

The only difficulty that remains is with women.

To test out the new armband, Gantenbein naturally doesn't choose precisely that café which he always used to frequent before he went blind, but another one, where the waiters don't know him; he is delighted to see all these new faces, women such as he has never seen before. His delight leaves him no peace, he can see that. Gantenbein drinks his campari, the black stick between his knees,

45

the yellow armband on his arm; he puts his cigarette in the sugar basin and gets up to other little dodges. Don't they trust his official armband? He feels himself being scrutinized. He tries out all the postures of masculine nonchalance that give him away, and watches the result: she too, the lady at the next table, tries out nonchalant postures, either by suddenly powdering her nose, painting her lips or turning her head, as though she doesn't want to be stared at, or by suddenly putting him to the test with a smile. It's going to be difficult. Women never quite believe in his blindness, armband or no armband; women feel it in their backs, when they are being seen.

I'm sitting in a bar, afternoon, so I'm alone with the barman, who is telling me his life story. A first-class raconteur! I'm waiting for someone. As he rinses the glasses he says: That's how it was. I drink. So it was a true story. I believe you, I say. He dries the rinsed glasses. Yes, he says again, that's how it was. I drink and envy him — not for having been a prisoner of war in Russia, but for his doubt-free relationship to his story. . .

"H'm," he says. "Just listen to that rain again!"

I don't respond to this, but drink.

"Every story is an invention," I say after a while, without on that account doubting the horrors of being a prisoner of war in Russia, as a general principle: "every ego that expresses itself in words is a rôle — "

"Herr Doktor," he says, "another whisky?"

Herr Doktor!

"Our greed for stories," I say and notice that I have already drunk a great deal; this is evident from the fact that I don't finish my sentences, but assume that I have been understood thanks to my insight: "— perhaps a man has two or three experiences," I say, "two or three experiences at the outside, that's what a man has had when he tells stories about himself, when he tells stories at all: a pattern of experience — but not a story," I say, "not a story." I drink, but my glass is empty. "One can't see oneself, that's the

46

trouble, stories only exist from outside," I say, "hence our greed for stories." I don't know whether the barman is listening to me after being six years in the Urals, and take a cigarette in order to be independent. "Have you a story?" I ask, after he has just told me what he obviously considers to be his story, and say: "I haven't one." I smoke – I watch him take my empty glass from the zinc, dip it in the rinsing water, and pick up another, a fresh, dry one. I can't prevent him from pouring me another whisky: precisely because I'm watching I can't prevent him. . . I think of the man on the Kesch, a story which until today I have never told anyone, although it pursues me constantly, the story of a murder I didn't commit. I twist my glass round as I ask:

"Have you ever been on the Kesch?"

"Kesch," he asks, "what's that?"

"Piz Kesch," I say, "a mountain."

"No," he says. "Why?"

Nonsense! I think. Why should he be the man I met in 1942 on the Kesch? I fall silent. Nonsense. I drink.

"Sooner or later everyone invents for himself a story which he regards as his life," I say, "or a whole series of stories," I say, but I'm too drunk really to follow my own thoughts and this annoys me, so that I fall silent.

I'm waiting for someone.

"I knew a man," I say, in order to talk about something else, "a milkman, who came to a bad end. He ended up in a lunatic asylum, although he didn't think he was Napoleon or Einstein; on the contrary, he definitely thought he was a milkman. And he looked like a milkman. In his spare time he collected stamps, but that was the only fanatical streak he had; he was a captain in the Fire Brigade, because he was so reliable. In his youth, I believe, he was a gymnast, anyhow a healthy and peaceable man, widower, teetotal, and no one in our community would ever have guessed that he would one day have to be put in a lunatic asylum." I smoke. "His name was Otto," I say. "Otto." I smoke. "The ego this good man had invented for himself remained uncontested all his life long, especi-

47

ally as it demanded no sacrifices from his environment; on the contrary," I say, "he brought milk and butter into every house. For twenty-one years. Even on Sundays. We children loved him, because he often used to let us ride on his three-wheeler." I smoke. I go on with my story: "It was one evening in spring, a Saturday, as Otto, smoking his pipe as all through the years, was standing on the balcony of his detached house, which, although it was on the village street, had so much little garden round it that the pieces couldn't hurt anybody. You see, for reasons unknown even to himself, Otto suddenly seized a flowerpot, a geranium if I'm not mistaken, and threw it pretty well vertically down into his little garden, which immediately caused not only broken pieces, but also a sensation. All the neighbours immediately turned their heads; they were standing on their balconies, in their shirtsleeves just like him, enjoying their Saturday, or in their little gardens watering the flowers, and they all immediately turned their heads. This public sensation, it seems, so vexed our milkman that he hurled all the flowerpots, seventeen in number, down into the little garden, which after all, like the flowerpots themselves, was entirely his own property. Nevertheless they took him away. After that Otto was considered mad. And no doubt he was," I say. "It was impossible to talk to him any more." I smoke, while my barman gives a suitable smile, though he isn't sure what I'm getting at. "Well," I say, stubbing out my cigarette in the ashtray on the bar counter, "his ego was worn out, that can happen, and he couldn't think of another one. It was horrible."

I don't know whether he understands me.

"Yes," I say, "that's how it was."

I take my next cigarette.

I'm waiting for someone –

My barman gives me a light.

"I knew a man," I say, "another one, who didn't end up in a lunatic asylum," I say, "although he lived completely and utterly in fantasy." I smoke. "He imagined he was dogged by bad luck, a decent man, but one for whom everything went wrong. We were all sorry for him. No sooner had he saved up some money than there was devaluation. And it went like that all the time. No tile ever fell from the roof when he wasn't passing. The invention that one is dogged by bad luck is one of the favourites, because it's comfortable. Not a month passed for this man without his having cause for complaint, not a week, scarcely a day. Anyone who knew him a bit was afraid to ask: How are things? And yet he didn't really complain, he merely smiled about his legendary bad luck. And in fact things were always happening to him that other people were spared. Simply bad luck, there was no denying it, in big things as in small. And all the time he bore it manfully," I say and smoke "– till the miracle happened." I smoke and wait until the barman, mainly occupied with his glasses, has asked what kind of a miracle. "It was a blow for him," I say, "a real blow, when this man won the big prize in the lottery. It was in the newspaper, so he couldn't deny it. When I met him in the street he was pale, dumbfounded, he didn't doubt his invention that he was a man dogged by bad luck, but he did doubt the lottery, in fact the world altogether. It was no laughing matter, he actually had to be comforted. In vain. He couldn't grasp the fact that he was not dogged by bad luck, wouldn't grasp it and was so confused that on his way back from the bank he actually lost his wallet. And I believe he preferred it that way," I say. "Otherwise he would have had to invent a different ego for himself, the poor fellow, he couldn't have gone on seeing himself as a man dogged by bad luck. Another ego is more expensive than the loss of a full wallet, of course; he would have had to abandon the whole story of his life, live through all its events again and differently, since they would no longer have gone with his ego –"

I drink.

"Shortly afterwards his wife deceived him too," I say. "I felt sorry for the man, he really was dogged by bad luck."

I smoke.

Outside it is still raining. . . . I no longer know what it was I was trying to say with this story and I look at my barman. Perhaps it is him after all? I think, although he denies it; I can't remember any more what he looked like, my man on the Kesch, perhaps for that reason I shall never get rid of him; I smoke, think about it in silence, smoke.

That was in 1942, a Sunday in April or May, we were stationed at Samaden, Grisons, a cloudless day, I had weekend leave, but I didn't go home, I wanted to be away from people and went up into the mountains. Actually, soldiers on leave were strictly forbidden to go into the mountains alone, because of the danger; but I went notwithstanding, and up the Piz Kesch. I had spent the night in a hay barn, where it was as cold as hell, no hay, draught blowing through, a clear, starry night; I wanted to avoid the Kesch hut, because there were probably officers there to whom I, a simple gunner, would have had to report my destination, which was just what I didn't want to do. What I wanted was real leave, leave from all compulsion to report. Since I was as cold as hell all night, I was up and about early, long before sunrise; against the grey scree of the mountainside no one could see me, field-grey as I was, and I climbed pretty quickly, and when I reached the snow it was still crisp and hard. I rested on the Kesch Gap just as the sun was rising, not a soul in sight, I breakfasted on dry Ovomaltine. I had an ice axe with me, that was why I hadn't wanted to be seen by anyone in the valley, a lone climber with an ice axe. I was glad to have this shiny little axe; I might have managed without it, since the ice quickly softened in the sun, but in the shade I had to cut steps. I had taken off my floppy battle tunic and slung it from my belt; every now and then I stopped and peered round to see if anyone was coming, an officer perhaps. Once on the peak, they couldn't stop me any more, I thought, at most they might ask if I didn't know the regulation and then say no more about it, moved by the comradeship between fellow mountaineers. But I saw no one, anyhow not on the snowfield, and when I wasn't actually hacking away with my axe I heard nothing either. I was as much alone as on the moon. I heard chunks of snow rolling down over the rocks,

50

nothing else, from time to time the ring of my axe against the sharp rocks, wind, nothing else, wind over the chine. Later, when I reached the peak, I found myself alone with the cross on the summit, happy. It was getting warmer and warmer, and after I had built up a shelter of loose stones behind which I was out of the wind, I actually took off my sweaty shirt and rolled my tunic into a pillow. Later I slept, tired after the night, I don't know how long; at least I shut my eyes and dozed, having no other plans. The man who had suddenly spoken to me, a civilian – he said *Grüssi!* which he imagined to be Swiss; obviously a German – didn't want to disturb me, as he said, when he saw my amazement; but naturally I immediately sat up, at first without saying a word. He had evidently been here some time; he put down his rucksack a little way away. I said good morning, as I rose to my feet so that we were now standing side by side. He wanted to know, a pair of field-glasses to his face, which was the Bernina. You're a soldier! he said, when he saw my impossible drainpipe trousers, with a certain smile, and as I showed him what he wanted to know I soon noticed how well he knew the district. A lover of the Engadine obviously, a foreigner, but a connoisseur; at least he was familiar with the names, Bernina and Palüff and Rosatsch, but also with the names of the villages down in the valley. He was carrying a map in the approved manner, although maps had been confiscated at that time, and also a Leica. His stubborn insistence on imitating our national speech and making it sound like a form of baby talk, an attempt to curry favour without any talent for catching the alien intonation, patronisingly benevolent without noticing that it set my teeth on edge, did more to make conversation difficult than the wind. Naturally I answered in High German, even if with an Alemannic accent, but without success. He even knew what a kitchen cupboard was in Swiss: *Chuchichäschtli.* This in passing; it had nothing to do with the conversation. A lot of soldiers here, yes. He was trying hard, I could see, to take my military uniform seriously. Perhaps the embarrassment is my fault, I thought, as he offered me his field-glasses, and in return I offered him my waterbottle, filled

51

with Veltliner. I now saw through his field-glasses that he had used my tracks. No one else came. I thanked him for the field-glasses. He stayed for about half an hour, and we chatted above all about the mountains, also about the flora, of which he spoke in a tone of great appreciation. I had an inhibition (why, actually?) against looking him in the face, as though prepared for some tactless remark that embarrassed me in advance, and I couldn't think of much to say. I don't know what he thought of me, anyhow he thought me gauche; he was very surprised indeed when it turned out that I knew Berlin. The more fluently the conversation now went, more fluently because he reverted to his own natural intonation, the more urgently I waited for the moment when he would pick up his rucksack. My advice as to how he could best get down to the Madulein proved superfluous. He had spent the night in the Kesch hut, which he praised as though I had built it. A lot of officers, yes, very nice lads. I left it to the wind to answer his question as to whether we were trained in mountaineering. That he would get to Madulein by four, he left me in no doubt. All the same, he now packed his rucksack, not without bequeathing me an apple. I felt somewhat ashamed. An apple up here was something. After he had buckled on his rucksack, I was no longer prepared for it; we had already shaken hands when he was seized by that outburst of frankness the exact wording of which I have forgotten. The Reich, that was enough for me; the meaning was plain. I said nothing, nor did I contradict him; I simply stood in silence, my hands in the pockets of my field-grey drainpipe trousers, which I hated, looking out over the land which soon, as he said, would also belong to the Reich. What I saw: rock, blackish, in places also reddish, snow in the midday light and scree, slopes covered in grey scree, then meadows, treeless, stony, streams glittering in the sun, pastures, cattle that looked in the distance like tiny grubs, a valley with a wood and cloud shadows; close by, the black choughs. It was only after a while, after he had put away his Leica and finally disappeared round a rock with a cordial wave and wishing me a good time in the army, that I felt angry at not having told him to shut his trap and began to take an interest in his special characteristics; I now stepped out onto the projecting ledge, but too late: I didn't see him again until he came round the ridge, now a hundred feet below me, so that all I could see was his green felt hat. He slipped, but managed to steady himself; then he climbed more carefully. I shouted to him, to make him raise his face again; but he heard nothing. I wanted to tell him kindly not to dislodge stones. They kept rolling down, which obviously didn't worry him; he was up above. The more I forbade myself to get indignant about what he had said, the more wildly indignant I now became over the way this idiot climbed. Stones were rolling down again! I whistled through my fingers; he probably took it for the whistle of a marmot that would also soon belong to Hitler's Reich, and looked round. I stood out on the rock until he reached the Kesch Gap, a little black man in the snow; he was probably taking photographs again, anyhow he spent a long time tramping to and fro. I picked up my battle tunic, suddenly resolved to climb down and catch up with him. What for? I remained on the peak. All the same, I watched him till he left the snowfield, and went on watching him on the scree slope; on the meadow he was camouflaged by his loden jacket and I abandoned my senseless watching.

Later I fell asleep –

When I woke, probably because I was cold, I was dismayed by the thought: I pushed that man over the rocks. I knew I hadn't done it. But why didn't I? I hadn't dreamed it either; I merely woke with the waking thought: A push with the hand as he bent down for his rucksack would have been enough.

Then I ate his apple.

Of course I'm glad I didn't do it. It would have been murder. I have never talked to anyone about it, never, not even tête-à-tête, although I didn't do it. . . I saw no one far and wide. A few black choughs. No eye-witness. No one. Wind and no listening ear. That evening at Samaden during roll-call I would have stepped into the back row, head to the right, dress by the right, hand on the seam, at attention, good and straight, afterwards I'd have drunk

53

beer. No one would ever have noticed from looking at me, I don't think. Since then I have talked to a lot of murderers, in a dining-car or during the interval at a concert or elsewhere; you can't tell by looking at them. . . When I had eaten the apple I stepped out onto the projecting ledge to see how far he would have fallen. A snow-drift, harshly glittering, then nothing. The choughs, black, were soaring soundlessly above the distant glacier, black and close. A low north wall, pretty well vertical. I looked at my watch; time to go down. I picked up my floppy battle tunic, belt, ice axe. The snow was now pretty soft, and I admit that I too occasionally sent a stone rolling down. By the time I reached the Kesch Gap I had really forgotten the man already. Apart from the fact that the descent in the soft snow at times demanded my full attention, I hardly need say that I also had thoroughly real worries which it was more sensible to think about, beginning with the beast of a sergeant-major, who would try to put me on guard duty again, but above all the profession that had been left at home, my profession wasn't soldiering. In the Kesch Gap in the afternoon light, when I saw his footprints running this way and that across the snow, I couldn't remember what he had really said up there, where now the white cross stood all alone on the summit, only that one could have done something that I hadn't done. And that, one might have thought, was the end of it; precisely because I didn't do it. But I was interested to see where he would most likely have fallen. Just to have a look. Although I had come to the little glacier, I trudged northwards under the Piz Kesch. Not far; only to see; only a few steps. The snow here was so soft that I sank in up to my knees; I was sweating. I should have had skis. I knew the run down over the glacier. Without a pack and a carbine on one's back it must be magnificent. Right towards Sertig, left towards Bergün. I didn't get far trudging around; besides, it was time I was going. Three o'clock! By this time he must already be far below in the valley, taking a look at Madulein, on the other side of the watershed; if he walked as sturdily as he talked, he must already have reached the first pines. While I was here sinking up to my knees in the snow! All the

54

same, I was now more or less under the low wall, and as I didn't know how I should feel at the sight of a shattered skull, I pondered in a matter-of-fact way on whether the man would really have fallen on this slope. I climbed up a few yards, to get a better view of the wall and also to be able to stand better; a chasm below me made me anxious. I was panting. Perhaps he might have got wedged among the rocks, only his Leica would have fallen in the snow, or perhaps not. Seen from nearby, it wasn't really a wall; probably he would have got stuck up above in the couloir. I didn't know why I was worried about what hadn't happened. Here, where the wind on the summits didn't reach, it was deathly quiet, only the soft dripping of melted snow, since the afternoon sun was now shining into the couloir. It was hot, and not for the first time I cursed our army's impractical battle tunic. The rock, now in the afternoon light, looked like amber, the sky overhead violet, the little glacier by contrast bluish, at least the cracks, the snow more like milk, only my deep footprints in it looked glassy blue. Everything motionless. Only the choughs, black, were soaring high overhead. The cross on the summit wasn't visible from here. I went back to the Kesch Gap. My hope of being able to slide in places was disappointed; I tried it again and again, but the snow was too mushy. I followed his tracks to the end of the snowfield, but even on the slaty rubble I could still make them out, marks of slipping, but also other marks, footprints like rubber stamps, I saw that he had first-class climbing-boots; it was only on the meadows that I lost his trail for good.

That was all.

That evening at Samaden, during roll-call, I got into the back row, but in vain; I was put on guard duty, and there was nothing doing with the beer and nothing doing with sleep either, I had a hellish sunburn, fever. Although I slowly became convinced that the man on the Kesch was no harmless tourist I said nothing about it. I was on guard in the village square, so I had nothing to do but look, with my carbine on my arm, to look and see whether a green felt hat crossed the square. Naturally my belletristic hope was not fulfilled. I did sentry-go in vain, ten steps this way, ten steps that. At that time, 1942, there really weren't any tourists. I should have recognized him, but he didn't come through Samaden –

So forget it!

Forget what?

In the following years, as everyone knows, a great deal happened. Real things. I never thought of it again, it was no time for trifles, God knows, and certainly not for figments of the imagination, for imaginary murders, when, as I soon knew, there were enough of the other sort every day. So I thought no more about it and never told anyone about that blue Sunday on the Piz Kesch; it was too ridiculous. Nor did I ever go on the Piz Kesch again. Nevertheless, as it turned out later, I haven't forgotten it, whereas I have forgotten so much that I have really done. That's strange. It seems that more than anything else it is our real deeds that most easily slip our memories; only the world, since it knows nothing about my non-deeds, has a predilection for remembering my deeds, which really only bore me. The temptation to exaggerate one's deeds, whether good or evil, springs from this boredom. I can't bear to listen to anyone reminding me that I did this, that or the other, whether it is shameful or praiseworthy. It is only as an unforgettable future, even if I displace it into the past as an invention, a figment of the imagination, that my life doesn't bore me – as a figment of the imagination: if I had pushed the man on the Kesch over the cornice. . .

I didn't do it.

The hand of the law will not descend upon my shoulder.

So forget it!

Not till much later, while reading a newspaper, did I suddenly think of it again. I read there, among other things, that the Germans had planned to set up a concentration camp in the vicinity of Klosters, Grisons; the plans were ready, and it's safe to assume that such plans were not prepared without a thorough study of the terrain. Who reconnoitred the terrain round Klosters? Perhaps it was the man who, on that Sunday in 1942, also made an excursion to the Piz Kesch to enjoy the view, and whom I didn't push over the cornice –

I don't know.

I shall never find out who he was.

Another time I couldn't help thinking about it when Burri, then a young doctor, came back from Greece, where he had been working for the International Red Cross, and when he told us all the things he had seen, among other things how a starving Greek child, who tried to steal a loaf from a Wehrmacht car in the middle of Athens, was grabbed by a soldier and shot in the middle of the street. Naturally Burri had seen other things too; not every soldier merely shot a Greek child or a Polish child. I know that. I simply asked him what that particular soldier in Athens looked like, asked, as though I might have recognized him –

What for?

We just chatted the way people do on the top of a mountain, like comrades, so to speak, two men who are the only ones for miles around, comradely but sparing with words, the continual wind of the peaks makes long sentences impossible. Without formalities, naturally, a handshake without any introductions. Both of them have reached this peak, that's enough; both have the same wide panorama. Handshake or no handshake, I don't even remember that for sure now; perhaps I kept my hands in my trouser pockets. Later I ate his apple, that's all, and looked down over the cornice. I know for sure what I didn't do. Perhaps he was a good fellow, a splendid fellow even; I keep telling myself, to take the weight off my mind, that I didn't do it. Perhaps I've actually met him again, without knowing it, after the war, dressed differently and so that with the best will in the world we couldn't recognize each other again, and he is one of the many people whom I esteem, whom I wouldn't like to be without. Only sometimes I'm so uncertain. Suddenly. And yet it's twenty years ago. I know it's ridiculous. Not to be able to forget an act one never performed is ridiculous. And I never tell anyone about it. And sometimes I completely forget him again. . .

Only his voice remains in my ear.

I empty my glass.

Time to pay.

"Yes," I say. "The Russians!"

My barman too, I see, has meanwhile been thinking of other things. . . . His story of the Russian mine, linked by a short circuit with my story that didn't happen – forget it.

"Herr Doktor," he asks, "another whisky?"

"Tell me," I say, while he is emptying the ashtrays and running a wet rag over the zinc, which I have evidently dirtied with ash, "– have you ever been on the Piz Kesch?"

"No," he says. "You've already asked me that."

I've drunk too much. . . The lady who has meanwhile come in and reminds me with her searching look round that I have been waiting for somebody for an hour and a half is, I realize, the wife of this somebody, who has unfortunately had to leave town, and has come to apologize for him, as I slip down off my stool to take off her wet coat. To be polite. To show I forgive her husband. As a matter of course. Really I ought to apologize; I've quite forgotten to wait. To be polite:

"Will you have a drink?"

I am just a bit confused, because I've never seen her husband, who is in London while I ought to have been waiting for him, and I'm now seeing his wife.

"Is it still raining?" I ask.

Actually I was just going to settle up.

"But I don't want to keep you!" she says, sitting down on the stool at the bar. "I really don't want to keep you –"

"What will you have?" I ask.

"No," she says, "what a downpour!"

First she has to tidy her hair, and since she has evidently noticed that I have already drunk too much, she orders a ginger ale. What shall we talk about now? I immediately take her for an actress, I don't know why. I'm seeing this woman for the first time, probably also for the last time. In order not to be impolite, I don't enquire what she does for a living; she may actually be a well-known actress, and my question would be a downright insult. So I nibble pretzels, as many as I can get hold of from left and right, and listen as she tells me why Svoboda, her husband, has had to leave town, give her a light between whiles and accept her apology again with a wordless gesture. She smokes rather hurriedly as she talks about her husband. Her hair, wet with rain, gleams black. I am determined not to fall in love. Her eyes are blue and big. From time to time it is up to me to say something, in order not to appear awkward or sullen. My uncertainty whether to take her for an actress or not is making me feel more and more embarrassed, as she now, I don't know why, talks about Peru. I ask myself what part I would give this woman. My silence filled with glances manifestly gives her the feeling of being understood; anyhow, she too becomes rather embarrassed. She drinks her ginger ale as though she were suddenly in a hurry. She doesn't want to keep the strange gentleman. I enquire about Peru, but she really doesn't want to keep the strange gentleman, she came to apologize for her Svoboda, and tries gradually to pay, which I don't allow. Certainly not! I say, and since Pepe, the barman, is now playing deaf and keeping in the background, we don't get round to paying and have to go on chatting. What about? I enquire about her husband, whom I should have met. Her husband, as I have said, is at present in London. Now, as though in response to an alarm signal, I am suddenly very sober; only the strange gentleman, whom she doesn't want to keep, is still drunk, not badly, but enough for me to differentiate myself from him. Peru, he says, is the land of his hope! Whereas I think he's talking rubbish, she listens big-eyed; it seems to please her, so they chat about Peru, which I don't know. She has travelled through Peru with her husband. I have to confess something to myself, namely that there is rarely a woman whose conversation interests me if she doesn't interest me in some degree as a woman. That's why I keep watching her mouth. When I hear in passing that she is faithful, I don't know why she said that; I wasn't listening. Her face is lively and beautiful when she is speaking, and I watch her in silence (while the strange

59

gentleman is speaking) smiling, till she blushes, tosses back her hair
and carefully taps the almost non-existent ash from her cigarette,
pretends to be deciphering an advertisement over the bar, *Johnnie
Walker highest awards*, blinking her eyes, because her own smoke is
rising into her face, *guaranteed same quality throughout the world*, her
face well worth looking at from the side too, her hand not strange;
even her hair, that most curious substance in a human being, does
not strike me as strange. . . She looks at her tiny watch.

"Oh," she says, "three o'clock already!"

But I've got plenty of time.

Actually she has plenty of time too.

"Won't you really have a whisky?" I ask, and since Pepe, like
every barman, is quick to sum people up, he has already taken a
fresh glass, so all I can say is: "Two then."

I ask myself what's going to happen next –

Three in the afternoon is a terrible hour, an hour without a slope,
flat and with no outlook. I remember my distant childhood, when
I was ill in bed and it was three in the afternoon, picture books,
stewed apple, eternity. . . Simply for something to say, I ask whether
she has any children, which is really none of my business. We
watch the barman doing his stuff: ice, whisky, soda. . . The strange
gentleman, as he later (ca. 3.30) takes hold of her bare arm, is
embarrassed not in relation to her, but in relation to me. She doesn't
look at me, as I had expected, with a mocking expression: What's
the idea? Nor does she withdraw her warm arm, and as she doesn't
say anything there is nothing for it but to persist in the strange
gentleman's action. I honestly regret that I feel nothing as I do it.
More than that: I'm staggered. And when the strange gentleman
finally takes his hand away, because I need it to take hold of my
whisky before it gets warm, she has already noticed my secret
dismay, I think, and misunderstood it. Anyhow, she now, as she
also picks up her glass, draws rather too deep a breath, as though
something had happened to her, and pushes the hair back from her
forehead, looks at me – me! – with her big blue eyes, without
seeing that I would like to be alone. We smoke, outside it is still

raining, we smoke. I can feel it, now I am going to relapse into the melancholy that suits men so, that renders them irresistible. It's no good my keeping a close watch on the strange gentleman. As I expected (I know him!) he now talks with playful frankness, more intimately than I feel like doing, getting right down to the problems of life. Should a woman who has a profession have a child? What is meant by marriage? I see through the game. To utter words before they have any meaning in relation to one's own personal life story, that's the point, words like love, man and woman, sex, friendship, bed and profession, fidelity, jealousy, species and individual and so on and so on. And since my own views, thus diluted into general principles, bore me to death, the strange gentleman spices them with little examples, which he makes up. Let us suppose, he says, that two people like us fall into each other's arms. Or: We agree that it shan't develop into an affair, we swear in advance that there shall be no repetition. He goes a step further in order to make the example, meant to illustrate a principle, more vivid; he invents dialogues that enable him to address her with the familiar *Du*, the example demands it, and she understands that the strange gentleman only means it as an example when he says, We. Or, you and I. Or, you knew that we should part, and I knew it too. She smokes as he talks, she understands that he is speaking in inverted commas, and she smokes away, and when he picks up my glass again to show that we are in this dreary bar and nowhere else, he addresses her with the formal *Sie* again. The game is over. And she remains silent for a long time now, intoxication rises from her half-open mouth like a bluish veil over her face that is full of understanding for his views, for the universal validity of his views in general principle. They are not in love, oh no, that's clear. But the game of using *Du* has brought an experience that somewhat changes the conversation; this can't be reversed by reverting to *Sie*. I occasionally look at my watch, to warn the strange gentleman; but in vain. The *Sie*, no matter how strictly it is adhered to henceforth, has acquired a magic that dispels boredom. So I talk now about innocuous things, world events, in a monologue. Every now and then, as though the

61

smoke were forcing her to, she half closes her eyes like a woman in an embrace, and it would be only natural if the strange gentleman, either with a joke or a mute doglike gaze, should take hold of her bare arm again, her hand, her hand with the cigarette lying by the ashtray, her further shoulder, the back of her neck. He doesn't do it. If I weren't keeping watch on him he might try it – involuntarily. . .

Now I really did want to settle up.

"Pepe?" I called out.

In order to treat us like a couple, the barman had made himself indispensable over by the window, was acting as though he had never seen traffic in the rain before, and pretended to be deaf, no matter how often I banged with the coin on the zinc. Suddenly I was very bored indeed again. For that very reason I only dared tap very softly, un-urgently.

"You must go," she said.

"Unfortunately," I admitted.

"So must I," she said.

I banged with the coin again.

Why the strange gentleman, who was boring me even more than her, since I wasn't listening to his remarks for the first time, suddenly started talking about the charm of homosexual men, I don't know; I wasn't listening very closely, because I was trying to catch the attention of the inattentive barman – she agrees with him, oh yes, regarding the charm of such men who like to dress up (I remember now, we were talking about a particular actor, then about actors in general) and who have a feeling for women's costumes, a feeling for perfumes. She is wearing a yellow costume. He admits that he likes her costume, but adds this: if he liked it less, he wouldn't have the slightest idea how it could be improved. He swears to that. By contrast, that kind of man, he thinks, would immediately – and he does it purely as an example – would immediately take hold of her collar, alter something and transform it as though by magic. He does it. Her amazement makes her even more beautiful, I can see that, different from hitherto. . .

Now I pay.

I don't want a love story.

I want to work.

She had her handbag, black, which went splendidly with the yellow costume, black like her hair, under her arm already, as I put the change in my pocket and she said how glad she was to have met me. After this I held her coat for her. To invite her to dine with me would have been very natural, especially as her husband was away; I didn't do so while she tied her scarf round her hair. I also said how glad I was to have met her, as I now, before she slipped into her coat, saw her whole figure for the first and, as I hoped, last time. Most love stories need never happen, I believe. Have you got everything? I asked, as though I already knew how forgetful she was. She liked that. I don't know whether it was the strange gentleman who now – she looked so bewildered each time he addressed her with the intimate *Du* – stroked her forehead, jestingly so to speak, arbitrarily, altogether mockingly, in order affectionately to stress the absence of destiny; anyhow, it happened. Our parting out in the rain, when a taxi finally stopped, was swift and formal. Not until she was sitting in the dry, inconsiderately preoccupied with her black handbag, was one struck by what one calls emotion. She saw it in my face, I believe, and after the surly driver, surly because he wasn't really allowed to stop here, had driven off with the lady in the rain, while I waited in vain to see if she would wave with her glove, I was paralysed by the fear that my freedom of action might be at an end...

I pulled my cap over my head.

I turned on my heel – I don't want to be the ego that experiences my stories, stories that I can imagine – I turned on my heel in order to part, as quickly as possible, from the strange gentleman.

I turned on my heel – when I looked round, her taxi in a flower-bed of rain-splashes was a taxi like all the others, no longer distinguishable as it stopped at a crossing, suddenly there were lots of taxis, each one sending up splashes like the next...

63

I strolled to my hotel.

Down below in the street outside the hotel, where I lay on the bed in my clothes, a pneumatic drill was yammering; it seemed to me demonic, since I was trying to sleep; it was no use my shutting the windows and even lowering the roller blinds; the panes shook. I didn't know what to do. When the drill occasionally stopped, the tone of the yammering merely changed; then it was the compressor that was yammering. I really didn't know what to do in this town and dialled her number as though for a joke. She was at home. As though for a joke, I handed the receiver over to the strange gentleman, so to speak, as soon as her voice answered. Go ahead! I had absolutely nothing to say, nor as a matter of fact had she. What to do? I was witty. Her laughter (without a face) bored me. As I carried on a laborious chit-chat, I lay on the bed looking at my left trouser-leg dangling like a puppet's, looking at the blue sock of the strange gentleman, whose toes I could move at will, the big toe on its own even, and I heard, not without malicious pleasure, that she wasn't free this evening, she had to go to the opera, to a guest performance at the Scala, I believe, at least that's what I understood. On the other hand, her husband's ticket was free, since, as I knew, he had had to go away. The demonic yammering had suddenly stopped. When her voice, now low, since the town between her and me was suddenly quiet, and incidentally not a voice that inevitably conjured up the picture of a beautiful woman, asked rather hesitantly what I was doing this evening, I said in the tone of a confession that I wasn't interested in opera. Nevertheless the strange gentleman went on chatting. I had no urge to see her again. When I had put down the receiver I had a funny feeling – as one usually does after an action: I didn't feel that the vague date the strange gentleman had made was binding on me; burdensome, but not binding. Was that necessary? I thought, after my dark suit had been taken out of the suitcase and hung on a hanger, and I lay down on the bed again to smoke, suddenly sober. . . I saw the strange gentleman in my dark evening suit, sitting in her husband's seat, and myself as her husband, who has gone on a trip,

64

who doesn't know what to do with himself in a strange town, because it's raining, and who is lying in shirt and trousers in a hotel room that is indistinguishable from this one, smoking –

I tried to read.

(I, too, often have the feeling that any book which isn't concerned with the prevention of war, with the creation of a better society and so on, is senseless, futile, irresponsible, tedious, not worth reading, inadmissible. This is no time for ego stories. And yet human life is fulfilled or goes wrong in the individual ego, nowhere else.)

I simply didn't know what to do.

Soon after six (I didn't want to be there to receive her promised phone call between six and seven) I left the hotel to go to the cinema, to escape from the sound of the pneumatic drill, which was in action again. The rain had stopped, the wet tarmac reflected a blue sky, spring. Without an overcoat, after changing for the opera, that is to say in a dark suit, my hands in my pockets, I walked into the middle of a film, so that I didn't understand what the shooting was all about and got bored; later into a bar, another one, where I played with a slot-machine. . .

The strange gentleman: Enderlin.

Next morning, when he found himself out in the street and the world again, earlier than usual, it was seven when he, a gentleman in a dark evening suit, walked down the alien street like others who were going to their daily work, coatless, his hands in his trouser pockets, trying to look as inconspicuous as possible, and when he went into a bar, surrounded by workmen sipping their coffee, and also had a coffee and bought cigarettes, because they had smoked all the others during the night, he knew: a night with a woman that will go into that strange number which one never mentions. *Mille e tre!* He knew and ate rolls, without counting them, and ordered a second coffee. He believed it was over, he hoped he believed it. Even if there was nothing to be seen from his pale face behind bottles, he nevertheless had the feeling that everyone could see by looking at him; this confused him like the sun outside, like the mirror behind bottles, like the traffic in the strange town, like the fact that it was Tuesday, Tuesday the such and such, and he didn't know why it confused him. No one knew him here. Even if it was too late to escape invisible under cover of night, he had succeeded, he hoped, in leaving the house without being seen by anyone. He hoped it for her sake. Later, zigzagging through the streets and probably seen only by a roadsweeper, he had washed his face at a public fountain that would remain in his memory. . . The wet handkerchief in his trouser pocket was bothering him now, he stood and drank his second coffee, and the fact that now and here, where the espresso machine was hissing, where there was a din of cups and voices, he still felt it necessary to walk on tiptoe confused him utterly. As though the men on his left and right, lorry drivers in leather aprons, had never made love to a woman! Incidentally, the arrangement about her key had gone off all right; the key of her flat now lay in the letterbox, as agreed, and the little key of the letterbox lay on the bedside table. If she didn't oversleep, everything would be all right. . . After the second coffee he was awake, as though he had slept, and not tired at all. Above all, he was glad now to be alone. Alone among men. She was probably asleep, and sleep is the most distant country there is; he didn't think this, but felt it: so long as she was asleep, she wasn't in this town. And he was in this town like yesterday: alone. After he had slit open the little blue packet, looking forward to the first cigarette he was going to smoke alone, he discovered that he had no lighter, only the wet handkerchief in his right trouser pocket; he had left the lighter somewhere during the night. Actually, feeling quite happy, because he really believed that they would escape repetition, he looked round with the unlit cigarette between his lips, absent-minded since the discovery that he had left his lighter behind. One of the lorry drivers kept spitting on the floor, *terrazzo* with saw-dust over it. Where do they have that, *terrazzo* with sawdust over it, in which countries? Suddenly seized by a limp fatigue, which

66

threatened to link him with her again, he abandoned his hesitation and asked a workman for matches, but all that was held out to him, in a cracked, oily fist, was a lighter, a little flame for this one first cigarette that he was allowed to smoke alone again, nothing else. He thanked the back of the man's head. The only face in this bar that watched him from time to time was his own in the mirror behind bottles, a narrow face with hornrimmed spectacles and a brush cut. He didn't know what there was about it that often appealed to women. Only the two water-grey eyes – they were looking out of the mirror as though they were really there in the mirror – are such that he recognizes himself in them. . . He enjoyed smoking a cigarette that did not pass from mouth to mouth in a tender game, and at the same time reading a foreign newspaper that he had just bought. After all, the world does exist. Her cunning, which yesterday evening looked practical and almost jovial, her long-distance call to see if her husband really was in London, suddenly struck him, as he now involuntarily recalled it, as unpleasant, while he stood with his cup in his left hand once more reading about Algeria. He didn't know why he thought of it now. After all, it was her affair. What made him sad was simply the thought that one far-off day, which had actually already begun, he would remember her cunning more clearly than all the rest, the way she chatted with London from the bed, the receiver in her left hand, her right hand on his chest. He had shut his eyes, in order not to be there. He couldn't shut his ears. For a long time afterwards they had only smoked in silence. After all, it really wasn't his affair how she had built it into her marriage, and he didn't want to think about it now, as he stood with his cup in his left hand reading about Algeria. But Algeria wasn't his affair either and he now felt the need to pay. After only a quarter of an hour he was like everyone else in this bar, there was nothing to distinguish him, no sort of distinction that made him feel confused in front of everyone else, and when he had paid he no longer walked on tiptoe, and he was no longer surprised that it was Tuesday, Tuesday the such and such. He was definitely leaving today. With the foreign newspaper over his mouth, because he suddenly had to yawn, he sauntered out and hailed a taxi, in order to go to the hotel. Now he wanted to sleep, to have a bath and sleep. . . The mere fact that he knows her name is too much. . . In the moving car, his hand in the shabby loop, he tried to tidy up his memory. It was yesterday, afternoon in a bar, it was raining, he was waiting for someone, he met this someone's wife, her yellow costume and her wet hair, ginger ale, the game played by that strange gentleman which bored him, which he knows, which has nothing to do with him, the cleft between him and that strange gentleman; he wanted to go on his way. . .

That was yesterday.

There is a demon, so it seems to him today, and the demon won't allow any game apart from his own, he makes our game his own, and we are the blood and the life that is no rôle, and the flesh that dies, and the spirit that is blind for evermore, amen. . . From the moving taxi, his hand in the shabby loop, he looked out at the world: yesterday's house-fronts, yesterday's squares, unchanged, the same streets and crossings as yesterday, the monstrous advertisement of an airways company that had caught his eye yesterday already. Everything unchanged: only it isn't yesterday, but today. Why is it always today? The vain question whether it was really necessary bothered him like the wet handkerchief in his trouser pocket. He wound the windows down, so that at least he could inconspicuously get rid of the handkerchief as they drove along; he didn't dare. He wasn't in the least bothered by the infidelity they had committed, both of them, he didn't need to think about that yet; he was simply bothered that it was now a fact, on a par with all the other facts in the world. He was a trifle surprised. A man of average experience – what had he expected? Even before eight in the morning, while she still slept with her hair loose, the world, namelessly scorched in a night of embraces, was already present again, more real than their embraces. A world unchanged with dirty green buses and advertisements, monstrous, with street names and monuments and a date of which he didn't want to take

68

note. And nevertheless it remains a fact, however unimportant; invisible; impossible to throw away like a wet handkerchief. He had no regrets. None whatever. He was merely bewildered that today isn't yesterday. It doesn't show when you look at the town. He was glad about it. He is himself. Really he was very glad. There is no sense in seeing each other again, and he would like to see her again, but he won't phone her, not even from the airport, because he knows there's no sense in it. . . He didn't go to the hotel, but stopped the taxi, paid, got out; he wanted to go to the museum. In order not to be in the world. He wanted to be alone and beyond time. But the museum was still shut at this hour, and there he stood, after the taxi had disappeared, on a flight of steps, his hands in his trouser pockets, coatless, a gentleman still dressed in a dark evening suit, unshaven, a cigarette in his mouth, but he hadn't any matches, nor anything in his pockets with which to feed the cooing pigeons, nothing but a wet handkerchief.

He sniffed at the backs of his hands:

Her perfume was gone –

It will come to an end if they see each other again, and it will come to an end if he flies off for ever; in any case, he knew that, it will come to an end, and there is no hope against time. . . There he stood now, and since it was cool he turned up the collar of his jacket, later he sat down on the base of a column, surrounded by cooing white and grey pigeons which every now and then, startled – what by? – flew up with a great flapping of wings to the classicistic cornices.

Was she still asleep?

They had promised each other not to write letters, never, they didn't want a future, that was their oath:

No repetition –

No story –

They wanted what is possible only once: the now. . . That had been soon after midnight and it also applied to him, who was now sitting on the base of the column, surrounded by cooing white and grey pigeons that had come fluttering down again into the empty

69

square and onto the steps, one after the other, this time without a great flapping of wings, and who didn't know how to ward off the future – because the future, he knew, that's me, her husband, I am the repetition, the story, the finitude and the curse in everything, I am the process of ageing minute by minute. . .

Then he looked at his watch, which, however, wasn't on his wrist; in order to get out of her flat quicker he had simply stuffed his watch into his trouser pocket. It was now 9.05. Provided his watch was still going. At 11.30 he had an appointment, a business discussion to be followed by lunch probably. Before strapping it on his wrist, he held his watch to his ear; it was going. So it was 9.05. Less than twenty-four hours had passed since they first met – yesterday afternoon in that dreary bar. Up to now there had been no repetition for them, not even of the time of day. No yesterday, no today, no past, no rounding-off by time; everything is now. Their first morning, their first midday. Apart from the few insignificant words when he ordered coffee and bought cigarettes and asked the workman for a light, not a word had come between them, no conversation with other people. The world was still simply outside. He was smoking now; suddenly he had found matches after all beside the wet handkerchief, and one of them still lit. So now he sat and smoked, his eyes on his black patent-leather shoes, which were now dusty, and didn't know how to ward off the future that was already beginning with his remembering. . . He remembered the flat. She wanted to show him the maps of Brazil, when he called for her to go to the opera, and she refused to be put off, although it was already high time for the opera. He stood in the hall waiting, not without a touch of impatience, although she was the one who was interested in opera, not he. He would have preferred a film, a film and afterwards dinner. He waited, his superfluous hands in his jacket pockets, for the information about Peru which in her opinion might be useful; in particular she hunted everywhere for the road map of Peru, because he intended to travel by car, if the occasion ever arose. Only a second before it happened he wouldn't have thought it possible; she stood there carefully

70

unfolding the road map of Peru. He wouldn't have thought it possible; to be more exact, he wasn't thinking about it at all, and when he felt that his hand, which he imagined to be in his jacket pocket, was stroking her forehead, he was more astounded than she. She acted as though she didn't feel it. Hadn't this gesture, light and like an insignificant joke, occurred once before? He had forgotten it, now recalled it and was ashamed of the repetition. That afternoon already, in the bar, his hand had unexpectedly stroked her forehead – as though in jest. As though in farewell. She acted as though she took it for everyday good manners on his part, and so they studied the tattered road map of Peru, which I had preserved for years as a memento, and even if his gesture hadn't hurt her feelings, nevertheless there was a silence, before they discussed road conditions in Peru, now in a more matter-of-fact tone than ever. This was at eight o'clock. She was wearing her overcoat, they meant to go to the opera, and this was no pretence; they still thought they were going to the opera, even if they missed the first act. Her car, which she hadn't even locked, was standing down below in the street, where only vans were allowed to load and unload, and she hadn't even (as he saw next morning) switched off the lights. Bent over the map of Peru, which still lay spread out on a chest next morning, they talked differently from the way they had talked that afternoon in the dreary bar, where it was a flirtation out of embarrassment, all on his side; in the bar he hadn't known what to talk about to her. Now they talked like two sensible people, bent over the map of Peru. She was sorry her husband was away; because her husband, she said, could have given him much more accurate information about Peru. She took it for granted that he really did want to go to Peru. He smiled. Peru! This was later to be the only name which he uttered during their embrace; but he didn't know that yet, when he smiled, and his smile confused her a little. Although he made a polite effort to display a knowledge of the Incas, while she, but without sitting down or offering him a chair, took a cigarette, they didn't really know what they were talking about. They looked at one another. It must have been

71

about nine and she still hadn't offered him anything; they were still standing smoking and she still had her coat on. She seemed to have an urge to keep mentioning the name of her husband, as though she were in danger of forgetting him; she was visibly reassured when he too took the name of her husband, whom he only knew by name but had never met face to face, in his mouth, and she thought it funny that they didn't sit down. He reminded her of the opera, which was inexorably proceeding, while she sat down, but without taking off her coat. He didn't sit down until much later. He found the fact that he wasn't also wearing an overcoat embarrassing; it looked as though he hadn't just come up for a minute. He talked standing, talked a great deal, but for his part on the verge of boredom, his hands in his trouser pockets; he was afraid of his hands, which weren't listening to him. He was afraid of the silences. It was already the third time they had looked at one another, a man and a woman, without a word, without even a smile. Without embarrassment. In the meantime he had sat down after all, but in such a way that a table stood between them, as though both of them shrank from any undertaking that might have outwardly changed anything, from putting on a record, for example. They sat and smoked. He talked about cats, he didn't know why. It was almost eleven when they both admitted to being thirsty. She immediately stubbed out her cigarette in the ashtray. Although it would have been more comfortable to have a drink here in her flat, they both felt they ought to go into town for a drink, to some bar again. Their agreement took them back, their wordless agreement. Glad to be thirsty, they both stood up, although, he felt, it would not have been flying in the face of convention for her to have given a visitor a drink at midnight. She put out the standard lamp. Up to now the whole flat had been lit up and all the doors had been open for hours, ever since she looked for the map of Peru, even the kitchen door, as though they were afraid of closed doors. It was strange when she put out the standard lamp, then the ceiling light as well; he was standing in the hall, while she walked to and fro in her open coat. For the first time – she was just putting out

72

the light in the studio – he saw her figure with the sweet awareness that he would never forget this figure – he will forget it! he knew that as he sat on the base of the column surrounded by cooing white and grey pigeons, undecided whether to see her again or not. He wanted to go. Where to? He rose like yesterday and stood with his hands in his dark evening suit, like yesterday in her flat. He was thirsty. That was yesterday. They both wanted to go. Where to? They were already standing in the hall, ready to go, and he was just waiting for her to find her car key. The only light still on was the one in the hall. As she looked round, as though there might have been something not in order, her left hand was already on the switch. Let's go! she said as his hand, as though saying goodbye to a possibility, involuntarily and at the same time ironically, because he was conscious of the repetition, stroked her forehead. Let's go! he said too, and she put out the light, and there was no more light until dawn came through the window. She was still standing in her coat when all clothes, destroyed by kissing, had long since become ridiculous, a lie made of fur and wool and silk which wasn't so easy to take off, although to do so was demanded by the decorum of passion. She would have to pay a fine, she said, there'd be a ticket on her car. She said it while he, engaged apparently casually in operations that betrayed his knowledge of ladies' underwear and yet would have come to nothing without her mocking aid, thought to himself in sober solitude that he knew it would be no different from the way it always was. He was sober, yes, but without irony, sober and mute. A streetlamp was lighting up the ceiling and the ceiling lit up the room, as he, a gentleman in black patent-leather shoes for the opera and a white shirt with a tie and still with his watch on his wrist, but without his glasses, which she had taken from his face, felt her unfamiliar body; she read his smile with her fingers from his unfamiliar lips. Not to know one another to a degree that went beyond all possibility of knowing one another was beautiful.

At ten o'clock, exactly, the museum opened.

He shut his eyes like the child who has said it will shut its eyes

73

now so that the darkness of the night shall not enter its eyes and extinguish them. . . He was now sitting on a bench in the room with the skylight. . . He heard whistles from a goods station that he had never seen, the steaming of a small locomotive, puffing, whistles, and echoes of whistles, then again the trundling of a goods train with creaking axles, the pounding of the wheels over the points, whistles, brakes, the echo of whistles, the puffing again, then silence, then steaming again. And so on all through the night. When he woke the whistling had stopped, he didn't know where he was, the cooing of the pigeons had stopped too – the pigeons weren't there any more, not a white pigeon and not a grey pigeon, not one single pigeon. . . He was sitting on a bench in the room with the skylight, where an attendant was walking to and fro watching him; he had evidently been asleep.

This dismayed him.

Probably he had only slept for two or three minutes, sitting, as one sleeps in the train or in an aeroplane, with his mouth open, idiotic, with his face slipped sideways; perhaps people had passed through the room, a group with a guide, he could hear voices. . . Not the night, not her body in the night, but his presence in this skylighted room seemed to him like a dream, the cooing of the pigeons like a distant memory; only the absence of her little body was real, present, as he stood with his arms crossed over his chest, while from far away the town sounded like surf, a dull boom, monotonous, like waves, those were the green waves. Perhaps the attendant was disturbed by his wearing a dark evening suit in the morning, and with the collar turned up. That was it! He turned down his collar.

He forced himself to read:

"Hermes. Probably beginning of the 3rd century BC, partially reconstructed, left leg replaced, also the neck. Posture of the head (original) is contested."

He looked at the posture of the head.

It was Tuesday.

He didn't know what it was that was getting lost hour by hour,

74

he merely felt that his memory was detaching itself from her real person, and blamed himself for it. At the same time it gave him a sense of relief. He was free. Once he took out his wallet to see if he still had his flight ticket. He had. He had to be at the airport at 18.40. Till then he was free. What his memory told him about the woman who filled his mind was correct and irrelevant, like a "wanted" notice, saying nothing when the person isn't there: colour of hair such and such, wearing a yellow costume (but that was during the afternoon in the bar, in the evening she wore a white one), handbag black, speaks with a slight accent, probably from Alsace, age about thirty, slim. . .

The attendant had gone.

From time to time he heard voices again, someone came into the skylighted room and left again, from time to time he heard an aeroplane over the skylight. Then it was quiet again. And outside the sun was shining. But at times, too, clouds passed over the foreign town; he could see this by the way the room suddenly became greyer, the marble flatter, then the room became very light again, the marble granular –

Why didn't he move along?

Alone in this great skylighted hall, leaning back on his arms as he studied the marble statue with the contested posture of the head, he was still sitting on the upholstered bench – suddenly very much alone. But he didn't go and ring her. He knew what would happen. The day comes when people ask each other questions, if it's only: What did you do yesterday evening? I rang three times. Where were you? The question is still quite innocent, indeed one feels flattered by the other's curiosity; the other doesn't want to know, merely to show how much he or she was longing –

Now he had risen.

In order not to fall victim to the future. . .

It was ridiculous: I stand up, I sit down, I smoke, I stand still, I sleep, I wake up, I stand up, I walk, I sit down, I stand up.

Outside the pigeons were cooing again –

75

He hailed a taxi.

During the night, even if they scarcely slept, they had said practically nothing to each other, in order not to let the world get at them through words and names; they hadn't remained silent, oh no, but they had whispered, as though nothing existed but them, no before, no after, not a single name, only them, nameless.

Now the clock struck eleven.

He decided to cancel the business meeting at 11.30.

In his pigeon-hole at the hotel lay a note, which was handed to him along with his key, a message. Who from? The way the two were handed over together, the air of discretion, offended him on her behalf. He might just as well have come from a stag party. The note said that a lady had rung him and wanted him to ring her and gave him her number and her name, which now, since he had just come from her embrace, had a strangely puzzling effect on him. More than that. He felt her request that he should call her – he read the note in the lift, forgetting his floor and his room number – to be a breach of promise, infamous, an infidelity. While he kept the oath they had sworn during the night, the only thing they had in common, she entered into an alliance with the world. That was how he felt it when he reached his room, where he intended to sleep until his departure; he wouldn't ring her, a disillusioned man, as he slipped off his black patent-leather shoes, suddenly weary with disillusion, also a bit glad of the disillusion, which freed him from her, a woman who entered into the namelessness of all women who just happen to need a man. Only now did he read the note carefully, to increase his bitterness, and notice the time the message had been received, 7.10 p.m., and hence his mistake. Her call and request that he should ring back had been made yesterday. That altered everything. He worked it out: at 7.10 yesterday he had been on his way to her. What he read in this note was a request from a lady who no longer existed, who would never exist again, an unknown woman in a yellow costume in the afternoon on the stool in an empty bar. Why this resurrection? He had already crumpled up the slip of paper and thrown it into the wastepaper basket,

76

displeased not with her, displeased with time, which announces its presence everywhere and over every trifle, time, which is forever overtaking us, transience in a trifle; he put his dark evening suit in the suitcase, folded its limp sleeves as though it were a corpse, and laid his dark trousers on top of it, had sat down on the edge of the bed and taken his wristwatch off his wrist, when he saw the crumpled note in the wastepaper basket again as the only thing he had of her, apart from his dream. As he uncrumpled and smoothed it, he examined the note again; it wasn't her writing. He didn't even know her writing. As though what he feared and what he hoped were now changing places, he was seized by a certain feeling of melancholy that her urgent request that he should call her had not been made today; 7.10 p.m., that could only be yesterday. The pneumatic drill was now yammering again in the street outside, but the silence which he now heard was louder than the pneumatic drill; her silence. Not his silence, which he would have enjoyed, but her silence. Suppose he rang her now? To break her silence. He sat with his hand on the telephone. His bed was turned back but untouched. Finally he pulled himself together. He took a shower. . . Every woman, he thought, every one he had made love to, had felt herself loved; but every one he was really beginning to love had told him sooner or later that, like every man, he didn't know the first thing about love. . . He was standing under the swishing shower when the telephone rang, for an instant hesitatingly, then resolutely. When he had picked up the receiver, because the ringing didn't stop there was a call for him, just a minute, they would put it through, not without a pounding heart, at the same time amused, the telephone crackled. Hallo? He stood naked like Adam and wet and waited for it to ring again, and was rendered speechless by his pounding heart. He could no longer imagine her voice. Ready, contrary to all their promises, to see her again, he saw the curtains, which were not drawn, so that perhaps he could be seen, but he stayed at the phone till he heard the voice of a man who, as arranged, was waiting for him downstairs in the lobby.

Yes, he said slowly, he was coming.

77

Let my name be Gantenbein.
I imagine:
my life with a great actress, whom I love and hence cause to
believe that I am blind; our happiness in consequence.
Let her name be Lila.

The world considers it sheer madness when, in order to marry,
we stand in front of the flash-light, an actress and a blind man;
people give this marriage (I can see it by the way they wish us
luck) a brief summer at best, and the only thing they aren't sure
about is which of the two, Lila or Gantenbein, really deserves
their pity.

We are happy as very few couples can be.
I imagine:
Lila deceives me (to use this very stupid word) from the beginning, but she doesn't know that I see it, and is as pleased as a child
when I meet her out at the airport every time. I wait on the spectators' terrace, leaning on my black stick, my glasses on my face,
equipped with a yellow armband. She doesn't wave as she crosses
the wide concrete field in the guided throng of passengers, and
naturally I don't wave either. In order not to act out of character
for joy. I see a gentleman carrying her coat, and Lila, as she looks
round for me, slips her arm through his. Now she has seen me!
I see that. Then they disappear into the customs hall down below.
I shall never ask who the man was. Because Lila never mentions
him and I couldn't explain how I know of his existence, not without
giving up my rôle. If I ask how my Lila is going to carry all her
stuff, bags and coats, umbrella, magazines and all the other things
she takes with her on the trip, she assures me there is always
someone there who will help a lady. I needn't worry about that.
Sometimes it takes a very long time to get through the customs,
Lila can't help that. I love waiting at airports, I like seeing the jet
planes whether it's raining or not, and I like hearing the rever-
berating loudspeakers, the world is full of destinations: Vienna,

Cairo, Stuttgart, Athens, Beirut, Bangkok, Tokio, Stockholm, Lisbon, Caracas, Prague, London, New York. . . Before going to the customs hall, I naturally make sure everything is in order; I go to a mirror and push my tie slightly to the left or the right, so that after the first exuberant greeting she can push it straight again.

No doubt my heart is pounding.

The others who are waiting with Lila to pass through the customs, also awaited by their husbands or wives, wave through the glass and try to communicate in deaf and dumb language, which we, Lila and I, don't need. At last it is Lila's turn. The gentleman who is carrying her heavy overcoat is always the same one, even when Lila has had to fly a day later than planned. Why is he shaking his head? That's the last straw, these customs fellows mixing up the cases. A good thing my Lila has someone to look after her! All the other men are bothering only about their own luggage. Now they part; I see that they do so without a kiss. Does she doubt my blindness after all? Then the gentleman walks past me while Lila, now loaded up with coat and bags and magazines, walks more slowly than he. Since he always looks to the other side when he passes me, I can say nothing about his face. What a load she has to lug along! And I can't even go to meet her, but stand like a shop-window dummy, until her kiss strikes me, then I say: Lila? and reach for her things. What has she forgotten? Lila hasn't even time to straighten my crooked tie. Is she looking for her porter? He is following ten paces behind us, and to draw this to her attention I ask her if she has a porter already. But that's not it. My question as to how the filming went is premature. She'll tell me about that later. She asks me to wait for a moment, not to leave the spot, otherwise she won't find me again. A paper, she says, she just wants a paper. So I don't move from the spot, a shop-window dummy, decked out with her coat and her umbrella, in everyone's way. Obviously she has forgotten something; he'll miss his bus, I think to myself, and it isn't the custom for him to travel in our car. I see him start, then feel in his pockets, left, right, shaking his head, continuing to hunt, I don't know what for. I see all this as if it were a film: not without intense interest, not without that advance participation one has at the beginning of a film, hoping that one will soon get to understand what is happening on the screen. And as in a film, the people on the screen are alone, without me even though I can see them; I can only imagine their feelings, but I'm outside, not involved, hence unperturbed. Perhaps he still has her passport? I'm more patient than the porter. Right! Now they're laughing. Of course her passport (why didn't Lila ask me?) is in her own handbag. To laugh too is outside my rôle. I ask the porter about the weather, to distract his gaze, in case Lila and the gentleman, who now really has missed his bus, should kiss each other after all out of sheer relief at finding the passport. I'm not yet as free as I should like to be; it might upset me if this porter (society) were to think he saw more than I. Now Lila, free from worry, on my arm again, is entirely mine, I can feel that. Did you get your paper? I ask without any undertone, but now she answers my question as to how the filming went. Oh that! We now look for her car, which I can see, but Lila remembers clearly having parked it further away and I don't argue. I go this way, I go that way, it's no laughing matter for the disgruntled porter. There, she says, there it is! I don't say: You see! Scoring little points like that wears away a great love. In the car, with Lila at the wheel, I know that I am the happiest of lovers.

I hope Gantenbein will never abandon his rôle, which consists in believing. How tender Lila always is, when she comes back from a guest star appearance. She sits on his knee, as relaxed as he is himself, and overflowing with affection, because there are no eyes to make her stubborn and untruthful; happy as she has never been with a man, free from hypocrisy, since she does not feel spied upon by suspicion. Then she takes off my dark glasses, in order to kiss Gantenbein on the eyes, and her love is true, I can feel that, because she doesn't have to lie to Gantenbein. How gaily loving she can be! She wouldn't like to live with any other man, she says, and I

80

believe her. It won't always be easy, but it's worth while; you can't pull the wool over the eyes of a blind man.

I don't trust my eyes.

Her suitcase, whose zip is only half open, spews out its contents into the corridor, scripts, letters, shoes, and it will remain like this for days, but Gantenbein won't say anything; our flat is like a waste-paper basket the moment Lila gets home from shopping, and it will stay like that, I know, until Gantenbein secretly collects the string and gets rid of the paper. Without saying anything. Lila thinks the place gets tidy of its own accord in time; she believes in pixies, and that is touching.
What's tidiness!
Only a person who is not at one with the world needs tidiness, in order not to go under; Lila is at one with the world.

Lila is beautiful. Plenty of people tell her that. When Gantenbein tells her, he shuts his eyes, combs her hair with his fingers and fills the hollows above her collarbone with kisses.

Lila in front of the mirror.
"Heavens above," she says. "I'll be late!"
She can't find her necklace.
"What time is it?" she asks.
She will always arrive late, Gantenbein can't prevent that, but she won't arrive without a necklace; since he has secretly tidied up, he knows where her necklace is, and since he loves, he puts it in a place where Lila finds it.
"Ah," she says, "I've got it!"
So it always works out all right.
Somehow.

I imagine:
Sometimes we have company, and that's more difficult – because the others are watching – for example when Lila doesn't see that

it's high time the ashtrays were emptied, that the sugar for the black coffee is unfortunately missing, that our dog (I think we have a dog) isn't contributing anything with his snoring under the table to the question whether Ernst Jünger has undergone a transformation, then I have to take care not to give myself away, not simply to get up and empty the overfilled ashtrays. Someone switches over to Joyce. So I stroke our snoring dog (dachshund or Great Dane?) and see how our guests squint about for sugar, saying nothing myself, saved by my dark glasses from hypocritically having to pretend that I too have read *Finnegan's Wake*. When will the ashtrays be emptied? Someone switches over to Benn, which doesn't surprise me; Kafka has already had his turn. Lila with her blue, open, beautiful, big, blue eyes! She doesn't see that the implacable gentleman who cuts across every conversation with the great example of Brecht has the same face as a gentleman who, up to the very last, was a member of the Reich Chamber of Writers, and of course I pretend not to see it either. Things like this are an effort. Occasionally I do get up and empty the ashtrays. . . My fear that I might give myself away by such actions, a blind man who sees that it's time the ashtrays were empty, does not apply to Lila; Lila is so used to it; only the guests, who don't know me yet, are something of a danger to me, and in the kitchen, as I empty the ashtrays, my heart pounds. I hear from outside:

"Tell me, Lila, is he really blind?"

"He makes an enormous effort," says Lila, "to prevent people from noticing it. I always pretend not to notice."

"How blind is he actually?"

"It's astonishing," says someone, "how he notices when somebody is looking at him. It's only when he is speaking himself that you really have the feeling he's blind. Don't you agree? When he gets excited like just now."

(– about Little Rock.)

"You're right," says the gentleman who has now discovered Brecht. "It's amazing, when he sits there like that stroking his dog, you keep getting the feeling you're being watched."

"Yes, you do, don't you?"

"How long has he been blind?"

"Ever since we've known each other," says Lila simply. "At first I thought he was pulling my leg." Pause. "Haven't I ever told you about that?"

"No."

And then Lila tells our story, more amusing each time she tells it, I enjoy listening to it, she tells it in all the greater detail the less true it is, this ever-successful anecdote of our first meeting. How Gantenbein comes into her dressing-room, a gentleman with the usual flowers of enthusiasm, Lila unwilling to receive him, if the old dresser hadn't told her it was a blind man. Lila just removing her make-up, wearing only her underclothes with an open dressing-gown over them. A blind man? She looks (Lila always says) like a witch, oily. What do you mean, blind? she asks, but before she can form any definite idea of how a blind man can be enthusiastic about her acting, Gantenbein is already standing in the doorway, irresistible as the blind can be; he doesn't see how impossible it is, doesn't even see the disgruntled expression of the dresser. Simply stands there holding roses, three of them, and says how enthusiastic he is. One has to believe him. And yet on that particular evening (this too she always says) Lila was worse than usual, positively catastrophic. He doesn't know what to do with the roses. Lila before the make-up mirror, oily as she has said, a witch with her hair down; she offers him an unfortunately wobbly chair and the dresser takes the three roses from him, whereupon he kisses the dresser's hand (Lila only includes this detail when I'm not present) and doesn't notice his slip, somehow poignant, and how then, sitting on the wobbly chair, he talks about Ionesco, profoundly, the first visitor to her dressing-room who doesn't let his eyes wander, but keeps them exclusively on art, while Lila combs her hair and later dresses in his presence, yes, after only a quarter of an hour one feels as though one were married with a blind man. Someone laughs stupidly. . . Then I bring in the clean ashtrays. Silence. I see their astonishment when Gantenbein places the clean ashtrays on the

83

table, one here, one there, without knocking over their cups or glasses. Why aren't you drinking? he asks and fills the empty glasses; they watch him, I can see quite clearly whether there is any lurking doubt or not. When someone doubts, I fill his glass till it overflows. Such dodges are more and more rarely necessary. Someone switches over to Musil.

An important point:
I let Lila keep me.
Reason:
There is scarcely a couple who don't discover, at the latest when they separate, that the money question between man and woman has never been solved, and are not bitterly hurt by it. What I mean is not the fortunate couple who have too little money; that isn't the money question between man and woman, which only starts where both are earning enough for themselves, and hence enough for both, so they think. Experiments have been made with a joint account, everyone gives and takes equally, but they are wrecked on present-day society which, from the receiver of tips to the State, continues to turn to the man –
I imagine:
Lila and Gantenbein in a restaurant, Lila, who is keeping me, and the waiter brings the bill. I see the slip of paper bashfully folded on the plate and play the blind man, carrying on with the conversation like a woman when the bill comes, talking while Lila looks for her handbag and pays, talking as though nothing had happened. When the waiter comes back with the change I ask him if he has any cigars. This takes a bit of time. So we talk. Lila is magnificent, as silent as a man, not a word about money, so that we can really converse. On my side at most the question: Have we paid already? Sometimes I really don't see, since it isn't my business. Lila talks about her childhood, while I choose my cigar, and I'm intensely interested in her childhood. But now, while I cut the cigar, Lila has to pick up her handbag again in order to pay again, since otherwise the cigar boy, whom her childhood really doesn't concern,

84

won't go away. I have no idea what my cigar costs. I only know that it is paid for, and wait eagerly but not impatiently to hear the rest of the story about her childhood, smoking. When we get out of the taxi I say: The rain has stopped at last! While Lila rummages in her handbag again and pays and has to work out the tip. I wait on her arm. When the post brings nothing but bills, I say: I've got no post at all today! We only talk about bills when they're grotesque; but the rent, the calendar-determined bills for telephone and electricity, for heating, for garbage disposal and road tax and everything that is recurrent, are not grotesque and hence not a topic of conversation, any more than the contributions to the involuntary old-age insurance. For these I am blind. When Lila isn't at home, I pay from the money in the drawer. Lila doesn't demand an account, nevertheless whenever the drawer is empty again I report the fact, if I don't forget. Lila is either horrified or not. Although I make it a principle, in order not to allow any question of money to arise between us, not to bother about the relation between income and expenditure, I can always feel when Lila, without being miserly, suddenly has the feeling that we ought to save. I respect her feelings. I do without cigars, without showing my displeasure, knowing there are whole strata of the population who never smoke cigars. I am prepared, she knows, for every renunciation. If Lila nevertheless brings me cigars, a whole boxful, even if unfortunately not quite the right ones, I naturally smoke them; Lila must know what we can afford. That it's time I had a dinner jacket isn't my idea, and I put off the enterprise as long as I can; the fact is, I haven't any patent-leather shoes to go with it either. On the other hand I must go to the dentist, that can't be helped, I don't need to say how bad I feel about it. I don't ask how much my Lila earns; she doesn't know herself, and I only see how hard she works and keep thinking Lila ought to allow herself a holiday. Without fail. She needs it, a blind man can see that. The pocket money Lila gives me is variable, but on the average enough for me to buy her a present for her birthday or Christmas, which Lila herself would never do; she is moved by it every time, and then

I kiss her on the hair. If I go out with another lady, which can happen, she doesn't pay for me; to this extent, the exchange of rôles is not quite complete. Every lady, the more certain she is that I don't consider her venal, allows herself to be paid for. That's the way it is, and I enjoy it. Moreover it evens itself out, because when Lila goes out with other men they insist on paying, and I know Lila enjoys that, if only because she doesn't have to keep putting her hand in her handbag for every coffee, every taxi, every cloakroom attendant, every newspaper, every cinema, every parking meter. Sometimes I feel sorry for Lila. Then I wangle, by paying behind her back; Lila never notices, she is a woman, even if an independent one. I can't carry my wangling too far, in order not to take away her feeling of independence. Lila doesn't know that I have a bank account of my own, and I shall never tell her. If I did, it would be the end of everything. To make the situation clear: I have never yet paid from my account for anything that concerned me. I live utterly and completely, from head to toe, on Lila. And she knows that, and that's enough. What I pay for out of my secret account are everyday things, not worth talking about – the dog licence and occasional payments that would depress her, changing the engine oil and greasing, stamps, fees, beggars, porters, Salvation Army, mere trifles. I simply can't bear to see a woman forever having to reach for her purse, just like a man. It is sufficient for the principle of the thing if Lila feeds and clothes me and I do nothing to provide her food, her clothes, her cosmetics, her and our amusements. If Lila says: Shall we have lobster today? I fall in with her gay mood. Why should the man decide when luxury is in place? Everyone has his need for luxury at a different time, and one of the two has to fall in with the other. Lila is as unreasonable as a man who is paying. But she is paying. In being reasonable, the one who isn't paying is being a spoilsport and I take care to avoid that, even if it isn't always easy to eat lobster simply out of love for the other person; but he who lets himself be kept must subordinate himself. I let myself be kept. Lila is happy with the situation.

Our everyday life is jolly.

At the concert I see Madame Stoffel lying in wait for us on the stairs and interrupt our conversation to say: Do you happen to know what Madame Stoffel is doing these days? This is the last thing Lila is worrying about. I hope she isn't here! I say, and soon afterwards Lila plucks my sleeve. You'll laugh, she says, she's standing up there! And I laugh, as though I didn't believe it, while we take the other stairs.

Lila believes in my sixth sense.

She has read that a blind man knows his way about his house better than anyone who has to rely on his eyes; a blind man never reaches for the doorknob or the tap and misses it; thanks to a sense of space that is never a fraction of an inch out, he moves about like an angel who never breaks anything. This, if in more scientific terms, was in an American magazine, written by a professor who had carried out over a thousand tests. Lila read it out to me. And I stick to it. Only once, when a short circuit threw our flat into darkness, did I have trouble like a man who can see, or cannot see, precisely because it is pitch dark. But as it was pitch dark, Lila also couldn't see the trouble I was having, and when I finally appeared with a saving candle, I once more seemed like an angel to her.

I imagine:

Lila buying clothes, Gantenbein has to go with her, it helps her to make up her mind, so I sit there all afternoon, the only man in the small but expensive shop esteemed by connoisseurs from all over the world, surrounded by costumes on hangers, and mirrors; wherever I look I see Gantenbein with his black stick between his knees and his sombre spectacles on his face. I see that Gantenbein is more smartly dressed since I have let myself be kept; I owe this to Lila; a blind man of the world. Lila is now trying on the next model, the fifth to be submitted to his judgment. I am all eagerness, not to see the model but to hear Gantenbein's verdict. The lady who runs the esteemed shop, not a businesswoman but an artist and at the same time a friend, a little too plump herself to compete with her customers in elegance, but also a woman of the world, who doesn't really treat Lila like a customer but as a sister, so to speak, as a connoisseur, as a human being, as someone capable of sharing her enthusiasms, and who really, as she constantly lets us see, wants nothing but understanding for her disinterested and spontaneous joy in just this model which Lila is about to try on, this lady, whom I don't like, is enchanted with Gantenbein. Not every gentleman, whether husband or lover, would give up so much time. Then we, Lila and I, are always rather embarrassed about the blatancy of our love. Now the lady draws the curtain; at the same time she is convinced that I am blind to the prices, which Lila pays with bundles of notes, unseen, as they both think, and since, in spite of the knowledge of human nature with which she credits herself, she has no idea which of us is keeping the other, I am in her eyes not only the most patient, but also the most generous of men who has ever smoked out her small, but expensive shop, which of course is not called a shop but a studio or boutique. So long as Lila is in the cubicle the dressmaker always acts as though I were not blind. You'll see! she says and sends out for a coffee from across the street, so that my enthusiasm shall not flag. You'll see! This is just a phrase of hers. But Lila, behind the curtain, also behaves as though the whole performance were exclusively for my enjoyment. Drinking my coffee, I sit there like a pasha shopping for his whole harem; Lila being merely a model for a whole harem. A whole Bible of silk patterns – what am I supposed to do with that? No one doubts my blindness, on the contrary; but they want to give me the feeling of being taken seriously, in spite of it. Naturally I never take off my glasses. If necessary, I see the colour of the material by squinting round the sides of the glasses. I don't do it for long at a time, because it makes me dizzy. I squint only at the crucial moment.

"Darling," says Lila, "I've made up my mind."

"Fine."

"I'm sure you won't regret it," chatters the lady. "As I told you, I saw the costume at Dior's and I thought of you at once, Madame Gantenbein –"

88

Now I squint.

"Who could wear that," I hear, "if not you, Madame Gantenbein! Only the collar, as I said –"

I consider it impossible.

"Darling," says Lila "– I've made up my mind!"

Her reiteration is a sign that she in unsure, needs help. Lila has taste, but like everyone she also has an origin. Assuming that Lila is a banker's daughter: naturally she shies away from every collar that makes her too lady-like and invariably falls for anything simple. Or assume that she is the daughter of an Alsatian hardware merchant: whether it suits her or not, she falls for everything that creates a great-lady effect, and over such things she becomes colour-blind at the crucial moment. I have to help her. Whether Monsieur Dior, who made this model as though just for Lila, loves her I don't know. I love Lila, whether she is a banker's daughter or the daughter of a Puritan pastor – which is also conceivable. I say:

"Fine."

"We've just got to pin it, you know –"

Lila is pinned.

"Is it the yellow one?" I ask.

"No," she says. "The wine-red one."

The lady and sister and artist, who now has to squat in order to pin the hem – I see that when she squats her own skirt almost bursts – thinks it's incredible how well it suits my Lila, and I see how hard Lila, who can now scarcely move for pins, is trying to believe in the incredible in spite of all the pins, by twisting her head round towards the nearest mirror.

"Wine-red?" I ask. "Like burgundy?"

"So to speak."

"Oh yes," I say, "that suits you."

It's difficult with a blind man!

"Like burgundy?" I ask. "Or what?"

Gantenbein, the blind man, remembers many kinds of red. A salmon red would also suit her, he thinks, even a dry brick-red, perhaps a dark-red too, such as you see in withering roses, a slag-red or something like that. He loves red. He remembers one single red that wouldn't suit her: an insipid, false, chemical, lemonade-red. He remembers: blood is red, red is the colour of warning, the flag that warns of blasting operations for example, the mouths of fish are red, so are the moon and the sun when they rise and set, fire is red, so is iron in the fire, sometimes the earth is red and daylight from behind closed lids, a headscarf in Corot's brown and green and grey landscapes is red, so are wounds, poppies, shame and anger, a great many things are red, the plush in theatres, rose hips, the Pope, the cloths in bull fights, the Devil is supposed to be red, and red awakes out of green, yes, red is the colour above all colours – for Gantenbein.

Her dress has been pinned.

"Darling," she says, "it isn't lemonade-red."

I smoke and wait.

"No," says the lady. "Good heavens no!"

I smoke and wait.

"Or do you think," asks Lila, looking in the mirror and addressing the squatting woman, "that it's lemonade-red –"

"Certainly not!"

In the mirror I can see that Lila is hesitating.

"Don't worry," the dressmaker says to me, impatiently, she thinks all men are blind. "Don't worry," she says and turns to Lila, "– the gentleman would be enchanted if he could see you."

As a blind man, under no obligation to be enchanted, I ask further questions, which Lila answers with a confidence that she does not live up to in the mirror; for instance:

"It isn't too simple, is it?"

It's bombastic.

"No," says Lila. "It isn't that."

I smoke.

"Do you mind," says Lila in a small voice, "I'd like to try the yellow one on again –"

Perhaps Lila has known for a long time that I'm not blind, and is merely letting me stick to my rôle out of love for me?

I imagine:
Lila, wearing her coat, crosses the stage, rehearsals, Lila is rehearsing Lady Macbeth, I am sitting in the darkness of a box, my legs resting on the upholstery of the front seat, chewing Spanish nuts which, so as not to leave refuse lying about, I crack in the darkness of my jacket pocket, hence blindly; the refuse stays in my pocket, and finding a nut in this refuse gets more and more exciting. The management have approved my presence, though they weren't pleased about it; no doubt they had to, in order to be able to talk Lila, who always gets her own way here, out of something else. Probably the management are asking themselves why I, a blind man, have to come to rehearsals. Lila wants it. I'm a help to her, she says. . . So Lila crosses the stage, wearing her coat, greeting and being greeted, as though she were not late. I don't know how she does it; we entered the theatre together and almost on time, because once again Lila couldn't find her watch and I didn't arrange for her to come across it, so that we should be in time for a change. She must have felt this when she came to the stage door. Perhaps she had a conversation on the stairs or picked up a letter from the doorkeeper, I don't know, anyhow Lila managed to re-establish her customary lateness; we wait, silence before the rehearsal, hammering backstage, silence, the producer at his desk is discussing things with his assistants, which is not urgent, but necessary, in order not to give himself and the waiting actors the feeling that they are merely waiting for Lila. She'll be there any minute, she has walked across the stage, she is already in her dressing-room. Silence, then curses from the producer, which I understand in my box. Lila doesn't set out to keep people waiting, it's just a gift she has. They wait. If I told her later what I had heard, Lila wouldn't believe it; she has never heard these curses, on the contrary, everyone will be enchanted when Lila comes, disarmed,

enchanted. So I wait and chew my Spanish nuts, since one isn't allowed to smoke in the box, and wait. . .

Enter Lady Macbeth.

In a sweater; but people believe her –

Of course, Gantenbein can't intervene when the producer gets some unfortunate idea into his head; no producer is going to let a blind man tell him what to do. Nevertheless I am a help to her. Secretly. After the rehearsal.

For example:

The producer, ordinarily a man who works in visual terms, has the idea of leading Lila right up to the footlights when she wants to wash the dreamed blood from her hands. It's different, granted, but bad. I'm amazed that he can't see it and go on chewing my Spanish nuts, while Lila is quite willing, hence right up by the footlights. . . Later, during lunch after the rehearsal, I ask why the Doctor and the Gentlewoman, whom Shakespeare has provided for this famous scene, have been cut; a question even a blind man is entitled to ask, because I didn't hear the Doctor and the Gentlewoman, who, although they don't have much to say, stand beside Lady Macbeth while she speaks in her frenzied dream. In fact, I'm told, they have been cut precisely because they don't have much to say. What I think about that is simple; but how is Gantenbein (without betraying that he sees what everyone could see) to communicate his impression to the man who, blind with ideas, is just eating his *filet mignon?* So as not to betray that I see, I ask the waiter if there's any *filet mignon.* . . During the next rehearsal, when my Lady appears again and puts the candlestick down by the footlights, washing her hands not in front of the Doctor and the Gentlewoman, whom Shakespeare invented as hidden spectators, but only before the audience, I close my eyes to test my impression. I hear the difference. When Lila was practising at home, not knowing that Gantenbein, hidden like the Gentlewoman and the Doctor, was listening, she sounded like a person in the solitude of her fear, and I found it shattering. Not now. Now I chew my Spanish nuts as she speaks. The same text, the same voice; yet not the same.

Because she is standing at the footlights, not overheard by Doctor and Gentlewoman, whom in her madness she doesn't see, but alone at the footlights: overheard by critics and the audience. I must tell her. You sound like a lady of the Oxford Group communicating her anguish of soul as a party piece, I tell her during a break, too dreary for words, and as the producer comes up to console Lila, I ask him if he doesn't agree that Lila sounds like a lady of the Oxford Group, an exhibitionist, it sounds as though she were standing right by the footlights, yes, as though she were standing right by the footlights –

Sometimes they change things.

Without telling Gantenbein: in order to test his ear... After the rehearsal I always wait at the stage door, leaning on my little black stick, pretending not to know the most famous actors, and in the early days they always used to walk past without nodding, not in an unfriendly way; but what good does it do a blind man to nod? At most one might say: Your wife's just coming. In passing. What could an actor talk about to somebody who has never seen him? After a time they begin to nod, to which, in order not to act out of character, I unfortunately cannot respond; then I stare straight ahead like a scarecrow, without greeting them, but not without seeing how their respect grows. Respect for my ear. On one occasion someone speaks to me and wants to know whether the conspiracy in the third act sounds more like a conspiracy now that they are no longer standing twenty feet apart. Obviously Lila has been talking. He introduces himself:

"I'm Macduff."

"Yes," I say. "It sounded different today."

"You see," says Macduff.

"Don't you also think," says another, and I see that he is addressing himself exclusively to the blind Gantenbein, "that it comes off better, much better, that it's just right, when he" – and he points at a third – "doesn't look at the witches, since they are, so to speak, only a vision seen by me?"

I'm speechless.

93

"Or don't you think so?" he asks and remembers that I can't see him. "I'm Macbeth."
I also introduce myself:
"Gantenbein."
They take my blind man's hand.
"I'm Banquo," says the third.
"Pleased to meet you," I say.
Lila is always the last to come out.

I imagine:
From time to time I get fed up with playing Gantenbein and go out into the country. Afternoon in the Grunewald. I collect pine cones and throw them as far out as I can into the Krumme Lanke, and Patsch, our dog, jumps into the brownish, still, bubbly water. I see the floating pine cone, but he doesn't, blind with eagerness, paddling. I throw a second. Point with outstretched arm, so that he shan't swim into emptiness, and now he snaps at it, turns round. Two ears and a muzzle holding the pine cone, two eyes above water. . . I'm very fond of these Havel lakes, memories, and Gantenbein doesn't need to see how things really stand with Berlin; there's a lot of life, I hear. . . Two eyes above water while his four legs kick away out of sight, that's Patsch, not a trained blind-dog; I have to train him myself, and of course I can only do it when there's no one around, for example during the morning in the Grunewald, while Lila is rehearsing at the theatre. A great deal of work is being done there and here. The scene in which Patsch finds his blind master's little black stick still doesn't go right. Is he too stupid or too clever? Now he comes ashore, our pine cone in his jaws. Then he stalks through the bushes on the bank, wagging his tail, panting, stands in front of the pine cone in the sand, shakes a brief shower of rain out of his hair. Good dog, Patsch, good dog! We haven't reached the point where I carry on whole conversations with my dog yet. As we walk on — there's absolutely no one about — I use my black blind man's stick to play a kind of baseball with pine cones. So: pine cone in the left hand, stick in the right

94

hand, now I throw a pine cone into the air – hit it with the stick. . .
Seven hits out of ten, not bad, and Patsch runs through the Brandenburg sand to look for the hits. A relaxing game. I need that
from time to time. A Catholic has confession in order to recover
from his secret, a splendid arrangement; he kneels and breaks his
silence, without giving himself into the hands of men, and afterwards he gets up and enters into his rôle among men again, redeemed
from the unfortunate desire to be recognized by men. I just have
my dog, which keeps silent like a priest, and by the first human
habitations I stroke him. Good dog, Patsch, good dog! And we take
each other on the lead again. No more games with pine cones!
Patsch understands, and after I have put my paperback (I read in
order to know men by their judgments) in the first wastepaper
basket, we walk along once more in the proper manner, a blind
man and his dog. At Onkel-Toms-Hütte we take the Under-
ground.

Coffee on the Kurfürstendamm:

Journalists, actors, cameramen, a doctor, admirers from every
intellectual sphere, at times I feel spasms of impatience, a downright
anger, over the way they take me for blind, just because I'm her
husband, the way they feel it necessary to instruct me:

"Lila is a wonderful woman!"

I stroke the dog.

"You don't know," says one of them, "what a wonderful wife
you have –"

Pause.

What can Lila say to that?

And what can I say to that?

Lila straightens my tie.

I see:

Lila, courted by everyone with eyes in his head, and as they look
at her their eyes become glassier than their horn-rimmed spectacles;
Lila is defenceless, so that they hold her hand or her arm, and I
know that actually Lila doesn't like it. How can I tell the gentlemen? Now I could read a newspaper without exciting attention;

95

they feel so safe in front of me. Why do men in love always look rather stupid? I stand up. What's the matter, asks Lila, the centre of enthusiasm, so that the enthusiasts have to turn their heads too. Nothing! Her coat has slipped off the chair, no one has seen it, I say: Excuse me, Doctor, you keep treading on the lady's coat. Oh! he says and immediately draws his foot back, but no conclusions from my remark. He apologizes to Lila. The simple assumption that the husband is blind is unshakable.

There are times when I don't find it easy.

But the advantages, I tell myself at such times, the advantages, you must never forget the advantages of your rôle, the advantages in big things as in little; you can't pull the wool over the eyes of a blind man. . . Another plays the part of a writer whose name is irresistibly rising in the monthly sales charts, in fact is really at the top since, between ourselves, the other titles are not to be taken seriously. His name is hovering just at the point where one cannot yet talk about a best-seller, exactly at the upper limit of literary significance. But he is not to know that I have seen the sales charts, and he is the only one at the table who turns to the blind Gantenbein, and I for my part am the only one who is under no obligation to know his book. I treat everyone who needs it as a famous man.

"You see," says the famous man –

I see, while I hold Patsch, who always wants to get away from the all too human, on the lead, I see how his eyes, as he talks about himself to the blind Gantenbein, keep looking round to make quite sure that no one else is listening. I see that the man takes me seriously because Gantenbein can't contradict, and since he, who is taking me seriously, is at the moment famous, all the others suddenly take me seriously too. Suddenly Gantenbein is asked how he sees the future of Germany, yes, Gantenbein of all people. I start in dismay. I don't want to be taken seriously, but it is precisely the blind whom they do take seriously.

"How do you see the whole situation?"

I behave as though I had never seen the West, and everyone knows about the East. . . Then in the car, when Lila looks for her key again, I give her the handbag, she left it on the chair, I saw it, and we can set off to have a bottle of champagne with the infatuated doctor, just two pairs of eyes, so to speak: Lila and the doctor and I. The infatuated doctor, who is sitting at the back, talks nonstop, as though I were not only blind but also dumb. I am sitting beside Lila and see a hand on her shoulder, a hand that comes from behind, full of sympathy over a stupid criticism in the Press. It would be heartless if I were to keep completely silent about it; the criticism was really very unjustly witty, and I put my hand, the blind one, on the other hand, which has been lying on her weak shoulder ever since we passed the Gedächtniskirche, and say: Don't worry about it! We drive on in silence.

And so on.

What I have learnt in the theatre:

An actor who has to play the part of a man with a limp need not limp with every step. It is enough if he limps at the right moment. The more sparing, the more credible. But it depends on the right moment. If he limps only when he knows he is being watched, he appears a hypocrite. If he limps all the time we forget that he limps. But if he sometimes pretends not to limp at all, and limps as soon as he is alone, we believe in it. This is a fundamental rule. A wooden leg, in reality, limps all the time, but we don't notice it all the time, and this is what the art of acting has to mirror: the moments of surprise, these alone. Suddenly reminded that this man limps, we are ashamed of having forgotten his disability, and through our shame convinced, so that for quite a time the actor has no need to limp; he can take it easy.

An old passion of Gantenbein's, I assume, is chess. And that too is no problem.

Have you moved? I ask.

Just a moment, says my opponent, just a moment!

I see and wait. . .

Yes, says my opponent, I've moved.

Well?

B 1 x A 3, announces my opponent.

Aha, the knight! I say, and especially those opponents who aren't used to the fact that I have the board in my head are generally flabbergasted when, filling my pipe, I say: Aha, the knight! And most of all they are flabbergasted to find that I still know the positions of my own men, which of course I never touch; I now light my pipe as I say:

F 8 x B 3.

My opponent has been hoping that I've forgotten my bishop and is ashamed of it; consequently he not only loses his knight but also his good conscience, I can see that, he begins to make mistakes.

Well? asks Lila. Who's winning?

Gantenbein! he says, his voice as gay as possible, but on edge, I see his fingers, he is surreptitiously counting the pieces, he can't understand it, in the past my opponent always used to beat me, and I've learnt nothing in the meantime, nothing to do with chess. He is just surprised. He doesn't think, he is surprised.

Have you moved? I ask.

It's as though he couldn't see any more.

Right, he says, B 2 x A 3!

My opponent really thinks me blind.

B 5 x A 1, I request, and while my opponent is forced to throw out his castle with his own hand, to put my queen in line with his king – he shakes his head, and in case Gantenbein isn't in the picture, he himself says: Check! – I tell Lila not to disturb us, but too late; my opponent lays his king down flat, which I'm not supposed to see; I wait, sucking my pipe.

Checkmate! he announces.

How's that?

Checkmate! he announces.

I'm becoming a phenomenon.

The point has been reached where Lila even leaves her letters about, letters from a foreign gentleman that would smash up our marriage, if Gantenbein were to read them. He doesn't do so. At most he puts an ashtray or a whisky glass on them, so that the wind can't leaf through them.

Let's hope I never act out of character. What use is seeing! It may be that Gantenbein, not equal to the magnitude of his love, occasionally tears the glasses from his face – and immediately puts his hand over his eyes, as though they were hurting him.

"What's the matter?"

"Nothing," I say, "my dear –"

"Headache?"

If Lila knew that I can see, she would doubt my love, and it would be hell, a man and a woman, but not a couple; it is the secret that a man and a woman keep from each other that makes them a couple.

I am happier than I have ever been with a woman.

When Lila, suddenly harassed and hurried, obviously late for something, says as she goes out that she has to go to the hairdresser today, her hair looks like a witch's, and when Lila comes back from the hairdresser, who is well known for keeping people waiting, and I can see at a glance that her hair has not been to the hairdresser, and when Lila, without actually stressing that she heard it under the hair-drier, tells me of some event in town such as one does hear about at the hairdresser's, I never say: Lilalein, why are you lying? For however lovingly I said it, humorously so to speak, she would be offended; she would ask Gantenbein what right he had to make the unheard-of statement that she hadn't been to the hairdresser, he, Gantenbein, who can't see her hair. I can see it, but I don't think Lila looks like a witch. So I don't say anything, not even anything humorous. Do I have to know where Lila has been since four in the afternoon? At most I say, without touching her beloved hair of course, just in passing: You look magnificent! and she doesn't ask how Gantenbein can say such a thing; it makes her happy, whoever says it. And I mean it quite honestly; Lila looks magnificent, precisely when she hasn't been to the hairdresser.

Lila too is happier than she has ever been.

99

I mention flowers that suddenly appear in our flat only when I know who has sent them; when I know from Lila. Then I can perfectly well say: I think we can throw those orchids the management gave you into the garbage pail now. And Lila agrees. Every now and then, however, there are flowers it's better for me not to mention, roses that Lila herself doesn't mention, thirty long-stemmed roses, and although their scent inevitably fills the flat, I say nothing. When a visitor bursts out: What marvellous roses! I don't hear, and there is no need for Lila now to say who sent them. When I hear who sent them, I don't understand why she has kept quiet till now about the roses I have been seeing for three days. A harmless admirer of her art. Lila is never at a loss for names; there are many admirers of her art who not only pity Gantenbein, because he doesn't see her art, but also pity Lila; they admire this woman not only because of her art, but just as much in a human way because she loves a husband who doesn't see her art. Hence the roses. Or whatever they are. I never ask who gave her the jolly bracelet. What I see and what I don't see is a question of tact. Perhaps marriage is altogether only a question of tact.

Sometimes Lila, like every sensitive and intelligent woman, has her breakdowns. It begins with a depression which I see at once, and any man who wasn't pretending to be blind would ask after a while what was wrong, tenderly at first, then roughly, since she keeps silent, more and more loudly silent, in order not to come out of her depression, and finally conscious of guilt, without being conscious of any definite guilt:
Have I upset you?
For heaven's sake say something!
And so on.
All these questions, tender or rough or tender again or rebellious, since after a torturing silence she says in an undertone and close to sobbing that it's nothing, don't lead to a relaxation of tension, I know that, but only to a sleepless night; finally, in order to leave Lila alone, as she wants, I take my pillow without a word and sleep

in the living-room on the floor, but soon afterwards I hear a loud sob and after half an hour I go back to Lila. But now she can't speak at all any more; my demand to be sensible makes too great a demand on myself, I yell, which puts me in the wrong, until dawn breaks, and in the course of the following day I shall ask her to forgive me, without finding out the reason for her depression.

Gantenbein is spared all this.

I simply don't see her depression, which renders anyone who does see it helpless; I chat blindly or remain silent blindly, ignoring her sudden muteness – unless Lila, forced to it by my blindness, announces right out what has depressed her this time; but that is something one can talk about.

A situation in which Gantenbein takes off his dark glasses without thereby striking a false note in his rôle as a lover: lovemaking.

A man, a woman.

She probably knows many men, of various types, including those who fail because they feel under an obligation to provide something which the woman does not primarily expect, rapists not out of frenzy but by an act of will, ambitious men who fail out of ambition, tedious, playful men are the exception, once perhaps an Italian fisherman, but for the most part intellectuals, neurotics, easily disturbed and difficult when they see Lila's eyes, they kiss with closed eyes in order to be blind with ecstasy, but they aren't blind, they're scared and are deaf, they haven't the hands of a blind man, surrender, but not unconditionally, not proof against being disturbed, tenderness, but not the tenderness of a blind man who is released from everything that frightens when one knows that it is also seen by the other; a blind man doesn't come from outside; a blind man, at one with his dream, doesn't compare her with other women, not for the space of a breath, he believes his skin –

A man, a woman.

Not until next morning, when Lila is still asleep or pretending to be asleep in order not to wake him from his dream, does Gantenbein silently take his glasses from the bedside table, to protect Lila from any doubt; it is only the secret which they keep from each other that makes them a couple.

I imagine:

Gantenbein is standing in the kitchen; Lila is in despair, she can't bear to see Gantenbein, her husband, standing in the kitchen all the time. Lila is touching. She simply can't believe that there isn't a clean cup left in the world, not one single one. Let's go out, she says, to give the "little people" a chance. . . So they go out. . . Lila can't bear dirt, the sight of dirt destroys her. If you could see the state this kitchen is in again! says Lila. Sometimes Lila goes into the kitchen to wash a glass or two, a spoon or two, while Gantenbein, a know-all like most men, thinks mass-production speeds things up. During an hour in the kitchen, whistling or not, he washes all the spoons and all the cups and all the glasses, to clear the decks for a while. He knows that again and again they will need a spoon or a glass, generally a glass, if possible one that isn't sticky, and if Lila goes into the kitchen Gantenbein isn't free either; he knows how impractical she is about it. And more than that; he knows that one shouldn't give a woman practical advice, it merely hurts her feelings and changes nothing. What to do? A man who notices a certain inefficiency in a woman he loves always seems loveless. There is only one solution: to see in it her specific and special charm, although it isn't really anything special. But what to do? So long as no housekeeper falls from heaven, it doesn't help matters if Lila is cut to the quick to see Gantenbein standing in the kitchen with an apron round his waist, and fetching the dustbin every day, removing the empty bottles and the crumpled newspapers, the printed matter, the string from parcels, the disgusting peel of an orange full of lipstick-smeared cigarette ends –

I think I've found the solution!

Since Lila really doesn't want Gantenbein, her blind man, to wash the dishes merely because they don't wash themselves, indeed, they don't even take themselves into the kitchen, and since every time everything in the kitchen is as clean and shiny as in a shop selling kitchen furniture Lila is saddened as if it were a secret reproach, Gantenbein has taken to never cleaning the whole kitchen. In fact, I admit, there was generally a little bit of malicious masculine pleasure involved, a scornful enjoyment arising out of masculine self-pity that made the kitchen shine like a new pin. It will never happen again! Now Gantenbein never washes another plate or another spoon, when Lila is at home, but always in secret and then only so many as will not be noticed. The kitchen looks as though no one bothered about it, and yet, lo and behold, there are always a few glasses left, a few clean knives, always just enough, and the ashtrays are never so shiny that they gleam like a reproach, only the ash doesn't pile up into mountains, the repulsive date stones have evaporated, so have the sticky rings left by the wine glasses on the little marble table; the printed matter, last month's magazines, have disappeared, as though they themselves had finally been forced to admit their yellowed out-of-dateness — but Gantenbein is sitting in the rocking-chair smoking a cigar when Lila comes home, and Lila is relieved that he no longer imagines he has to worry about the kitchen.

"You see," she says. "It gets along all right on its own."

Only miracles make everyday life bearable.

I love September mornings, dew-grey-blue, sun as though behind smoke, houses in the country look as though they were wrapped in tissue paper, the lake flashes, the opposite bank is as though wrapped in a haze, autumn, I stand among the greenhouses, Patsch on the lead, among the beds of a rural market-garden, without my glasses in order to see the colours of the flowers correctly, and I have hidden the yellow armband in my trouser pocket, so that the friendly gardener shouldn't think he can sell me wilting flowers. His knife flashes like the lake. Delphiniums, yes, or whatever it is, I nod and every stem, which I greet with a nod, meets the knife and falls with a low crack, flowers for Lila, crack, crack, crack, a whole gardener's arm full of blue delphiniums, crack, till I say: Enough! I'd like something yellow to go with it, no, something paler, not too much, and a few red blossoms, asters, yes, also dahlias, yes, wine-red, a lot of wine-red, a lot. . .

Today Lila is coming back from guest performances.

If she knew how Gantenbein enjoys the glowing or glimmering colours of this world when she is away, and how he deceives her with every flower he sees!

Her plane is due at 15.40.

Now, at home, I bunch the flowers into the vase, step back with my head on one side, without my glasses, so as to study the interplay of the colours, bunch them again, I've got plenty of time, days of yearning are long, the hours even longer, I like doing this, bunching the flowers, waiting and changing the bunch, and although I know that Lila never comes earlier than she has promised, and sometimes later, but never earlier, I am nevertheless on edge. Away with this cloud of rustling tissue paper, away with the stalks, away with them! When I am ready the clock is striking eleven, a last look without glasses: I'm enchanted, one shouldn't praise oneself, but I'm enchanted by my taste, inactive now, since there is nothing left to put in a bunch, I whistle perhaps, too restless to be able to sit down and read a newspaper, therefore standing up, two or three times I bend down again to pick up a fallen blossom from the carpet, then that too is finished. I know Lila isn't even in the plane yet, and bend down a fourth and fifth time, because another blue flower has fallen off, an impatient delphinium, Lila is probably still in bed, and I think: Let's hope she doesn't miss her plane! and I stand up, a cigarette in my mouth which I forget to light, because I am looking now at the clock, now at the flowers, there's always a twig, a blossom, a colour that disturbs me, it doesn't look like blind chance, and it must do that without fail, I think, without fail, I want Lila later, not as soon as she gets back, but later, when this room is already full of handbags and magazines and gloves, to be able to take pleasure in what she sees without having to praise Gantenbein, on the contrary, I want her to tell me how beautiful chance looks, yes, it often takes me hours to get it right – I arrange the bunch again, again and again a blossom flutters down, looking beautiful on the carpet too, yellow and blue flakes, still dewy, of course I always have my dark glasses handy, in case Lila comes early, sometimes I hold them between my teeth, when I need both hands for the bouquet, and I listen like a child stealing from the pantry, trembling to the depths of my soul. . .

I believe I really love her.

Next day, when I have interpreted the telegram (NOT ARRIV-ING TILL FRIDAY 10.45) as meaning that the last outdoor shots have probably had to be postponed because of the autumn mist, my bouquet has unfortunately lost some of its freshness; I once more sweep up from the carpet the blossoms it has lost overnight, the heavy-headed dahlias in particular are bending their heads thoughtfully. I arrange the others in a fresh bunch – in vain. . . I see that my bouquet, by showing that it is from yesterday, is now standing in the vase like a reproach, mute, Lila will be dejected, although I shan't see anything, shan't ask any questions. One can see straight away that it isn't a spontaneous bouquet any longer. So I throw it away before going out to the airport; naturally not into the dustbin, where Lila might see it, but into the cellar, where it can wither unseen, covered with old magazines. I want it to look as though I simply didn't think of flowers. That means the vase has to be washed before I go to the airport –

Lila has already landed.

Gantenbein almost got there too late (the stairs also had to be cleared of yellow and blue flowers at the last moment), and I'm just in time to see that the gentleman who is carrying her things to the customs shed is still the same one. Patsch whines as the strange gentleman and Lila, Patsch's mistress, say goodbye fifteen feet from his blind master; I have to exert all my strength to keep him on the lead, my silly dog.

I hope I shall never get jealous!

A master baker at O, a man in his forties, known in the village as good-natured and reliable, acted as follows out of jealousy: first he shot his wife's lover, a twenty-one-year-old Tyrolese, with the

105

regulation rifle every Swiss has in his cupboard, not at random, but straight in the loins; then he took the stainless steel soldier's knife, which is also part of the equipment kept in the cupboard, and slashed the face of his wife, the mother of two children and pregnant at the time; after this the master baker himself took his two victims to the nearest hospital, laying them in his van like loaves; the lovers are out of danger – according to the newspapers. . . . A week later Burri, my doctor, tells me why he didn't come over for chess. That evening he had a phone call from a woman who asked him if it was dangerous to take ten sleeping tablets. When the doctor enquired who was on the line the caller hung up. Soon afterwards a second call came in the same woman's voice asking the doctor to come at once, now giving the name and address and saying it was urgent. (It was our Thursday, I had already set out the chess men and was waiting.) In the parlour he finds the baker's wife, who is pregnant, and the young journeyman baker. They love each other. Therefore the master baker of O can't sleep, that's all; he is lying upstairs. But when the doctor goes up, he finds the room empty. There follows a long discussion between the doctor and the wife in the parlour. The shirtsleeved Tyrolese, asked by Burri whether he wants to marry the baker's pregnant wife, stands there with his legs apart and says: How can I, when I can't earn a living? The master baker really seems to have lost his head. Ten sleeping tablets? At this moment – Burri can't believe his eyes – the cupboard opens and out steps the good-natured and trustworthy baker in a white apron, as in a farce. At last! he says, at last he knows for sure. So I'm right! he says, at this moment the most composed of all of them, dignified in spite of his ludicrous appearance, sensible, satisfied, now that he knows his long-felt jealousy is not groundless. At last she has admitted it! he says. In spite of a long consultation with the doctor, who doesn't have to open his little black bag after all, they cannot agree as to who is in the right, and the doctor's sober suggestion that the journeyman should leave the house and find himself another job fails to convince the journeyman, and the woman, who is standing between two fathers, thinks above all

106

that the master baker ought to be ashamed of himself, a demand which, for his part, fails to convince the baker. Nevertheless, everyone has calmed down when Burri (too late for our chess, I understand) finally leaves the house, on the homeward journey amused in retrospect at the emergence of the flour-covered baker from the cupboard. . . Days later, when the doctor happens to be passing through O again and sees the familiar light in the parlour, he feels obliged to pay a call and enquire what solution they came to. This time he finds the master baker alone in the parlour. How are things? The man is sitting there calm and sober. Doesn't the doctor read the newspaper? They drink a plum-brandy man to man. The baker himself doesn't know much more than was in the paper. Only this much: after the doctor had gone, he asked his Anneli to come up to their bedroom, in order to begin a new life at once, as the doctor had suggested as he stood in the doorway. She did not fail his hopes; for the first time he slept without sleeping tablets again, and hence not so deeply, so that he was woken by the emptiness of the bed, the coolness beside him. This was at about one o'clock, an hour after Burri had gone. Now he was furious. Simply to frighten them, he took the rifle and the pocket knife out of the cupboard and went down to the parlour. They didn't let him down, no, he found them here on this sofa together in the dark parlour as white as shirts in the moonlight, four-legged. When he switched on the light it was already done: the journeyman, who wouldn't look for another job, twisted round screaming, and he felt very sorry for his Anneli because of her face, which was bleeding from every lie. Although the perpetrator, as he saw for himself, couldn't possibly be anyone but he, the master baker behaved like a person who has come from outside and is completely in his right mind; he immediately rang the doctor, who however was not at home, then, as described in the papers, he drove the lovers in his delivery van to the nearest hospital, where he was known as a trustworthy master baker, and himself to the police, where he was similarly known.

Naturally he will have to appear in court.

I wonder why he shot the journeyman in the loins and why, on the other hand, he did not mutilate the woman's body but her face: the body is innocent, the body is the species, the face is the person. . . When I went to O recently to see the baker, he was not in the shop. Nevertheless I bought a loaf which I later fed to some chickens. A second loaf, which the shop assistant also sold me, I fed to the swans on the lake. I didn't know why I felt I had to see this baker. When I ventured to try again just before closing time I was already familiar with the sound of the bell on the door, then this bready air in the country shop, the silence till at last someone comes; I saw already that there was no bread lying in the racks, not even rolls, there were only wafers and sweets, and I was just wondering what else I could buy for the swans, biscuits perhaps, and I started when suddenly – as I had hoped – the master baker in person shuffled into the shop in his floury slippers. A man with a deed, as baffled as a policeman who always sees such deeds from the outside only, a man of the old stamp, probably a gymnast, even though bakery-pale, a native of the country in the way that makes crime look like something foreign, a man whom one simply wouldn't credit with such a thing – like the majority of perpetrators – he asked me what I would like. His deed, I could see, didn't fit him at all. That sort of thing happens: someone suddenly performs a deed that will put him in prison, and I stand there terror-stricken. I bought a bar of chocolate, as if nothing had happened, and paid in some confusion, went on my way and saw him staring after me distrustfully.

Camilla Huber is beyond price: she believes in true stories, she is crazy about true stories, she is gripped by everything that she believes really happened, however insignificant, which I tell her during the manicure – but it must have really happened. . . Naturally I never visit her without making an appointment in advance, and then I politely arrive late, equipped with my little black stick and yellow armband, the dark glasses on my face; I never meet Camilla Huber in a negligé; she keeps me waiting in the corridor until she has combed her hair and dressed, until the room has been tidied. She doesn't want to see any more of her life than I do. When she is ready for Gantenbein to enter, I see no brassières and no stockings any more, occasionally perhaps a hundred franc note beside the cognac, occasionally a man's wrist watch. Let's hope the forgetful fellow doesn't come back for it! Obviously Gantenbein is the only client who really has a manicure. And Camilla rejoices in me, I believe, as in an alibi, and my manicure is really carried out with a great many instruments, which she possesses for the benefit of the police, and with a touching patience on both sides, since good Camilla, as I can feel, has had absolutely no practice. I should have my fingernails cut more often, if Camilla Huber didn't always expect a story, if possible a serial story; at the very first finger I present to her, or at the second at the latest, she asks straight out:

"What happened next?"

"I've had a talk with him."

"Oh."

"Yes."

Camilla Huber, now in a white overall, sits on a low stool, while Gantenbein, his hand on a velvet cushion, has his nails filed, his pipe in the other hand.

"You've really talked with him?"

"Yes," I say. "A fine man."

"You see," she says and laughs, without looking up from my fingers. "And you wanted to shoot him in the loins!"

I lapse into silence, ashamed.

"You see!" she says and files and can't restrain herself from asking: "What did he say?"

"He worships my wife."

"And what then?"

"I can understand him," I report. "We talked about mythology, he knows a great deal, he has been invited to Harvard, but I don't think he's going, because of my wife." Pause. "A fine mind," I say and smoke, "really."

Camilla is surprised.

"Didn't you challenge him?" she asks filing, as a woman, entirely on the side of her blind client. "I can't believe that he's a fine man!"

109

"Why not?" I ask, nobly objective.

"Otherwise he wouldn't do that."

"What," I ask, "what wouldn't he do?"

"Just what you imagine," she says.

I report:

"We talked about mythology, yes, for almost an hour, we couldn't think of anything else to talk about, it was interesting. It wasn't till we had drunk the third campari that he said he worshipped my wife, I was just paying –"

Camilla files.

"In the end he presented me with his essay," I say, "an essay on Hermes," I say in that unshakably restrained tone that in no way stresses the gulf between a comparatively educated and a comparatively uneducated person, but also in no way conceals it. "He really is a clever fellow."

"What about your wife?"

I don't understand her question.

"How does she picture the future?"

Now Gantenbein has to give his other hand, while Camilla Huber pulls her little stool over to the other side, everything as in a mirror, my pipe too now moves across to the other corner of my mouth.

"She loves him?"

"I presume so."

"What does he look like?"

She forgets that Gantenbein is blind.

"Are you sure," she asks after a period of painful work, "that it's him?"

"By no means."

"You are funny!" she says. "You keep talking all the time about a man who is having an affair with your wife, and yet you don't know who it is."

"I'm blind."

I see her lower her head, see her peroxide-blond hair; Gantenbein makes use of the moment to study his finished fingernails.

Sometimes Camilla Huber apologizes when she notices that Gantenbein winces; then they talk about something else, about manicure; but her curiosity won't leave her alone.

"– but you can imagine," she says filing, "that it's him, this Herr Enderlin or whatever his name is?"

I nod.

"Why just him?"

"I ask myself that too."

Camilla won't let go.

"Such uncertainty," she says and looks at Gantenbein as though he were the only man in his position. "That must be terrible!"

"It is," I say, "it is."

Later, after completion of the manicure has been celebrated with a cosy cognac, and after I have already picked up my little black stick, she comes back to it again.

"– but you're sure," she asks with the indiscretion of sympathetic involvement, "you're sure that your wife is having an affair with someone else?"

"Not at all."

Camilla is disappointed, as though that meant that it was not a true story, and seems to be asking herself why, in that case, I told it.

"I can only imagine it."

That's the true thing about the story.

P.S.

One day a policeman comes. They come in plain clothes, that's the mean thing. The moment Huber the manicurist (that's what the police call her) opens the door he walks into the room uninvited. Without taking his hat off. Instead, he merely shows his warrant-card, especially to the blind Gantenbein: Canton Police! In reply, Gantenbein shows his certificate of blindness, and this certificate of blindness is the only thing in which the fat little man with the hat on his head really believes. Everything else here seems to him dubious, even the manicure implements, the white overall that Fräulein Huber wears at work. He observes that some game is being played here. But what? Finally he says: Oh well. A third document, which Camilla has meanwhile dug up, her labour permit, as she declares pertly, he doesn't want to look at, as though ashamed to do so in front of the blind man. He mutters: All right. They don't feel comfortable with a blind man, I find this over and over again. For example, not one of them has ever dared really to look at the certificate, when Gantenbein shows it to them. In the end he leaves without writing a report in his notebook, not exactly polite, only embarrassed and feeling somehow magnanimous. He didn't want to show Camilla up in front of a blind man.

Enderlin and his invitation to Harvard – when asked by friends when he is going to Harvard he shrugs his shoulders and changes the subject –

Why doesn't he go?

Soon it looks as though it was a swindle, this invitation to Harvard, a three-line hoax, on which everyone has been congratulating him. People who feel friendly towards Enderlin have stopped talking about it to him. And he prefers it that way. Enderlin doesn't believe in it himself, and no document that he carries in his pocket and can show to people – as Gantenbein shows his certificate of blindness – is any help. . . He can't. He ought to have written long ago to say when he is coming, for the summer term or the winter term or whatever they call it at Harvard. He can't. Weeks pass. Enderlin is simply not the man to whom this invitation to Harvard applies, and every time Enderlin has to think about settling dates, he takes fright, as though he had to mount a plinth, and he can't. Modesty? It's not that. This invitation to Harvard (Enderlin can't bear to hear this word any more!) is pretty exactly what Enderlin has been wanting for a long time. Perhaps that was why the newspaper report confused him so: a secret wish suddenly made so public! And that's no hoax. Nevertheless he appears to himself a swindler. And people scent that, of course; that's why no one really believes in the invitation any longer, apart from the dean of Harvard University, but no one who knows Enderlin. And yet we know his achievements; they absolutely compel our recognition. That's just it! Anyone who, like Enderlin, has once designed himself in such a way that he has to legitimate himself by his achievements, never seems fundamentally trustworthy. We congratulate him on his success right enough. Only this doesn't help him at all. The lecture which Enderlin is supposed to deliver at Harvard is already written. All he has to do is to pack it in his case. But he can't. What convinces is not a person's achievements, but the rôle he plays. This is what Enderlin feels, what scares him. To fall ill, so that he can't go to Harvard, would be the simplest thing. Enderlin can't play any rôle –

I know an example of the opposite:

A man, the ambassador of a Great Power, breaks down during his summer holidays, but it turns out that what he suffered was not a heart attack but merely an insight, and no sick leave helps him to get over it, no new decoration helps him to rise above it. He has realized that he is not the Excellency for which the world, received under chandeliers, pretends to take him. By virtue of the office he holds he must be taken seriously, at least so long as he holds that office, so long as he has to take himself seriously in the name of his Great Power and for the sake of his title. Why has to? A letter to his Government, typed by his own hand so that no secretary shall find out that for years he has been serving a fake, is already written – tendering his resignation. . . But he never resigns. He chooses that which is greater: the rôle. His self-knowledge remains his secret. He fulfils his office. He even allows himself to be promoted and goes on fulfilling his office without blinking. What he henceforth thinks of himself does not concern the world. So he continues to act the part of an ambassador, transferred to Washington or Peking or Moscow, knowing that he is acting a part, and he does not deprive the people around him, who believe that he is the right man in the right place, of their belief, which is useful. It is enough that he himself does not believe. He is serene and dignified, and those who doubt him do not wound him; he has no need to fear them or to hate them, only to combat them. And something happens

113

that looks like a miracle: while he is really only acting a part he not only achieves good solid results as heretofore, but exceptional results. His name appears in the headlines of the world press; that does not mislead either. He masters his rôle, which is that of a confidence trickster, by virtue of the secret which he does not give away, never, not even in a tête-à-tête. He knows that every piece of self-knowledge which one cannot keep to oneself makes one smaller and smaller. He knows that he who cannot keep silent wishes to be recognized in the greatness of his self-knowledge, which is no self-knowledge if it cannot be kept silent, and one becomes hypersensitive, one feels betrayed because one wants to be recognized by people, one becomes ridiculous, ambitious in inverse ratio to one's self-knowledge. This is important: not even in a tête-à-tête. What has once been said cannot be unsaid. So he acts as though he believes in his own Excellency, and refuses to let himself hobnob with anyone, particularly friends, who set the same value on him as he sets on himself. No confession renders him subservient. Thanks to his personality, which he is acting, a city is saved from destruction from bombers, and his name will go down in history, he knows that without smiling, his name will be written in marble when he dies, as the name of a street or a square, and one day he does die. No diary is found, no letter and no slip of paper, that betrays to us what he knew all these years, namely that he was a confidence trickster, a charlatan. He takes his secret, the fact that he knew, into the grave, does not lack honourable ribbons, big wreaths and long speeches that cover up his self-knowledge for ever. But he doesn't squint up out of his grave; when we look at his death-mask, which like many death-masks seems somehow to be smiling, we are surprised: it has a touch of greatness, undeniably. And even we, who never thought much of him, silently change our verdict, because he never asked what it was, as we look at his death-mask.

Yesterday, at a party at Burri's, people were once more talking about Communism and imperialism, about Cuba, someone talked about the Berlin wall, opinions, counter-opinions, passionate, a game of chess, this too, move and counter-move, a party game, until someone, silent till then, told us about his flight. Holding no views. Just like that: an action involving bullets that struck his comrades, and a fiancée who stayed behind. When asked later what news he had of his fiancée, he said nothing. We all fell silent – then I ask myself, sucking my cold pipe in the silence, confronted by this real story, what I am really doing: – making sketches for an ego! ...

– having woken up again, my hair still uncombed, but having had a shower and dressed, even if still without jacket or tie, I suppose, because the first actions are mechanical, helpless habit, I only know that I am once again sitting on the edge of a bed, yes, I have once more woken up, but I am still encircled by dreams which, if I look at them closely, I fear, will prove not to be dreams at all but memory, not memory of the night, however, but memory as such, the sediment of experience, and yet I am awake, as I have said, even washed and free of emotion, perhaps even whistling, I don't know exactly, it's unimportant, and if at this moment I am softly whistling, it's only so as not to have to speak, even to myself, I have nothing to say to myself now, I have to get to the airport, heavens above it's high time, so I assume, and yet I am in no hurry, as though this had already happened before, long ago, I'm surprised that no pneumatic drill is chugging, I listen, silence, nor are any hens clucking, I listen, there's no cheap music-hall to be heard, memory, steaming and puffing in a night-time goods station, that was once upon a time, whistles and echoes of whistles, I hold my breath, silence, for the space of a breath I sit as motionless as a statue, in the pose of a man pulling out a thorn, I'm not pulling out a thorn, however, but putting on a shoe, the second incidentally, every now and then there's the sound of a lift, but I'm not even sure if this sound of a lift doesn't come only from memory, the memory of a night, another one, it doesn't worry me, I merely see that my tie is still hanging over the chair, on the other hand my watch is on my wrist, yes, it's time, so I assume, time as always, time to set out into the future, I am resolved and shaved, actually gay, without exactly showing it, once again awake, free from longing, free, evidently I have meanwhile lit a cigarette, anyhow the smoke is making me blink, and if it isn't I who am smoking, I don't know who is smoking, I only know when my plane leaves, a Caravelle I hope, yes, the weather, I'll see about that once I've left this room, I mustn't leave anything behind, no words now either that remain behind, no thoughts, I'm sitting on the edge of a bed tying my right shoe, I've had an idea for half an eternity already. . . for a moment, now before I put my foot down on the carpet, I pause: again and again, I know it already and yet I am startled into immobility, I am Enderlin, I shall die as Enderlin.

So I drive out to the airport.

In the taxi, my hand in the shabby loop, I see outside the world, shop fronts, advertisements, monuments, buses –

Déjà vu!

I try to think something.

For instance:

What I could have said the other day during our conversation about Communism and capitalism, about China, about Cuba, about atomic death and about mankind's food situation in the event of its multiplying tenfold, particularly about Cuba, I was in Cuba once – but now I'm here, being asked how many cases I have, as I show Enderlin's passport and am given a green card, *Flight Number Seven-O-Five*, the plane is late, I hear, due to fog over Hamburg, while here the sun is shining.

Will she confess to her husband?

Enderlin is not the only one waiting here, and I try to entertain him, which isn't easy, because he is secretly thinking of the night, and I can't think of anything to say about that –

A model airport!

I buy newspapers:

Another atom bomb test!

– Enderlin can't think of anything to say about that.

Will he confess to anyone?

I try to think something – this inner life of love, to tell the truth, is boring, too familiar – for example, how this hall is constructed, reinforced concrete, the shape is convincing, stylish, light and floating. Beautiful. As regards the construction: in technical language, I believe, that's called a three-pinned arch . . . but Enderlin isn't interested in that, I see, Enderlin would like to fly. The faster, the better. Enderlin is once more passing the time left to him on earth with coffee, later with cognac. His luggage has been handed in, so I am free and unencumbered, apart from his briefcase, which I put on the counter. I look round: other people are now flying to Lisbon, others to London, others are coming from Zürich, loud-speakers are booming: *This is our last call,* but not for Enderlin. I reassure him, I heard it quite clearly. Enderlin is jumpy, I am merely bored, because it really is impossible to have a conversation with Enderlin. I make sure I don't forget his briefcase. Enderlin buys perfume, in order not to go home empty-handed, Chanel 5, I know that. Is Enderlin really thinking of his home? Anyhow Chanel 5. Others are called for Rome-Athens-Cairo-Nairobi, while there is evidently still fog in Hamburg, yes, it's boring. . .

I imagine hell:

I'm Enderlin, whose briefcase I am carrying, but immortal, so that I have to live through his life again, or if you like only a part of his life, a year, if you like even a happy year, for example the year that is just beginning, to live through it again in the full knowledge of what is coming and without the expectation that is alone capable of making life bearable, without the openness, the uncertainty compounded of hope and fear. I imagine it as hellish. Once again: your conversation in the bar, gesture by gesture, his hand on her arm, the way she looks at him, his hand that for the first time strokes her forehead, later a second time, your conversation about fidelity, about Peru, which he describes as a land of hope, everything word by word, first of all the talk about the opera, which you then miss, the whistles from a night-time goods station, whistles and echoes of whistles, and nothing can be skipped, not a sound, not a kiss, not a feeling and not a silence, not a fright, not a

117

cigarette, not a visit to the kitchen to fetch water that won't quench your thirst, no shame, not even the telephone conversation from the bed, everything over again, minute by minute, and we know what follows, we know and have to live it again, otherwise it's death, live without hope of things happening differently, the business of the key in the letterbox, you know it will go off all right, afterwards the public wash at the fountain, the workmen's bar, sawdust on the stone floor, not one minute is different from the way I know it was, not a minute is left out, not a step and not an espresso and not the four rolls, the wet handkerchief in my trouser pocket, Enderlin waves, it's the same taxi, but I know that later he will get out to feed pigeons, all that over again, including the fright with the note, the mistake, the melancholy, the sleep accompanied by pneumatic drills tearing up the sunlit surface of a street outside, and later the waiting at the airport, *Flight Number Seven-O-Five*, fog at Hamburg, and what follows: Goodbye in the hope that there will be no story, reunion, end and embrace, parting, letters and reunion in Strassburg, difficulties on all sides, passion, enchantment with no future, yes, with no future – but I know the future: the happiness in Colmar (after looking at the Isenheim Altar and on the way to Ronchamp) is neither your last, as you fear, nor your highest; nevertheless, it has to be lived again, just as it was, including the goodbye in Basle, the goodbye for ever, just as it was, yes, but with the knowledge of what follows. All the presents you gave each other have to be given over again, packed and tied with ribbon again, undone and admired and thanked for with delight. Misunderstandings that ruin half a journey have to take place again, quarrels about which you cannot laugh until later, everything has to be thought and felt again, every conversation spoken again, although I know how often it will be repeated, and the same letters have to be taken out of the letterbox again, torn open with a beating heart, and all plans have to be planned again in the knowledge of how differently things will turn out, for weeks you look for a plot of land, you negotiate, you buy and have worries that prove unnecessary, hopes that fill you with bliss, I know that

118

nothing will ever be built, nevertheless the plot of land has to be measured, all for the birds, but you can't change destiny, although you know it, and again I go to the door and cordially greet the man who comes between us, again I ask what he would like, whisky or gin, again my jokes, my suspicion, my magnanimity, my innocent victory, again your trip when the car broke down, my worried night, again the familiar times of indifference, I write him my greetings again on a picture postcard, those moody greetings that I wrote without knowing, just the same, but now I know, and again the coffee boils, only to grow cold after your confession, I know, I know, and yet I have to curse again and stride up and down the room and curse, just the same, once again the glass that shatters against the wall, the pieces that I sweep up, just the same, yes, but everything with the knowledge of what happens next: without the curiosity as to what happens next, without the blind expectation, without the uncertainty that makes everything bearable –

That would be hell.

Enderlin, leafing through a newspaper, pretends not to be listening; the situation is tense; he enjoys not knowing what will be in the paper tomorrow, not knowing for sure –

That would be hell.

Experience is a foretaste of it, but only a foretaste; my experience doesn't tell me what is going to happen, it merely reduces my expectation, my curiosity –

Flight Number Seven-O-Five.

The plane has just landed, I hear, and will be taking off again in half an hour, and now I'm curious after all to see what Enderlin will do; whether he will really fly without ringing her again, without seeing her again.

You don't want a story.

You don't want a past, don't want any repetition.

Enderlin, I see, is now paying for his cognacs, there were three of them, the barman knows that, Enderlin pretends to be in a hurry, and yet there's another half an hour before passengers can go aboard, and even the man who hasn't made up his mind can be in a hurry. . . I see the plane, a Caravelle, that is just having its tank filled. A fine plane. In two hours Enderlin will be at home, if he really flies. What does at home mean? Anyhow the plane is having its tank filled, time to sit down again, to cross his legs, even to open his briefcase and take out a book; anyway, the beginning is good, in my opinion. A technical book that Enderlin would have to read in any case, and he will read it too, no doubt about that, perhaps in the plane, if Enderlin really flies, and at home there's post waiting for him, no doubt about that, perhaps very pleasant post. . .

Let's hope she never writes!

Now, so I imagine, she is no longer lying in that bed either, but has dressed in clothes Enderlin has never seen, a pair of slacks perhaps; she is convinced that Enderlin is already soaring high above the clouds, and for her part falls from the clouds when his phone call comes.

"Where are you?"

"Here," he says. "At the airport."

Outside there is a booming, the sound of jets, and also the loud-speakers, which, however, are not calling Enderlin, there's time to talk, much too much time; there's nothing to say. . .

I knew it.

When Enderlin leaves the glass booth, determined to fly, I see that our Caravelle is still taking in petrol; the white-clad mechanics are still on the plane, and the doll's face with a blue tie and rasp-berry-red lips and a little blue cap on silver-blonde hair, a stewardess from whom Enderlin makes enquiries, can't alter the fact that it is indeed (I knew it) our Caravelle that is still taking in petrol. The luggage is just being loaded on to a conveyor belt. More determined than ever not to see her again, the woman who is occupying his feelings, Enderlin is the first to take up a position in front of *Gate Number Three*, alone, glancing at his wrist-watch, which he com-pares with the public clock in the hall, as though every half minute mattered – as though he were making an escape. . .

I understand his escape from the future.

Beware of names!

Sooner or later comes the day when you know what to talk about, even if it is only that you say whom you met yesterday, an acquaintance whose name you mention because it is of no importance. You are still the only reality far and wide, other people are puppets of your mood; you still hold the strings in your hands and anyone who would disturb the situation just doesn't come into your conversation, or comes into it in such a way that he doesn't disturb it. You are still careful and say: a Pole, a refugee, who lived with us and was my sister's boy friend. Or: my first husband. Or: a colleague of mine; an aunt of mine; a young girl I once met on the Via Appia. All nameless. This is all right for a time, then it becomes too complicated, and the doctor who is my friend becomes Burri. Why should I conceal his name? That's the man who always comes to play chess. The process goes on, names are like weeds, the seed spreads in all directions and the jungle grows; you don't see it yet; you go on talking, until suddenly Burri has a former wife. Anita? You laugh: how small the world is! You lie on your backs and chat about Anita, who now was Scholl's mistress, and Scholl is the first person you both know, Hannes Scholl, who went to Baghdad. You lie on your backs and smoke. How is Scholl getting on in Baghdad, you wonder. You never bothered about it before, but now it is a pretext to talk, and it's strange to think that suddenly there is someone in the world, even if a long way from here where you are lying side by side on your backs, who knows you both without having the least idea that you are a couple. What would Scholl have to say about it! It's strange how often henceforth you talk about this Scholl – till one day he writes from Baghdad that he is coming back to Europe soon. He writes to both of you, each of you, since he knows you both and would like to see you both. Is that necessary? The process continues, it's impossible to prevent the circle from forming; the best thing would be to lie where you are and say nothing, but that's impossible. Every now and then you go out into the street and a man named Hagen says good morning to you. How do you know this Hagen? He's a friend of her brother's. You've got a brother? One ought to flee. Where to?

121

Ibiza is no longer what it used to be. When were you in Ibiza? One ought to go to Africa. You laugh! I know a man who has a farm near Nairobi and is scared of Mau-Mau, his name is Ramsegger, you've guessed it, James Ramsegger. How do you know his name? His wife didn't want to go to Nairobi, which you can understand, and is now living in London with a Pole who has also cropped up in your conversations already; now his name is Vladimir, and since he's in the ballet it can only be the same Vladimir whom I know through Frau Löwbeer. Isn't that funny? I don't mention Frau Löwbeer; but a dressmaker, as an advertisement, tells you she also works for Frau Löwbeer. Is that necessary? Unexpectedly everything hangs together, and the future turns out to be the past. You lie on your backs and smoke, in order not to mention any names. In vain! In Vienna there's a concert in a private house; her brother is playing the first violin and I am introduced to him. Is that necessary? In Strassburg, when you meet for a secret week-end, Frau Löwbeer steps out of the lift that is to take you to your room. Nothing fails to happen. Even Burri, the man whose name wasn't mentioned, now enters into the service of the demons; suddenly at a party he meets the woman who loves Enderlin and talks to her about Enderlin, his friend. Why is that necessary? You lie on your backs and smoke and tell each other your past, just so that the world, that has no idea about you, shan't know more about it than you do yourselves; this brings further names to light. Pity! The demons scarcely let a week pass without catching you: Scholl, back from Baghdad, forces you to have your first lunch à trois. Further: the professor who has just got half the Nobel Prize for chemistry and stares out of every newspaper is her father. Further: on the occasion of a private view, which is unavoidable, you are at last introduced to each other in public; her husband, who has no idea, is also there; the ever-cheerful Frau Löwbeer arrives later –

etc.

Mankind seems to be a family, as soon as one is a couple; everyone else seems to know one another in this way or that, and only the couple, who have come from making love, don't yet know each other from outside; you still smile, because no one who knows you has any idea; you still walk upon soles that do not touch the ground. For how long? Every third person encircles you; every dream is ground down.

Flight Seven-O-Five.

Enderlin (I see him looking out through the glass pane, his face in the blue reflection of the pane) is now no longer the only one waiting; a whole herd, all with green or red cards in their hands, is crowding in front of the doll's face of the stewardess, who isn't allowed to open the door yet; Enderlin is no longer at the front –

He is still free to choose.

I'm in favour of flying.

At last the door opens and the herd moves, some hurry, others wave back, the doll's face repeats:

Flight Seven-O-Five.

I can imagine both:

Enderlin flies.

Enderlin stays.

I'm gradually getting tired of this game that I now know: to act or not to act, and in any case I know it is only a part of my life, and the other part I must imagine; action and inaction are interchangeable; sometimes I act merely because inaction, equally possible, also makes no difference to the fact that time is passing, that I am growing older. . .

So Enderlin stays.

I don't. . .

Why he and not I?

Or the other way round:

Why I?

Either way:

One will fly –

One will stay –

It's all the same:

The one who stays imagines how it would have been if he had

flown, and the one who flies imagines how it would have been if he had stayed, and what he really experiences, either way, is the split that runs through his person, the split between me and him, whatever I do, either way – unless the Caravelle, which now has a free runway and is starting to move, for some inexplicable reason explodes and the bodies are identified; but our Caravelle, I see, is climbing and climbing. . .

I imagine:

In the taxi, his hand in the loop, Enderlin is proud that he hasn't chosen inaction, at the same time bewildered; his body is sitting in the taxi, but desire has left his body – it is with me, as I fly, high above the clouds – and Enderlin doesn't really know why he is going to this woman, who suddenly has no present any more; the only present is the endless drive into the town, bumper to bumper, Enderlin is sitting as though he were in a hurry, and the driver, eyes to the front, as though the future were always in front, is doing all he can to move forwards, while Enderlin, now lighting a cigarette, is secretly glad of every red light, every convoy, every delay; there's no hurry about the past. . .

I imagine:

my fingers touching her forehead for the first time; her surprised face that no longer exists, not like that. . .

I imagine:

Enderlin after paying his taxi, confused for a moment because he has no luggage, horrified, as though it had been stolen, his luggage that is now flying over the clouds, but then reassured and positively delighted to be without luggage, but at a loss, but with both feet on the ground, actually on the pavement, so that really nothing can happen to him, Enderlin doesn't know exactly where he is in the unfamiliar city, but roughly, Enderlin remembers the kiosk, provided it's the same one, and if he doesn't now go in the wrong direction her house can't be far away, Enderlin calls himself an ass, he could have gone there in the taxi, but no, he suddenly told the driver to stop, obviously in the belief that he could still choose inaction. So why does he need to find her house, yes, why?

124

Enderlin at the kiosk: he asks the way to her street, so as not to go there, but they don't know, obviously it's a different kiosk, and Enderlin is really at a loss. Why didn't he fly! All the same, Enderlin recognizes the advantage in not having (like me) to eat on the plane, and it's a pity he hasn't my hunger; Enderlin has the choice of eating French or Italian, even Chinese, because he has plenty of time, a whole evening in a foreign town, no one knows where Enderlin is at this moment, even she doesn't know, since he isn't going to call on her, he doesn't even know himself, no, the kiosk is the same, but the bar next to it is missing. Why is he walking? He might just as well sit down on the pavement. Why doesn't he simply go into a restaurant? Suddenly everything is so senseless, including eating, when one isn't hungry, I understand; Enderlin strolls not to look for her house, but to find it by chance. Until he has, he can't sit alone in a restaurant and read the menu, the wine list, to celebrate having seen her house again – without ringing the bell. . .

I imagine:

Her house from outside. . .

Enderlin hasn't seen it from outside before, not yesterday, when he went in to fetch her for the opera, it was just any house, not yet a monument, and this morning, when Enderlin left it, he must have seen the front door with its brass fittings, but afterwards he didn't look back; really all Enderlin remembers is the front door.

I imagine:

The front stucco, four storeys, string courses of sandstone, built in the eighteenth or seventeenth century, renovated (I know there's a lift inside) in the spirit of the preservation of ancient monuments, height of each storey aristocratic except on the fourth floor, gargoyles, roof with pantiles; light in places on the fourth floor –

Or:

The front faced, travertine, height of each storey democratic, a modern building but with a tiled roof to tone in with the Old City, on the ground floor is a confectioner's that surprises me; the string courses of sandstone are on the next house, so are the gargoyles; a front door with pointed arches, probably built in the fifties of our century, reinforced concrete, but lacking the shapes of modern architecture; light in places on the fourth floor –

Or:

The house has no fourth floor at all (I'm sure it was on the fourth floor) on this side and one can't walk round the house; a front that was once genteel, now dilapidated, Biedermeier, later devalued by the proximity of the goods station with its whistling and puffing, business nameplates on the first and second floors, mullioned windows; light in places on the third floor –

Possibly:

A postman, who is just coming out of the door, asks Enderlin who he is looking for, and Enderlin, speechless, pretends to have come to the wrong place and walks on – without even saying thank you. . .

(Possible but not probable.)

Certainly:

I remember the swaying reflection of a streetlamp in the wind, swaying all night long, reflection in the curtains and on the ceiling, to be exact: when the streetlamp didn't sway its light didn't pass over the balustrade of the window, and only when the wind blew did the public light beat into our room like spray into a ship, and in the reflection from the ceiling lay a woman, that's to say, looked at from outside it will be the windows just above this streetlamp, whether they're on the third or the fourth floor. . .

I imagine:

Enderlin has rung the bell.

(– while I in the plane, wedged in between strange elbows with the familiar tray in front of me, am just taking the knife and fork and spoon out of the cellophane, looking at the oxtail soup and cold chicken and fruit salad.)

I imagine:

An evening without lovemaking, for a long time not even a kiss, you are meeting from outside, which forces you to make conversation, until you scarcely misunderstand each other any more, yes, it's terrifying. . .

126

I order wine.

We are flying, according to a handwritten report from our captain, 9,000 metres above sea level at an average speed of 800 kilometres per hour.

The wine is too cold.

I imagine:

Your wine is warmer. . .

I drink mine nevertheless.

I imagine:

You are living, you people on earth. . .

The stewardess, when she finally takes my tray, is smiling. Why? They always smile, one knows that, and they're always young, even if ten years have passed between the cigarette I have just finished and the next which I light from it.

I imagine:

Ten years –

I imagine:

So there you rest, a couple with bodies dead to love all night long in your joint bedroom, apart from short trips like this one. So there you live. Whether it is a flat or a house, furnished in this way or that, probably a mixture of antique and modern with the usual Japanese-made lamp, in any case there is a shared bathroom, the daily sight of utensils for the varying care of two bodies, one female, one male. Sometimes you are filled with longing. Neither of you has anyone with whom you are more familiar, no, not even in memory; not even in hope. Can one be more closely linked than you? One cannot. But sometimes you are filled with longing. What for? It makes you shudder. What does? You live through the endless, swiftly passing years lovingly, a couple, tenderly, without showing your feelings before your guests, because you really are loving and tender, a real couple with two bodies dead to love that rarely seek each other again. Only after a trip perhaps, a separation for the duration of a congress, does it happen that in broad daylight, soon after getting back, before the cases have been unpacked and the essential news exchanged, you make love.

What business is that of other people's? It's refreshing, but it's not worth a confession. Then once again, as in the old days, you have an hourless day in a dressing-gown and with gramophone records. Then again the gentle disappearance of all curiosity on both sides, not uttered and scarcely shown; only camouflaged behind the demands of the day. Thus you live away your lives. Your letters, when you happen to be separated, almost frighten you, fill you with bliss, as you write with a storm of forgotten words, in a language you have ceased to speak. From an hotel room with an empty double bed you ring each other up, cost no object, from London or Hamburg or Sils, to chat in the middle of the night, urgent with love. Then you hear your past voices once again and tremble. Until you meet again at home. What remains is affection, the quiet and deep and almost unshakable affection. Is that nothing? You have survived almost everything, except the end, it's nothing new to you that one of you runs off in the middle of the night, that anger breaks out again, that it doesn't help if you don't speak to each other for two days, you're a couple, at any time free, but a couple. There's nothing much to be done. Often there comes the thought: why just you? You look round for other men, for other women. Not much comes into consideration, or everything. Nothing will be wilder than your love in the old days, at best it will be just the same. Was it wild? You don't speak about that. In tender protection of the present. Or else with reproach, which is false like every reproach against life. Who can help habituation? How it once was is known only to a mirror in an impossible hotel room, a rusty-silvery-smoky mirror that never stops showing a pair of lovers, many-armed, man and woman, nameless, two bodies drunk with love. Which of you saw it remains a secret. Both? That wasn't you two in particular. Why does it pursue you, what that mirror shows? It might be another man, another woman, you know that and look at each other, you two in particular, trying to achieve magnanimity through irony, in vain. How can you bear the fact that you understand each other so well, better and better, so sexlessly, as though you weren't still, seen as bodies, a man and a woman? Then you suddenly seek grounds for jealousy. Without it, God knows, your deadly comradeship would be complete. A stupid incident on the beach, a natural, easy embrace among pine trees, which remain the unforgettable thing about it, an infidelity that happened years ago, cursed in anguish, then of course forgotten, her name or his name is preserved in silence like the Crown Jewels, uttered only in extreme conversations, hence rarely, once or twice a year, so that it shan't get worn out like the love of your bodies. Oh that name! It alone produces once more the wild feeling for the other one, the sweet, the hot, the immoderate feeling, or at least the reverse side of it. The rest is affection, a great blessing really; only madness dares shake it with sudden suspicion during a sleepless night. Then what is wrong? You pretend to be tired, you put out the light, because what can be wrong? Then, while the other is asleep again, you make plans of the sort prisoners make, during the night you are resolved to take action, to break out, recklessly and childishly, it isn't desire but the longing for desire; then you pack your bags. One time she, another time he. It balances itself out. Adultery doesn't lead far, it remains part of marriage. You are a couple, fundamentally certain that you will never more lose each other, a couple with bodies dead to love, and it's no good packing your bags; a phone call by the beloved voice is enough to make you turn back, to confess or not; then you live in the everyday again, which is truth, with pyjamas and a toothbrush in your foamy mouth in front of the other, with classical nakedness in the bath that does not excite, intimate, you talk in the bathroom about the guests who have just left, and about the intellectual world that links you. You understand each other, without having to agree. You are alive, you develop your views, but you know each other's body as one knows one's furniture; then you go to bed, because it's two o'clock again and tomorrow is a strenuous day. Now isn't Now, but Always. There are moments of excitement, tender excitement, but one of you is tired or full of thoughts that are only now, whereas your bodies are always. Then you're alone in a house, the two of you, but you're often alone, so often. There's nothing to it. Marriage has got you

129

again and you give each other a kiss that is like a full stop. You are filled with longing – not for each other, because you're both there, you long for something beyond each other, but you long jointly. You talk about a trip in autumn, a trip together, you suddenly long for a country that actually exists, you could go there in autumn. No one will stop you. You don't need a rope ladder in order to kiss, and no hiding place, and there are no nightingales and no lark to warn you it is time to leave, no myrmidons force you together, no prohibition, no fear that your amorous sin will be found out. You are approved of. All that prevents you is your bodies. Now you smoke another cigarette, you talk, you read the newspaper in bed. You don't enquire into your story; that is well known, so to speak. The calendar of your early times has long since been emended; a selection of names and dates and places, at first bold in its incompleteness, then carefully completed, has been closed for years. Why should you now, at two in the morning before a strenuous week-day, explore your past again? Confession with its joys has been used up, trust is complete, curiosity abandoned; the other's early life is a book you think you know as you know a classic, a bit dusty already and only when you move house and are faced with the empty rooms, which echo, do you pick up such books again and are surprised to find out who you have been living with all these years. You can't be surprised throughout all the years. Now you put out your cigarette. The past is no secret any longer, the present is thin because it is worn out day by day, and the future means growing old. . .

I am flying.

Please fasten your seat belts, we're coming in to land again, *stop smoking, thank you*, I not only stop smoking but also imagining, now is now, I wait for the usual bump as the plane touches down, that's the present, *we hope you have enjoyed your flight and that we shall see you again*, the present is already past again, *thank you*.

But I'm waiting with interest:

to see who has come to meet me at the airport.

130

I look:
if she has black hair and water-grey eyes, big eyes and lips that are full but never cover her upper teeth, and a tiny birth-mark behind her left ear, then it is I who didn't fly when it came to the point.

I'm growing older –
Via Appia Antica.
She could be my daughter, and there's no sense in our meeting again. I should like to, I've fallen for her, but there's no sense. We are standing on a Roman burial mound, afternoon, actually they're waiting for us in town. The whole time I see nothing but her eyes, a child, once I ask what she is thinking, and her eyes look at me and I know already that she is not a child. We dare not sit down on the summery earth lest we become a couple. I don't kiss her. There's no sense, we both know that, it doesn't have to be. In order to do something, she looks for a clover, a four-leaved one, as is appropriate to moments of happiness; but in vain. An aeroplane is droning in the sky; our gaze remains in the branches of the pine. With her leather bag hung on her shoulder and a three-leaved clover in her hand, she stands and turns round in the wind, which rumples her hair, and looks out over the brown countryside, Campagna with proliferating suburbs, which would have provided a pretext to talk about town-planning; she keeps silent. I give her a resinous pine cone. I really can't guess what she is thinking and repeat my question. She says: The same as you! But I'm not thinking anything. Her eyes: they are shining with present that can't be touched. Where shall we now throw these resinous pine cones? Once I jokingly press her head to my head, without kissing, and we both laugh. What about? There is simply no target for our resinous pine cones; so we take them with us. No doubt people can see us from far away, as we stand on this burial mound, a man and a girl, now arm in arm. Jokingly? For something to say I say: Shall we go? Because of the climb, I take her bag, she gives me her hand, sticky with resin, once I take hold of her foot, because it

doesn't find the foothold between the tufts of dry grass, and then we are at the bottom, clap the dry earth from our hands longer than necessary. In the car, after we have been driving for quite a while, with the roof down, so that she can bathe her reddish hair in the wind, I ask for her address just as I am changing gear, that's to say casually. And she writes it down on a letter from my pocket. I drive slowly, because of the old Roman road surface. Now, as she looks at me silently from the side, I could say something about the road surface: about the legions who marched over this surface, the thousands of years and so on. I don't say it, because I've said it often before. On the other hand I ask: What can one do with a day-dream? as we are held up by a red light, my hand on the quivering gear lever, and she answers: Take it! And then, after I have changed gear, we drive on –

Basta!

Today I threw away the pine cone, which was still lying in my car, because it had no scent any more, and her address too; one day I shall see her again, I know that, by chance in the street, a young woman, chatting animatedly about this and that, about her marriage and so on.

Burri, the doctor, often talks about cases while I would rather play a game of chess, and then I am gripped after all by what Burri, slowly cutting a cigar, tells me about everyday events in his clinic, while I equally slowly set out the pieces for our chess, the box with the ivory figures on my knee. . . But for the means of modern medicine which, unquestioningly employed, cause most of us as it were to outlive ourselves, I know that I too would twice have died a natural death, and one would be spared the question of how to get through one's old age, no doubt of that. . . Now I hold out my two fists so that Burri can choose black or white; I'm listening, but even so I can hold out my two fists. As the guest, naturally, Burri has the choice. It's our Thursday. Burri, as always, has come to play chess. I'm waiting. But Burri, leaning back in his armchair, first lights his cigar, obviously with his thoughts still in his clinic; I see the burning match, which very soon, if he doesn't put it down, will burn his fingers: – what does a man of my age do when he knows, or thinks he knows, that according to medical opinion he has a year to live, at most a year? . . . I hold out my two fists again and Burri chooses: so I get black. Later, after having for hours thought only with bishops and knights and castles, I begin to think about what Burri told me; with the box containing the ivory figures on my knee, now alone once more, because Burri had to visit another patient, I don't know what I myself would do in a case like that.

– live. . .

But how?

I imagine:

Enderlin, Felix, Ph.D., at the age of forty-one years, eleven months and seventeen days and with an expectation of life of one year, Enderlin alone, outside the open window spring is in full swing, the scent of lilac mingled with the scent of the hospital, which is simply always and everywhere, even when you gaze out at the distant mountains or into the future, and it is morning, the hour of courage, a lawn-spray in the sunlight, fans of water with rainbows in them, drops are glittering on the grass, from time to time a white or yellow butterfly, its zigzag, life a park. Enderlin hasn't yet read the note in question, he still believes himself cured. To be sure, he feels weak, but cured for good and all. He has been lucky, Burri told him that. Why shouldn't one be lucky! He got a bit of a shock, when Burri said that. Why lucky? Enderlin didn't expect anything else. The air coming in through the open window makes him shiver a little, and yet it seems to be a warm day, almost hot, south wind, the mountains are near enough to touch. Actually he's sweating, weakness, that's understandable after seven weeks in bed. The mountains still snow-covered, the ploughed fields dark, almost black, streaky like bacon, a wedge of flashing lake with sailing boats on it. In the foreground blossoms a magnolia. A gardener in a green apron and carrying a watering-can, there's nothing missing. And somewhere a halleluia; the singing of the nurses who are off duty at the moment. At the same time workmen are mixing mortar on a scaffold; the hospital has to be enlarged; the workmen are rattling a pulley, Italians, their voices, their brown torsos. So the doctor, Burri, has gone out for a moment, after just announcing to Enderlin his complete cure and early discharge from the hospital; Enderlin in an easy chair by the desk, pale in a blue dressing-gown, Enderlin is still holding a damp strip of film in his hand, his cardio-gram which the friendly doctor has shown him, looking like Arabic writing, beautiful but enigmatic, it reminds him of a signpost in the desert between Damascus and Jerusalem, illegible but beautiful, so that Enderlin is delighted by the calligraphy of his heart, which, he wouldn't have credited himself with, he can't look at it enough, and it is only when a wind blows in through the open window that he catches sight of the note on the desk, gets up to put an ashtray on the slip of paper, which is threatening to blow away; not to read the note. But he has already read it. This note wasn't intended for him. At first he merely finds it embarrassing. His name, obviously just covered by the ashtray, is now out of sight as Ender-lin looks again; what he can read, on the other hand, is the technical expression that death has chosen, written with a ballpoint pen, a word Enderlin doesn't know, and in the margin, evidently scribbled on afterwards, the words: expectation of life approx. one year.

Enderlin alone in the room:

Oh no, one doesn't believe in one's death as easily as that. Perhaps this note doesn't refer to him at all? When the doctor comes back into the room, Enderlin has already sat down in the armchair again, his proper place, his arms on the upholstered arm-rests to left and right, two dressing-gowned arms with two white hands dangling from them, and the doctor says:

"Sorry about that."

Enderlin, more embarrassed than dismayed, gazing out of the window, acts as though nothing had happened.

"Sorry about that," says Burri.

"That's all right," says Enderlin.

Then, after shutting the window, Burri, that colossus of masculine kindness, sits down again at his desk, puts the cigar which he had previously laid in the ashtray decorated with the silver lizard in his mouth again, it is still just alight, so he hasn't kept Enderlin waiting too long. "I understand," says Burri and seems to be looking for something, absent-mindedly, the stump of his cigar between his lips which he has to get going again before he can go on speaking, "I understand," he repeats and, when the cigar is at last properly alight, he seems to have forgotten what he was going to say, instead he picks up the note, without looking at it, and says: "You want to know the result of our last examination." Enderlin smiles. "What was it?" Enderlin asks and is surprised by his own calm, while the doctor evidently feels an urgent need to demonstrate by exact figures why Enderlin can now regard himself as so to speak cured. "I understand," he says for the third time and remembers what he was going to say, "You've no patience left, but I shan't let you out before Saturday," he says with a comradely, rough laugh, the roughness is intended to show that he really considers Enderlin cured and capable of standing up to things, no need to treat him with kid gloves any more. "Saturday at the earliest," he says with a threatening hint of authority and follows this up with figures giving the percentages of white blood corpuscles, percentages of bilirubin, figures which Enderlin has often heard and eventually has come to use himself, so that, although he doesn't really know what these figures mean, he himself can judge how much these figures have indeed improved, to the delight of Burri, who is reading them from the reverse side of the slip of paper. "Yes," says Enderlin, "that's fine," while outside he sees the healthy workmen. "My dear fellow," says Burri, finding himself alone with his delight, "things might have worked out quite differently −!"

Enderlin nods.

Secretly, while they pretend to look one another in the eye, he works out dates: one year, so it'll be one year, and now it's April −

Enderlin nods.

"Look," says Burri, as though conscious of some mistrust, and shows the figures in black and white, that's to say red and white.

"Here," he says, handing over the slip of paper, then Burri leans back in his chair, smoking, waiting, as he adds: "Six weeks ago we still had twenty-seven per cent." Enderlin reads: Bilirubin two point three per cent, but he dare not turn the slip of paper over and challenge Burri straight out, so he says nothing; as a doctor, Burri knows that a certain apathy is part of the clinical picture, all the same, good old Enderlin might have shown a little enthusiasm over his luck, he thinks, Burri doesn't want applause, all the same, Enderlin strikes him as a bit too apathetic as he sits there holding the slip of paper. "My dear fellow," he says, "we've been lucky." Enderlin gives him back the note. "Twenty-seven per cent!" says the doctor. "We didn't tell you at the time, but that was the truth," he says, as he picks up the buzzing telephone, annoyed by the interruption. It's not a professional call, it's about the regatta the Sunday after next, and Burri, not without a glance of apology at Enderlin, leafs through the calendar, it isn't a long conversation, but still long enough for them not to talk any more afterwards, having once been interrupted, about bilirubin, but about the future, first about the June regatta, but above all about Enderlin's future, about his visit to Harvard, which has been delayed because of his illness, that's to say about his career, Enderlin makes an effort to talk about it as about a reality, the effort of a conspirator who has to conceal his secret knowledge of what the future will bring. "Two months," says Burri, "two or three months in Tarasp or Chianciano, of course you'll have to look after yourself, that's obvious," he says leafing through the same calendar in which he has marked his regattas. "Mergentheim is a good place too." He becomes aware that he is repeating himself, that's not like him, Enderlin is making him unsure of himself, really he isn't saying anything he hasn't said already. "Of course you'll have to look after yourself," he says unbuttoning his white coat. Enderlin is trying hard. "I should prefer Chianciano," he says. "As you like," says Burri taking off his white coat, actually in a hurry, but he daren't show his hurry. "Today is Tuesday," he says. "On Friday we'll take another check." This too he has already said once. "Harvard is a

136

fine opportunity!" says Burri, now washing his hands, then drying them, and Enderlin nods. "Two point three per cent," says Burri, as though he has to come back to that again, and crumples up the little slip of paper, he asked for the figures over the telephone before Enderlin came into the consulting-room, the figures have already been entered in the hospital report, he throws the slip of paper into the wastepaper basket and says: "There's nothing to worry about." As he says this he puts his jacket on. "I know," he says with some hesitation because of the jacket, "I always talked about one point five per cent and said I wouldn't let you go until then, I know, but you'll see," he says looking round to make sure he has got everything, "on Friday we'll take another check." Burri has to go now, and Enderlin, who hasn't the strength to stand up, would be glad if he went, Enderlin feels like a dummy put there to conceal his breakdown as the friendly Burri, in order not to hurt his feelings by haste, goes on talking – about Harvard again! – and asks with absent-minded cordiality how old Enderlin is. "Forty-two," says Burri, "is no age." Burri is older. "My dear fellow," says Burri, now in a raincoat, "I didn't start living till I was forty-two!" A hearty handshake. "Don't you believe me?" asks Burri and is not to be stopped in his praises of a man's life precisely after his forty-second year, yes, even in the sphere of love fulfilment still lies ahead, it's a question of experience, Enderlin must be prepared for that, he laughs and goes. . .

Enderlin alone. . .

But the door is open and he daren't go to the wastepaper basket to take the slip of paper out again. To read it again in black and white. What for? Enderlin gets up, acts as though he has been dreaming or something. In the corridor, where he has been building up his strength by daily walks, he meets Elke and smiles too, in order not to shatter her sisterly confidence that he is getting better and better every day.

I imagine:

Although Enderlin believes that the note refers to him, he doesn't believe that the oracle will be fulfilled; he simply doesn't believe it.

Even Burri can make a mistake! . . . Alone in his white room, which has meanwhile been tidied, he works out that Harvard, which in any case was only intended as a jumping-off point, would be pointless. But what is he to do if he doesn't go to Harvard? And when the nurse comes to bring in yesterday's flowers from the corridor, Enderlin, in order not to have to chat with her, slowly opens the post that arrived while he was talking to the doctor; he actually reads it – so this is the first thing one does during one's last year! – reads and knows what he is reading, even knows what he ought to answer. Will he still answer? When the same nurse comes into the room again, this time to leave him a glass of fruit juice, Enderlin doesn't even notice her any more; he is now no longer sitting (evidently he has meanwhile walked across the room) on the bed, but in an armchair by the window, the letters on the dressing-gown and his white hands on the arms of the chair: as though on a throne. Unapproachable. As though on a throne: high above his contemporaries. If he believes in the ballpoint oracle, yes, greatness is the only thing left to him, the only thing that still makes any sense: not to betray to anyone that he knows about his imminent demise, and to act in front of all his friends as if. And to go to Harvard as if. And to make plans and everything, as if –

One knows of men who have been able to do that.

– and to deliver his lectures:

"Ladies and gentlemen,"

In the words of the manuscript:

"Hermes is a figure of multiple significance. Notorious as the god of thieves and rogues, himself a rogue who, on the very day of his birth, stole the calves of Apollo, famed for his astuteness, a gay and crafty astuteness which he enjoys employing to make fools of mortals, he is involved everywhere, his whole being and demeanour stand in the sign of magic, a friend of herdsmen, a god of the herds, which he protects from falling into ravines, a bestower of fertility. The herm, his original symbol, has the shape of a phallus. That he is at the same time, which seems incompatible, the god of merchants, is well known and understandable when we recall what the herm, a cairn of stones, was to wandering merchants: a signpost. The fertility of the herds, that is one thing; it stands for fertility in general, the blessing in all human commerce. Hermes is a master of cunning. He is a helper, a bringer of luck, but also a misleader. In love too he plays this rôle; it is he who brings unexpected luck, the opportunity. Hermes is a friendly god, closer to men than the other gods, hence the messenger of the gods. Homer also calls him the guide of dreams. He likes, so it is often said, to be invisible when he approaches a mortal; and the sudden, the improbable, the incalculable and unhoped-for, even the capricious, all this belongs to Hermes and his domain, the sinister element in all gaiety, for Hermes is also the god who fetches the departing, silent as always, unexpected, omnipresent, the messenger of death who leads us to Hades. . ."

And so on.

Once the telephone rings, after some hesitation he lifts the receiver to answer the brief enquiry as to how he is (the other person really wants to know something different) with detailed confidence; a bit too detailed. Why should his voice be different? different from yesterday? He denies it, talks about being discharged next Saturday, about Chianciano, about bilirubin, about Harvard, while the other says nothing, because he already knows all the plans of which Enderlin is now boasting, and more than this: to prove that he is cured, Enderlin now actually enquires about things that lie beyond his expectation of life, at length and stubbornly, as though he wants to know, and precisely, what the situation now is regarding finances, which publisher, guaranteed for two or three years, further if the arrangement is quarterly or monthly; once more he is talking about starting a magazine of which Enderlin, who was asked long ago if he would act as editor, will at best see only the galley-proofs of the first number. Enderlin agrees.

"Yes," he says, "I give you my word."

That's settled.

– then the conversation has been prolonged by his gratifying acceptance, Enderlin as editor can't simply ring off, there's the question of the title, again and again the question of the title, the question of which contributors to invite and which not, Enderlin has to express his opinion, but he expresses himself less and less, finally he gives his word again, then as soon as he puts down the receiver he lets his head fall back against the heaped-up pillows, exhausted as the other day after an over-confident walk in the park; he tries to think about the magazine, but in vain . . . the question of the title, yes, the question of the title . . . the question of whether Burri is mistaken . . . the lawn-spray in the sun . . . the question of whether I am really attached to everything that is called life – but I shall take care of myself, even if disintegration is already visible; I shall cling to it; I shall believe every lie; in the night I shall know everything, but during the day I shall believe the opposite, and the nurses in white will say: There's a good boy, Herr Enderlin, there's a good boy! And those who come to sit by my bed will see it, and what no one says, the pain will shout at me, the pain from time to time, the pain more often, pain all the time, but every injection brings relief which I transmute into hope, injection after injection until I die like a dog in injected hope –

Enderlin can still think.

Why don't they tell him the truth?

He's still human.

Don't they credit him with greatness?

The little white table with the so-called lunch in front of him, savoy with hygiene, cream cheese, everything tastes of taking care – just so that Enderlin shall live to see the first galley-proofs of the magazine! He tastes it. Cream cheese! He tastes the thought that now, if Burri is not mistaken, he can write everything he thinks. What, for example? Yesterday fish, today cream cheese, tomorrow fish, everything tastes the same, protein, salt-free and insipid like the calculation of whether, if Burri is not mistaken, he needs to earn any money at all for this remaining year, and what dismays him is not the balance-sheet but the dreary commonplaceness of his thinking. A man dedicated to death, he feels, couldn't think like that. Burri is mistaken! He tries savoy, in order to fortify himself.

Why hasn't anyone, certain of his imminent death, ever performed an act of great daring? An assassination, for instance. My life for his life! But mine isn't a life any more, merely an existence with injections in the arm and pap between my teeth, halleluia, and how the lilac blooms again – outside. . . When the nurse comes, Nurse Euphemia, and asks maternally why he hasn't eaten anything, more exactly: why we haven't eaten anything (till just before you kick the bucket they talk in the first person plural: Haven't we an appetite? Shall we have a nap? Have we passed water? etc.), Enderlin takes a few spoonfuls but brings everything up again and as soon as he has been cleaned up he implores the nurse not to tell the doctor about it. Suddenly he is afraid of Burri, who hitherto was his friend. Enderlin will show him how healthy he is. He wants to get away from here. He wants simply to refute the results of the examination that are being concealed from him. Oh no, Enderlin won't go to Chianciano, nor to Tarasp, he will laugh, write a card from Paris, with a dietetic joke in the margin, or if he does go to Tarasp, then for seven days at the most, to please Burri, but not by train, Enderlin will drive there in his own car and in such a way that it squeals round corners, and on Friday already, and in Tarasp he won't drink the waters that stink of rotten sulphur, but he'll play tennis, get to know a woman, a very young one whom he marries on the spot, over the apéritif, a blonde Baltic woman perhaps, for whom he builds a house with a swimming pool, and exactly one year from today the house-warming will take place with a piglet on a spit, whisky beforehand, whisky afterwards, yes, and with Burri as a guest, and Enderlin, a Havana in his brown face, will nudge him in the ribs, his oracle-doctor, laughing. . .

Why just a Baltic woman?

Elke, the night nurse, is from the Baltic and that scares him; the fantasy of a sick man who has no choice any more, of a helpless man who won't go much further.

Outside, the birds.

Women –

Lots of women!

He can't think in the singular.

All women!

And he only thinks of their sex, into their sex; he doesn't think of any woman he knows, but of all those he has missed; sexes; mouths and his tongue in their mouths; even if their faces are indistinguishably alike; and words which he has never uttered and whose obscenity satisfies him strangely by arousing dissatisfaction; sexes, lips, thighs, hair, breasts, eyes that narrow, and sexes, sexes, all sexes – and all the time he is sweating with weakness as he sits on the edge of the bed, his arms spread out as supports, helpless, looking out of the window: trees, roofs, an aeroplane invisible in the sky, only its white trail that bores sharply into the blue and then turns into a tail that grows slowly flocculent and disappears, chimneys which, on the other hand, remain, washing flapping on a flat roof, wires, mountains behind wires with sparrows on them, many roofs, chimneys, balconies, trees rising from an avenue, a fragment of glittering lake, the face of a tower-clock, hands that are imperceptibly moving, nothing else – what he has been seeing every day for weeks . . . the Italians on the scaffolding, every now and then they hang a bucket on the pulley and haul it up, men with naked torsos, muscular. It's no good Enderlin looking elsewhere. Near or far, it's all one, his bed, the clock-face, the rattling pulley: things that will outlive Enderlin. The demonstration of a trivial piece of knowledge; without any messenger of the gods. The hope of greatness proves to be sentimental nonsense; only self-pity is revealed unconcealed and shameless. Not that Enderlin is now crying! He is only sweating. Then there is a knock at the door.

"Come in," says Enderlin, getting into bed and covering himself up, and when there is another knock at the inner door he says in a louder voice: "Come in!"

It's me.

"Sit down," he says. "How are you?" I ask, and so that I shan't forget it again I put the notebook down, without waiting for his answer, on the white table with the medicines and instruments; I see ampoules, a hypodermic syringe, needles under alcohol. "Your essay!" I say. "I've read it, I think it's brilliant." Enderlin mute. "Well," I say, stepping out onto the little balcony, "you really have got a lovely view here." As though this were my first visit. I feel embarrassed, but I don't know why, rubbing my hands. "Yes," asks Enderlin, "and how are you?" I think it's a wonderful day today. Perhaps Enderlin is expecting me to say more about his essay; but when I try to do so, Enderlin looks past me and no conversation comes of it. "What I find particularly excellent," I say and see that he isn't listening. "All right, thank you," I say as I step back into the room, "I'm working." Now I fill my pipe, a man who is standing with both feet in life, then sits down, his pipe in his tobacco pouch, I shan't smoke, a sick-room is a sick-room, however wide open the window is, a visitor with a sense of what is fitting, but healthy; not inconsiderate, but healthy, someone who talks about objective questions, world questions, egoless, his filled pipe in his mouth, without lighting it, not worried about Enderlin, who has his medical attention and his flowers and his fruit juice, worried about Europe, worried about mankind as a whole, this time particularly from a town planning point of view, town planning as a political problem, on this subject I have a few things to say, although Enderlin isn't hearing them for the first time. This doesn't turn into a conversation but into a lecture, because Enderlin says nothing. It must have been out of embarrassment that I lit my pipe. "How is your magazine getting on?" I ask. To draw Enderlin out of his apathy. I can't know that this morning Enderlin considers himself a man dedicated to death; his self-pity, mute, but perceptible, gradually makes me edgy, even rough. I stop smoking to be sure, but I let fall sentences that are supposed to show him that he is now cured: "You and your paper!" brutally: "Did you ever believe in that paper?" I'm getting rough now, I know. "We know all about that," I say. "Everyone promises to contribute, in order to have his name connected with it, but no sooner is the egg laid than they've got other things to do and you, as the editor, are stuck with it." I don't know what's the matter with Enderlin, and I succeed less and less in striking the right note, but I talk all the more.

"Yes," I say, "we must do that again some time, our walking tour on the Etzel!" His smile. "As soon as you're fit again," I say and really it's time for me to go. But how? The best thing would be to say: "Well, I must go now," while Enderlin is sipping his fruit juice, and I'm already standing up, holding his bed with both hands like a pram, looking into the future that has to be planned, town planning as a political problem. I ask Enderlin how our children's children are to live, I ask how, for example, Enderlin pictures the traffic in ten years, in thirty years, in fifty years, that really is a question – not for Enderlin, but for the world, especially for our Western world, whereas Enderlin (but I can't see this by looking at him) can think only of his own expectation of life: one year, one year at the outside. . . When the nurse comes in to give Herr Enderlin his daily injection in the forearm I say nothing for a while, as is right and proper, and hide my pipe on account of the nurse, who has to repeat the injection a second time. Poor Enderlin! I can understand him not listening to me properly, I imagine I can understand him; these daily injections, one day in the left and one day in the right arm, get on one's nerves, especially when they don't always hit the vein first time, I understand. When Enderlin rolls down the sleeve of his pyjama jacket again without a word, I ask him, to take his mind off things, what he thinks of a book I see on his locker. I can smoke if I like, he says. Somehow or other he would like me to stay; but now I really do have to go, which is difficult, because Enderlin doesn't say a word. And yet he is thinking, I can see that, thinking incessantly. Out of embarrassment I talk about people. Gossip. Who has recently started an affair with whom. He listens but he looks past me. The workmen outside on the scaffolding, I look out, Italians. That's also a problem; if it goes on it will mean the sapping of our country by immigration. Enderlin makes no comment on this either. When I try another way, for example ask how many lectures he has to give at Harvard, he does answer, but as if it had nothing to do with him, as if I were gossiping. So what's left? Once he asks what day of the week it is, what the date is; otherwise nothing. . .

Eventually I left.

He has survived the first visitor, the first person on whom he has had to test his power to keep a secret. . .

The tower-clock strikes four.

A year is a long time –

If only he could scream!

Burri is right:

Forty-two is no age.

Later in the evening, after Enderlin, drowsy from the injection, has tried to think with his eyes open, looking at this hygienic gallows in the dusk. . . Why doesn't one hang oneself? – perhaps that is what he is thinking, his eyes on the white pulley over his head, while the room grows darker quarter of an hour by quarter of an hour. What is there to think? Death can't be thought. . . His face, when he has switched on the light, his face in the mirror on the cupboard, where his suit has been hanging for weeks, his face and his bare neck and his skin need sun, that's all, sun in the Engadine or by the sea. Or in Peru! Suddenly he thinks it without irony: Peru as the land of his hope! Perhaps Enderlin pictures himself on a neighing horse, a year in Peru, a man who rode away – I don't know. . . What can be pictured: old age, which he will be spared if Burri is not mistaken and not spared if Burri is mistaken. . . Sleepy from the injection, but wide awake with fright, while what has frightened him seems like a dream, he lies with closed eyes, his arms stretched out, his hands dangling over the edge of the bed – really he doesn't want to live, in order not to grow old – but when they bring him his dietetic supper, when the nurse, as always, arranges the pillows so that Herr Enderlin can sit up, he feeds his body, and when the nurse comes back after half an hour to fetch the tray, she says:

"Good boy, Herr Enderlin, good boy!"

He won't hang himself –

For Burri, I can understand, it's a tricky situation. All he knows is that the note lay on his desk, and he is so preoccupied by the suspicion that Enderlin might have read this note that when we

145

play chess in the evening he does hopelessly badly. Anyhow, our good Enderlin's behaviour in the morning, when he told him he was completely cured and would soon be discharged, was a bit odd. The suspicion only came to Burri in the course of the afternoon, when he couldn't lay his hands on the note, which he had written not for Enderlin but for another patient who was about to be transferred to a sanatorium, and when he found the slip of paper in the wastepaper basket, with the favourable results of Enderlin's examination on the back. A stupid piece of carelessness! My advice that he should speak to Enderlin straight out seems to him entirely wrong. That would only reinforce Enderlin's conviction that he isn't being told the truth. I can see that. Burri sees no other possibility: he will simply discharge Enderlin and keep him under observation. If a man thinks he has only a year to live, a year at the outside, he won't go on living as he has up to now, thinks Burri. And I don't contradict, so that we can now continue playing, a second game, a better one it's to be hoped. I'm white this time. Burri can't leave it alone; that's why he sets his pieces out so slowly, as if he had to think where the bishops and the knights go. Would I go on living as before, he asks, after I have already opened with the king's pawn, if I knew that I should be dead in a year at the latest? I don't know. Word of honour, I can't imagine it. To make him think about something else, I play a gambit.

What I can imagine:

(because I have experienced it)

his awakening next morning, the grey dawn outside the open window (it is raining) grey and fissureless like granite: out of this granite, like a scream, but silent, suddenly a horse's head with a red mane, neighing, but soundlessly, foam on its teeth, but its body remains inside, only the head is out, the eyes big and mad, seeking mercy – for an instant – then terra-cotta artistically painted, its black nostrils and chalk-white teeth, all only painted, the red mane rigid, it slowly withdraws into the rock that closes without a sound, fissureless like the grey dawn outside the window, grey like granite on the St. Gotthard; in the valley, far below, a distant road,

146

bends full of brightly coloured tiny cars speeding towards Jerusalem. . .

I was in Jerusalem once.

An hour earlier, when I had crossed the Jordan, a rivulet, and then, after a winding road through an arid valley with camels, suddenly caught sight of the distant walls high above the desert, amber-yellow, walls in the morning sun, it was Jerusalem – as I had pictured it . . . now I'm standing here, having got out of my car, a tourist. Not the only one, but alone. Damascus Gate. As I lock the car a thought strikes me: the Mount of Olives, I've driven past it, not through indifference, but through expectation, that must have been the Mount of Olives. The moment you stop driving it's hot. I've been driving for a fortnight, in order to stand here, in order to unlock the car again, to drink tea from the Thermos flask, to lock the car again; but then that's done too. Damascus Gate: huge, beautiful, the familiar Roman masonry. What's the point of this journey? I ask myself; but now I'm here. And it's not true that I'm here. Damascus Gate in the morning sun, Arabs, the braying of an ass. My being here is a fact; I'm not somewhere else. I see my car number in Jerusalem, barbed wire on a wall, machine guns behind sandbags. In order to cross the frontiers of the Arab states I have used up no fewer than six baptism certificates, this by the way; merely to say that I really have made this journey. A few thousand miles. And I already know now that hours later, when I have been sightseeing to the point of exhaustion, it won't be true. I see: Pontius Pilate's house, at least it's the site, it's Friday, a court-yard, shade, so that I stay awhile, branches with lemons among the leaves, a view through an arcade of the Arab mosque on the site of Solomon's Temple, its cupola like a gleaming soap bubble. I don't know whether this happens every Friday: I see monks kneeling in Pontius Pilate's courtyard, Franciscans, all in brown cowls, some with white or yellowish sola topis, faces with pince-nez, here and there a camera is humming, filming their worship, pilgrims in shorts, northmen who think the south is the place for summer holidays,

147

cross themselves and kneel down, until the Franciscans rise and set off along the Via Dolorosa. I follow the murmuring procession. A procession through the Arab Suk, a procession of the minority, approved by law, the Arab policemen make sure they can pass, heat, in the narrow alleys it is sunny in parts and shady in parts, and where the sun is shining hazy, you can't see through, in the darkness someone is hammering copper, asses are braying here too, the Arabs squat in front of their shops mutely with long water-pipes, market, I see meat, a sheep slit open, meat bloody in the sun, stinking and covered in flies, the Franciscans kneel and pray at every station, the tourists likewise, the holy kerchief of St Veronica, and there are always some who cross themselves more quickly and then stand up and film the others, including monks who film their brothers. I merely watch. I am apprehensive of Golgotha. (Our painters, Breughel and the rest, have deceived me; Golgotha does not lie outside the walls.) We are on Golgotha. (I expected rock or stony ground, shadeless for thousands of years, perhaps a few thistles, grasses in the hot desert wind.) Here Jesus fell with the cross, I see the spot, here the cross was stuck into the ground, a marble staircase leads down into the tomb, candle-lit darkness, Golgotha as an interior, architecture that one has to imagine away, the shuffling of the pilgrims on marble, now you have to take off your sunglasses in order to be able to see anything. And it is getting less and less true that I am here. Marble, iron bars, marble, candles, marble, incense, pompous and stuffy. I can't get used to the incense, but I stay here till those who are praying have gone; a tourist. I see the spot where the cross stood, the marble is slit open like a piece of clothing, the naked rock like flesh, the hole in the rock, the hole for the cross. . . Then I go on sightseeing, also Gethsemane, midday, it's too hot to eat anything, all round nothing but desert, valleys and mountains of yellow sand, no other village, no farm, Jerusalem is the only city under the sky, the sun circles round Jerusalem, I go on foot, Gethsemane is a little garden, a boon of shade, but I don't sit down. I see this is the olive tree where Jesus prayed, a dried-up, stunted trunk, silver-grey. An attendant in uniform, an Arab Christian, points out to me the legendary foot-prints in the rock, and I give him a coin, as he expects. Architecture here too, marble and incense, here too the marble floor has been slit open, so that one can see the sacred rock –

Everything remains mere appearance.

Towards evening, when I am driving down and stop at a bend to look back again at Jerusalem, its walls outlined against the light, I only know what I already knew when I arrived, and when I drive on I am determined never to talk about it. Later I do so all the same.

A celebration takes place:

No one knows what is being celebrated, not even Burri, who has come late as usual ("I just had a birth to see to"), a gay celebration, ladies in evening dress are lying on the floor, a witty cock of the roost (Siebenhagen?) with his legs crossed, in the garden they are dancing, standard lamps, the poison-green lawn under standard lamps, Burri in a dinner jacket, he has fallen for the joke, the only one who could have guessed the reason for the celebration, the oracle-doctor –

The year is up.

Enderlin, the host, has bought a house with a garden and a swimming pool that is lit up, and a young lady is just being thrown into it, her screams, because the water is cold, a terrific joke, it seems; only Burri, the obstetrician in a dinner jacket, is standing about feeling hungry, gramophone records "Rien de rien, non, je ne regrette rien", while Burri helps himself to the remnants and still can't figure out what it is all about, friends with glassy eyes and crooked ties, a couple embracing on the divan, Enderlin outside in a hammock, Enderlin aged exactly forty-two years and eleven months and seventeen days; his dejection at having remained just the same –

So he'll grow old!

Grey dawn –

but without a horse's head –

grey horror –

but without a scream –
Don't be silly, says Burri, you'll catch cold.
The oracle-doctor!
Don't be silly, says Enderlin, I shall live to seventy.
The guests have gone –
Come on in, says Burri.
Birds are twittering –
Burri has gone –
So he'll grow old!

Enderlin hasn't been drinking. He can't take it any more. Certain limitations impose themselves without doctor's orders, as it were voluntarily; that doesn't mean that one doesn't feel a wreck next morning every time. It's come to that. He still feels so to speak young. Only he has to take care of himself. He is flattered when people take him for younger than he is. It's come to that. He gives presents of jewellery when he's in love. He wouldn't have thought of that in the past. At the jeweller's, when he looks up from the rings and beads, he gets a shock: they are all elderly gentlemen who are giving presents of jewellery. Nobody stands up to give him a seat in the tram yet. That will come too. One can't talk of old age yet. Only he is dismayed when he happens to see a photo from the past, a face that no longer exists. He still competes with younger men. But it's come to the point where he looks at every man to see if he is younger, and people rightly contradict when he talks about old age. There's no sign of it yet so to speak. And that people of his age-group no longer enjoy an advance supply of expectations is something no one notices but him. The slack skin and the bags under the eyes, when he is forced to look in the mirror while shaving, still look merely like signs of passing tiredness. He refuses to be shocked by them. Only his teeth, which have often fallen out already in dreams, we know what that means, his teeth shock him, so do his eyes: everything white is becoming ashen or yellowish. It's come to that. His hair isn't falling out yet, it just lies flatter, and what is growing is his forehead; there's no need to call it a bald patch yet. But that will come. His lips are becoming thinner, more expressive, so to speak, but colourless. Fulfilment still lies ahead, Burri is right. And women offer themselves as never before. The hair on his chest is growing silvery; but that only shows in the bath. Fasting and some sport, practised with moderation and vigour, prevent the development of flabby fat; but that doesn't make the muscles young. He still walks without effort, but he sees it in his shadow: a man of fifty, his walk is getting more thrifty, the movements no longer run through his whole body. His face is growing livelier than his body, more personal year by year, more important so to speak, when it isn't tired, and it's often tired. He hides his tiredness as much as he can, if necessary with pills. He hasn't reached the point of having to rest after lunch. But all this will come. He still does a full day's work. Definitely. He actually gets more done than in the past, because experience enables him to see more quickly what cannot succeed, and professionally this is his best period. Definitely. And the moment will come which he fears: when he is treated with respect. Respect for his years. People will let him speak, because he is the older, and no camaraderie, no wooing of the young will be any help. They are getting younger and younger. They listen out of politeness and more and more rarely say what they think. All this will come. He will try to win their favour, but at the same time refuse when they want to help him on with his coat, and will pay heed to their inexperience and exaggerated expectations. They will find him touching and also a bit of a nuisance, without his noticing. He will admire, in order not to appear envious, and he will be envious of everything that he himself has already had, envious because it can no longer seem to him worth striving for. All this will come. Accustomed to the natural increase in deaths in his age-group and accustomed to certain marks of honour due to his past, a sexagenarian whom people are beginning to assure of his mental freshness and this more and more frankly, he won't complain about his age, on the contrary, he will turn it into dignity, dismayed that this assumption of dignity does not seem in the least ridiculous but entirely appropriate. All this cannot be delayed. And perhaps he will live to be seventy, thanks to modern medical science. Things haven't gone so far yet that he has to be watched over at every step. Naturally he needs help. Naturally he has to take care of himself. What for? His memory, although it is no longer good enough to enable him to learn a foreign language, will be astonishing; he will remember the most distant things that once preoccupied him. The young men (of forty) will argue among themselves, while he sits apart under protection. His views are no longer capable of changing. He will go for a walk every day, perhaps with a stick, anyhow with a hat, read the paper every day, in order not to go for a walk in the past. Present? He knows how things have led up to this present. Sometimes he will talk about his personal meetings with men who have brought this present into being, about his time, which is history, always the same. . .

Why didn't he hang himself?

Camilla Huber, asked what she would do or leave undone if she had only a year to live, a year at the outside, knows at once:

"– not work any more."

Naturally Gantenbein doesn't ask what she means by work, but acts as though they were talking about manicure.

"Well," I ask, "what would you do instead?"

Camilla doesn't tell me what she would do, but it can be guessed through her peroxide-blonde hair when soon afterwards another customer rings up:

"Sorry," she says. "You've dialled the wrong number." And when the telephone rings again a minute later: "I told you, you've got the wrong number."

She carries on with the manicure.

It's the first time Camilla doesn't need a story; she is making one up herself, it seems, without words: her last year on earth, a story that probably includes a transformation scene, a story with a meaningful ending, a comforting story.

I have given Enderlin up –

152

(There are other people I can't give up, even if I rarely or never meet them any more. I don't mean they pursue me in my imagination, but I pursue them, I remain curious as to how they would behave in this, that or the other situation, at the same time uncertain as to how they are really behaving. Their real behaviour may disappoint, but that doesn't matter; they still have the scope afforded by my expectation. Such people I can't give up. I need them, even if they have treated me badly. They may even be dead people. They grip me all my life long through my idea that they, if placed in my position, would feel differently and act differently and come out of it differently from me, who cannot give up myself. But I can give up Enderlin.)

A story for Camilla:
(a comforting one)
Ali, as the name indicates, was an Arab, a young shepherd on the Upper Euphrates, and the time came when he wanted to take a wife. But Ali was poor. In that region at that time a decent girl cost £15, a lot of money for a shepherd. Ali had only £10. When he heard that in the south brides were cheaper, he didn't hesitate long, he took his ass, filled his waterskin with water and rode south for many weeks on end. It was simply time for him to take a wife, he was young and healthy. So he rode full of hope, £10 in his pocket, down the Euphrates, as I said, for many weeks on end, living on dates. When Ali finally came into the district that had been so highly spoken of, there was no lack of daughters whom he liked, nor of fathers who wanted to sell; but the price of brides had meanwhile risen in the south too, and there was nothing to be married for £10, not even an ugly girl. £12 was the regular price, £11 a unique opportunity; Ali bargained for days on end, but without success, £10 was not an offer but an insult, and when Ali realized that there was nothing to be had he took his ass again, filled his waterskin with water and rode north, grieved to death with his £10 in his pocket, for he hadn't used any of it, as though he still believed in a miracle. And naturally the miracle did not fail to occur, which

153

Ali deserved for recognizing it. Midway between south and north, when he was bathing his sorry ass and himself at a well, Ali caught sight of a girl like none he had ever seen before, more beautiful than all of those whom he had been unable to get for his £10, a blind girl. That was a pity. The girl was not only more beautiful, however, but also sweeter, since she was blind and had never seen in any well how beautiful she was, and when Ali told her how beautiful she was with all the words familiar to an Arab shepherd, she loved him on the spot and asked her father to sell her to Ali. She was cheap, because of her blindness her father wanted to get rid of her, terribly cheap: £6. Because no one on the whole of the Euphrates wanted a blind bride. But Ali took her, put her on the ass he had bathed and called her Alil, while he himself went on foot. In the villages, wherever Ali went with his Alil, the people couldn't believe their eyes, no one had ever seen or even dreamed of a more beautiful girl; only unfortunately she was blind. But Ali still had £4 in his pocket, and when he came home he took her to a miracle doctor and said: Here are £4, now make Alil see her Ali. When the miracle doctor had succeeded and when Alil saw that compared with the other shepherds round about Ali was not handsome at all, she loved him nevertheless, because he had given her all the colours of this world through his love, and she was happy, and he was happy, and Ali and Alil were the happiest couple on the edge of the desert. . .

Camilla is disappointed.

"Yes," she says, without looking up and without interrupting the manicure, "but that's a fairy story."

Camilla doesn't want to hear any more.

"Wait!" I say. "Wait!"

Camilla files.

. . .the fairy story lasted a year, then it was over; through being with Alil, Ali had become infected, so that he slowly but surely went blind, and there came a bad time, because no sooner was Ali blind than he could no longer believe that she loved him, and every time Alil left the tent he became jealous. It was no use her swearing

154

to him. Perhaps she really went to the other shepherds, we don't know. Ali couldn't see, and since he couldn't bear such uncertainty, he began to beat her. That was bad. Otherwise he didn't touch his Alil any more. So it went on for a long time, until Ali took revenge by making love to another girl who slipped into his tent more and more often. But that didn't make him well either, on the contrary, things got worse and worse. When he knew that it was his Alil who was now lying in his tent, he beat her, and she wept so that people could hear outside, and Ali and Alil were the unhappiest couple on the edge of the desert. That was well known. When the miracle doctor heard about it he took pity on them and came to heal Ali, although he couldn't pay another pound. Ali was able to see again, but he didn't tell his Alil that he could see, because he wanted to creep after her, and so he did. But what did he see? He saw Alil crying because he had beaten her in the tent, and he saw her wash her face and slip into his tent as the other girl, so that the blind Ali should make love to her –

"No!" says Camilla. "Really?"

The manicure is finished.

"Seriously," she asks, putting away the little scissors and the little file, "is that a true story?"

"Yes," I say, "it seems so to me."

The game with the dark glasses and the little black stick on the kerb and the armband that is always on the sleeve of another suit every time Gantenbein goes out, so that he has to go back again, is thoroughly tedious, in my view too; I should understand it if Gantenbein suddenly gave up his rôle, and I ask myself in particular how Lila would take it if Gantenbein suddenly confessed one evening that he could see.

The temptation is getting greater and greater.

What's the sense of the pretence?

I am sitting by the fireplace at midnight, a glass in my hand, ice in the glass, so that it clinks when I swill it round. Perhaps I have drunk too much already. Our guests have gone at last; once again

155

it was an effort to play Gantenbein and not to tell people what I see. I have just put a log on the fire, while Lila is reading the newspaper, and I watch the log on the fire slowly begin to smoke on top of the glowing embers of the evening: suddenly the first flame jumps up, a little fleeting bluish wild caprice that immediately disappears again, but after smoking awhile is there again, now a crackling, blazing flame. Otherwise nothing happens. Lila has once again told our guests the anecdote, successful as usual, of the blind Gantenbein in her dressing-room. The guests, as I said, have gone; we too will soon go to bed, it seems. My glass in my hand, ice in the glass so that it clinks gaily when I swill it round, I see our happiness. Does Lila really still believe in my blindness? I see her legs, the left crossed over the right, her knee, next to this her taut skirt, further I see her two hands with which she is holding the open newspaper: headlines with murder.

"Look," she says. "Did you read this – ?"

She has nothing special in mind when she asks a question like that. She does it often, with no intention of putting Gantenbein to the test.

"Yes," I say "– I've read it."

Pause.

"No," she says, "how is that possible?"

She means the murder.

"Horrible!" she considers it.

I drink till there's nothing but ice in the glass, and wait, the glass in my hand, waiting intently to see if Lila won't suddenly realize what I have just said; but I wait in vain, and since nothing happens, I repeat:

"Yes – I've read it."

She simply doesn't hear it.

"Is there any whisky left?" she asks.

There is.

"Thanks," she says later, "thanks."

Silence.

"Lila," I say, "I said something to you."

156

"Sorry," she says.

At last she puts down the paper, but her face shows no surprise at all, I see, she merely reaches for her whisky, to listen, to ask:

"What did you say?"

I hesitate.

"I said," I smile slowly and put my glass to my mouth again, insipid melted ice, so that my smile vanishes: "– I said that I had read it."

"Don't you think it's horrible?"

She still means the murder.

I see that all Gantenbein need do now is to keep silent and smoke and everything would remain as it was, but perhaps he is seized with rage – I could imagine that – a rage that will come to no good end, I know that and hold my empty whisky glass with both hands, so that Gantenbein shan't smash it against the wall. What's the good of that? I see the blazing log in the fireplace, I see Lila drink, then pick up the paper again, the headlines with murder.

I merely imagine it:

Wordless at first, apparently in control of himself, after smashing his whisky glass against the wall, pale with agitation, not knowing himself what he really wants, he only knows that he would do better to say nothing, but a smashed glass is a smashed glass, there's no changing that, even if he says nothing, Gantenbein in a state that really scares poor Lila, without his glasses (as usually only while making love or swimming) and trembling with remorse that he is now (why?) yielding up his secret, his glasses in his hand, he isn't blind, he says, striding up and down the room, oh no, he isn't blind, he laughs, without looking at Lila, blind with rage, yelling himself hoarse and enumerating all the things he has been seeing for years, yes, seeing, whether Lila believes it or not, oh no, he isn't blind, he yells, so that the whole neighbourhood hears it, foaming with fury that Lila doesn't sink into the ground at his revelation but merely sweeps up the broken glass, while Gantenbein, to show that he isn't blind, kicks over the armchairs, without a word, then he says again that he has seen everything, everything, and her silence doesn't pacify him, he bangs the table that he has been seeing for years, acts as though during all these years it hadn't been he who was pretending but she, Lila, he grabs hold of her, shakes her till she cries; he is out of his mind, yes, he can see himself that he is out of his mind, he sees the armchairs on the floor and it's no help that Gantenbein himself picks them up, what's said is said, Lila is sobbing as if he had deceived her, her pearl necklace is broken too, oh no, he isn't blind, he says, trying to calm himself with a cigarette, but it doesn't last long, not half a cigarette long, then he starts hitting out again if only with words, as crazy as a horse that has slipped and scared itself –

How does it go on?

Whereas for Lila, after he has calmed down and apologized about the pearl necklace, nothing has really changed – because for her his confession has not made him any blinder or any less blind than she knows him – for Gantenbein, now that he is no longer playing the blind man, another life begins. . .

I imagine:

One day (soon afterwards) Lila comes home in a strange mood. This isn't the first time, but for the first time she knows that I have already seen it on the platform. I call a taxi while she says: Best wishes from Henry. I thank her. Otherwise nothing new? Terrible weather for three days, I've been working. I ask: What have you been doing? It's none of the taxi man's business. Tell you about that later! So the day before yesterday she was with Henry and his wife, who also sends me her best wishes. Lila tells me more than ever before after a trip. I've never seen a Russian ballet, but I believe immediately that it is magnificent. Tell me; I'm on tenterhooks. Why don't I kiss her? Because I'm smoking. My father is better, thank you, and the weather, yes, it's unbelievable how different the weather can be in different countries. In Hamburg, for example, the sun was shining, yes, in Hamburg of all places. Well here, I say, it's been raining for the last three days. I learn

that incidentally Lila met her first husband. Why incidentally?
He was dreary, she says frankly. Why so frankly? Well, Svoboda
was dreary. Who would have expected that! For the first time since
I have heard of Svoboda, he was absolutely dreary. What else? By
the way, Svoboda sends his best wishes; everyone sends me their
best wishes. By the way, I too have a confession to make: an accident due to black ice! The car just spun round. Black ice! Now it's
raining, but the day before yesterday there was black ice; our taxi
driver can bear me out. Back home I take off her coat and hang it
on a hanger with the question: Well, Lilalein, what's the matter?
I fetch two glasses, and Lila is glad that only the car got damaged,
not me. To repeat: I was doing thirty, at the most forty, but there's
nothing you can do about black ice. Well, cheers! But Lila can't
get over her first husband, who now sends me his best wishes for
the second time. How can a first husband become so dreary! I
fetch ice. Why Lila missed the plane is a question that remains
open, since, as I've said, I just went to fetch ice, while Lila is wondering who else sent me their good wishes. There were a few more
people, I can believe that. The only one who didn't send his good
wishes has no name, I don't know him, that's why he doesn't send
me his good wishes. I understand. It was after the Russian ballet,
as I hear, a group of young students. I misunderstand. Of course
it isn't a whole group who want to marry Lila, but just one. How
does he figure that out? Lila too, I hear, thinks it crazy, but counts
on my understanding. How is one to understand what one doesn't
know? I demand knowledge, I become petty, which Gantenbein
never was, and this is a painful disappointment for Lila. She remains
silent, to show her disappointment. Are we to become an ordinary
couple? Well, on Monday, or was it on Sunday, no, it makes no
difference, anyhow it was after the performance, which incidentally
was a success. What? Lila is just telling me: a group of students,
but also of dancers. I try to imagine it: I too was once a student,
but not so courageous as this one whom Lila, to make it short,
calls a pig. I suspect a touch of genius when I listen to Lila making
her unwilling report, and fill my glass. I understand, oh yes, I find

it impressive when a student, twenty-one or so, tells a lady whose
coat he is holding, after having had no opportunity to speak to her,
without beating about the bush, that he wants to fly with her to
Uruguay, in order to live there with her, and that this lady, namely
Lila, is still a bit upset. Why do I misunderstand everything? All right,
not a student, a dancer, no, not that either; simply a pig. It really
doesn't matter what the pig's name is. So he took her home, that's
to say to her hotel. What then? I misunderstand again. Nothing
then! So I content myself with a student or dancer, who is probably
a genius, since he considers everything that has a name old hat,
including the Russian ballet, and who wants to marry Lila and
right away. Destiny! I merely ask whether he knows Lila is married.
Why am I being impossible? I don't ask whether he has money; I
drink and say nothing; everything I think of is banal. Where love
is, there is also a plane to Uruguay. So Lila calms me, although I
am calmer than she: not a dancer, no, not a student either, no,
Lila doesn't know either what he is. That's the magnificent thing
about him. It's not a question of marriage in the bourgeois sense, I
understand, but of something else, Lila won't give it a name, I say
it: something absolute. Lila admits that that's the way it's meant
on his side. The idea that I might now smack her face, for the first
time of course, bewilders me. When I enquire objectively how Lila
imagines the climate in Uruguay, she who is so sensitive to the
climate, it turns out that he didn't talk about Uruguay at all, but
about Paraguay; it was simply a slip of the tongue on Lila's part.
I've made Lila all confused. I'm being altogether unfair to him;
he didn't say he wanted to marry Lila on the first evening, I'm
twisting everything, but on the platform just before she left. I feel
ashamed. Instead of a confession that would open the floodgates
of my masculine self-pity, I am merely hearing about an experience
that cannot be put into words at all. Then let's leave words out of it!
Lila is simply touched. I can see that. It's definite that she doesn't
like him, and furthermore that he is handsome, but impossible, but
handsome, a pig, she says, heavens above, and the things he says,
the things he talks about, it all nauseates her, his arrogance is

160

childish, she says, and Lila finds him a nuisance, but she couldn't get a grip on herself when he looked at her. The guinea-pig and the snake! Lila doesn't put it like that, but I understand. I don't know Paraguay, but I can understand that for his part he can't understand why Lila, a woman like Lila, is going back to Gantenbein. Shall we put on a record? I just thought we might. If we were at least hungry! I don't consider my question what is to happen now so out of place that Lila has to yell at me because of it. Nothing is going to happen now, God above, nothing whatever! And nothing has happened. Is it Lila's fault if she meets a madman? The word is hers. I put a record on, I place the needle on the record, without trembling, after all nothing happened, Lila finds me impossible, she told me she can't stand him, can't stand him. Unfortunately she couldn't tell him that; she's telling me. That was the experience: how can one find a pig so handsome? The record is playing, but we don't hear it. I hear: when he looked into her eyes he could say what he wanted to, that ape! She repeats: That ape! For my part, I don't want to adopt this designation, I'm not entitled to; nor do I know whether he is an ape. Time will tell. Perhaps he will be coming over here during the next few days? I ask, at last lighting my pipe, and Lila thinks the question in bad taste. Why should he come over here? I think: to fetch Lila. Lila thinks humour is out of place. It's a Brandenburg Concerto we're listening to, the fifth, I think, and what I should like to know is this: how they said goodbye to each other this afternoon, I don't mean did they kiss on the platform in sunny Hamburg, I merely mean with what in mind? Lila doesn't answer my question but repeats: A madman! What I want to know is this: did Lila let him know in any way that Gantenbein exists? Lila prefers to listen to Brahms. Naturally he can imagine that Lila isn't living without a man. I look for Brahms, Lila is right, my question is stupid. Why should she tell an unknown man the intimate details of her life, just because he wants to marry her? Lila is right. What business was it of that fellow's that Lila and Gantenbein, as I know, are happy? I put the record on, Lila is right, I place the needle on the revolving record. . .

The telegram next morning doesn't surprise me. The Post Office, unsuspecting, gives it over the telephone. I write down:

ARRIVING TOMORROW EINHORN.

I thank the Post Office, Lila is asleep, and if she is going to Uruguay today it's time she packed, that's to say I ought to wake her. Perhaps I ought to wait till I'm more relaxed; perhaps I shall never again be as relaxed as I am now. For a while I go on with my breakfast, then I dress, not forgetting my tie. It's possible that the telegram was sent off yesterday, while we were still listening to Brahms; that would mean that tomorrow is today. Lila thinks me crazy, yes, completely crazy; she is indignant, as though I had sent this telegram. It's out of the question, she says, but that's easy to say. I fetch her dressing-gown. *Einhorn* = unicorn. Does Lila expect me to step in front of the unicorn and say Lila can't see anyone? Yes, that's what she does expect. Won't the unicorn laugh? Lila thinks I'm mean because I refer to him as the unicorn instead of the ape. Nothing of the sort, she says, of course they didn't make any arrangement! Lila is more surprised than I am that he can't tear himself away from her eyes, and tells me straight out what she omitted to tell the unicorn: that she has absolutely no desire to see him again. But suppose he's already on the way? Lila simply can't understand where he got hold of her address. Our address. Naturally I wonder how I shall behave towards a unicorn, and now I'm the madman, because Lila has had an experience of the eyes which he takes seriously. I'm still holding her dressing-gown. But Lila doesn't want him to come here, no question of it! I don't understand why she now rebukes me. She wants to send a telegram at once. Have you got his address? I ask objectively, while Lila is looking through her handbag. She has it. Thank God. Her first idea: GONE AWAY. When asked if I think that's the right thing, I must admit that if I were a unicorn it wouldn't convince me. I've nothing against lies! But I'm surprised, not to say flabber-gasted, that such intimacy already exists between Lila and this unicorn as to make this lie necessary. Second version: VISIT UNFORTUNATELY IMPOSSIBLE. When asked I must say that

I don't find his visit impossible, but perfectly logical. But Lila doesn't want to see him! He won't be able to guess that, I suggest, when he reads VISIT UNFORTUNATELY IMPOSSIBLE. Why UNFORTUNATELY? He will deduce from this that Lila has a narrow-minded husband. Right, then: VISIT IMPOSSIBLE. Lila really doesn't want to see him, that's agreed, but I would like to see him. I've never seen a unicorn. Third version: I'M MARRIED. That won't surprise him. In what way am I making it difficult for Lila? Perhaps it would be a good idea if the two of them were to make love once, before going to Uruguay or Paraguay. I haven't put this into words, no, I'm ashamed of even thinking it. If Lila doesn't put on her dressing-gown it strikes me she'll catch cold. Right then: PLEASE DON'T PLEASE. That's clear. Am I satisfied with it? As though that were the point. He will be satisfied with it. What a *cri de coeur*! I agree to it, oh yes, I've nothing against pathos where it is felt. That's the kind of telegram not every twenty-one-year-old can stick into the frame of his mirror. If I'm asked, it makes me think of Donna Proeza, whom Lila once played, but above all of how I am to behave if the unicorn comes in spite of it. His name isn't unicorn at all! I'm making a scene, thinks Lila. And yet all I want is to know what to be prepared for. Maybe I too have difficulty in finding the right word. I don't know what's going on. I merely see the confusion of a mature woman. I conjecture. A bagatelle or destiny? I have to be prepared for anything, it seems to me, that's why I listen tensely as Lila gets up and goes without a word (angry with me!) to the telephone to send the telegram. Which version will it be? But Lila shuts the door; I can't hear as I stand and smoke. . .

So much for the scene.

Gantenbein, since he has stopped playing the blind man, is impossible. I'm worried. . . In the evening, Thursday, they talk sensibly and frankly as though about something that is over and done with and not worth discussing, even with a humour that doesn't wound; they drink wine with their talk, not too much, but a special bottle, and they don't play records, but suddenly talk openly about past events that have never been mentioned before; Gantenbein and Lila are close to each other as they haven't been for a long time. . .

So far, so wonderful.

Next morning, Friday, comes a telegram which Lila, as I see, immediately tears in pieces before my eyes. That's at breakfast. She puts the pieces in the pocket of her dressing-gown. Will you have some more toast? she asks, and I talk about world events, until Lila suddenly gets up to fetch a handkerchief; she needs the handkerchief to stuff into the pocket of her dressing-gown, so that the pieces shan't fly away. I ask about her rehearsals. Later, the pieces don't find their way into the wastepaper basket, but disappear to the last scrap down the lavatory. I have to go, indeed I've already got my coat on, when Lila begs me to go off on a trip with her this very day. I catch on: so he's coming! During the coming week Lila has only one single rehearsal, which she will get out of; she doesn't want to see this madman. A trip? I ask why she doesn't want to go on a trip alone. Is she afraid that I shall clout the first man who rings our doorbell? I don't intend to, but one never knows oneself, and since I see how apprehensive Lila is I succeed in talking her out of this sudden trip, which doesn't fit in with my plans at all, until she cries, but it seems to me that I can't evade her entreaty, which she opposes to my common sense, especially just now. So we go on a trip! It's true that it's raining, but somewhere the sun will be shining, in Elba or the Engadine or Majorca. . .

I imagine:

Gantenbein and Lila on the beach, which is almost empty, sun, but windy, and Lila is not wearing a bikini as she usually does, but a model Gantenbein has never seen before, which attracts the attention not only of Gantenbein, but also of the brown, barefoot lads who are hiring out a sunshade, but above all of the other holiday-makers on the beach, who, on the pretext of looking for shells, saunter to and fro, particularly of ladies who are wearing bikinis and feel themselves to be unattractive, to Gantenbein's mind quite

164

rightly; what Lila is wearing is an anti-bikini: only her thighs are bare, and her calves naturally, her body is covered, jersey, taut, a white like gull's down, a bathing-costume with long sleeves, yes, right down to the wrists, and with a décolleté such as you see in fine evening-dresses, that's to say open from shoulder to shoulder, and with it her black hair, wet, since Lila swims without a bathing-cap, formed into strands by the water like the hair of Greek sculptures. . . Like this Lila lies in the sand, her hand on my knee, Gantenbein is squatting, not a word about the unicorn, or Lila lies on her stomach and smokes and reads, while Gantenbein harpoons, happy too, because now he can harpoon again too, since he has given up his rôle as a blind man, and doesn't have to keep quiet about all the things he has seen in the way of polyps and urchins and jelly-fish. He sees that Lila isn't thinking about the unicorn either, not for an instant. He can see by looking at her. Good. For hours on end they play with a bright-coloured ball, Lila and Gantenbein, or hop about in the surf, without knowing what day of the week it is. No one knows their address (Hotel Formentor, Majorca), no one in the world and no one in the theatre, no one can even send a tele-gram. Lila dreams of a house by the sea, a life without rôles, far from films and television, not necessarily in Formentor but some-where or other, simply a house by the sea, such a thing must exist, it's purely a matter of money, a matter of films. They draw ground-plans that are rubbed out by the curling of a wave that runs up the beach, but that doesn't matter, they draw a new ground-plan. Where are you going? Gantenbein comes back with twigs, oleander, to make it easier to visualize the garden. Men are so inventive and skilful, while Lila in her gull's-down-white beach evening dress, smoking a cigarette and enchanted with the ground-plan which she can't read, merely knows that it is to be a house with many rooms and its own olives and its own vineyard of course and at the same time very simple, oh yes, but with baths of course and with fitted carpets, that's something you need and while you're about it you might as well do things properly. They talk with complete seriousness, Gantenbein and Lila, they actually talk about their ultimate old age, their shared old age, Philemon and Baucis. . .

I imagine:

No more yelling ever!

I imagine:

Philemon and Baucis, when they come home a week later, are awaited by a mass of letters, but Philemon only bothers about his own, Philemon once more a man of intellect . . .

And Baucis?

She has a drawer with an antique lock, which is always locked. How do I know? I have never tried to open the drawer. I wouldn't think of such a thing! I merely see that Baucis opens it with a key, every time she wants something from this drawer, and always says to Philemon that this drawer simply doesn't concern him. Only the care with which she puts the little key away out of sight amuses him more and more, and one morning chance wills that this drawer stands open, an oversight obviously. Or does she want to put him to the test? God knows, he has other things to do. Shall he go and push the drawer shut, so that Baucis doesn't get a shock later? That won't do either, in my opinion, and I'm in favour of Philemon sitting down to the damned income tax declaration, or whatever the demand of the day happens to be. She has just rung up to say she is at the hairdresser's and will be back later. I refuse to think that this is a ruse. For Philemon to go and ring the hairdresser to make sure that Baucis won't be back for two hours is not permissible. This isn't the style between Philemon and Baucis. And if he later does so all the same, this is only because he really does need a piece of information for the purposes of the tax declaration, which of course she can't give from under the hair drier. Did Philemon doubt? He can't walk past without seeing a drawer full of letters. He could read them for two hours on end. Letters from the unicorn? Now there are two possibilities: he does it or he controls himself. Naturally he doesn't do it. But it makes him irritated with Baucis to have to control himself. Really, as I have said, he has other things to do. In short, he doesn't do it.

166

I'm relieved.

There is nothing in a film actress, seen by millions on the television screen, receiving letters. That's clear; but it isn't immediately clear why so many of the letters have Danish stamps. The Danes seem to be particularly keen on television and to possess only one single kind of typewriter. It isn't immediately clear why there is never a letter with a Danish stamp among all the letters that Baucis often leaves lying around for weeks on end. To take no notice, that is the only advice I can give the good Philemon. Has he got unpleasant post, she asks at breakfast, as she puts the letter with the Danish stamp (Philemon can now recognize Danish stamps at a distance of three to four yards) in her dressing-gown without reading it, so that the toast shan't burn. His question: What news is there? refers exclusively to letters without Danish stamps, and it is answered by Baucis in this sense. On an average two to three letters come a week, Danish, all without a sender's name. Naturally Philemon is ashamed of himself for counting them, and there is no need for me to tell him that, to put it mildly, he is a fool.

Let's worry about something else!

For example:

divided Germany, in connexion with which we must ask ourselves under what conditions satisfaction of the real or apparent demand for reunification would not represent a danger to Europe, a threat to peace; why don't we do everything to create conditions –

Or:

conditions in Spain –

Or:

the silting-up of our lakes –

Let's worry about that!

As to Philemon and Baucis, we know that jealousy, founded or unfounded, is still rarely eliminated by the dignity of silent self-control, more easily by one's own infidelity, even if the classical fairy tale of Philemon and Baucis says nothing about this, and quite rightly; it is enough that Philemon knows. He didn't know how uninhibitedly he could lie; he is amazed. For too long Philemon hasn't lied any more; this is what has made him so sensitive. Only at the first moment, when he sees his Baucis, does he feel awkward; he thinks her lips are bound to notice. But Baucis notices nothing that her lips notice, and is happy that Philemon is once more a high-spirited man, and when he says he loves her, it is true, even though three hours ago he was loving another woman; he is amazed how true it is, oh yes, as true as his secret.

So far, so good.

It's pure fooling when, for a whole week, Philemon simply doesn't hand over the Danish letters, which keep on coming just the same. I don't know what he hopes to gain by this. Pure fooling. Perhaps he just wants to show me how reckless he feels about the whole business now. He asks: What's the news? and Baucis takes the top off her egg or pours out the tea, without even asking: Isn't there any post for me? After a week it is Philemon who feels ill at ease; the fact is he is now carrying three letters around in his breast pocket, letters with Danish stamps. Fortunately Baucis doesn't bother about his suits. What a fool he would look! A casual word from her, no more than a look, and Philemon would immediately put his hand in his breast pocket, apologize for his forget-fulness and hand over the Danish letters. Unopened! Instead, an express letter arrives, brought by a messenger, so that Baucis receives it in person. She reads, without on that account forgetting the toast, and doesn't ask with a single word whether he has inter-cepted letters, at least three. Not a word. Philemon butters his toast, glances at the morning paper. I ask myself: what is he going to do now with the three letters? For a moment, when he is already sitting in his car and operating the starter, Philemon wonders whether he shouldn't go back indoors and challenge Baucis, that arch-actress of a woman, straight out. Philemon! I say and remain with my hand on the starter. Isn't it an honour for him that these letters come so openly into the house? I try to pacify him. Doesn't that mean that at least they don't think him petty? I say: Drive off! The engine has been running for a long time already, and I'm relieved that he finally puts on his gloves; only his face in the driving mirror worries me. Why so grim? He doesn't say what he's thinking, probably nothing at all. I think: up to now Philemon has behaved irreproachably. Up to now! When two Danish letters arrived at the same time, he simply laid them beside the table napkin, without smiling, and Baucis, generally so free and easy, pretended to be sulky, bored, irritated, annoyed. What more can anyone want? I understand: Philemon wants to get rid of the three letters. Without reading them! I should hope so. Why is he disconcerted to discover that for her part, as may be deduced from the Danish alarm, his Baucis is evidently in the habit of writing at least twice a week? He really is disconcerted by this. Did he think a Dane could play ping-pong with balls that didn't come back? I must reiterate that up to now Philemon has behaved irreproachably; he never, which would have been tactless, put the Danish letters on top. What angers him is this registered letter, her superior silence over the fact that letters are missing. Ought he perhaps to go and apologize? Finally he has his first idea: I'll go to the main post office and simply post the three intercepted letters again. Full stop. I'm merely afraid that the post office, orderly as it is, will postmark them again, a postmark with a date. So what is he to do? There's only one thing: for Philemon, although he really has other things to do, to drive up into the forest and burn the three letters.

So Philemon drives.

Why does he have to go so far?

Philemon doesn't want to be seen, not even by forestry labourers. It's raining, morning, there's no one else in the forest. It's a pity one doesn't go into the forest more often when it's raining and take the time to trudge through the green ferns, knee-deep in wet fronds, or stand under a beech, dry as in a tent, while all round you hear the green harps of the rain: an anthill in the rain, a hillock of pine needles, brown and wet, or moss, blackish and spongy, sponges according to the season, tree trunks, and it is dripping, you keep away from bushes, every twig is a shower, not a bird is stirring, silence under green umbrellas, motionless, spiders' webs, but without spiders, roots that are black and glistening with wetness, at times it is slippery, then again as dry as a carpet, it is raining somewhere high above, a rustling that never arrives, there are brown puddles in the path, that's where it gets to, you can see that, splashes, and the thick drops roll slowly down the branches, wood in bundles, there the beetles live free from drips, the wood has been dried many times, the bark mossy, the round crosscuts gleam yellow like poached eggs, apart from that the world is grey steam between wet columns linked by green filigree, and the sky above, which is raining, is lilac . . . It's a tragedy that Philemon doesn't see any of this, anxious about forestry labourers, whom he has just seen, men in boots sitting like cobolds under a tarpaulin; but that was a mile or two from here, yes, just where he wanted to burn the letters. In the meantime Philemon has been wondering how it would be if he went to the bank and put the letters in a safe. Advantage: if they were ever mentioned, they would be immediately deliverable. Disadvantage: they would remain readable at any time, apart from Sundays and general holidays. I'm in favour of burning, but quickly. I should like to get on with the job. Why not in this gravel pit? I'm impatient, yes, and Philemon is absent-minded; when he gets out he forgets to switch off the windscreen wiper. The puddles in the gravel pit, it may be, are reminiscent of the shallow sea round the Danish coast. Right, out with the letters! The place is highly suitable, a bleak and abandoned gravel pit with a rusty notice saying *No Entry. Trespassers will be prosecuted*, a humming aeroplane passes over the forest, a Vampire, perhaps right over the gravel pit, low, but invisible in the rain clouds, then again the dripping silence; Philemon's black car, splashed by driving through many puddles, is standing askew up on the path with the windscreen wipers swaying to and fro; now a jay flutters up out of the undergrowth and squawks in the air, but that isn't why Philemon hesitates. The letters, not intended for the rain but for the drawer, look as though they had been drenched in tears. Will they still burn at all? It is to be foreseen that the letters, unopened, will only singe, and afterwards they will lie there, paper with brown edges, that at best glimmer and curl up into ashes, and Philemon will have to kneel down to blow and to read on his knees a few unburned words that don't concern him, the remains of a sentence to a scornful degree meaningless, so that he deciphers the ashes as well, words which, since he has to invent the context for himself, will go on burning unforgettably in his brain. He will regret not having read the letters properly, and when he has read them he will regret it too. Wouldn't it be better simply to dig a hole and bury the letters? I see him looking for a branch with which to dig a hole. But the branch breaks. A second breaks likewise; gravel is gravel. I see him go red with anger, yes, anger with you two. Now it's raining properly, he feels it, you're laughing at Philemon. You two! But that is the beginning of jealousy, that I think: you two, the couple, you two! Now he really tears up the letters, all three of them, unhurriedly, as I see, but resolutely. I can't prevent him. I merely think, he didn't have to go into the wet forest for that. What a sight Philemon looks now, his trousers, his muddy shoes! When he walks to the car, so that at least he can read the letters in the dry, I say again: Philemon? The letters with the Danish stamps are torn up, I see, but still unread. What can be in them? He hesitates –

I can tell him:

– Copenhagen in the spring, Paris of the north, but as empty of people (to judge by these letters) as the moon, not a single Danish woman appears in them, life in Copenhagen must be unbearable, unbearable without Baucis, but the main thing is that she has had a good rest, it's raining in Copenhagen too, not a word about Philemon, on the other hand a lot of nice things about Lila, a trip to Hamburg postponed out of understanding, exclamation marks, hope of a guest performance in Munich, question mark, Hotel Vier Jahreszeiten, at times there does dart through the Copenhagen of these letters, and vanishes before uttering a word, a person, a wraith, who threatens to take her life, hence the accommodation address, time will bring a solution, meanwhile professional success, mentioned lightly, naturally, not really worth talking about, a lot of intelligent things about films, agreement over a thousand

171

miles, Copenhagen is a city of millions, but the only person who understands isn't in Copenhagen and the way to the Central Post Office, where there hasn't been anything for several days, seems not to be bordered by any houses but by memories of the Jungfernstieg, and yet there are some very beautiful flats in Copenhagen, precisely for women who want to live independently, thanks for the photo, an aeroplane is just flying over the house, and so time passes, time, thanks again for the photo, longing for a cold whisky in a hot bath, etc.

Well then:

Philemon hasn't read the letter, he puts the car in first gear and releases the brake, the last straw would be if because of you two he couldn't get out of this rut; the wheels spin round in the mud, but then he does make it and the car is long ago out of the rut, but Philemon is still in the mud of his feelings, his thoughts spin round and round without moving from the spot –

And it's like that the whole day!

Baucis's free and easy, everyday cordiality, her casual and unreproachful question why he's so late, her pleased comment that he has at last bought himself a new pair of shoes and that the car has been washed again, this entirely natural and real and in no way feigned easiness, with which Baucis greets her Philemon, cries out to heaven – I admit – on the assumption that the three Danish letters contain more or less what I suppose; but I can't swear to it! . . . The car has been washed, yes, but it has a dent; at some point he must have brushed against the trunk of a tree, probably as he drove out of the slippery rut; a very noticeable dent. That by the way.

Philemon lies:

"Oh," he says, "that's an old one."

This is the last straw, that he, Philemon, has to have a bad conscience, yes, that it is he who can't look the other in the eye –

Philemon drinks too much whisky.

She doesn't say he's not as young as he was, a man of his age ought to start taking care of himself. Not a word about that! But he hears it –

172

Philemon is working too much.

"Yes," he says, "let's go to the cinema."

"There's a film on at the moment," she says, "that's supposed to be exceptional, stylistically quite exceptional, people say –"

"Who says so?"

"Don't you feel like it?"

"What do you mean by stylistically?"

"A film," she says, "that has no story at all, you understand, the only incident is, so to speak, the camera itself, nothing happens at all, you understand, only the movements of the camera, the connexions which the camera establishes –"

"Who says that?"

For a moment it looks as though he were going to challenge her outright, because she already knows of a film that is being shown in this country for the first time not merely the non-existent story, but also its stylistic characteristics –

"I've read about it."

Read!

"Yes," she says, "yesterday in the newspaper."

The continuation:

He throws the three torn-up letters down a drain in Baucis's presence; but she takes no notice, although three times, once for each letter, he has to help the pieces down with his toe; she sees that they are letters, but she doesn't bother about his post.

So far, so good.

Longing for a cold whisky in a hot bath, of course I shouldn't have said that, I don't know what was in the letters, it was only a guess, and now I see Philemon, a cold whisky in his hand, standing in front of the curtains and staring.

I ask what Philemon is thinking.

No answer.

Are you jealous?

Why should I be?

I'm asking.

It depends, he says, what you mean by jealousy. The thought, for example, that the woman I love drinks cold whisky in a warm bath with another man – my mistake if I imagine it, I know! he says. But?

To tell you the honest truth, he says, I find the idea unpleasant – I laugh.

He stares.

I ask Philemon why he imagines things which, as I assure him, are pure fantasy, speculation, no more. Or does he suddenly believe I am a clairvoyant who can see through letters without reading them? Apart from the fact that such things don't concern us at all –

Philemon, I say, go and work!

It is good that these things are now down a drain, otherwise I believe he would actually read them now, just to see my conjecture refuted.

Philemon, I say –

Enter Baucis.

I ask what Philemon is really after.

Baucis is humming.

A cold whisky in a warm bath, I must say again that this is a blind speculation, no more, without any real evidence, a conjecture drawn from the arsenal of my own secrets, nothing more.

Baucis hums.

Why doesn't he challenge her?

No answer.

Scared?

I imagine: Philemon challenges her and Baucis has something to confess – Philemon won't shout. I know him. He will act as though there were nothing to it, and later he will relight his pipe, which has gone out. So I was right! That's the only thing he will think of to say: So I was right! It's like an injection that hasn't worked yet, and it's even possible that I shall smile, and Baucis will feel a fool for not having talked about it in January already. In January? he asks, in January? But dates, she considers, are beside the point; at the moment she is content with the relief she feels that I am keeping calm. Why does Philemon want to know now what the other man's name is? Perhaps he only insists on it because he can't think of anything else. What difference does it make to me if his name is Nils or Olaf! But Philemon wants to know. He would rather I wasn't present. I know already that he will survive it. Does she really love the other man and how does she picture the future, a lot of questions that I too have asked before, I can't prevent Philemon from asking them nevertheless; but without my participation. Why do I always have to be present? I don't hear her answers, but pour myself another coffee and can understand that Baucis, controlling herself, doesn't pass me the sugar; it is a painful tact that now forbids her this accustomed gesture; she doesn't want to make an idyll of it. Now he knows! she says, while I take sugar, with a taste on my tongue which I know. It's two o'clock, really time to go back to work; Baucis puts the cups together. Why doesn't he slap her face? The ability to distinguish between feelings one has and feelings one once had improves. This has nothing to do with maturity. I experience the moment like memory. That's all. I remember how years ago I didn't shout, because it wasn't the first time either, and the first time I heard from a woman that she had been with another man, I only shouted because it tallied so exactly with my suspicion, as since then it has tallied with my memory of the first time. . .

Well then:

Philemon doesn't challenge her.

I go to work.

A week later, unexpectedly, Baucis gets a car of her own, which she has always wanted, yes, a little Austin-Healey Sprite. How can she understand, she who can have no idea about the scene over black coffee that didn't take place? I see her in the chic Austin-Healey Sprite as the gears are being explained to her, blissful over the present without pretext, a bit confused all the same and with no idea how it all works –

So far, so good.

I'm relieved that Philemon didn't challenge her – assuming he had done so, I know that within ten days, although he wouldn't have forgotten what Baucis confessed to him, he would have got over it, as is right and proper, or at least he would think he had, after apologizing to Baucis. I have never known a woman who didn't expect an apology when she has been with another man, and has also obtained one, that's to say an apology on my part, so that nothing shall stand in the way of the future. What future? The future of Philemon and Baucis. What else? Well then. Why not champagne? We only live once. Why save? She scarcely recognizes him, her Philemon, he is in such a free and easy mood, it's almost uncanny, and he shows such felicity with words she really has to laugh, the grace of a conqueror, he notices it himself, she now looks at him when he talks, lost like a girl in the close splendour of the only possible man. Conversationwise to gamble everything while he cracks lobster legs – he can afford to do that now. Only in secret does he occasionally take fright when he sees how for her part Baucis, without hypocrisy, forgets her invisible Dane whom they have to thank for so much. The waiters in evening dress, who are the devil when one is sitting there at odds with oneself, bow to his mood and flit off to fetch another lemon. The moon too comes as if to order, not any old moon, but full moon. Baucis is blissful; she feels protected. For the first time Philemon dares, not to approve of an opened bottle with a confused nod, but to refuse it and without long explanations which lead to nothing, which as is well known only cause an angry quarrel, a scene that ends after a second and third sip with one giving up and nodding with ironic magnanimity, no, for the first time a mute look is enough, a wrinkling of the forehead, a casual and brief smile that doesn't interrupt the conversation between Philemon and Baucis for an instant, and the dust-covered bottle has vanished in the white-gloved hand of the waiter. Why shouldn't the woman one loves have other men as well? It is in the nature of the matter. Do you like it? he asks, without giving the meal too much importance. At one point he makes a play on words that cuts him himself like a knife; but Baucis hasn't caught the reference, fortunately, and the pheasant tastes delicious, pheasant with orange, and with it a full moon as I have said, and Philemon's

176

serene vision of living alone. How does he mean? she asks; now he has to taste the new wine. Why alone? He nods, approves by silence, whereat the waiter, with the grace of relief, slowly fills the burgundy glasses. They enjoy the silence of this act. Baucis talks about plots of land again, while Philemon sees himself as a bachelor in New York. It's a pity Baucis has absolutely no appetite. What does he want to go to New York for, she asks; but now he needs a cigar: Romeo y Julieta. The problem of what would happen if Baucis were now to have a child, in particular the question whose child it would be, doesn't seem to preoccupy Philemon; anyhow, he smokes his cigar and talks, his eyes on the night-time lake, about the silting-up of our lakes, which is a serious problem. Philemon hasn't talked so much for a long time. Over cognac, naturally rather more languid through the processes of digestion, he sees no reason for Baucis to cry, and when he has paid – he only has to wait for the change – it is clear that Philemon and Baucis will go home together. . .

I imagine:

One day, long afterwards, I have driven to Munich to meet Lila and am waiting in the lobby for her luggage, Hotel Vier Jahreszeiten, when I see a young man who has just paid his bill, I can't hear if it's for a single or a double room, and of course it's ridiculous of me immediately to think of the Dane, apart from the fact that this young man isn't blond at all. I wait, reading a newspaper in order to hang on to reality. I am aware that I don't know what was in those Danish letters; it was merely to keep Philemon from reading the letters that I pictured to him what might have been in those letters which he later threw down a drain: Copenhagen in spring, professional success, longing for a whisky in the bath, opinion about a film, hope for Munich, Hotel Vier Jahreszeiten. Absolute invention on my part. The fact is that I am now sitting in this lobby, Hotel Vier Jahreszeiten, and that a young fop (why a fop?) has just paid his bill. No doubt there are also Danes with black hair, I don't even know whether Kierkegaard was fair; and I have just as little idea whether this young fop (he must be a fop to judge by his clothes!) is a Dane. Nor does the fact that he is waving a German newspaper about prove the contrary; all Danes read German and there aren't any Danish papers here. Moreover, so far as I know, Lila knows no Danish; so he must know German. On the other hand, I tell myself, not every handsome young man has to be Lila's lover, just because he knows German. Furthermore, I don't find him as worthy of attention as he seems to think himself. The way he waves the newspaper about, the way he bangs his thigh with it, merely shows that he is nervous. Because I've come? There may be other reasons. Why should he recognize me? There may also be other reasons for his having looked at me twice; anybody one stares at occasionally returns one's stare. . . There you are! says Lila, suddenly standing beside me ready for the journey. She is, as I see, pretty worn out by the filming, as always. My question as to whether she has already paid the bill, she doesn't hear, busy at the moment with her luggage, while I fold up my newspaper and observe that the fop has disappeared. I should have liked to have seen his face now, but he has gone through the glass doors before us, to stand banging his thigh with his newspaper outside on the pavement. It's going to be another awful film, reports Lila, when we are sitting in the car; I pull on my gloves, look in the rear-view mirror, without a word. Unfortunately I see only shoes and two trouser legs. The upper part, the more personal part so to speak, is cut off, and I daren't adjust the rear-view mirror. I switch on the engine and wait, as though the engine were cold. Why shouldn't I now light a cigarette before we start? Now I don't even know whether the young man has a beard; it's possible, but I'm suddenly uncertain. We shall be blocking the traffic, says Lila, if we don't move off; but I don't see any traffic, only the lower half of a man wearing a waistcoat, and now he has put his right hand in his trouser pocket, in order not to wave, I understand, a man of tact. What can he be thinking about the back of my head? I fiddle with the ashtray, which is stuck again. Why shouldn't the young man wear a waistcoat? Then I ask Lila again if she really has paid her bill. A man has to think of everything. Right then: I put the car in first, release the brake, switch on the blinker, everything as it should be done, look into the rear-view mirror to make sure no traffic is coming, but the mirror really has got displaced, it's pointing too low, I have to straighten it up, word of honour, for objective reasons. Meanwhile the supposed Dane has stepped sideways out of my mirror. What do I care if he has a beard or not! When I involuntarily look back out of the open side window as I swing out, as I always do, to make certain once more that no danger threatens, he has turned round. So the beard question remains unsettled. Lila tells me not to drive like a madman. How are you? I ask nonchalantly, to indicate that there can be no question of my speeding. When I ask again about the bill, Lila gets almost annoyed: Of course I have! I should hate anyone to cheat a hotel-keeper in my name. When Lila threatens to get out as I am doing a hundred on an open stretch of road, I immediately slow down to sixty to make it easier for her to do so; once, when she complains again, I pull up: Go ahead! I know I'm being unbearable. . .

What has actually happened?

Baucis now has her own Austin-Healey Sprite, and everything else hasn't happened: no frank discussion over black coffee, no lobster eaten with the full moon shining over the lake, no stupid behaviour on an open stretch of road. None of all that! The one single fact remains: Baucis now has her white Austin-Healey Sprite that delights her and runs perfectly.

So far, so good.

And Philemon is a man who can let people see him again, a man among men, a contemporary between East and West, a citizen who speaks out against atomic weapons even if without success, a reader, a friend who helps, a chess player, a brain, a member of society the changing of which seems to him essential, a worker from morning till evening, a man of action, a participant and an opponent, a man who is concerned with world questions, the want of the peoples, the hope of the peoples, the lies of those in power, ideologies, technology, history and the future, space travel – a human being. . .
What fascinates him: the thought that in millions of years, when our

earth grows cold, and Venus on the other hand has cooled down and in its turn acquired an atmosphere, human life could be transplanted into space (*Science and the Future*).

I'm relieved.

As regards the letters with Danish stamps, I see in their sudden cessation no reason for further stupidity on my part. Every exchange of love letters peters out in time. It is solely his dreary conscience that impels Philemon to think about this extremely natural circumstance at all. His suspicion, derived from his own experience, is simple enough: they have noticed that three letters have been intercepted and now they are writing to each other at an accommodation address. Suppose they are! – I see no reason on that account to break open her locked drawer with a crowbar. It is three in the morning. I say: You're drunk! It must have come very suddenly; he couldn't sleep, while Baucis was asleep, and looked for a sleeping tablet. What has this drawer to do with it? Open is open. And now? That it is full of letters, we know already. What next? He almost hopes that Baucis will wake up, come into the room and catch him at her writing desk. What then? But Baucis sleeps, the three strokes of the cathedral clock don't wake her, she leaves him alone in his shame. He hates her. He is shivering. Philemon in pyjamas and barefoot, but glad that he hates. That is once more like the first feeling, so hot, so unambiguous. He hates her. She has brought him to that. How, actually? He hates her, and that gives him more and more right to break open her drawer, which, however, he has already done – I can't stop Philemon now. . . *Darling*, there's no objection to be made to that, that isn't unsurpassable, *my darling*, he really only wants to know how you two address each other, *my dearest darling*, it doesn't take a brain from Denmark to think of that, *my Lilalil*, that too has been said before, Philemon has written to her like that himself before now, and altogether men seem to resemble each other, apart from their handwriting. It's fabulous what this man manages to produce in the way of personal calligraphy, much of it can't be deciphered at all in the haste of breaking in, and on top of that there is his pounding heart,

and where the eyes do suddenly get caught up like a dragging anchor, he doesn't really find out very much, the characters of a love that are easy enough to decipher, but unrewarding when he stops and reads; it is incomprehensible how little there is in a genuine love letter, almost nothing at all, if you don't count the exclamation marks as feelings, a single statement: *I shall wait by the kiosk*, time of writing in the top right-hand corner: *Thursday afternoon after your visit*, there is no date, yes, all pleasure desires eternity, I know, deep, deep eternity, but that's the end of it. Perhaps the postmark knows when that was? But the envelopes have gone, that's just it, a drawer full of naked letters, and Philemon is too drunk to sit down and sort the material out and work like a historian; standing, only in this way, shivering and without even shutting the door of the room, just as if no intention were involved, only in this way does he permit himself the impermissible nosing through letters that are so illegible with passion, even if they say nothing, so tender that he doesn't recognize them as his own. One single letter is still in its envelope, one single letter in the whole drawer; but this, it turns out, is a letter from her first husband, *Your old Svob*, a beautiful letter actually, simple and to the point. It is also dated. It is the only letter which Philemon, now sitting on the back of the armchair, is able to read right through, simultaneously dismayed and reassured. The tenderness that does not take itself as its own subject, that is merely contained in the way a thing is written about, the way the writer really takes account of the recipient and of nothing else, I too find that such tenderness lasts better than these ecstatic telegrams: SOON STOP EVENING AFTER NEXT STOP SOON STOP ONLY TWO MORE DAYS STOP SOON SOON. Well there it is. If Philemon is going to nose through letters, why won't he see the date of the telegrams? He has no rest, he is thirsting for an enormity, but what he finds: *Your voice, your voice yesterday on the telephone, your faraway voice, but your voice, suddenly your voice*, that's boring, I consider, sentimental trash, but as soon as a real personality appears in these letters, not merely a little man playing with a ballpoint pen or a
181

typewriter, a personality that surpasses him in intelligence, at least in his drunken state, no, he doesn't read that, admiration for his sleeping wife, and understanding homage to which he could give his support, no, he doesn't read that. What he is looking for is something like this: *Write and tell me where I can write to you so that you don't have any difficulties.* That comes closer to the wound. *So that you don't have any difficulties,* continued on the next page, *if Svoboda doesn't want us to write to each other* . . . Why Svoboda? That would mean that they are his own letters. Too true, I say, have you only just noticed that? It is odd how strange our own handwriting can appear to us at times, especially when we are not prepared for it, when we break open a drawer in order to spy on a sleeping woman and end up by merely spying on ourselves.

Philemon, I say, go back to bed!

The lock is broken –

That's one thing.

Philemon will not be able to avoid making a confession that will warn Baucis for all time, while he knows from now on that somewhere in this flat there must be another hiding place. . .

That's the other thing.

Philemon, I say, give it up!

I see the sleeping woman:

Her loose hair black, she has just turned over onto the other side, her ear coral-red, her hand with outspread fingers on the pillow by her face, she is breathing slowly and regularly like someone who is really asleep, and with motionless lips, her lips slightly open and childlike, her left shoulder and the beginning of the breast are bare, her body covered only by a sheet, her body under the sheet as clearly defined as that of a Nike under the betraying drapery of marble, but warm, even hot from sleep, dry, glowing, her coral-red ear under the black hair that I could touch without her noticing, once the lashes twitch, but she is asleep, her closed eyelids bluish and waxen coolly gleaming like the pallor of autumn crocuses over the sleeping eyes, motionless, only the hair seems sleepless, the tips of the fingers by the face might also almost be awake, but she is asleep, sleep is in the nape of her neck, there quite deep, dreamless, moist, deeper than in the face that seems to be floating on dark sleep like a destructible reflection –

Lilalil.

Philemon, I say, you love her!

Everything else is nonsense.

In Africa (so a guest tells us) there is said to be a primitive tribe in which lots are drawn to determine which man shall belong to which woman, in the sense that he has to look after this woman when she is young and healthy, when she is ill, when she has children, when she grows old; apart from this, however, everyone couples with everyone. And (according to the guest) it is supposed to be the most peaceful tribe in this Dark Continent. Eros as common property, as Nature intended, sex and person are not subject to the same law; hence it never happens among the Tuholi (or whatever they are called) that men shoot at each other on account of a woman. They need both their minds and their arrows for hunting; quarrels occur only over the spoils of the hunt. Theft is punished by death, the manner of death decided by the value of the object stolen. A simple death, cutting of the jugular vein, awaits the thief of household utensils. The thief of jewellery, for example a woman's earrings, is tied between two palm trees until the next wind, by swaying the two palms to and fro, tears his thieving body apart. A thief of arrows, which evidently represent the highest possession, is emasculated, then buried alive. Women thieves are burned to death by their husbands. Apart from theft, however, there is nothing which these people regard as despicable or punishable or which even worries them –

Baucis is delighted!

Apart from this delight, which incidentally is shared by other ladies present, and apart from those Danish letters, which likewise prove nothing so long as we don't know what's in them and which moreover, as I have said, have stopped coming, nothing has really happened, nothing factual, which, thinking logically, would in any way justify Philemon in supposing that Baucis is leading a Tuholi marriage, nothing whatever –

Philemon, I say, I want to work!

And what about the waistcoated fop in the rear-view mirror?

Philemon, I say, you really mustn't blindly treat every speculation that passes through my head as a fact.

But he can't leave it alone:

To re-establish trust he employs the method of frankness; without any compelling reason, unasked, he suddenly reports his affair with the little typist, and lo and behold, Baucis didn't know about it, but she doesn't want to know about it, no, she doesn't want to know about it in future either. . .

A misfire!

I don't think much of frankness, I know my Philemon, I know that confessions are more masklike than silence, one can say everything and the secret merely slips back behind our words, lack of shame isn't the same thing as truth, quite apart from the fact that one never tells everything, for instance not the business of the drawer; our honesty, when it displays itself as such, is mostly only a crooked transaction involving lies, a cover for other secrets.

Her silence is more hygienic.

The confession regarding the broken-open drawer, which unfortunately has to be made one day so that the charwoman shall not be dismissed on a false suspicion, takes place over black coffee, yes, in the two armchairs and just as I had pictured Baucis's confession, only with the rôles reversed, which for her part she can't know; now it is she who turns pale, speechless, as she stubs out her cigarette in the ashtray, and it is he who pours out the black coffee but daren't pass the sugar; she can't look at him, eagerly as he is waiting for her to do so. Only love mourns inwardly like this. She can't manage a smile as he apologizes for reading his own letters one evening, she doesn't even find it funny.

"Yes," she asks, "and what now?"

Philemon takes her hand.

"No," she says, "please."

Baucis doesn't want a kiss from a man who reads his own letters; she never thought him capable of it; she thought she knew him; she is sitting in front of a stranger –

What next?

Baucis is ill, not seriously, a high temperature and headaches, anyhow she stays in bed and I make tea, I stand in the kitchen thinking of my work till the water boils, I sit on the end of her bed, Philemon and Baucis, like in the book. I believe in aspirin, but can't find any. Baucis feels wretched; she asks me to look in her handbag. She doesn't only allow me to, she asks me to, wretched as she feels. But her handbag isn't in the room, I'm sorry, her handbag is over in the living-room. I have always been surprised by the muddle in her handbags, and if I were to find the aspirin by feeling for it blindly, as the poor thing expects, it would be a miracle; I try it, but the miracle doesn't take place. What I find: keys, banknotes, lipstick, a little notebook, passport, coins, another lipstick, gloves, an airline ticket, a case containing tweezers, coins of various currencies, two tickets for a museum in Munich, a ballpoint pen, driving licence, comb, cigarettes, compact, hotel bill Vier Jahreszeiten single room with bath, car key, a newspaper cutting, earrings, a letter bearing Danish stamps dated the day before yesterday addressed poste restante, the envelope has been slit open –

Philemon, I say, stop that!

It would be too cheap.

Yes, I call out, I've got them!

I'm already sitting on the edge of her bed again, an empty tumbler in my hand, my other hand on her hot sweating forehead...

Philemon is unpredictable.

On the day before her trip to Hamburg he suddenly decides it would be more sensible if she went alone, suddenly his enlightenment; a cheerful enlightenment; he has thought it over. To be frank, it really wouldn't suit me at all to go to Hamburg just now. No, she says, then I shan't go either. Why not? Anyhow, not to Kampen. That's nonsense, he says, I think a week in Kampen would do you good. Without you? she asks, and he won't budge, however sincerely she asks him to change his mind. Does he hope she won't dare? That would be stupid. Why doesn't he mind? He doesn't mind. Cunning? Contempt? Nothing like that. What does he intend to do? Work. What could I do in Hamburg? he says and he won't budge; next day he drives her to the airport, with unfeigned cheerfulness; Kampen is a healthy place, everything is clear and right and doesn't need to be discussed –

There's no other solution.

Just like that: latitude –

Until one fine morning the bell rings and since Lila is asleep I go to the door, and outside is a young man whom I imagine I recognize at once, although I have never seen him before. I ask him to come in. I'm glad I'm already dressed, even if I haven't put on a tie yet. He comes in, doesn't hesitate, takes his pipe in his hand. Presumably there's no need for me to introduce myself, since he doesn't do so either. So he stands there smiling, a loose-limbed fellow, young, compared with us, a student with tousled hair or a dancer, but without a beard, also without a waistcoat. Whether he is handsome I cannot judge; he certainly isn't a pig. His eyes have no sort of power over me, but then it isn't me he has come to see. I ask him if he has any luggage. His answer is confused. But he doesn't want to be a nuisance, he says, he could come back at eleven. Perhaps he has left his luggage out at the airport in order to have both hands free for Lila's luggage; it will be no small amount, if they are flying to Uruguay. He doesn't take off his coat. He is a bit embarrassed, but probably only on my account; perhaps she wrote to him that I make scenes. I shall control myself, I shall astound him, but I shan't change anything, he seems to know that Lila won't be able to say No when she sees his eyes. So let's keep it short! I simply say: You'd like to see Lila? He smiles at my conventional dialogue. I add: Lila is here. As I lead him up to the bedroom: Go ahead. The last remark sounds a bit sharp, so that the young man doesn't know what to do. Has his luck deserted him? All the same, he follows me, holding his pipe, which now, as I knock, he puts in his pocket, presumably in order to have both

186

hands free. At the moment I do it I don't know why I'm doing it, no idea, I do it because it's the only possible thing to do, and my heart doesn't pound. I knock at the door again, either to avoid giving my Lila a shock, or to avoid making myself look ridiculous by putting on the air of an owner in front of the young man, who knows that in love there is of course no ownership. So I knock at the door. No answer. Then I press the latch very slowly, in order not to wake her with a noise; that's something she can't bear. He should make a note of that. Why does he remain standing on the threshold? I switch the light on, because the curtains are still drawn. Didn't he know that we share a bedroom? He really seems rather confused, I see, otherwise he wouldn't now put his pipe back in his mouth again. As always, when Lila doesn't want to be woken, she rolls over onto the other side; I take hold of her shoulder. Time for reality, my dear friends, time for reality! It's quite a time before she stretches in cosy bliss. I say: Lilalein? And since she hasn't yet seen out of her eyes: the unicorn is here! I talk to her as to a child. Who's there? she asks with a yawn, and the student in the open overcoat, student or dancer, who expected things to work out differently, it seems, acts as though he knew nothing about any-thing, his pipe in his hand again; but Lila screams, as though there were a chimney sweep in the bedroom, and screams one single word: my name, which, it seems to me, has little to do with the situation. I laugh, but get a grip on myself at once. Excuse me, I say, as I go out, then I lock the door from outside, put the key in my trouser pocket, gradually horrified that I have really done it, not merely imagined but done it, I take my tie from the bathroom door, tie my tie, take a jacket and stand there, make sure that the car key is in my pocket, stand there, and since nothing happens I go and sit in my car, which I start up without haste, drive off. And since it is a sunny morning, I drive with the top open, wind in my hair, whistling, only my right hand on the steering wheel, whistling, I let my left arm dangle out of the car, which glides quietly and slowly through the landscape; I've got plenty of time. Something painful that can't be whistled away, a doubt that catches up with

187

me, even when I drive faster, a sudden doubt whether the stranger whom I have locked in with Lila is really the person I think he is, forces me slowly and stubbornly, like a policeman cutting across me, to stop on an open stretch of road, so that I can produce papers to show to my own suspicion. And suppose it isn't him? In fact I have no papers to prove that it is, none at all. How should I know what a unicorn looks like in reality? I put my hand in my right trouser pocket; I really have got the key to her room in my right trouser pocket. It isn't a dream. I pretend for a while to be thinking things over. What things? A cigarette, which was supposed to calm my nerves, I throw away before I have lit it, and put the car in reverse, turn the wheel with both hands, change gear and step on the accelerator, as though speed could wipe out what has happened. . . The bedroom door has been burst open, the room is empty, they are sitting down-stairs in the living-room, Lila in her blue dressing-gown, he has meanwhile taken off his overcoat, it is lying rolled up on his knees, a young man who is studying medicine but would like to go into the theatre and has come to get advice from Lila, still a bit taken aback by the customs of our house but not showing it. The conversation, conducted by Lila with an objectivity that enables her negligé to be forgotten, lasts another half an hour. When he has gone, she says:

"– I'm leaving."

A week later (unfortunately in life superfluous conversations can't be left out) Lila has gone; she can't live with a madman, I understand that.

What help is it to see!

I sit on the arm of an upholstered chair and play with the cork-screw. All the upholstered furniture has been covered with white sheets, the ashtrays emptied, all the flower vases emptied so that the place doesn't smell mouldy, I sit there in coat and cap because it's raining outside. The carpets have been rolled up, the shutters closed. Of the people who lived here this much is certain: one was male, one was female. I see blouses in the cupboard, some ladies' under-clothes that wouldn't go into the trunk, ties on the other side, my jackets; at the bottom of the cupboard stand my shoes, some with shoe-trees in, lined up as though for roll call. All the doors are open; in the kitchen the tap is dripping, but otherwise it is as quiet as at Pompeii. I am still sitting there in coat and cap, both hands in my trouser pockets. As at Pompeii one can stroll through the rooms, hands in one's trouser pockets, one tries to picture how people lived here before the hot ash smothered them. Everything is still here, only life has gone. It can't have been long ago. Her blue dressing-gown is still hanging in the bathroom. I don't know what really happened. . .

We are still sitting by the fire, past midnight, I haven't said anything for a long time. Lila behind the outspread newspaper she has in her hands. I'm glad I'm still holding my whisky glass, even if it's empty. Lila yawns and the log on top of the glowing ash has gone out again. Time for bed. I remember exactly what we were last talking about:

"Did you read it?"

"Yes," I said, "I read it."

Pause.

"No," she said, "how is that possible?"

She meant the murder.

"Can you imagine how anyone can do such a thing?" she asked. "I think it's awful."

"Yes," I said, "I read it."

"Is there any whisky left?" she asked.

"Lila," I said, "I said something."

"Sorry," she said, and I saw her face as she asked: "What did you say?"

"I said I had read it," I said.

"Don't you think it's awful?"

"Yes —"

Since then we have neither of us spoken.

"Yes," says Lila now, "let's go to bed!"

I remain Gantenbein.

I ask myself what professions can be considered for Gantenbein that would not necessitate his giving up his rôle as a blind man; there are many possibilities, it seems to me, for example the profession of travel guide: Gantenbein, equipped with his dark glasses and his little black stick, which he taps on the marble steps of the Acropolis, surrounded by a group, Gantenbein as the only man of our day who hasn't already seen what the tourists see, no, not even in films or on photos – he doesn't tell the people what they are now seeing to left and right, he asks them what they see and they have to describe it in words in response to his questions. From time to time he sits down and wipes the sweat from his brow; Gantenbein doesn't point out to them all the things they are not seeing. They take snaps. Gantenbein doesn't see that there's so much to snap, and fills his pipe until they have snapped all they want to. His questions are touching. Are all the columns of the Parthenon the same height? He refuses to believe it; he has reasons for his doubt that make them prick up their ears. Is the space between these columns the same everywhere? Someone does him the favour and measures. No! Gantenbein isn't surprised, the ancient Greeks weren't blind. Sometimes the group doesn't move from the spot, Gantenbein has so many questions, questions that can't be answered with a camera; he doesn't see the bus that is waiting to take them on to Cape Sunion. He acts as though they were not waiting for him; he fills himself another pipe and acts as though he were waiting for the people who can't see enough of this Acropolis. Above all, it is by his lack of delight that he makes the group observant. It's tragic all the things Gantenbein can't see! He sits on the fragment of a column as though he were not on the Acropolis, busy only with his pipe, bored and not even inspired by the hope that colour films will show him later where he was today. Someone takes him by the arm to show him the Erechtheion, the little Temple of Nike outside, in the distance the violet bay of Salamis, the Theatre of Dionysos, and it is sufficient for Gantenbein again and again to face in the wrong direction to bring the sights home to them. One or two feel so sorry for him that, in their search for words that will give him an idea of the sacred atmosphere of the place, they themselves begin to see. Their words are lame, but their eyes come to life; Gantenbein nods and listens and nods and lets his pipe go out; his sorrow that he will die without ever having seen this Acropolis makes the others for the first time really grateful to have made this trip, cost what it may. It is an effort to travel with a blind guide, but it's worth while: inwardly for the tourists, financially for Gantenbein, because what they save in colour films adds up to a pretty fair fee –

I shall put in an advertisement:

"Travel with a blind man! The greatest experience of your life! I shall open your eyes! Trips to Spain, Morocco, Greece, etc."

I remain Gantenbein:

And Lila is happy. . .

How do I know?

Naturally this Gantenbein isn't as fine as I pretend, and once, it seems, he did read a Danish letter, of which he has retained two or three sentences in his memory.

"*I shall always be there.*"

(Unfortunately without a date.)

"*It's good like this. Why do you cry? I understand everything. Why should I be angry, since you tell me you are happy there? It's good like this.*"

So Lila is happy.

What more does Gantenbein want?

"*Then shall we journey into the Seventh Heaven? Your Nils.*"

Gantenbein as a travel guide –
Gantenbein taking trout to pieces –
Gantenbein as a chess player –
Gantenbein by the Krumme Lanke –
Gantenbein as a host –
Gantenbein before the municipal medical officer –
Gantenbein when there is a short circuit in the house –

Gantenbein in the Dior boutique –
Gantenbein arranging flowers –
Gantenbein at the airport –
Gantenbein as a blind husband –
I can imagine all this.
– but Gantenbein as a friend?
We meet in the street, Gantenbein with his yellow armband, so
that I feel sorry for him, and we talk about the world that he doesn't
see. It's true he always asks me how I am; but I never dare tell him.
We know each other from the past. One doesn't talk about one's
own career when the other person doesn't see it. Gantenbein knows
my views from the old days, and since I'm convinced that Gantenbein doesn't see how my way of life is changing year by year I act
as though we were the men we used to be from one handshake to
the next, and Gantenbein does the same. . .
But one day Gantenbein will come to visit me.
I have forgotten how my way of life has changed, have got used
to it, come home and am whistling to myself when it suddenly
strikes me as I hang up my cap: that's mine, no doubt about it,
but it's so new. A beret without a sweat-stained artificial leather
band inside. My jacket too, I see as soon as I have found the way
back into my whistling mood, is new: suède leather, but without a
sweat-stained collar. I obviously possess several such jackets that
are sent to be cleaned without my knowledge; after all, one can't
help sweating, and as I remember it suède is very sensitive. However that may be, I chuck my jacket down any old how, slovenly,
as though it were my scruffy jacket of the old days and as though I
were coming into my student's digs of the old days. But I hear a
barking outside. I see myself with a dog's lead in my hand, pigskin,
likewise new. The barking brings me up sharp. Perhaps we have
recently acquired a boxer? I hope it doesn't bite anyone. As I am
about to pick up my suède jacket, the one I chucked down any old
how, because the barking suggests to me that someone is coming,
I see in spite of my absent-mindedness: the suède jacket is already
hanging on a hanger. Obviously there are servants. Without look-

ing round any more I ask why the boxer is barking like that. A gentleman is waiting in the hall. That's new too, I must say, that we have a hall. And the maid, who is wearing a cap, says: A gentleman by the name of Gantenbein. Her intonation indicates that in case my dog and his dog don't get on, she is entirely on my side, which proves that we pay her well, this girl who is now holding my suède jacket for me. I am a bit confused by the barking and Gantenbein, who has evidently been shown into the hall by a second servant, has to excuse me; first I have to put the boxer, or whatever it is, on the lead. Excuse me! I say to the blind man, who has come to our new house for the first time, and I see not one boxer but three boxers, which calm down at once as soon as they see their master. Sit! I say, and the pigskin lead proves superfluous; so I throw it on a chest that isn't new, on the contrary the chest is very definitely antique. Excuse me! I say again, and Gantenbein acts as though it was not a maid who had meanwhile taken off his coat and also hung it on a hanger but myself, who now greets him with a handshake. Our handshake of the old days. My pleasure is genuine. It was just the boxers that confused me. Since he makes no comment on the Matisse that is hanging in the hall, I can assume that he really is blind, and that gradually restores my equanimity; only the suède jacket still worries me. Make yourself at home! I say, and since he doesn't see the armchair I lead him to it, relieved that Gantenbein doesn't see our living-room; only I see it as though for the first time. What's new? I ask, as though everything here were the same as it used to be. How's your Lila? As I ask I take a good look at Gantenbein, my friend of the old days. Is he really not looking round? All the same, he seems to sense that there is more than one bottle standing on the cocktail cabinet, and says he'd rather have a campari when I offer him a cognac. Haven't got any, I say with a certain relief, and it's true. On the other hand I have an armagnac, ninety years old, which I needn't tell him. But he tastes it. Well I'm damned! he says, as though he had seen the bottle too, a special bottle, a seven-litre bottle that perhaps looks ostentatious; and yet it's cheaper to buy in bulk –

193

I don't know what to talk about.

I only see fitted carpet –

Gantenbein, happy with armagnac, talks about Lila, thank God, as always with a tenderness that switches over to homage to her art (in order not to bore with intimate feelings) and that makes mince-meat of the gossip surrounding this woman, which I naturally know about as everyone does. Let's hope he isn't deceiving himself! I wish him all the best. She's a great actress, no doubt about it.

So we talk about art –

I see:

A fitted carpet bilberry-blue, in front of it my left shoe, which is new, it doesn't help to cross my legs the other way, the right shoe is also new, a fine mouse-grey with socks to match; only the skin and hair on my shinbone are not new. Our children, who burst in unexpectedly and then greet Herr Gantenbein rather sheepishly, because he acts the blind man so excellently, are not new either, they only look as if they were because everything they are wearing is as new as in the shop window and of the very best quality, even the slippers. Out with you! I say, but that makes no difference either to the fact that my cuff links are gold; I inconspicuously pull the sleeves of my sweater down over the silk cuffs, cashmere. What were we talking about? The children, yes, and how they grow up, and I remember a heart-warming little remark one of them once made, but since the point wouldn't come over without mentioning that we have been in the Canary Isles I don't quote it, I laugh and ask Gantenbein about his worries which I hope have nothing to do with money; otherwise I could easily help him and it would be obvious that I had become a rich man.

Silence.

Politically we are still in agreement, differing only in the degree of our seriousness; we are both left, but I have become the more serious; Gantenbein makes jokes about the left that I can't afford to make –

At one point a pendulum clock strikes.

An heirloom! I say –

194

Gantenbein doesn't look round, merely listens until the heirloom falls silent again, then he asks for another armagnac. Don't you find it very warm here? I ask casually and take off my suède jacket, also my tie. What I can't take off are the curtains, the tapestries, the fitted carpets. Gantenbein doesn't find it particularly warm, on the contrary, a bit on the cool side, and I wonder whether I ought to light an open fire. To distract attention from the fireplace, which comes from a Tuscan *palazzo*, and since I just happen to catch sight of the book-lined wall, I now talk about a Balzac first edition I came across recently. Ridiculously cheap! I say, and also quote the price, so that he shouldn't imagine it cost more than it did, and since I happen to be standing I offer cigars. What have you got? he asks, and suddenly I see no reason why I should pull the wool over his eyes. I've got everything. Even something special that Gantenbein has never seen: a Havana, but plaited like a pigtail, yes, there are such things; my tobacconist spoils me. Try it! I say, without interrupting our conversation to say it. Our conversation about what? Anyhow I bite the end off my cigar, as though I didn't see the silver cigar cutter, and sit down again. There's an ashtray, too, porcelain, Chinese, another gem that Gantenbein doesn't see; but I see everything. I think we're talking about music, about the electronic composers. I just hope my wife doesn't come in; sooner or later, when music is mentioned, she shows every guest her harp that I found recently. Likewise not dear. And then she plays it, and the chest in which the music is kept is also a find, medieval, from the South of France I believe. When Gantenbein doesn't talk the room is silent, but not really silent; then it is as though the white buckskin sofa were talking, and wherever I look I see good taste, nothing showy, no, but there is nothing that could be even better, more beautiful or even more useful. I am almost pleased about the hole that Gantenbein, in order to play the blind man, is burning in our white buckskin; I say nothing. How about a burgundy? Gantenbein is still talking, not without having casually praised the pigtail Havana, about art, and I don't close my mind to the view that art must become free of content, devoid of preconditions, obviously it isn't art's task to change the world. Fortunately there's a bottle in the room, so that I don't have to call a maid who would interrupt us. I draw the cork, open to the absurd. I don't know what Gantenbein takes me for. It isn't views and insights that separate us, but only this ashtray that he doesn't see, and all the rest of it. Has wealth changed me? That I have good taste isn't new; only in the past I didn't translate it into fact. What is it then? My wife's good taste has been added to my own... But Gantenbein doesn't say anything, apart from praising the burgundy. I'm glad about that. Why shouldn't I send Gantenbein a crate? It would give me pleasure, so long as he didn't misunderstand. That by the way. I too find it a bit on the cool side, an open fire is called for. I'm surprised to find that the matches I take out of a jade jar are still made of wood; the pine logs and beech billets that I pile up in the *palazzo* fireplace are also ordinary wood, dirt cheap; it is always the cheap things that keep reminding me of money –

Later my wife arrives.

She doesn't seem quite to believe that Gantenbein is really blind, and this creates a certain tension between us; for my part I believe that Gantenbein sees nothing of her jewellery; anyway, he doesn't show any sign of doing so, as if he were already used to it like me.

I talk about my work.

I work a great deal: not to get richer. But that's inevitable. Whatever I touch now makes me richer. At the same time I spend as much as I can within reason. I buy a hill in the Tessin, a bay near Malaga, a forest in Austria. I keep a lawyer who gets rich out of me and wants to do something in return, so that he makes me rich too, and he isn't the only one, everybody wants to make me rich. I can't help it, money has started to flow in a new direction: towards me. What's the good of the hill in the Tessin, which I have only seen once? I have given the grass to an old peasant to mow, likewise the chestnuts, which I don't need, and the blackberries. But what does this hill do? It has trebled its value. The simplest way of life makes no difference to this; I could go about in sackcloth and ashes, I eat sausage and potato salad whenever I'm alone, I don't only work five days a week like my employees, but six, yes, even Sundays and often into the night; it doesn't stop me from getting richer and richer. Or ought I perhaps to play golf? – I don't say this, of course, but merely think it as I talk about my work which is boring for my wife, she knows all that.

"You work too much."

But I am talking to Gantenbein, so that he should understand me. Why doesn't he say anything? He merely forces me to see for myself all the things I am keeping quiet about. Why doesn't he say that everything here, from the Matisse in the hall to the platinum watch on my wife, makes him sick?

We aren't friends any more.

This makes me sad.

And although he plays the blind man it isn't a good evening, and later, when I drive him to the station, I take our Volkswagen, not the Jaguar, so that he shan't hear the change in our way of life, in case he really is blind.

Gantenbein makes me unsure of myself.

I ask myself whether I like him. . .

A conversation with Burri, after a game of chess that I lost, about women, apparently about women, but really about men who cause disaster by taking women too seriously –

Burri (in so far as I understood him):

It is the man himself who is to blame when he suffers because of a woman. . . What makes men subservient: their contempt for woman which they don't admit to themselves; therefore they have to glorify her and pretend to be blind; when reality gives them the facts they run to the next one, as though the next one were not also a woman, and they can't give up their dream. . . What one despises in women: their passivity, the coquetry they still keep up where quite other things are at stake, the permanence of their woman-man position, all other interests reveal themselves as pretext or camouflage or interlude, their insatiable need for love, the way they become accustomed to being served (matches) and always having a special right to feel disappointed, altogether their tendency to reproach, leaving the nature of the reproach to be guessed at, their ability to keep silent, they wish and are able to remain a mystery to themselves, their ability to suffer, their trick of being the victim and with it their awful ability to be consoled at any moment, their readiness to flirt even in the midst of happiness, their willingness and at the same time their craftiness in leaving it to the man to decide what happens, and when the man, in order to be able to act, would like to know where he stands, their art of leaving things open, they leave the decision and hence the guilt to him from the outset, the ease with which they are offended, their need for protection and security and with it the wraithlike inconstancy on their part, in a word: their magic. . . The man behaves all the more chivalrously the more contempt he has to hide. . . The biological difference: a woman can be together with ten men in one night, a man can't be together with ten women; he has to have desire, she can let it happen even without desire; for this reason the whore is possible, but not the male counterpart. The woman, forced by the man's vanity to put on an act, feigns her release in pleasure even if it doesn't take place; the man never knows for sure what has really happened to the woman; it is the man who surrenders himself, not the woman; this makes him distrustful. . . The woman is a person before one loves her, sometimes afterwards as well; as soon as one loves her she is a miracle and hence untenable –

"Yes," I say. "Let's play."

"You agree?"

"Not entirely," I say. "It's your move."

Burri after his move:

"As far as your Lila is concerned –"

"Mine?"

I have moved.

"Aha," says Burri. "Ahaaa."

I change Lila's profession.

(I'm sick of the theatre.)

Lila is not an actress by profession but a scientist, a medical research worker, Lila in a white overall, assistant at the University Radiological Institute, everything is completely different, Lila is attractive but instead of black hair she has blond, her different vocabulary that often startles Gantenbein, and at least to begin with Lila is almost unrecognizable, she says the things an actress keeps to herself and remains silent where an actress speaks out, displacement of modesty, her different interests, the different circle of friends, but above all her vocabulary which is so different that all the conversations between Lila and Gantenbein will have to be gone through over again, from the first kiss onwards. Her utensils in the bathroom, which Gantenbein sees, remain the same –
Or:
Lila is a *contessa*, Catholic, a Venetian *contessa*, a morphia addict, breakfasts in bed waited on by a manservant in a blue tunic. Eyes like deadly nightshade berries. Her vocabulary is different again, so is her circle of friends, who believe Gantenbein to be blind; the scenery is a *palazzo*. Her utensils in the bathroom, which Gantenbein sees, remain the same.
N.B.
Gantenbein remains the same.

The new magazine has appeared, Enderlin is the editor, the first number isn't bad, in fact it's amazing; but the fact remains that I have given Enderlin up.

Lila as a *contessa*:
(why it won't do either)
She really is a *contessa*, for centuries not used to being shouted at, and I should never think of shouting at her if she herself weren't always telling me not to shout at her – and yet I only asked her if she didn't hear the gong. That was at the beginning of our happiness; now that I know how sensitive she is, how easily frightened, with what acute hearing for the undertone in such a question, I have never again asked her if she didn't hear the gong. I simply wait

until she comes to the table. She simply has no feeling for time, but so much feeling for other things that are more important, heaven knows; for example a feeling for style! Not merely the Venetian furniture, not merely her vocabulary that comes out without a single vulgar word and is yet able to express everything she doesn't want to keep silent about, even her silence has style; it is simply unthinkable that anyone should not treat her like a *contessa*. Even the people who come into contact with her acquire style. I see this over and over again. I can even see it in Gantenbein; he isn't a *conte*, but he behaves like one, and yet I've never in my life seen a *conte* who behaves like one. So I wait.

I'm not waiting for lunch. I'm merely waiting because it's time for lunch. I'm waiting for the Contessa, who may appear at any moment, because it's time for lunch. I can't work when I'm waiting. So I wait – not for the Contessa, but for the moment when she will appear from the loggia or on the stairs. . . Perhaps she is still asleep and hasn't heard the gong. . . To pass the time, I could already describe how she will appear from the loggia or on the stairs: in a dressing-gown but with her hair combed, in a dressing-gown or in slacks, with a childlike surprise that it's already midday again in the world and in need of a comforting reception, pale but beautiful, in her mouth a long cigarette-holder (amber) with a cigarette waiting for a light. . . So I wait. . . Perhaps she is just combing her hair. . . So I wait, without looking at the clock, and try to guess what she is doing with time, with my time, with her time; she has a different time, therefore it's no use my looking at the clock; clocks offend her, clocks always act as though there were one single time, a universal time so to speak. . . Perhaps she is reading a book that is just getting exciting, or she is playing with the dog or she is already on her way – it would be a pity if I were now (after three-quarters of an hour, I estimate) to get impatient during the last half minute. She feels any impatience, even if it is controlled, to be a reproof; any reproof as shouting. So I wait and wait, without looking at the clock; in order not to become impatient, I enjoy the view –

It's like this every day.

If I ever shout at her again, she says, she will pack her bags and probably never come back –

And yet we're so happy.

Antonio, our servant with the white gloves, opens the mirror-door to the dining-room, the marital meal is ready, but since it is summer probably a cold meal, and in any case Gantenbein doesn't display any sort of hurry, and since the perfect servant (we've only had him a month) naturally thinks Gantenbein can't see him, he doesn't say *pronto*, but merely looks round in silence to see if the Contessa is there too. She's asleep. And although Antonio knows after only a month that we may have to wait till three o'clock, he still doesn't say *pronto* but looks at his watch. Antonio is touching, he doesn't know that Gantenbein can see him in the mirror and retires on tiptoe, acts as though it were just getting on for twelve. And Gantenbein does the same. Unfortunately there is a baroque pendulum-clock which doesn't conceal even from a blind man that it is two o'clock. Something has to happen; it's true Gantenbein isn't hungry, but he is a man who wants to work, and Antonio too, whose afternoon off it is, has to be at the football ground or with a girl by four, it's his right.

Antonio! I call –

He doesn't merely act as though he had come from the distant kitchen to say *pronto* at last – he actually pretends to be saying it to the Contessa; he already knows that the master gets annoyed when the Contessa sleeps all day, and yet the good lad has only been one month in the house, which of course is a *palazzo*, Renaissance.

Lila, I say, come along!

And everything is done to prevent Gantenbein from getting annoyed, to prevent him from noticing that once again he is sitting down to lunch alone; Gantenbein wears a relaxed expression, as he silently gropes for the table napkin, and the servant with the white gloves, also wearing a relaxed expression because his free afternoon has been saved, omits nothing that will make the presence of the Contessa, whom Gantenbein can't see, at least audible. I see him shift the chair with his knee. Everyone knows what acute hearing the blind have. He does it magnificently; he even snaps a grissini before going to fetch the cold bouillon, and I can see how he hurries in order not to prolong our marital silence too far before it is justified by eating. All the same, he is quite a while.

Have you been riding? I ask.

Lila says nothing; she is asleep, probably she took her dope again yesterday, the unfortunate woman, and since she is convinced that Gantenbein can't see her drugs, she can't explain the after-effects.

Have you been to the doctor? I ask.

Antonio in the doorway, I see him in the mirror waiting rather uncertainly to make his entrance; it is an enchanting dining-room, full of Gobelins and mirrors, so that one can even converse with the back of one's own head; I don't know why Antonio is plucking at his white gloves and hesitating.

What did your doctor say? I ask.

Now he comes with the bowls, and it is clear that the Contessa, even if she were present, wouldn't report the doctor's findings in the presence of a servant; thus the silence is quite natural again. This makes Antonio too feel sure of himself once more. As is right and proper, he puts the first bowl down on the plate of our Contessa, who is asleep, loudly enough for Gantenbein to hear. He does it really splendidly, this son of a poor fisherman with his white jacket and the golden tassels; he remains in the dining-room the whole time as Gantenbein spoons up his soup. People don't like to talk in the presence of a servant. All that's lacking is for him to tap her spoon against her bowl. He doesn't do so, and all one hears is Gantenbein sipping the cold bouillon; one doesn't hear a *contessa...*

But what happens then?

I only hope Lila doesn't turn up now, so I press for speed, but there's fish and Gantenbein has no alternative but to take the magnificent fish to pieces; to divert Antonio from doubts as to whether Gantenbein is really blind, I ask the name of the fish, whether it is common in Venetian waters, all sorts of things connected with fishing, how the nets are cast, about prices, about the poverty of the fishermen; it is not only interesting to hear how much Antonio, the fisherman's son, knows, but also splendid the way he keeps on acting as though the subject also interested our Contessa, whose fish is growing cold untouched on the china. But Gantenbein can't talk only to the servant, naturally; that would look as though we had quarrelled. Especially now, when the servant goes out, Gantenbein simply has to talk till the cheese comes. What about? I talk about Communism and anti-Communism, a topic that in any case, wherever one stands, calls for no counter-argument, since the counter-arguments are well known and are just being refuted. At the same time I don't talk without a break, not without occasionally snapping a grissini or sipping my wine, not like a filibuster, but with such lapidary conviction that the Contessa's silence doesn't seem incomprehensible. What Antonio, who may be listening from the service room, thinks about it doesn't interest me; Gantenbein is talking to Lila, whose brother is a purer Communist. If Antonio is listening outside he must realize that there can be no question of class arrogance among the people he serves, at least not towards a poor fisherman's son; we're in Italy. Of course there are one or two *conti* who are Fascists and hence embittered; but the bright brains of the family are not, on the contrary. An aristocratic outlook (in Italy) is more likely to find expression in not sharing the bourgeois fear of Communism about which, like every mass fear, there is something vulgar. To this extent Gantenbein could speak quite openly, even if the Contessa were present, so the fact that she is not present is not strikingly evident, as he talks and talks. What on earth is making Antonio take such a long time? When you talk and talk, without hearing any contradiction, you yourself start contradicting; that is almost inevitable. But whom is Gantenbein to contradict, since the Contessa is asleep? He contradicts her brother; he finds it grotesque that Dino, that young landowner, is a Communist, and not even a romantic one, oh no, Dino is a bright boy, with the looks of a curly-haired pagan god, a Hermes perhaps, who never gives offence, he clings to his Catholic upbringing, I mean Dino, her brother, and not even his servants notice that the Conte (he himself uses this title only during clashes with the police) is a Communist. Dino is no proletarian with a raised fist, Dino smiles almost imperceptibly about people who condemn the strike of his agricultural workers, and he doesn't preach, he doesn't make a nuisance of himself with his Communism, he merely understands Communism, one of the few who could afford to study the subject, and he serves Communism precisely by behaving like a capitalist. Oh no, Dino is no dreamer, oh no, he knows that the world can't be revolutionized by private actions – there's a lot to be said on this topic, and Gantenbein really doesn't see that the cheese has come long ago; the servant is holding out the board with white gloves and the appearance of not listening. Gorgonzola or Mozzarella? Gantenbein only nods, without on that account interrupting his conversation with the Contessa, who is asleep, while Antonio refills his glass.

Yes, I ask, or am I wrong?

Silence.

Gantenbein goes on talking, I see Antonio pick up the sleeping Contessa's glass again and empty it; that's the only way he can refill it again, I understand, and when he does fill it up again he does so from a height, so that Gantenbein can clearly hear the gurgling.

Does he really believe that Gantenbein doesn't notice anything?

Or is it merely Gantenbein who believes that the servant believes this?

Later over black coffee, which is taken out on the loggia, the game really isn't necessary any more; Antonio has gone off, his last service has been performed when he pours the coffee into the two precious little cups, carrying out the marital duty of the Contessa. At the same time he actually gave the Contessa, who is not present, a short answer; Gantenbein might not have heard her casual question because of the fluttering of the pigeons, especially as she always speaks softly.

"*Come no*, Contessa, *come no!*"

A gifted lad.

"*Come mai,*" he laughs, "*come mai!*"

This second answer is given from quite a distance, I see him peeling off his white gloves as he speaks; he would never do that in the Contessa's presence. Then he goes off, but now things have gone so far that Gantenbein really (not merely for the servant's benefit) talks to the Contessa, who is still asleep, because she has taken her drug again, and she takes the drug because she is unhappy.

Lila, I ask, why are you unhappy?

Fortunately Gantenbein doesn't take sugar in his coffee, the Contessa knows that, consequently her absence doesn't attract attention when she doesn't put the sugar in for him.

Am I not a man? I ask.

As he speaks, Gantenbein smokes a cigar and gazes at the Canale Grande, which one can also get tired of.

Am I the one who is making her unhappy?

Since the Contessa remains silent, this question at least is answered, and frankness creates frankness. The truth is painful, but it goes without saying that now he wants to know more exactly. In for a penny in for a pound. Alone with the two precious little cups, both of which Gantenbein drains before he can continue speaking, I ask whether and how far lovemaking with other men is different, a question that a woman of taste in any case never answers, and once again her silence doesn't mean that the Contessa isn't present.

The pigeons of Venice are cooing.

Lila, I say, this can't go on!

She doesn't answer:

Why not? What do you mean?

She isn't present, but her absence isn't noticeable; even if she were present she would now, thus challenged, maintain a pregnant silence, until I ask straight out:

What's really going on between you and Nils?

Silence.

Or is it someone else? I ask, and it's the first time we speak so openly and at the same time perfectly calmly; she can't say I'm shouting at her and so she keeps silent, while Gantenbein smiles; I enjoy his calm, his masculinity, his blind readiness to look any fact in the face, and I ask again: Or is it someone else?

No answer.

Well, who is it? I ask.

But I understand that she can't reply to this; it's none of Gantenbein's business. Or is she still afraid that I shall shout at her? Simply for the sake of saying something and to demonstrate Gantenbein's calm, I say after a while to the accompaniment of the cooing of the famous pigeons:

I always thought it was Nils.

It's the first time I have uttered this name, prepared to see the Contessa pack her bags probably never to return, and to do so this very day, even if she doesn't go to Nils, because that was a long time ago and to that extent funny, but no laughing matter, at least the Contessa doesn't laugh, and since Gantenbein, alone on the Venetian loggia, has at last uttered this name I can't avoid a confession:

I once read a Danish letter —

What is the Contessa to answer to this monstrous statement I have just made? — the Contessa who is asleep. . .

A conversation with Burri recently; I should have liked to know how he sees "my" Lila. He speaks of her with an adoration that flatters me. And at the same time I was startled. When Burri had gone I sat for hours as though stuffed, my chin on my interlocked hands. He talked about her (though only briefly) as about a real person, and I seem to be the only one who doesn't see her.

Lila is an actress:
(postscript.)
Her charming game with the kitchen apron when guests come, and up to now no guest has ever seen through it, not even the sober and crafty Burri, probably Lila believes in it herself — a quarter of an hour before the guests arrive Lila comes home, dog tired from

her Macbeth rehearsals that took place in the morning, and now it's evening, she slumps into an armchair and immediately, dog tired, reads the new magazines, without taking off her coat, without a glance at the table, which Gantenbein meanwhile lays; she can rely on Gantenbein. Possibly an anxious question at the last moment: Did you remember the mayonnaise? He did. It's a good thing guests are generally late; after all, Lila has to comb her hair. He remembered not only the mayonnaise but even bread, which nobody notices when it's there. Lila ordered the lobster, which has actually arrived, so really there can be nothing missing. She is proud of the beautiful lobster, a terrible pity Gantenbein can't see how beautiful it is, the lobster that she chose over the telephone. A miraculous beast, purple, a lobster who thinks of everything: not only of the mayonnaise but also of the wine that goes with him, but also of the cold meat in case anyone doesn't like him, and of the fruit that will be welcome later, when his remnants are already in the waste bucket. Fortunately, as I have said, guests are always late, so that while she is combing her hair Lila can inform the blind Gantenbein of who is coming; in every gathering there are always those who never open their mouths, and it's embarrassing if Gantenbein deduces from this that one can talk about some people as if they weren't there. It is essential for him to make a mental note of the list of names. When the doorbell finally rings Lila, although her hair is combed to perfection, cannot go to the door; this is the moment when she has to put on an apron to receive the guests. Gantenbein now distributes the names he has made a mental note of, and a chair to each name. Lila scarcely has time to say hullo, while for their part the guests are speechless with surprise: Lady Macbeth in an apron. They're touched, they all want to help, except Gantenbein, because he knows that everything has already been done.

It's all right, she says, I'll do it!

She scarcely has time for an apéritif.

It's all right, she says, I'll do everything!

Gantenbein's job is then to share the guests' delight, or at least not to spoil it, while Lila runs to and fro in her apron, in, out, in, Gantenbein as a pasha. What Lila does in the kitchen while the guests, drinking whisky, feel ashamed at the thought of how much trouble this great actress is taking, is to prepare the salad which Gantenbein, to be on the safe side, has washed in advance. Gantenbein as a pasha with crossed legs in a rocking-chair, hoping she doesn't forget anything. She is utterly confused, but it suits her. I'm afraid there are no lemons, she says, and that's a pity; the lemons are lying in the kitchen, but Lila doesn't see them. From this moment on, Gantenbein knows that he can do anything he likes without destroying the first impression; he fetches the lemons, etc.

I change the story again:

Lila isn't a *contessa*, any more than she is an actress. I don't know how I ever got hold of that idea. Lila is simply a woman, married to a man whom I was supposed to meet in the bar that day. Thirty-one. Not a morphinist; not a Catholic; with no profession. A fascinating woman; there's no need for people to tell me that, as though I didn't know. Why should Lila have a profession? She may once have studied medicine as a young girl and even passed the first examinations, then marriage interrupted her studies, or she went to a school of acting, even acted throughout one winter alongside big names; all this is perfectly possible, but not in the least important. She can let it go, she is a woman. She feels independent even without an income of her own. Otherwise she would be ready at any time for any sort of work, she wouldn't have to go short, wouldn't have to go about in homemade clothes, with her knowledge of languages she could get a job as a secretary at any time, in a publishing house for example, not in commerce or in a welfare office, not a dreary job among the ordinary rank and file; for preference in a publishing house, she says, as an editor. She would be prepared to do that at any time. It isn't necessary, since she's married. At times she has a positive yearning for work, homesickness for the profession that became unnecessary. She isn't a housewife. She prefers reading.

She has her own car; otherwise she wouldn't feel independent, a present from her husband, who earns enough. This is still her first marriage. She is healthy, even robust, and at the same time delicate, so that one enjoys feeling a tender anxiety about her; an early tuberculosis has healed up, a memory that she only rarely uses to demand consideration, only in case of need. She is not incompetent (like the Contessa) and not ambitious (like the actress), but she too, as I have said, is no housewife; she is too intelligent for that and refuses to let herself be persuaded by men that women must have an inborn talent for every kind of work that the men themselves find too tedious. She is a woman, but not a subservient being, thus entirely a woman of today, a magnificent woman in my opinion, one of the first women of this century who admits to herself without fuss that she really has no urge whatever to exercise a profession.

P.S.

I don't know how her husband found out or will find out that Lila loves me, and it doesn't bother me. I don't know this Svoboda. It wasn't my fault that we didn't meet in the bar that day. To judge by the name, Frantisek Svoboda, he is a Bohemian. I don't know how a Bohemian behaves when the woman he loves loves another man –

I imagine:

They have guests, they drink and chat, Svoboda is the same as always, he is talking about London, Lila is the same as always, the guests are gay, Svoboda uncorks the bottles, they talk about the Russian lead in space, Lila is wearing the yellow costume (it is exactly a month since our first night) or another costume that I don't know yet, and the guests think she looks, wonderful someone is just talking about the opera that Lila unfortunately missed, and even if Lila doesn't agree with all the basic objections to opera that I raised she nevertheless considers that it is a point of view that can be thrown into the conversation, so as not to have to talk about the particular evening she missed but about opera in general principle; of course no one knows whose viewpoint it really is, but it's a viewpoint that Svoboda can't just sweep under the table. (Naturally opera as created by Mozart is wonderful and unimpeachable, but I wasn't talking about Mozart but about modern opera.) Svoboda is strange, positively on edge, as though my opinion were a personal insult to him; he puts on a record in order to refute my standpoint in front of all the guests: *Don Giovanni*. They listen, Lila beams, delighted not only with Fischer-Dieskau, although he is magnificent, but also with Zerlina: the only person in the whole confused affair who is simply right, who doesn't make a tragedy of it because she has nature on her side, the only one who is relaxed and free, which also finds expression musically. A guest, armed with her exposition, has to admit that she is right when they listen to the passage over again. Later they talk about people. . . At three in the morning, after he has already been asleep, Svoboda wakes up without putting on the light, wakes up as though a shot had rung out. But everything is quiet. As though a burglar were at work. But there's nobody there, only Lila and Svoboda.

"Are you asleep?"

"Why?"

"I don't know," he says. "I'm in despair."

Lila says nothing.

"I'm in despair," he says. "Did you hear?"

Lila says nothing.

"I think," he says, "you'll have to leave me."

"What are you talking about?"

"You'll have to leave me."

It's difficult to say, a knowledge based on nothing, not even on a suspicion, simply a certainty that has broken in. Perhaps he has had too much to drink, yes, there are tablets you can take against that, but not against her radiant beaming in front of the guest; that was what woke him up. As a dream might have woken him up.

"Why leave you?"

For weeks he has had the feeling that she is wearing a mask. Since when? That his presence compels her to wear a mask is an impossible situation; it must be due to some shortcoming on his part; he's impossible to live with.

"Come on," she says, "take a sleeping tablet."

When she switches the light on he believes that it was all a fantasy; he won't allow himself to be waited on, but fetches the water himself and says no more; really he has had too much to drink.

(I sleep.)

When Svoboda too is almost asleep, at least doesn't answer any more, she says in the darkness that she wrote him a letter, yes, to London, but didn't send it off, but tomorrow he can read it if he wants to, but now he should sleep. . .

I imagine:

Next day, harassed by professional matters, Svoboda inwardly has no time to think of the semi-dream conversation, he forgets it, he feels ashamed, anyhow he doesn't ask for the letter, but Lila doesn't believe that he has forgotten everything; her serene and totally ingenuous confidence that he suspects nothing has broken down. Unfortunately. She feels compelled to have a discussion, although Svoboda asks for nothing and makes it all too easy for himself. . .

I imagine:

It is his fault that the letter in question is handed over in a restaurant of all places, that is to say at a moment when they are escorted on both sides by waiters, looked at by other customers who, even if they are just laughing or poking a lobster, have ears – his fault because Lila didn't really want to go out, or perhaps it is his good fortune that he didn't get the letter to read in London but here in this restaurant, where Svoboda is known; the fish is excellent as always, a pity Lila has no appetite, the waiter is not without sympathy, Lila smokes, Svoboda can't simply drop his knife and fork, and so it takes a while before he starts to read the letter across the plate, yes, seriously but obviously without any particular tension, calm, he doesn't forget the salad, he knows this page of the letter already: roughly the same thing as in another letter that she really did post, comradeship, good wishes for his trip, concern about his stomach, items of news. Really an affectionate letter. Why didn't she send it? Lila smokes, while Svoboda can't give up his fish, otherwise he would have the waiter round his neck as he reads: I'm very fond of you as always, all I want is that you should feel the same towards me as always, even if another feeling has arisen in me. What business is that of the waiter's? Svoboda orders more wine in order to send him away for a few lines, in order to understand why actually, as this letter so much stresses, there is no cause for alarm. The wine comes already; the waiter pours out, another one comes to remove Svoboda's plate, so that the letter can no longer be read across the plate; nevertheless Svoboda holds it no differently from before, after interrupting the reading to light a cigarette before finishing it. It seems he is expecting too much. No cause for alarm: I would tell you if anything had changed between us. Here the letter breaks off and the waiter brushes the crumbs from the table. Really a sweet letter. What dessert? There are cherries. But who does this letter belong to now? It is still lying beside the ashtray. Should Svoboda put it in his pocket or hand it back to Lila? Cherries have the advantage that they keep the eater busy; cherries and a cigarette at the same time – how can anyone talk on top of that? Svoboda seems really to be sticking to the letter, no cause for alarm, Lila now regrets ever having shown him the letter at all, Svoboda pays, Svoboda buys a newspaper which he actually unfolds in the middle of the street, as if he had a desire for news, coffee in a bar, Svoboda goes over to the order of the day, Lila is relieved, she evidently didn't trust Svoboda to behave exactly as she hoped he would – there he stands sipping his coffee: calm and yet not mute, not shut-in, thoughtful but not unfriendly, with eyes for other things too, not unmoved but full of confidence and attentive towards Lila, who looks at him with big eyes.

(It's as though I had never existed.)

Perhaps they will now go to the cinema. . .

(I wait in vain for her phone call.)

Later they go home. . .

I imagine:

Svoboda, a strapping Bohemian but with a gentle voice (not soft but gentle) and always one degree more confident when he has undone the top button of his shirt and loosened his tie a bit, a man who will never understand when people tell him that his kindness (it isn't deliberate but innate) tyrannizes, in short Svoboda – I don't know why, but until the contrary has been proved to me I visualize him as a man with water-grey eyes and bushy, pale eyebrows – Svoboda, after going to the kitchen and fetching ice to make a whisky for his Lila, speaks almost jokingly, not sarcastically but as though to a child who has broken a window and remains apprehensively silent, as though this damage could never be paid for.

"Well," he says, "what's the matter?"

And yet it's all in the letter.

"There's no soda-water left," he says –

And yet it's all in the letter, thinks Lila who, to evade his importunate question, gets up and after absent-mindedly searching finds that there really isn't any soda-water left and actually makes a note to get some more; Svoboda is standing with his glass in his hand and for a time it looks as if he were busy with the post, but he doesn't open it, he merely looks at the sender's name, he is now holding the letters in his hand as though about to go to his room, and drinking.

"Say something!" he says.

What does he want? What's the matter with him?

"You wrote in your letter," he says, "that there's a different feeling in you –"

Pause.

"I'm very fond of someone," she says.

Pause.

Her face is not ecstatic, only unfamiliar, her voice matter-of-fact. Very fond. Her face bears witness to it. Very fond. The simple expression tallies with the truth; hence there is nothing to add. Why does he put his post down on the table? It takes quite a time before Svoboda, filling his pipe, slowly perceives, as it were from the echo that goes on ringing in him, that the innocuousness of the expression is not a sly, defensive attempt to make the situation appear innocuous, but the appropriate description of a fact whose seriousness does not permit any bombastic phrases. Svoboda looks at her, still filling his pipe, for the space of a breath in the hope that it is an over-hasty misunderstanding on his part; only the unfamiliarity of her face refutes his brief hope. Very fond. There's no changing that. Very fond. The echo doesn't stop when Svoboda at last lights his pipe and then smokes; his voice too remains matter-of-fact as he asks:

"Who is it?"

Pause.

"Don't you want to tell me?"

"Of course," she says with a hint of resentment, but she waits. Doesn't he know? She delays the information as though she would prefer him to guess, so that she would only have to nod. Why doesn't he help? Svoboda waits, not without speculations that seem to him insane, and is at first glad when she finally says "You don't know him."

He drinks.

She finds it difficult –

He looks for matches, because his pipe isn't drawing, then a pipe cleaner; Svoboda has to do something with his hands now in order to find his way back into the relaxed, playfully encouraging tone, in order to be able to ask casually:

"What's his name?"

Pause.

"Enderlin."

Thankful that he doesn't repeat the name but says nothing, and with an expression that implies there is nothing else to be said, she now gets up, while Svoboda goes on cleaning his pipe... After the name has been said there is no need to say where and when Lila met me; Svoboda remembers our rendezvous in the bar which didn't take place, because he was away; Svoboda may now be regretting that he has never seen the man of whom Lila is very fond face to face. I waited for Svoboda. When was that incidentally? He works it out. When was he in London? The date's important, it seems to him. Beginning of March? The scales fall from his eyes, as he looks down at the carpet, with regard to her *joie de vivre* since March. So that was what had made him so happy recently? Lila doesn't guess his Bohemian thoughts, and it's now one o'clock, and since she doesn't want to hear any unseemly questions she says unasked:

"He's going to America, he's been invited to Harvard, he's a university lecturer." What else does he want to know? "He's the editor of a magazine, as you know –"

Svoboda says nothing.

"Yes," she says, "what else do you want to know?"

She speaks as though he has been pestering and inundating and tormenting her with questions; her demeanour exasperates him, but for a while, his pipe in his fist, Svoboda listens, till Lila falls silent, and after everything she has told him about my academic career she isn't prepared for his incongruous question:

"Have you already slept with each other?"

Silence.

"You don't answer?" he says. "So you have."

"Yes."

They're both calm.

"Yes," she says, "why?"

"Yes," he says, in order to hear the calmness of his own voice, but he really can't think of anything relevant to say with this voice, so Svoboda stops talking and sits down. Pain is still operating as an almost physical enjoyment. When Lila, sought by his eyes, lowers her own, she does so not out of shame, naturally, but as someone who has been hurt, hurt by Svoboda who has forced her to express herself like this and at this moment it isn't true that she is very fond of Svoboda, as she said in her letter. So far Svoboda hasn't done her the favour of offending her; he is still sitting with his hands in his trouser pockets, closed but with his face uncontorted; he still refuses to be drawn into claiming any sort of rights, even if only the right to frankness. He still has the strength simply to give life its due. For how long? But Svoboda has to say something. Anything. For example:

215

"How old is he?"

Lila is tired.

"Don't ask me now," she says. "That's all I can tell you, Svob."

"That you're very fond of him."

Unfortunately time doesn't stand still; unfortunately no curtain falls so long as Svoboda, now resting his elbows on his knees, his glass of lukewarm whisky in both hands, preserves the dignity of the loser in silence, even if only because he can't think of anything else to say. Even the question, what is to happen now, is premature; he only knows that it will ask itself. . . Altogether, he knows. Oh yes. But he doesn't feel anything, he merely tastes the insipid flavour of whisky that has been watered down with melted ice and that he is retaining in his mouth as though he were going to gargle with it.

"Svob," she says, "I'm tired enough to drop."

If he, Svob, wouldn't sit there like that, Lila could now behave with comradely affection; it's his fault that she remains frosty. She empties the ashtrays. He sees that something must have happened, something cataclysmic: she isn't merely emptying the ashtrays, she is tidying the whole flat, Lila as a housewife, she takes his jacket and puts it on a hanger. That startles him. Lila has never done that before. It shows the degree of her confusion; she doesn't seem to know any more what is customary in their marriage. Is she so far away already? He watches, his elbows resting on his knees.

"I told you that," she says. "I told you the garage rang up today, about the insurance."

"You told me that."

"About the bill," she says. "The bill has to be sent on to the insurance company —"

Svoboda says nothing.

"Just so we don't forget," she says —

"What?"

Lila now thinks of everything, even of his father's birthday, of visitors who are likely to turn up, of the parcel that is still at the customs, Lila will fetch it, yes, she has to go into town tomorrow anyhow, there are masses of urgent things to be attended to, Lila

216

thinks of them, and if it wasn't past midnight she would now ring the man about the refrigerator, but Lila has to go into town tomorrow anyhow, they've run out of salted almonds, the Hinrichsens are coming on Friday, on Sunday there's the Mahler concert, Lila will pick up the two tickets, she really thinks of everything now, not only of the mysterious parcel that is still at the customs, and of his father's birthday, even of the dog licence. . . life goes on – while Svoboda says nothing.

Svoboda at the window –

Svoboda is wondering when he could have noticed. What for? Of course he could have noticed. Every day! It's amusing to see all the things one has noticed, beginning with the fact that when he came back from London Lila was simply more beautiful, younger; then the disproportionate present for his birthday; even before that the disappearance of her migraine, her verve, her radiant high spirits especially at parties, her initiative, her complexion. All this Svoboda noticed. Like a miracle. Her letter to London, the other one which she really sent: short, but a love letter. Then her failure to say anything about the opera. Her fleeting mention of the man whom the absent Svoboda didn't meet: without commentary. Then the disappearance of her curiosity regarding the usual post, her omissions towards her own family, her obvious interest in the new magazine and her silence about what she thought of it. Her need to mention the other people she has met. Her new hairdo. Her fickleness in all their joint plans. Her lack of curiosity as to whom Svoboda for his part might have met, by contrast her sisterly joy in his professional success. Once he found her studying international flight timetables. Her nervous punctuality on certain days of the week. All this now strikes Svoboda, along with certain casual remarks, joking remarks, frank comments regarding man and woman in general, and her enthusiasm about a film that was daring, especially about the scene in which a woman, while her husband is kissing her, strokes another man with her foot; altogether her humour, linked with a veiled concern about Svoboda when he broods to himself; on top of this her pity for the captive animals in the Zoo, her remark about swans, which always swim along together so demurely, and so on . . . It's not her fault that Svoboda didn't catch on; she didn't conceal her *joie de vivre*; it's his fault that he attributed it to himself or to a miracle, and moreover it was a happy period for him too, yes, precisely since his return from London.

"I'm going to bed," she says.

Why does he shake his head?

Enderlin –!

He can't yet bring himself to utter the name. It's funny the way some name or other suddenly detaches itself from all other names and hooks itself on to us. And yet I might have had a different name.

"I don't know," she says, "why you're laughing."

In order not to take the situation tragically.

Svoboda, I fancy, is one of those men whose women, when they need a nickname, are likely to call Bear. Svoboda has never had any other nickname from the animal kingdom applied to him; women of very different kinds have called him their Bear, independently of one another. There must be something in it. They are probably referring to the sweet pertness but also the strength and slowness and ponderousness, the playful tenderness, the sly humour of a small-eyed beast that can suddenly be very vicious and violent, unpredictable, at one moment a touching mannikin who begs, who twists awkwardly around for the sake of a piece of sugar, so that on top of one's compassion one is enchanted by this shaggy paragon of innocuousness, and then, without any visible reason for the transformation, becomes a beast that no barrier holds in check and no sugar tames, that doesn't understand a game, that is not to be deterred from tearing his victim to shreds – Lila is afraid of him – next morning, sobered by his delirium which a whole night long (until the birds twitter and the sun shines) has talked everything to shreds, sobered and shamed by uncertainty as to what he has really said, then next day he apologizes with clawless paws, yes, he does that. Then he acts the begging mannikin again. But Lila knows that he will start off again, and his apology doesn't alter him;

again and again he will not shrink from tearing everything to shreds with his sharp words –

It hasn't come to that yet.

"Yes," he says, "go to bed."

He is still pretty sober.

"Yes," he says, "good night."

As he says this he pours himself whisky.

"Now I understand," he says, "now I understand why you phoned me in London that night –"

What has that got to do with it?

"Is he good looking," he smiles, "this Enderlin?"

Naturally Lila can't answer that. This Enderlin! That isn't the tone in which to speak of me, and Svoboda feels that too.

He drinks.

Why, yes, why doesn't a curtain come down?

We know what follows –

Around five in the morning (I'm asleep) things have gone so far that a whisky glass suddenly smashes in the fireplace. Why? Not because he doesn't understand that Lila likes making love to another man, but because she doesn't understand. What? She doesn't understand what there is to understand. Is Lila to put herself in Svoboda's place, who commits an injustice with every word he utters? She let him talk and talk without arguing. Why does he suddenly smash his whisky glass against her considerate silence? Lila really doesn't know what he wants. Does he know?

"I'm sorry," he says.

Outside day is breaking –

And at the same time Svoboda remembers as he would remember an innocence that he has thrown away, he knew himself that there was nothing to be said. From nine in the evening when in the restaurant, escorted by waiters, he read her friendly letter, till two in the night he held to his knowledge that Lila now has no interest in his feelings and ideas on basic principles, not even in his plans, certainly not in his magnanimity. That's how it started, it seems, with his magnanimity. Not that Lila would have yawned; and yet

219

she has been tired enough to drop since midnight. I don't even think that while Svoboda strides up and down the room, then sits down again and speaks more and more slowly, in order not to get worked up, she is thinking particularly of me; he would like her to, but Lila doesn't want me ("this Enderlin") to be the subject of a discussion between them. Can't Svoboda, so anxious for understanding, understand that? She doesn't remain silent because she isn't listening; she is listening, but she isn't here. She isn't with me either. But not here either. She is alone. The incident that moves him and that he would like to clarify with her help, is not one shared between them. That is the liberating thing about it, precisely that: Lila is alone. . .

Silence.

Outside the birds are twittering.

"Lila," he says, "do say something!"

"I can't say anything to you," she says. "I can see that in this whole affair you only see me as a woman, I can hear it in everything you say, you see everything simply and solely from that point of view."

"From what point of view?"

"You see me solely as a woman."

Svoboda thinks it over.

"I'm sorry!" he says, and it sounds really as though he is admitting a mistake; but then he laughs: "You're right. I'm sorry. You're right."

What does he mean by that?

"I only take you as a woman," he says, and his eyes nail her to the spot, so that Lila is scared; suddenly he has the evil eye, although he is quite calm: "I only take you as a woman," he repeats, as one repeats the words of a bad joke: – "whereas Herr Enderlin – I understand!" he says with another attempt to laugh, but set right by her look, he says: "I'm sorry!" and gets up and walks across the room, which is just receiving the first morning sun, and stands still: "I'm sorry!" he says, and it seems as though his own poison calms him at least for a while, then it is the whisky bottle that crashes into the fireplace: "I'm sorry," he says and trembles. "I'm sorry."

220

Lila looks at him.

Why does still no curtain fall?

Now he gets sentimental.

"Don't you think it's monstrous, what you're saying to me?" he asks. "You tell me I only take you as a woman, you say that now, after you've been with another man – evidently not as a woman – I'm not reproaching you, but you're reproaching me, I don't understand why you're reproaching me, but that's what you're doing, my dear, even if you don't speak, you say you can't talk to me because I only see you as a woman –"

"In this matter."

Lila is simply right.

"Yes," he says, "let's go to bed."

Meanwhile it has become Thursday, yes, but still no curtain falls; life, real life, doesn't permit us to skip things, not by a year and not by a month and not by a week, even when we know more or less what is going to follow. . .

(I shouldn't like to be Svoboda!)

A story for Camilla:

A man and a woman, when the first intoxication of impersonal love had worn off, discovered that they were made for one another. They understood each other so splendidly. Only the intoxication had worn off. And so they lived together, not high spiritedly, but without quarrelling. Only sometimes it happened that he saw their lovemaking, while it was taking place, as though from outside, as though he were sitting in an armchair beside them or just standing by the window, he had thoughts such as one has when one looks out into the street, not bad thoughts, but thoughts, then again he was one with himself and with her, and later, when she was making tea, he would call out to her using her nickname, and as she poured out the tea he said that he loved her. It was absolutely true. And she probably felt just the same. She too loved him, only him, even though differently from in the beginning, more personally. They were inseparable, they went on trips together. Once, in a hotel, he was dumbfounded when he saw their lovemaking, while it was taking place, in a mirror, and glad that it was his body with which she was deceiving him, and he looked in the mirror, in which he was likewise deceiving her. They started having crises over trifles. And yet they loved each other. One evening, later, he sat reading a newspaper while she was lying in bed; he had thoughts, everyday ones, such as he secretly had while they were making love, but he was really sitting in the armchair; she was asleep and, instructed by the mirror, he could without difficulty picture another man making love to her, and he sat at the side, in no way dismayed, rather pleased at the effacement of his person, actually gay: he wouldn't like to be the other man. Reading his paper while she was asleep and perhaps dreaming what he was imagining from outside, he was one with his great love. Their names were Philemon and Baucis: the couple.

Just assuming Svoboda looks more or less as I imagine: a strapping Bohemian, broad-shouldered, round-shouldered, a bit too tall for the delicate Lila in my opinion, even on her highest heels she just reaches to his shoulder and when she is barefoot they look almost indecent as a couple, a heavy man, yet not fat and by no means ponderous, athletic, a man incidentally whom one would immediately describe as blond, although actually he is completely bald, his bald head doesn't suggest fallen hair, however, but goes with his masculine face like his chin and his forehead, a good head, a head that might also have belonged to a Russian, a hard head, a bullet head, an unusual head, but he doesn't like looking at himself in the mirror because he can't understand what women see in him, Svoboda in a dinner jacket is thrilling, he knows that, and also a good dancer, a man who generally sweats and is never cold, who can hold his liquor without getting noisy, except when he has a three-hour rage, otherwise rather taciturn, a pipe-smoker, quiet and with a pleasant laugh in company, doesn't wear glasses, no doubt a brilliant cook, a melancholic, a bear, heavy but mobile, clumsy only because of the need (particularly in Lila's presence) not to show his strength. Lila is afraid of him, although he has never yet struck her. . . Just assuming that Svoboda looks like this, then I can guess how for his part he imagines Enderlin: a slender, delicate intellectual, not actually pigeon-chested, but delicate. No bear. More of a bird. No Bohemian. More of a Spanish or French type, possibly Italian, anyhow black-haired (which isn't true) with a delicate hawk's nose (which isn't true either) under a classically rectangular, low forehead such as you find among Mediterranean peoples. It's true the name sounds Alemannic, but Svoboda doesn't let himself be deceived by this for an instant; he knows her type. No bullet head. He understands. A narrow head with a perpetually surprising knowledge in all fields, hence entertaining. Perhaps with a touch of•the homosexual, so that Svoboda would never guess who he was if he saw him in the street, perhaps with a dog. No fop, but well cared for; he certainly never has black finger-nails. Nor freckles. With black hair, a type who will never go bald, that's quite certain. Unathletic, but to make up for it witty. It may be that he attracts women precisely because he has a certain amount of difficulty. That's quite possible. But not necessarily. Anyhow he's an intellectual. Highly conscious. Arm-in-arm with Lila he has a boyish gait. A beret. Anyhow he's younger, that's certain, and more educated than Svoboda. No cook. And helpless when a wall-socket gets broken; not a handyman. Lila isn't afraid of him. Without a doubt he reads seven languages, starting with Greek. In a bathing costume he is as pale as wax, yet not unmanly and in any case with black hair. And witty under all circumstances. Not a raconteur, but witty. In bed he behaves as in a French film. Politically? Probably half-left. When Lila takes off his Corbusier glasses, a rather soft face, but lean. Not a drinker. Not a colossus. Not weak he carries her cases without being any taller than her. No dancer. What fascinates Lila, she naturally doesn't know herself – it was unseemly to ask. . . Simply the type. The un-Bohemian. That was bound to happen. The black-haired type. The Latin. A *torero*, slender and large-eyed, a type which from the very beginning, even if till now only in jest, Svoboda has looked upon as the danger, black-haired and with a bird's face and black-haired not only on the head but also on the legs –

I shall disappoint Svoboda!

When I ask Lila how he behaved, she says nothing. In any event he has lost her, and from now on his behaviour makes no difference. And she doesn't want me to bother about it. Let him behave as he likes from now on. . .

I see several possibilities:

Svoboda crashes into a tree with his car.

Or:

Svoboda decides to be magnanimous. He puts his hope in the power of time, which is always against love and hence against us. At times he drinks, while we are on a trip within the latitude allowed by his magnanimity. When he is sober he forbids himself any atavistic feelings. It isn't rancour that makes him more domesticated than ever; sometimes he is already asleep when Lila comes home, or pretends to be asleep. Then again, all of a sudden he drinks, which isn't good for his liver; but Lila can't help that, and he knows it. Her concern for his liver is the only thing he declines to accept. He doesn't press for a decision. He understands life. He waits. This goes on for three months, six months. He is kind, as Lila wishes him to be, and Lila will esteem him. The danger of Lila becoming a matter of indifference to him exists only from time to time; her happiness with me, naturally, is not without variations, which Svoboda, of course, sees, and since it also makes an everyday difference to Svoboda whether she walks about their joint house-hold singing or turned to stone, he can't avoid a sympathy that is akin to love. This goes on for a year. Supported by his knowledge that there is no person without whom one cannot live, he shows her at all times that he can live without her; but he doesn't do so. He has grown accustomed to his magnanimity. He doesn't pester her with joint plans, but waits. What for? Lila is happy, so that no change is urgently necessary. She esteems Svoboda, as I have said, more than ever. For his magnanimity. Naturally he will lose her like this too. . .

Or:

224

Svoboda (after the stupid night when he smashed the whisky glasses in the fireplace, and after a week of brutally frank talks that don't alter the facts) chooses freedom in night-clubs. He dances. He is bored, but he dances. He goes to the swimming-pool and it is seething with women and girls who could easily replace Lila, in so far as he only takes her as a woman, if only he didn't keep thinking of her all the time. He swims, a Tarzan, then he stands about and looks, a man as tall as a tree with broad shoulders, his hands on his hips. He plays ball with the child of a lady in a bikini as a means of approaching her, but he gets no further than playing ball with her child. He buys an open car, ready at any time for hitch-hikers, but there are generally boys with them, once he picks up two girls but they speak a language Svoboda doesn't understand and they can only stammer to each other. He goes to every private view, he insists on giving a young woman photographer a lift home. He tries to fall in love, in order to create an equilibrium, if not an equilibrium of happiness at least an equilibrium of jealousy. As though Lila could become jealous now! He sees their mouths, but he can't fall in love; women can smell it, Svoboda now has the smell of a sick animal, and nature is against him. All the same, he can tell himself that he is now going his own way, and he lets it show. But Lila isn't inquisitive. She doesn't actually wish him good luck, that would be in bad taste; she doesn't want to know. She really doesn't care. Any more than about his fidelity. He will lose her in any case. . .

Or:

Svoboda doesn't take the matter more seriously than is usual among professionally active men; he has other worries. He doesn't think about it for more than a minute. Oh well. It happens. The usual thing. Sex. It doesn't affect his person, what the two of them do, and he doesn't let himself be intimidated. Sex. It makes him laugh, if Lila sees anything more in it. But go ahead. It's her affair. But for Lila, the woman, it's more serious, and even if right may be on his side in relation to me, he loses it precisely by having seen through her infatuation too quickly. . .

Or:

Svoboda sits in Salamanca, Plaza Mayor, where he has his shoes cleaned, a tourist whose function in life is to keep the shoeshine boys busy, they have known him for three days, he sits for hours at the same little table, looks at his watch, isn't waiting for anyone, but waits, without reading a newspaper, with no eyes for the famous architecture, looks at his watch and taps with a coin, pays and gets up and goes as slowly as possible to the post office, morning, afternoon, evening, comes back and sits down, orders a sherry, smokes and has his shoes cleaned, it need not be Salamanca, he doesn't see the place anyway, it could be Arles or Agrigento where he writes his letters, they're all the same, there's always the same grille where he shows his passport (which is no longer necessary: they know him already, they quite believe he is Svoboda) and asks in vain for a letter, she knows he is in Salamanca or Siena or somewhere else, it really makes no odds where Svoboda has his shoes cleaned to pass the time until the post office opens, it could be Brindisi (a horrible place; people come to Brindisi to go aboard ship, no one stays in Brindisi voluntarily) or in Cadiz –

What Svoboda sees:

Roads black, grey, white, yellow, asphalt or concrete, hot asphalt with mirages, gorse, bends round which one has already driven scores of times, milestones, avenues dappled with shadow, mule-carts, tar barrels, suburbs, ships in the harbour, people, traffic lights, poverty, railway embankments, a goods train with sea between the wheels, a shore road curving to the left, curving to the right, straight ahead, then right again and left and right, left, right and on, second gear, buses from behind, the dust of lorries from behind, level crossings, sea, cactuses, sea, gorse, sea, bridges, villages that keep coming again, small towns, squares with a memorial, will-o'-the-wisps in the dusk, trees in the headlights, milestones in the headlights, suddenly a team of white oxen, reeds in the headlights, sea as darkness, rear-lights, flocks of sheep as a swarm of green eyes in the headlights, hands on the wheel, tarmac in the moonlight, moonlight on the sea, milestones in the headlights, road, hands on the wheel, road and so on.

What Svoboda doesn't see:

– her face.

Once (I could imagine) one of his tyres bursts on the open road, midday, a change of wheels in this scorching heat, that's the last straw; he knows at once that it's not Lila's fault, but his rage, as he takes out the tools and attaches the jack, is directed against this woman as though she were present, as though it had been she who scattered these nails over the road, it's ridiculous, yes, he knows that, the whole trip is ridiculous. . . I've gone away for three weeks to give you time! That's what one says. Why just three weeks? The gesture (on the morning after the smashed whisky glasses) was not without sober and hence convincing magnificence, but three weeks is a long time. To give you time! She didn't send him away, but nor did she hold him back; she was a bit surprised that he took the matter so seriously, more seriously than she did, and a bit angry too, because he had never been able to take so long when they went on holiday together. Three or four weeks, he said, then we shall see more clearly, he said, one way or the other, he said and kissed her on the forehead, while Lila, who doesn't need his trip, seeks a different reason for it, a more sensible one; she welcomes the idea of Svoboda undergoing a cure, overworked as he is. Why Cadiz? She thought of Bolzano or the Engadine. Why so far? What's said is said and a man sticks to his word – 70 miles from Cadiz (or Brindisi) in the midday heat on a treeless stretch of road, as Svoboda, sweaty and smeared with grease, throws the tools into the boot along with the flat tyre, there is no turning back, although at just this point, as Svoboda sees, one could double back without making a three-point-turn; possibly there's a letter waiting for him in Cadiz (or Brindisi) . . .

What is Svoboda expecting?

He takes the matter more seriously than she. His trip and his letters above all, which are not without dignity, not without boldness and free from reproach, orgies of sober insight, compel Lila to

227

a seriousness that makes her resentful, to a decision that will in any case be premature.

Telegram:

LETTER FOLLOWS DAY AFTER TOMORROW STOP YOURS LILA

Svoboda has his shoes cleaned.

I know Cadiz, but I've never been there alone; this city, seen from the land a dream of white shells, is a disappointment as soon as you enter it, the beach is dreary and on top of that shingly, the food hopeless, when you're alone, only the sherry cheers you up. . .

I shouldn't like to be Svoboda.

Svoboda recognizes that he is incapable of seeing his own case in general terms and gives himself up to sherry, which puts feelings right without being able to understand them, that's to say gives himself up to a hangover. . .

Second telegram:

SENDING LETTER TO BARCELONA STOP DRIVE CAREFULLY WHEN YOU HAVE READ IT STOP PLEASE LET ME KNOW IN GOOD TIME WHEN YOU ARE AR-RIVING STOP LILA

Svoboda drives like a Neapolitan.

The wording of the letter which is waiting for him poste restante in Barcelona, where he arrives on Sunday, but which isn't handed over to him until Monday, is likewise not without dignity, not without a boldness of insight, sober (probably Svoboda feels it to be hostility when a woman also thinks soberly) and intelligent, even if still undecided. And that is enough to turn Svoboda's knees into cottonwool, so that he has to sit down. So it's gone that far! Filling a pipe, to keep himself in countenance, after skimming over the long letter and stuffing it in his pocket, he sits on in the hall of the post office. When, by his trip and above all by his letters, he challenged her to reach an early decision, didn't he reckon with his challenge being accepted? Smoking a pipe to keep himself in coun-tenance, as though he had not been disarmed and as though he had expected nothing else, he sits and sweats no less than when chang-

228

ing a wheel at midday: so Lila is seriously weighing up whether to live with Svoboda or with a man named Enderlin. Or alone. Her decision, as I have said, has not been taken yet. She feels herself drawn into precipitate action, it seems, not by the other man but by Svoboda; she asks for patience, apparently in no doubt that this man named Enderlin (without a Christian name; Svob is no longer interested in his Christian name) wouldn't hesitate to give up everything in order to live with Lila. Her reasons for not being able to live with Svoboda are intelligent, not unloving, but so intelligent that they are not to be refuted by love, reasons that are obviously not new, only uttered for the first time; on the other hand no reasons are required as to why she might live with Enderlin, that's a simple fact, Lila doesn't even need to sing this other man's praises, doesn't even need to know him, and what she reports about this man named Enderlin is very little, age, profession, nationality and the fact that he reciprocates her feelings. . . Svoboda, when he is finally sitting in his dusty car, not without having read the letter a second time, so that he knows certain sentences off by heart, inserts the key, slowly depresses the clutch, then starts the engine before putting the car into first gear, all like a learner driver doing his test, one thing after the other, but unfortunately forgetting to take off the hand brake, Svoboda is relieved, confused as after a fall, but un-harmed and relieved. Doesn't it always cheer one up when it seems that life is moving forward? In Nîmes he looks at the antique theatre, the only thing he has really seen on this long journey. In Vienne (shortly before Lyons) he dines at a three-star hotel. For the first time he thinks he can see the future, like an outsider who is not hindered by emotions; to be more exact, not the future but the end of a past that no longer runs out into any present. Lila is right. He drives along, his left arm dangling in the wind, one-handed and nonchalant. Lila is right. Like an outsider who, although he doesn't want to give advice nevertheless does so, he knows that for this couple there is no solution but divorce, the quicker the better, so get on with it. He whistles. Free for the problems of humanity, that is to say relieved, released from everything that one calls private life, he drives home, dawdling along at an average of 60 m.p.h., the past is in no hurry. . .

I imagine:

Svob, suntanned after three weeks in an open car, at the same time rather leaner, anyhow with his face taut, that is to say rejuvenated, so that Lila scarcely recognizes him as he comes in, is an unintentional conqueror, a stranger, gay, because he has nothing to lose, hence winning: Lila betrays me after only an hour, blissful, so long as he doesn't claim any sort of rights, not even the right to be melancholy. She meets me briefly next day to report his return, so that I shan't ring up any more, briefly and absent-mindedly, taciturn, while at home, Svoboda is opening his post and whistling. There follows a half honeymoon, not a half as regards their feelings, a half only as regards its duration, a happiness that makes no difference to the disarming intelligence of her Barcelona letter; then Svoboda is himself again, he wants to know where he stands.

I imagine:

Life goes on, but not forwards, and the question arises, even if it is not spoken, who is to blame, Svoboda with his demeanour of waiting to spring or Lila, who takes refuge behind social activity.

"Svob," laughs Lila, "are you mean?"

"Why?"

"No one has any wine."

"Sorry," he says, Lila is right, he was listening to Lila telling the story of the Greek snake. He remembers: it was a happy day that day, a day of love, which doesn't concern the thirsty guests, and Lila is right in so far as she conceals the truth. But in that case, why does she tell the story at all? She merely says that they were sleepy with the heat and got some awful wine and sunburn and couldn't even get any cigarettes or anything, and in the middle of this dusty road on their wedding trip there squirmed this snake they had run over —

Svoboda opens a bottle.

A friend of theirs has heard that Lila has no plans for the summer yet, and there is some casual talk of Lila perhaps going to Copenhagen. This is the first Svoboda has heard of it. Other people seem to be better informed. But, as the friend knows, it isn't certain that Lila is going to Copenhagen; it's possible, as the friend knows, that they may spend their holidays somewhere by the sea, that is to say Lila and Svoboda, "family style" (as the friend quotes, because he finds this expression she used amusing).

Svoboda fills the glasses.

Someone speaks briefly of Enderlin, who has been invited to Harvard, as everyone knows, but for some incomprehensible reason doesn't go –

And so on!

Lila is getting more and more sensitive.

"Your smoke!" she says. "Why do you always hold your pipe so that all the smoke always goes in my face?"

Or:

"Can't you drive so that I don't die of fright?" she says. "Is that impossible?"

Or:

"Svob," she says, "don't eat so much."

Or:

"Svob," she says, "look at your fingernails. What's the idea? I've been asking you for six years –"

Or:

"Have you taken my key again?"

"Me?" he says. "What makes you think that?"

"I can't find it."

He finds it.

"Sorry," she says. "I forgot where it was. I can't think of everything," she says. "Sorry!"

Or:

"Excuse me," she says, "I said good morning to you, but if you aren't listening –"

Or:

"Svob," she says, "I'm doing everything you want."

And so on.

And yet it's true that Lila does everything Svoboda wants, and even the summer holiday by the sea takes place. . .

What does Svoboda expect to gain from it?

"Family style":

I lie on the beach, reading a foreign newspaper, alone with foreign people, it is a hot midday, the time of Pan, sunshades, to the left a radio is droning, to the left lie a couple who are not speaking to each other – naturally not Svob and Lila, but just some couple or other! . . . He is sitting in the hot sand oiling his shoulders; she is lying on her stomach on the rug with her face turned to the other side. At one point I go for a swim, very nearly drowning incidentally. – When I come back to my place the silent couple are no longer there, only their brightly coloured things. It seems the man has succeeded in getting the woman to move; they are now playing with a ball, but it's too light, the wind blows it off course and the ball rolls over to me. I give it back. She thanks me (in Italian) with such an amiably cheerful face that she is scarcely recognizable. Really she is well worth looking at. At least for this moment, since someone is looking at her, almost girlish; she shakes her loose hair round her neck, so that I shall see it, and hops about, and when she throws the ball, which previously she did clumsily and wearily, it is now almost gracefully clumsy. She isn't tired at all, only listless towards the other side. Really an enchanting woman, or whatever you like to call it, gaiety personified. If only he wasn't there! To be sure, he throws the harlequin ball carefully, so that she ought to have been able to catch it as she caught it from me, but in vain; she doesn't pay attention, shakes her remarkable hair when he throws it, and then the ball rolls into the sea, which is irritating. In order not to make the couple feel uncomfortable by staring at them, I gaze straight ahead: on the horizon a black freighter is smoking, sea like tin foil, the sun glitters white over the steaming shore. A little while later when they return to their place, both of them mute, the woman is limping; her movements, as she sits down, make it plain that he alone is to blame.

232

Who else forced her to play ball? I lie down on my back and shut my eyes, but I hear:

"Of course it hurts!"

Later:

"What are you doing with the umbrella?"

"Making shade."

"I'm freezing," she says. "I'm sorry."

"I thought you had sunburn."

Later:

"Be so good and give me the sun oil, dear," she says. "And if you'd be so kind, dear, rub some on my back, but so that it doesn't hurt," she says. "You and your hands!" she says. "Ow!"

Later:

"Don't be angry," she says, "but now I'm getting all your smoke in my face again," she says, "the whole time."

Later:

"Please, can't you watch out?" And since he doesn't know what's wrong: "You keep throwing sand over me all the time," she says, and when he has proved that it can be no one else than the wind that has bothered the recumbent lady, and when he is about to blow the nasty stuff off her shoulders: "Don't do that," she says. "Why don't you go swimming?"

Like any outsider who heard such scraps of conversation, Svoboda knows that the invisible point at which parting becomes due has not merely been reached, but already passed, the point of no return, the only question now is who can make the break, in order not to suffer it, and both sides are simply waiting for the pretext for the great anger that makes people capable of acting; they know this; the love to which they must bid farewell is no longer sufficient to prevent each one from seeing through the other.

Something new:

Svoboda wants to see and talk to Enderlin! . . . I don't know how he pictures it, and when Lila tells me I wipe my hand over my mouth. Talk about what? Svoboda suggests Thursday or Friday or Saturday. Naturally I'm prepared to meet him, for Lila's sake, only Thursday is out of the question, after all I have a job, which Lila understands. Lila is all against it, which I can also understand; she feels no need to see Svoboda and Enderlin side by side. What does he hope to gain by it? He can't live with a ghost, I hear. I'm sorry I laugh. It won't even be embarrassing, our meeting *à trois*, only an effort, and certainly pointless. I'm sorry for Svoboda. If I answered with a blank No, Lila might be grateful to me; but that's impossible, it would look as if I were scared. Very well then! Only it just occurs to me that unfortunately Friday is impossible too. And that isn't an excuse. But I declare my willingness, and if Svoboda really sticks to the idea till then, all right, I'll drop in for a drink. Why a whole dinner? I shan't have much to say; I love his wife. Why does he act as though he didn't know that and wants me to tell him? I can imagine what he has to say, and however well he succeeds in speaking with control, with enlightened dignity and in a comradely tone, it makes no difference to the fact that for the moment his wife loves somebody else. That's the way it is. I really think a drink will be enough. I'd prefer to go to a bar, but I understand: I'm to see the Svoboda-Lila home as though I didn't know it. Very well then. Saturday at six, I'll be there. Svoboda at the cocktail cabinet that I know, will make us each a whisky, whisky on the rocks or with soda water, according to taste, while he himself drinks mineral water. Perhaps Svoboda won't understand what Lila sees in me –

The surf wasn't particularly stormy, two or three breakers as high as a man before they crashed down with a roar and a shower of spray, and then, after I had dived through the breakers and left their thundering behind me, big smooth billows without spray, blissful swimming, up and down and up again, billow after billow without struggle, every now and then a crest began to curl, but without toppling over, easy swimming, billow after billow beer-bottle green with a hissing ruche of sun-glitter, and if I had not been alone I should have shouted for joy, the troughs that follow are smoother and inky-blue-black with a white pattern of foam.

234

Once I swallowed water. I was the only swimmer. Behind me the dull thunder of the surf, out to sea silence, midday sun that dazzled; but as though from a violet night sky. Every now and then, when a billow lifted me up, I saw a freighter out on the horizon, behind me the flat beach with its motley sunshades not too far away, but on the other side of the surf, the yellow flag fluttering on a pole, and beyond this, above the billows fleeing towards the land, when they collapsed behind their spray, the land itself, mountains behind a milky haze, pink. . . When I swam back to the shore, not in the least tired, it was barely another hundred yards, I hoped I could already stand: suddenly there was no bottom, but a mass of brown and black seaweed, so that I had to swim, at one moment smothered by the billows that pushed me under and didn't carry me forward, the next moment in the middle of the breakers, but unable to touch bottom, now fighting with all my strength, without making any progress against the pull of the backwash. I became breathless with fear, but didn't want to believe the truth yet, didn't want to call for help a hundred yards from the beach with its sunshades. No one would have heard. No sooner had I got my breath back than the next breaker struck me. I still struggled, but at the same time I was sure it was all over, not really surprised, it was bound to happen some time, why here, why like this, why now, the consciousness that now it's all over, as the consciousness of something ridiculous, now I was only fighting against looking ridiculous until conscious-ness left me – suddenly sand. . . As I waded ashore I felt ashamed of myself. And yet no one had seen me. On the beach, now possibly seen, I pretended to be looking for shells. So as not to show my exhaustion. Then I had to sit down. I oiled my body, looking out to sea, sun, on the horizon the smoking freighter, a blue midday like any other. I tried to think: suppose I were now drowned? – and I couldn't think of anything. . . I oiled my body carefully, my shoulders and calves, my thighs too and my chest and forehead and arms and again my calves; on my left a radio was droning, on my right lay the Italian couple with the harlequin ball, bored, "family style".

A story for Camilla:

about a man who is always making up his mind to change his way of life but of course he never succeeds. . . One day when he was once again about to fly home, a man who no longer looks out of the window while the plane is standing on the runway waiting for permission to take off and who already unfolds his newspaper before take-off, he happened to read in a paper from his own country which, since he had bought it at a foreign airport, was naturally a bit out of date, his own obituary notice. No one had informed him of his demise; no one had known where he was at this time, not even his wife. He himself, no sooner had he read his obituary notice, did after all look out of the round window; but it was too late to think of getting out, the runway was whizzing past and the plane was just rising steeply from the ground. He still saw meadows, farms from above, a pine forest with roads, a vehicle on one road, soon afterwards a railway station with lines, but already like a toy. Then mist. A good thing no one was sitting next to him; he would scarcely have dared to open the newspaper again. Not merely the name, outlined in black, was exactly his; the names of those he had left behind were right too. He evidently turned pale, in spite of knowing better. The stewardess smiled as she asked if she could do anything for him and adjusted the ventilator nozzle above his head. He asked for fruit juice. The paper was dated the day before yesterday, his obituary notice repeated three times, as though to exclude all doubt: one in the name of his family, one in the name of the board of directors, one in the name of a professional association. God appeared only in the family's notice, on the other hand they were all agreed as to the cause of death: a tragic accident. Nothing more precise was to be gleaned from the newspaper, no matter how often he read it as he drank his fruit juice. Perhaps, as once before, some lout had pinched his car, only this time he had crashed into a petrol tanker and been burned beyond recognition. Funeral today. That is to say, if the plane arrived on schedule, the man just had time to get to his own funeral –

Never did a jet fly so slowly.

Perhaps he tried to think over the life he had lived on earth, as the plane flew above the sunlit clouds; but he couldn't manage it, and when the stewardess with her immobile smile brought the tray, he only shook his head; he couldn't eat, he couldn't really think either, only keep looking at the clock – as the widow now drew her black veil over her tear-stained face. . .

At last the loudspeaker crackled.

NO SMOKING.

The plane, shaken by gusts of wind, so that the wings flapped, cruised round for at least another twenty minutes in the mist; for the first time he was afraid.

As expected:

his car simply wasn't there any more; the car park attendant, to whom he showed his parking ticket, couldn't do anything about it and directed him to the police –

He took a taxi.

Without picking up his luggage.

He was the first at the cemetery; naturally he had rung home the moment he landed, but in vain, the mourners were already on their way. A gardener, who was raking up the rotting leaves from the path, otherwise there was no one in the cemetery. He read the ribbons on the wreaths. A rainy day. Perhaps certain ribbons that he missed were inside on the coffin; but he didn't dare go into the crematorium to see, especially as he was wearing a light-coloured raincoat. Of course he wanted to clear the matter up, that was his duty. When he enquired the name of the deceased from an attendant, he took his pipe out of his mouth, rather bewildered, then more and more confused as soon afterwards the first cars drove up. As though he had no right to be there, he stepped behind a cypress. He was rather shaken by the sight of all the people in black, their slow walk in silent groups or alone, there were quite a lot of them and some of them he didn't know at all, probably representatives of a guild or a firm, also children from the neighbourhood, friends whom he hadn't seen for ages, all in black, while he, the only one in a light-coloured raincoat, stood behind the cypress with his pipe in his hand. The moment to step forward had really been missed already. There were so many people, some of them from far away. Actually there was no real need for him to hide, since all of them gazed down at the ground as they walked past on the crunching gravel, mourners and those who were acting the part of mourners. Those who knew each other merely nodded gravely. And no one was smoking, of course not, so that he involuntarily stuffed his cold pipe into his pocket. That was bad; because he thereby acknowledged the ceremony even before the veiled widow had come, and he could only watch everything take its course, helpless. The emotion he had felt on reading the rainwet ribbons was past; now he felt the whole thing to be a conspiracy. The widow came, as expected, under a black veil, supported by two brothers-in-law who walked erect with sober dignity and protected her from greetings by nodding briefly in this direction and that on her behalf. There was nothing to be heard but the crunching of the gravel as the cars drove up, the banging of the car doors and in between the rain dripping from the cypresses. Who would have dared now to step forward in a light-coloured raincoat? And very soon after this the organ began to play. Really the man had no alternative but to follow on as the last in line, since it was too late now to stop the ceremony. It would have been perfectly possible to follow on as the last in line and to listen to the funeral oration; in a crematorium people don't look behind them, once they have taken their places on the benches, and so long as he behaved quietly there was nothing to stop the dead man from standing by the door. He just waited for the last stragglers. The car park, the organ, all this did not leave him indifferent; especially the organ. More and more people arrived, more than there were seats for; many of them had to stand in the doorway, hat in hand, and even outside. So it wasn't possible; they would have seen him if he had pushed his way in through the door to listen to the funeral oration. Now the organ had fallen silent. But all he heard were the raindrops falling from the cypresses, now with his pipe in his mouth again, though without smoking, and he didn't really know what he ought to do now in his position. Go to the cinema or home? He enquired from a chauffeur where the mourners were planning to go afterwards, and went on foot, his hands in his pockets, a man who suddenly has too much time, idling and at leisure, while a clergyman who never knew him was reading out his biography; a man in a light-coloured raincoat. Once he stopped. He watched some boys playing football among allotments and waited for a ball to fly over the fence. That would have appealed to him, and as he strolled on he kicked an empty tin, so that it flew like a football, then rolled down a slope, tinkling, while the mourners stood with bent heads, comforted anew by the organ, remembering him. He was half glad not to have had to listen to his biography, half depressed at not having been able to make some comment on it. He stood in the café where the mourners were going to forgather afterwards and drank a *grappa*, then a beer, then a second *grappa*, without taking off his coat. It was an impossible place, he thought, a café got up in Swiss national style. The top floor had been booked for the funeral repast. It took a long time for the lout to burn to ashes in his name. Any idea that came to him, for instance that he could go up to the top floor when the mourners came, had to be dismissed as impossible out of consideration for the widow, who had really been through it these last three days. Nor did he himself, to be frank, feel in a jesting mood. He was really at a loss what to do. He probably reproached himself for not having said anything about his aeroplane trip, and ordered another *grappa*, leafed through today's papers without, however, finding an obituary; after all, newspapers have to find something new to say every day. When the people, previously a single compact group of mourners, began to mount the stairs in professional groups and family groups or heterogeneous groups thrown together by the circumstances, they talked in everyday voices, but little. Everyone held the door open for everyone else. Undoubtedly there were two or three real friends among them whom he would have liked to have spared this funeral repast, this black-clad embarrassment that they felt obliged to endure not for his sake, but for his family's sake. Why didn't they come down to the ground floor? It made him sad. When later, obviously drunk, he had gone to the jukebox to let loose a blaring beat number, it wasn't long before the proprietor, also in black incidentally, came down and told him off, understandably. But once in motion, it was impossible to turn off the jukebox; they had to hear the beat number to an end. He could imagine how things were on the top floor: dignified, a horseshoe-shaped table, the widow now without a veil but tear-stained, a simple meal, ham and Clevner-Beerli accompanied by recollections of a personal kind. A woman who even in recollection will never make it up with him was certainly not there, and this relieved him, altogether the gathering up there had little to do with his life, could be a matter of indifference to him, of greater indifference than one can show during one's life-time. When he had to go to the lavatory, which was on the top floor, there was fortunately no one in the wash-room. He had to vomit. When someone did come his door was bolted. The mourner went away again. The man behind the bolted door suddenly felt awful, he feared that he would never get the door open again, but he didn't want to shout. No doubt they were now chatting quite naturally in the dining-room, only the widow was silent, which everyone understood but which put a damper on their mood. Once he heard voices in the wash-room, two men side-by-side in front of the basins, they were discussing professional matters, which also interested the man behind the door, and washed their hands at great length, dried their hands at great length, in order to have longer for their discussion, ending with a joke in the doorway— not about the dead man, naturally, far from that. . . The man was glad to hear the joke, although he knew it already. Now he could have gone into the dining-room: life was going on. The people there would now have been in the right mood for his appearance. But he felt too rotten, unfortunately, and he had no alternative but the street, where it was raining.

His luggage was still at the airport.

So he felt unencumbered.

Towards midnight, after he had slept as much as he wanted to in a waiting-room and was sober, he grew sad again. Homeless in one's hometown, that gets on one's nerves. To be sure, he could have gone to a hotel, room with a bath; without luggage, but with money. And with a passport. He dared not do so, as though every concierge knew who had been cremated today. The cinemas were shut. So he sat on a public bench, hatless in the rain, exhausted, freezing, gradually amused to think that he was alive and suddenly ready for a celebration, yes, a crazy celebration. But who with? Hatless in the rain alone, after he had politely refused the invitation of a street-walker, he discovered that for years he had neglected the few people who could still be considered as friends after today, and it was impossible to descend upon them now, shortly after midnight, like a ghost out of the grave. Perhaps one or other of them might have been glad to see him. He thought of them with remorse. But this was no place to sit about, and something had to happen. When finally he went into a booth and phoned home no one answered; probably the widow was sleeping at the brothers-in-law's, that is to say at her brothers', who never had much time for this brother-in-law. One can't blame them. The man in the light-coloured raincoat, who was now standing in the public phone box, never fitted properly into the family; he knew that himself. They had never been able quite to understand this marriage. Moved by her sorrow – the real breakdown usually takes place after the funeral – they probably didn't tell her even now what they had been thinking all these years, but comforted the unhappy widow. Fortunately there were no children. They comforted the unhappy widow with understanding; they didn't contradict when she sobbed and sobbed and talked like the Portuguese nun: not about him, but about her love. . .

Anyhow, no one answered.

The man in the light-coloured raincoat, when he had finally replaced the receiver and put the re-emerging coins back in his pocket, made sure he had the key of the flat and took a taxi home. He wanted to sleep. The flat was in darkness; he switched on the light and stood there . . . it was funny: the seven tea cups on the table, their last refreshment before the funeral, and the flowers everywhere, a box full of condolence cards and letters with black edges. He read some of them, without sitting down, his head on one side. Someone had left his black bowler behind. Otherwise everything was the same as always, apart from the open drawers; they had needed documents, naturally, had looked for and found a will. And then let a clergyman speak in spite of it. Oh well. He switched on the light in the bedroom: the double bed, her black veil on it. He put out the light. A cat, asleep in its basket, was the only living creature at home. He switched on the light in the kitchen, took a glass out of the cupboard and filled it with water, drank, refilled it. Back in the living-room, the glass in his hand, he looked round again, without taking off his raincoat, the other hand in his pocket in order not to interfere with his own things that had been cleared out of the chest-of-drawers: bundles of letters, receipts, an athletics badge from the old days, tax certificates, an insurance policy, photos, an honorary diploma. Trash. Surprised by all this evidence of a striving that was suddenly outdated, he drank his water, pleasantly surprised. When the cat, which had meanwhile woken up, crept into the room, he jumped with fright; then he laughed a little, gave the cat a biscuit from the mourners' tea table. He didn't stay long in the flat, he had nothing to attend to here, it seemed to him, nothing to touch. Only when he saw a pewter mug with seven pipes in it he couldn't help picking out the best and putting it in his coat pocket, not without putting the pipe he had had in his coat pocket in the pewter mug in its place. And that was about all. He looked round at everything once more and then switched off the light. In the well of the stairs he thought he heard something, immediately hid in an alcove, for a while breathless. Steps coming up the stairs! But then he heard a door on the floor below followed by silence. Tiptoeing like a lover, worried by every creak on the stair, he reached the front door unseen. He opened it cautiously. The rain had stopped. He turned up the collar of his raincoat, looked up at the housefront, walked away.

Apart from the fact that he had left the light on in the kitchen they found no trace of him; the tumbler on the desk attracted no attention; his front door key lay in the letterbox, which remained inexplicable. . .

I'm still preoccupied with Svoboda.

(– because I have wronged him. It is impossible to picture a person solely in his relationship to the opposite sex, impossible in the case of a man; most of our lives are spent working.)

I imagine:

Svoboda in a white coat. The two draughtsmen, whose work he is checking, don't notice anything different about him. Svoboda the same as every morning. He sits with his hairy hands resting to right and left on the corners of the drawing-board, thoughtful, while the two employees, waiting intently for his verdict, stand to right and left of Svoboda. Something seems not to please him; a proportion, perhaps, he doesn't know straight away, takes a ruler, measures, says nothing, looks and knows. It doesn't work. Pity. Svoboda isn't angry, only thoughtful. He must think of something else. So he is thoughtful, but without reproach; after all it's his own idea that has been drawn out there with a hard pencil and to scale in ground-plan and elevation. So it doesn't work. Well, the position has been clarified. And one abandons what proves unsuccessful; that's work, that's good. Svoboda with his hairy hands on the corners of the drawing-table as they wait, as a team so to speak, for an idea; he looks out of the window as for the moment he thinks of something else – of yesterday evening with Lila – but not for long. . . This here, a design for a public competition, is more urgent, and he asks for a roll of tracing paper, which he casually unrolls, also for a pencil, a soft one, a 5B. Perhaps the pencil will suddenly have an idea. Then a second roll of tracing paper, a third, on which he draws nonchalantly, which he nonchalantly spoils with a drawing that goes wrong. Nonchalantly. All the time with eyes alert, but nonchalantly; there must be a solution. Svoboda is no virtuoso, but he is a professional, a trained worker, and what he

243

puts down on paper this morning (after the night's rumpus with whisky bottles) is already better, at least clear; the two draughtsmen, now leaning forward with their heads on one side to read his sketch, begin to nod. . . Other matters interrupt, a phone call from a building site, Svoboda makes a decision; later they hear him laughing; later he has to go and see a government department, while the two draughtsmen stretch a fresh piece of paper and sharpen their pencils, and in the afternoon I see him again in his white coat, his hairy hands on the corners of the drawing-board. What he sketched out in the morning really seems to have been a good idea, even if too modest, he finds, too modest in scale, so that Svoboda once more spreads a rustling piece of paper over it, and now, lo and behold, it is merely a question of overtime. When one comes in, announced by a secretary, one sees the bald top of his head from the back; I wait, till the draughtsmen have completely understood, until he turns slowly on the revolving chair and then stands up, taking off his horn-rimmed glasses.

"Am I disturbing you?" I ask.

Washing his hands, then drying them, a crag of a man, for whom one need not fear, he describes my visit as welcome, although his thoughts are manifestly still on the tracing paper, heartily, and I believe him, since he immediately shows me a model in order to have the opinion of a layman.

"Excuse me," he says –

I see:

Svoboda, the receiver wedged between his ear and his shoulder, pulls out a chest-of-drawers on runners, leafs through an Eternit catalogue as he talks and asks the secretary to bring an estimate; in between he asks:

"What do you think about theatre in the round?"

"Nothing," I say. "Not much."

Perhaps I shall talk to Svoboda about it when he has time and tranquillity, perhaps afterwards in the car; now I remain squatting in front of his model, which I like very much. A working model, I hear, that is going to be modified. This in passing. The discussion of the catalogue, which obviously irritates him, takes a long time. When he has at last put the receiver down and shut the Eternit catalogue with a bang, he says:

"Crap."

I see Svoboda, not without glancing at his wrist-watch, take off his white coat, then take his jacket, now mute; the business of the Eternit catalogue seems to be a great nuisance.

"Thanks," he says "– I'm fine."

But before we can go, my hand is already on the latch, but there's no hurry, Svoboda goes into another room where people in white coats, some sitting, some standing, bent over T-squares or slide-rules, are working on solvable problems, an equally snow-bright studio; an old quantity surveyor is to calculate the whole project (from what I gathered during the phone talk, it is a house in a park) over again using Eternit, yes, I'm afraid so.

"How about you?" Svoboda asks in the car. "You've been to Jerusalem," he suddenly recalls. "What were you doing there?"

I see:

Svoboda at the wheel, both hands at the top, the way one relaxes on a long stretch of straight road, his face tired but wakeful; a sensible driver; he overtakes immediately when opportunity offers without breaking off the conversation, and when he can't overtake he drives slowly without getting edgy, as though it were the road that was driving, not he, while he talks.

Not a word about Lila.

On the way I see a building site and Svoboda walking over the bouncing planks, the shell of a building after work has stopped for the day, beside it stacks of Portland cement, a latrine under a flowering cherry tree, wheel-barrows, a hut with a paper placard under wire netting: UNAUTHORIZED PERSONS ARE STRICTLY FORBIDDEN TO ENTER THE BUILDING SITE. Svoboda in an overcoat. What he describes as a living-room is a jungle of vertical posts and beams called shuttering or false work, the ceiling has been concreted today, sacking over it, it is dripping. Material everywhere: rolls of tarfelt that feels like emery-paper, a water butt with cherry blossoms floating on the dirty water, shovels, bundles of reinforcing bars in the grass, hillocks of brown humus with weeds growing on them, heaps of bricks pale-pink like the dusk. Once Svoboda takes out a yellow folding rule. An oil tank waiting by its pit, and puddles everywhere, boards with the notice in stencilled lettering: *Scotoni & Co.*, a plumb-line scaffolding, pipes gleaming brown like fresh horse chestnuts, drains, a concrete tank, above it a tripod and pulley-block, a pile of gravel beside birches, and beer bottles in the grass, the paper from empty cement bags. Svoboda looks at it with satisfaction.

"Well," says Svoboda, "shall we go?"

At home:

"What will you have to drink?" he asks, not without having said thank you to Lila for bringing the ice, and for the whisky glasses that he smashed in the fireplace the night before. "You with your liver?"

"Whisky."

"You see," he says. "He thinks all this talk about theatre in the round is nonsense too –"

So that's her.

I tell them about Jerusalem. . .

After all, Lila is an actress!

If I were Svoboda:

I should fetch my gun from the cupboard and lie down on my stomach, perhaps stand up again to take off my jacket, then I take my pipe out of my mouth before lying down on my stomach again, then press the first round of ammunition into the gun with my thumb, everything the way I have learnt, close the breech, every-thing calmly. For a moment, as I put down the gun, it looks as though I were hesitating, as though I realized the stupidity of what I am doing; but I have only put the gun down because my trousers are pulling, moreover I have to polish my glasses before releasing the safety catch, then the butt to my cheek, then take aim

246

– with complete calm – for example at the Louis Quinze clock. Do you remember? White and round like a target, porcelain with gold hands: crack! and open the breech so that the empty cartridge tumbles out, I hope it won't burn our carpet, close the breech, it's important to breathe calmly and regularly as I aim, at the Venetian mirror, take first pressure, my eye with the medium sight trained on my reflected eye, then slowly bend my index finger: tinkle! and again open the breech, close the breech, everything the way I've learnt, only no haste as I aim – this time perhaps at the Hi-Fi loudspeaker that is still playing Schubert, Trio No. 1, and don't let your eye twitch before you squeeze the trigger: pumm! I undo my tie before going over to finer tasks, and place the gun-strap round my left elbow in order to stop it from trembling. Hit the nail on which your picture is hanging! I use up four cartridges before the picture so much as quivers. Am I drunk? I have to reload, catch back, cartridges in, catch forward, everything as I have learnt, gun to my shoulder. How about the books? My cheek enjoys the coolness of the butt as I aim at Miller. Puff! I've been hearing voices in the street for a long time, shouts, but I'm in my own home. Breech open, breech shut, carry on. What business is it of the people shouting in the street! Meanwhile I am having a go at slimmer targets, for example the letters of a Portuguese nun. That takes three cartridges. It's not the right thing, it seems to me, the bar strikes me as a better target: whisky-ping, gin-pong! It tinkles, and I'm amused by the way a hot cartridge-case hops out every time I whip open the breech; I don't understand why the telephone starts ringing now. I hesitate but I'm not longing for anyone. The telephone rings and rings, until I fire at it: tack! And still without knowing what my next target is to be I squeeze in the next round of ammunition, the last but one, breech shut, butt to the cheek. Silence. There is no possibility that it might have been you ringing me. Why should you? You are lying with the other man and I must carry on. Or was it some third party, an innocent person, who rang to tell me on your behalf (unwittingly; but people will do anything for you) that you have missed your train? I think it was. How about the keyhole on your drawer? But your secrets are out of date; I prefer the leather upholstery. Piff-paff-puff! The dull thuds of a buffalo hunt. Then a shameful failure to hit the earthenware Inca dog from Peru, and again I have to reload, looking round the site on which we used to live. To the last cartridge, yes, there's no doubt of that; retreat is impossible now. How about the electric light bulbs? For four bulbs I need five cartridges and plaster is raining down out of the darkness; the last cartridge is for the moon, which immediately tries to take the place of the electric light bulbs and evidently thinks itself safe on the other side of the window pane: tinkle! And there stands a policeman who is lucky there is no cartridge left in the barrel and who, armed with a shamelessly dazzling pocket torch, asks me for my particulars. . .

But I'm not Svoboda.

Let my name be Gantenbein.

My stories for Camilla – one fine morning that will be over, my last manicure.

"You and your stories!"

She laughs, just as she sets to work on Gantenbein's left thumb, laughs briefly and without looking up, so that all Gantenbein sees is her peroxide-blond hair, and incidentally this hair isn't peroxide-blond, not any longer. Perhaps not for a long time. Gantenbein has stopped seeing it, it seems, really seeing it.

"Camilla," I ask, "what's the matter with you?"

Her need for stories is satisfied; Camilla has a story of her own, it seems, a real story.

"Yes," she says, "you'll have to find someone else to do your manicure now," and files the nails of my left hand for the last time, without looking up, as she adds: "You see, I'm getting married –"

My congratulations on the news.

Her fiancé, a dentist whom she found through an advertisement, doesn't want his Camilla to go on being a manicurist. So that's the end of an independent woman.

"I'm going to help him," she says, "in his practice," she says with unmistakable respect for this word. "Anyhow so long as we have no children."

"You'd like children?"

So later, when I inspect the nails of my right hand too, I know that this has been my last visit to Camilla Huber. I'm sorry about that. I can understand the dentist not wanting her to go on manicuring. We shall never see each other again, I realize that, otherwise the dentist will get the wrong idea, and I don't want that to happen. I repeat my congratulations, but I'm sorry; Camilla and Gantenbein have become friends, as now becomes clear, real friends.

"Herr Gantenbein," she says –

"What is it?"

"You're not blind."

I don't ask her how long she has known.

"No," I say. "Why?"

When I have taken my black stick and we are standing in the corridor, really having said goodbye already, my hand is already on the latch, I see from her face that Camilla wants to say something else.

"Herr Gantenbein," she says –

I wait.

"I shall never tell anyone," she says, "that you're not blind, you can rely on that, and don't you tell anyone what you have seen."

That's a pact.

I have just noticed, not without dismay, that however I have tried to imagine her so far, Lila never has a child. I have simply never thought of it.

A child by whom?

I imagine:

Afternoon in a bar, asked by the strange gentleman if she has any children, naturally not asked with interest, but just for something to say, chat between one salted almond and the next, she did not by any means keep silent but told him exactly how old her child is now. Only he seems to have forgotten meanwhile, the strange gentleman in the dark suit, as he stands in her living-room, waiting to take her to the opera. With his head on one side to read the titles, he is standing in front of the book-case, his hands in his jacket pockets so as not to touch anything. He doesn't know what's keeping her so long, after he has already helped the lady into her fur coat. But he waits without impatience, without a trace of displeasure. Perhaps she can't find the key, while he becomes aware of the advantageous light in which he is appearing by com-parison with her husband, whose pipes are standing in an Inca beaker and who is now in London; no husband is so free from impatience when he is kept waiting. Not knowing, not having the slightest idea, what is keeping Lila so long, has a positive charm for the strange gentleman. Once he hears the clip-clop of her high-heeled shoes out in the hall. To be sure, when she went out she told him to help himself at the bar. But he doesn't like to. He doesn't want to touch anything here. His hands in his jacket pockets, a strange man who is here but doesn't want to know where he is, he waits nonchalantly; without curiosity. Even to have looked at the books was too much, an insight, a contact with her surround-ings which he doesn't want to know anything about. And then those pipes in an Inca beaker. He knows she didn't fall from heaven simply in order to go to the opera with him; no lady ever fell from heaven into an afternoon bar. We know that; sooner or later it makes its appearance: the reality of a milieu, a family, a story, real and complicatedly ordinary. But he doesn't want to know. Doesn't want even to sit down. Even using a lighter. Dunhill Gold, which she probably gave her husband, clouds his mood for the space of a breath; he doesn't want to become at home here. He smokes, stands and smokes. Doesn't know why this Svoboda-Lila flat somehow disturbs him; it is tasteful. The Louis Quinze clock. The white leather upholstery. The earthenware Inca dog. Every-thing entirely tasteful; but present. Why does a face one meets never float in the void? And he doesn't want to look round too closely. Rather go to the opera! – When she does come back he is standing by the window, in order not to look into the flat but outside; he has forgotten that she has a child that has to be comforted before Mummy goes to the opera.

"Why aren't you drinking anything?"

As she goes to the bar to get something for the strange gentleman, he hears that the child cried; but now it has been comforted, it seems, with the promise that Mummy will tell it the whole story of the opera when she comes home.

"How old is it?" he asks.

She tells him again.

"Thanks," he says, "thanks very much."

And they drink, talk about other things and smoke, they are far too late for the opera, Lila still in her overcoat, both of them feel that they ought to go out of the flat into the town, although it would not be an offence against convention for her to give someone a drink at midnight. Anyway it isn't midnight yet. . . The child is asleep. . . He has forgotten it again, apparently; not she. She is a mother. They don't talk about her child that is asleep, and don't think about the child either; but she knows why she isn't with Svob in London. Because she is the mother. That's the way it is. A blessing. Tomorrow she will drive the child to the kindergarten; she doesn't need to think about it, she knows. She can rely on it. Sometimes Lila (thirty-one) feels old. . . They stand up to go into town, for a moment dumbfounded by the mute agreement; she turns out the standard lamp. Up to now the whole flat has been lit up and all the doors, apart from the door to the nursery, have been open for hours, since she looked for the road map of Peru, even the door to the kitchen, as though she were afraid of closed doors. It is strange when she puts out the standard lamp, then the ceiling light as well; it forces them out into the hall, and he is only waiting until she has found her car key, ready to go. As she looks round, as though something might not be in order, her left hand is already on the light switch. Let's go! she whispers as his hand, as though saying goodbye to a possibility, involuntarily and at the

251

same time ironically, because he is conscious of the repetition, strokes her forehead. Let's go! he whispers. Where to? That isn't under discussion. They whisper in order not to wake the child. Whispering makes them seem allies. This dismays her, and she doesn't look at the strange man as she puts out the light in the hall, and then there is no more light until the grey of dawn comes in through the windows – once more with the exception of the nursery. It is three o'clock when she goes across, because she heard coughing, and switches on the light to make sure the child is asleep. It is asleep. Is it cunning of her to wake it? She does so. To say that Mummy is back, that she has been to the opera. She doesn't tell it the story of the opera in detail, but enough for the child to remember it. And when it is big, it can go to the opera too. In order to get bigger it must sleep now. She makes it some sugar-water. Later she puts out the light. Waits by its bed without kissing the child; but she says that Daddy will be back tomorrow and is bound to bring something with him, a doll with a tartan skirt (if it's a girl) or a sailing-boat (if it's a boy), but only if it goes to sleep now. And she waits until the clock strikes four; then she locks the door from outside, and when she comes back, not a word, not even whispered, she hides her face in his naked·arm, while he breathes regularly with his mouth open, listening, all is quiet. . .

Next day Svoboda comes back.

The child (it evidently didn't hear the bit about the Scottish doll and isn't disappointed that Daddy doesn't bring anything) tells him the story of the opera Mummy went to see, very comical.

The child as a guardian angel?

I have bought a tape-recorder to record your conversations, conversations without me. That is underhand, I know. And I'm ashamed every time I slip one of these brown bands, spoken in my absence, into the devilish machine with trembling fingers –

What for!

At times I believe I can imagine how my friends' conversations go on without me, at other times I know I can't. Now that I have gone, are they still talking about the history of the popes? Or about what? But above all: how are they talking now. Differently from before? Exactly the same? More seriously or more jokingly? I don't know why I want to know. There are people whom I trust to go on talking exactly the same after my departure as before, and to be frank there is something boring, almost inhuman about them. Of course, I may be wrong. That someone goes on talking exactly the same as before after Burri has said goodbye doesn't mean that he goes on talking exactly the same after I have gone. Certain people entice one to treachery, others don't. How does treachery come into it? I don't mean that the others, as soon as they are alone, start talking about me personally, and if they do, so what? What stimulates my curiosity is something different. Whether Burri, alone with my wife, hasn't also an entirely different face? By inventing conversations that take place when I'm not there, I run the risk of fearing or respecting or loving people according to the way they talk in my imagination when I'm not there. My almost blind trust in Burri, merely because in my invented conversations he speaks and remains silent and laughs in exactly the same way as when I am there, goes so far that I simply don't believe it when I hear by a roundabout route what Burri is supposed to have said recently. Gossip! I won't listen to gossip. The outcome: I don't suspect Burri, but only the people who tell me what Burri is supposed to have said in my absence recently. Perhaps he really said it, but not in the way gossip passes it on. Literally, perhaps, but not in that tone. Quite simply, I can't imagine Burri selling me for the sake of a witticism. And equally founded or unfounded, that's to say the product of my blind invention, which sooner or later forms round everyone, is my years-long distrust of others, for example my painful embarrassment in the presence of Dolf, merely because, as soon as he is speaking not in my presence but in my imagination, he suddenly speaks not only in a more refined and more intelligent manner, not only with far more knowledge as soon as he no longer has to suppress his great knowledge in the presence of my ignorance, but also with greater sparkle and wit. I'm convinced that certain people hide their wit from me; I don't hold it against them, I'm just repeatedly astonished that they aren't witty in my presence, not bubbling over with bright ideas, not gay to the point of reckless high spirits, not superior. I assume that they take revenge for this; I have no proof of it. Dolf is a case in point. For in conversations that I invent on my way home or when I am lying in the bath, Dolf is a regular prodigy of humour, a squanderer of knowledge which he always conceals from me. Why is that? Often the only reason I don't go to a party is because I should be there, however quiet I kept; as soon as I am there it is not the party in which I am interested, but a party of masks of which I am the cause –

Hence the tape recorder!

Hurriedly, while I feel negligently ashamed, my trembling fingers fiddle with the spool, I really do feel ashamed every time I switch the machine on, but I take no steps against myself. I always cut off the first yard, but in spite of this, on a few of the tapes, I catch the tail end of my own voice, a murmured lie: I'll go and fetch the cigarettes! which I do too, after setting in motion the infernal machine, hidden behind books. My oath never to make use of these tapes is cheap. The tape can be wiped off, not the memory. What do I actually expect? Mostly I don't understand very much, because they're all talking at the same time, a babble of voices, I smoke as I listen. I'm surprised that you can understand each other. Laughter! I don't see what about. Laughter upon laughter! There is nothing in the text that could have caused you so much amusement. Equally incomprehensible is a sudden silence. Suddenly it is as if the tape had torn. But it's running. Deathly silence. I've no idea what is going on now. Still deathly silence. Have you noticed that there's a machine hidden in the room, an ear, a memory? Now a voice, in an undertone, a lady: the servant problem. I smoke, waiting for the deep voice of Dolf, for his humour that doesn't come, and gradually I get disappointed; I might just as well be sitting there myself. And Lila? Lila alone sounds different, so that I hold my breath. But she too says nothing that I couldn't perfectly well

254

hear, and avoids the same names as when I am present. All the same: she sounds different. Freer. She laughs differently and more when someone is witty, louder. Is she afraid, when I'm there, that I might think she is laughing at me? She is more irresistible, I believe, when I'm not in the room. More girlish. But that's understandable. Then she sounds as she did in the old days, when I first got to know her, that was a long time ago. Just the same; and yet the tape I am listening to was made today. She dares to make jokes that would delight me too, and it happens that, although I am in the nasty position of an eavesdropper, I can't help laughing. Once, when I am scarcely listening, my name crops up. Shall I turn it off? Too late: someone has already praised me. What for, I didn't catch. I could turn the machine back in order to hear, but I don't. Perhaps you praised my cellar, since a conversation about wine follows now, Lila asks casually where I've gone. At this my pipe goes out. The tape is now played half through. You take your time, it seems, you wait till my spool is at an end before really talking, without masks. Now you're looking for the corkscrew, I hear, and can't help. The corkscrew was in the kitchen. Dolf thinks it's a pity I don't go into politics, a great pity. Why? His assertion that he had advised me to do so isn't true at all, at least I can't remember it, nor can I remember the brilliant (very successful on the tape) aperçu I am supposed to have made about social democracy today. Why does he deck me out in his own feathers? After this he lapses into silence, as though the author of his brilliant aperçu might come into the room at any moment, and Lila has meanwhile gone into the kitchen to fetch the corkscrew. I can hear that she isn't in the room now. I hear it like a blind man; she isn't silent, like all the others, she's not there. Our guests are on their own. Perhaps I hear it from the slight alteration in the tone. You are now talking about a Fellini film, all of you, it sounds gayer than before, livelier, at the same time constrained, since you are now on your own, free from the duty to talk about the supposed interests of the hosts, a babble of voices, it's as though up to now you weren't allowed to talk about Fellini. To avoid the risk of gossiping about your hosts you fight

255

shy of any silence. Someone calls out: Lila, what are you doing? and like an echo of the same voice: What is she doing? It's a good thing everyone has seen this Fellini film, a good thing above all that you disagree with one another. The Catholic element in Fellini –

End of the reel.

I relight my pipe.

That was all.

Betrayal (if one wants to call it that) has not taken place, I wipe out the spool, which has taught me only one thing: I am hankering after betrayal. I should like to know that I exist. That which does not betray me is subject to the suspicion that it exists only in my imagination, and I should like to come out from my imagination, I should like to be in the world. I should like to be betrayed in my innermost being. What's odd. (Reading the story of Jesus I often had the feeling that when Jesus spoke of betrayal at the Last Supper he was not only concerned to shame the traitor, but was also ordering one of his disciples to betray him in order that he should be in the world, in order to bear witness to his reality in the world. . .)

So I smoke my pipe.

Reassured?

The tape recorder proves a failure. It is true that I hear your conversations, but I do not see the betrayal, which must lie in your expressions, and even if I filmed your expressions in my absence, the film too would be a complete failure. Treachery is something very subtle, apparently, it can't be either seen or heard, unless magnified by madness.

P.S.

Jealousy as an example of this, jealousy as real pain that a being who fills us completely is at the same time outside. A dream-terror in broad daylight. Jealousy has far less to do with the love of the sexes than appears; it is the chasm between the world and madness, jealousy in the narrower sense is only a footnote to this, a shock: the world is identical with my partner, not with me, love has merely made me one with my madness.

Let my name be Gantenbein!
(But finally.)

I imagine:
Gantenbein as a blind witness before the assize court, armed with his glasses and his little black stick and his yellow armband, which he wears for all public appearances, otherwise not all the time, but as a voter at the Sunday ballotbox or at the register office or before the court, naturally; Gantenbein in the ante-room alone, his stick between his knees, as though he needed something to hold on to. What do they want to know from him?

The case, which for weeks has occupied columns in all the newspapers, is known to every reader and therefore also to Gantenbein; to begin with it was only a headline on the placard that the paper sellers carry on their stomachs, *Murder in Seefeld*, shouted out and immediately read in all the trams and then forgotten, while the Criminal Investigation Department got bogged down in investigations that went on for months and got nowhere, later a sensation when a well-known personality in public life was arrested, a scandal that stirred emotions and finally, unfolded before the jury, is threatening to become a political scandal –

"Herr Gantenbein," says a voice, "there's no hurry, but start getting ready."

What am I going to tell the court?

"Don't get up yet," says the voice. "I shall lead you when it's time."

It is the morning of the last day of the examination of witnesses; I don't know whether it is the prosecution or the defence that has called Gantenbein; I only know that the verdict which the jury have to reach has already been reached by the public at large, and as far as Gantenbein is concerned I know that he, like every witness, has one single interest: to maintain his rôle – hence the closed eyes . . . Outside, the eleven o'clock chimes, and when they have ceased, once again the cooing of the pigeons, their cosy cooing, their stupid cooing.

257

I know only one thing.

If Gantenbein, as a witness, were to tell the truth and Lila were to learn from the newspaper that I am not blind, Lila and all my friends –

"Here's water."

Evidently they have seen that I am sweating, but naturally I don't reach for the jug and the glass, I merely hear the court-attendant filling it; I seem not to be the first who, called solely as a witness, feels like a defendant.

"Herr Gantenbein," says the voice, "if I may ask you –"

I stand up.

"– but there's no hurry."

With closed eyes, in order not to mar my rôle in front of the court, with eyes already closed now, because I don't want under any circumstances to see the accused again, I stand, supported by my little black stick, at the disposition of the court, I merely have to be led. I feel the powerful hand on my elbow, the friendly hand that will not let go of me till I, Gantenbein, Theo, am standing or sitting in the witness box.

"Take it easy," I hear, "take it easy."

I hear my footsteps in the corridor.

"Careful," I hear. "There are steps here –"

I lift my foot.

"– three steps."

So that means right, left, right.

"That's it," I hear, as the hand leaves my elbow. "Wait here!"

I hear a door being opened; a soundless door; I suddenly hear a room.

"This way, please."

Once again held by the elbow and led, so that I really don't need to open my eyes, I tap my way along with my little stick in the spacious silence that is disturbed only by my tapping, a silence full of tension.

"Here," I hear. "Please sit down."

I feel for the bench and there it is, I sit down, now abandoned by the hand. Don't open your eyes now! I hear paper, it must be a big, high, bare room, a room with closed windows, no cooing of pigeons, a room full of breathing people; the accused must be among them. Does he recognize me? What I hear more than anything, or feel as though I hear it, is the pulse in my throat. Otherwise nothing happens for the moment. Every now and then someone clears his throat far behind me, in front of me whispering, then the rustle of paper again; all in all, however, silence. I know what I should see if I opened my eyes: a prisoner at the bar between two gendarmes, behind and above him the President of the Court, somewhere a public prosecutor in a gown, perhaps it's he who is still rustling papers, and a lawyer with pince-nez, also wearing a gown, the defence counsel, who is just leaning forward to pass a note down to the accused. Further, the jury, who must reach their verdict today, a row of strained faces of very different origins. And high up, in all probability, a classicist representation of Justice blindfold and holding a pair of scales. . . Now somebody is reading out the particulars of Gantenbein, which I have to confirm, then the admonition to me to speak the truth and nothing but the truth, I hear the echo of my oath, then coughing, paper, the cooing on the wooden benches, steps towards me, a voice:

"Herr Gantenbein, did you know Camilla Huber?" I hear. "And for how long?"

I nod.

"For how long?"

I think it over.

"Did you ever have the impression –?"

"I should like to point out," interrupted another voice, "that the witness is blind, that in consequence there is no point, gentlemen, in asking questions that a blind man cannot answer under oath, in particular the question –"

A bell.

"I protest against –"

A bell.

"Gentlemen –"

A confusion of voices, everyone seems to be overstrained; I wait till the President of the Court has an opportunity to speak again, of which, however, he does not make use but passes it on as silence, as a moment without echoes so to speak, to a voice on the right that I have not heard yet.

"Did you know the murdered woman?"

I open my eyes, but I don't see her.

"What was your relationship to her?"

"Manicure."

Laughter in the jury-box.

"That's true," I say.

They don't believe me.

"Did you visit Huber frequently?"

"Camilla Huber?"

"Yes."

"Regularly."

"For the purpose of manicure –"

Naturally I am relieved to see that they evidently don't want to know the truth, which as a witness I have sworn to tell.

President of the Court:

"To keep to the point –"

"I should like once again and with all possible emphasis to point out," says the other voice loudly in the courtroom, "that the witness is blind, that is to say he can never have seen the murdered woman."

Interruption:

"That's not the point!"

A bell.

"A blind man is not a witness!"

It is, as I have said, a case that stirs the emotions. Only the jury sit with rigid faces, so does the accused, but unlike the jury he is scarcely listening; his life is done for one way or the other.

What I know from the newspaper:

Strangulation with a curtain cord. Suicide unlikely. The murdered woman is portrayed as having led a gay life. Murder for robbery or murder as sexual violence. Her trade ("call-girl") and her previous history; the daughter of a middle-class family. Suspicion falls upon a man who gave her a Karmann car. There is a good deal of additional evidence, but this is contested; no alibi. Her correspondence with the accused. Her marriage advertisements. The murder took place on the eve of her wedding to a dentist –

Defence counsel:

"To come to the point," he asks, "you never heard Camilla Huber mention the name of the accused?"

Public prosecutor:

"Did you ever hear her speak, without mentioning any name, of a client who had been threatening Huber for years by letter with his jealousy?"

So that's what they want to know from me, and I don't know why I don't simply shake my head, but say:

"What do you understand by jealousy?"

Flashlight in the courtroom.

"Answer my question –"

Uncertain whether people didn't notice that Gantenbein too winced at the flashlight, I give my answer: No! But my fright at the flashlight has taken all credibility from my statement, I can feel that.

I see the accused:

A gentleman whom I have often seen, rather a personality, a cultured man, which doesn't mean that I don't credit him with the deed; I know the jealousy that no amount of culture can withstand. On the contrary, culture only dams it up, till it becomes utterly primitive. That's terrible, yes, perhaps I understand him. Rather a personality; now he is a ruin, faultlessly dressed and well kempt, silent with a twitch round the corner of his mouth when people talk about a curtain cord (as in a thriller). His nervous breakdowns, noted reproachfully in the newspaper reports, do not speak in his favour. Why doesn't he confess? And one can see that at times he suffers from severe remorse; then he puts his hand to his forehead, the posture of a man who no longer understands himself. The mere disclosure that this man had for years been carrying on a correspondence with a call-girl has done for him, although these letters, read out in the courtroom and quoted in the Press, are really very beautiful, actually something out of the ordinary; even in print they don't look ridiculous, testimonies to a passion about which there was something murderous, perhaps; this violence was not expressed in crude threats, however, but in a tender craving to discover who it was he loved. These letters form the basis of the defence, spirited as they are in their tireless courtship, and touching. How could a personality like this, the defence counsel has been saying for weeks and will repeat in his closing speech, have recourse to a curtain cord? But no one falls for this. What incriminates the accused more than anything is not the sum total of the evidence, not the conflicting opinions of experts regarding the finger-prints, not the business with the lift key, not even the fact that he is unable to provide a sound alibi for the quarter of an hour during which screams were heard in her flat, but the involuntary twitching of the corner of his mouth, his nervous breakdowns, above all the subtle feeling of guilt expressed in advance in his letters, the irony of his letters towards himself and towards everything that must surely be sacred to a public figure. A lost man, publicly lost, a man who takes the force out of his defence counsel's speeches by considering them too simple; you can see this by looking at him, even if he says nothing. And when he speaks, which happens less and less often, he is helpless, as though hampered by an experience which others can only acquire from action, not from listening to him. Well known as a brilliant speaker in Parliament, of which he is a member, the accused drew particular suspicion upon himself by the fact that several times, when pressed by the public prosecutor, who incidentally is a member of the same political party, he is said to have started to stammer, positively to stammer. He can't find the words in which to express complete innocence. It wasn't like that! Anyone can say that. But how was it? For weeks he has been saying that he didn't do it, he didn't do it, but as though he didn't consider it impossible that he could have done it. To begin with, as I have said, it was a scandal that suspicion had fallen upon this man at all

No one would have credited him with carrying on such a correspondence. Whereas during the first few sittings, although incriminated by damning evidence, he in no way tallied with the idea one has of the murderer of a tart, he succeeded (by means of his personality) in changing people's ideas on this subject, so that there is really no doubt now about the verdict. . .

President of the Court:

"This brings to an end the hearing of the witnesses. The court will meet again this afternoon at two o'clock," he says, his voice trailing off, "for the closing speeches of the prosecution and the defence."

I'm free —

The question, the only one I was afraid of, has not been asked, the question whether on the night in question and at the time in question (12.35 – 12.50) Gantenbein had seen the accused, either in the bar referred to or in the street. I don't know the bar referred to, according to the description a drearily dubious spot long familiar to the police, and Gantenbein could have replied on these lines and then left it at that. But naturally this question would never be asked in the face of his yellow armband. Other witnesses, who were in the bar, can't remember for sure; some of them, who thought at the beginning that they remembered, later grew unsure, when their mode of life had made them appear unworthy of credence. And now, at the end of the hearing of witnesses, to ask a blind man would have been a bad joke. No one contests the fact that the accused's car stood in the Feldeggstrasse; misled by this into seeking his alibi in this bar, the accused himself doesn't seem to be able to remember any more where he really was at the time in question. After the defence, once having been guided by his false memory, has for weeks been pinning its faith on this bar, no other alibi was likely to sound convincing, particularly not an alibi provided by Gantenbein with his yellow armband. We have often seen each other, when I went for my manicure, once in the lift, but since he couldn't know that Gantenbein saw him, we never greeted each other, which is a pity; otherwise that night between twelve and one,

263

when I was taking my Patsch for a walk along the Uto Quay and saw him feeding swans, we might have struck up an alibi conversation, which he could have remembered and which Gantenbein could without difficulty have substantiated, without thereby having to sacrifice his rôle as a blind man.

President of the Court:

"The sitting is closed."

A babble of voices.

Before I close my eyes, I once more see the accused, the twitch round the corner of his mouth, as though he had known for a long time what is really going on: the ruling class of a country, guilty of many things that cannot be confessed without thereby bringing its rule to an end, cannot afford to have one of its members, who has been leading a shameful life and is suspected of a crime, but a purely personal one, acquitted for lack of evidence in full view of the people; it might look as though everyone were not equal in the eyes of the law, and a vague suspicion would remain which would incriminate the ruling class itself; such a man cannot be preserved; the ruling class of a country must at least be represented at its summit by personalities whose private respectability covers up everything else; otherwise dictatorship would be the only way of ruling.

"Herr Gantenbein –"

I close my eyes.

"There are steps here," says the court-attendant, taking the blind witness's elbow, and when we are out in the street he asks: "Will you be able to find your way?"

I thank him.

"Here's the kerb."

I tap.

Every rôle has its guilt. . .

I am waiting intently for the verdict. . .

The only certainty about Lila: she doesn't exist in the way I imagine her; one day, perhaps, I too shall be able to see her, Lila from outside –

Once again I am standing on board a ship during the last minutes before it puts out into the open sea, cheerful in spite of the grey weather, filling a pipe, actually I don't know of any other gesture for these moments of excited satisfaction, one can't start singing or dancing in the middle of the people on deck; nor do I want to ask myself why I feel in such good spirits on board a white ship before departure, alone not only on board but also alone in the port, filling a pipe that has no wish to be lit, idle, while men are trying laboriously to cast off the long, heavy hawsers from the iron cleats on the mole, for my part idly contemplating idle days to come aboard this ship that has now raised its gangplank, my pipe in my mouth, without smoking, my hands in my trouser pockets. Why I feel in such good spirits: I have no one to wave to, I am waiting for the dull hooting that goes through the marrow of one's bones, the second, hoarser hooting; once already the ship has hooted through the marrow of my bones. I am thinking of no one, resting my elbows on the railing watching tugs beneath smoke like dogs on a lead, Naples behind a haze. Later I stroll across to the other side to see people, crowds of people who are staying ashore and waving, families, friends, fiancées, a little old woman sobbing. I can't see Vesuvius. A grey day, heavy, yet windy. And now the heavy hawser splashes into the dark water of the harbour, hoots reverberate and break in pieces among huts and customs houses, the waving increases, handkerchiefs like a bed of narcissi; beside me a lady who isn't waving either, while the fissure between the mole and the ship slowly widens; the feeling as I watch that it is the mole that is swinging out, not our ship; the tugs are sending out clouds of smoke and making themselves important with a great deal of spray. I can't see her face (what do I care about it!) because of the flapping headscarf. She is simply standing there, her hands in her jacket; she too has no one to wave to. We are slowly starting to move, I see, still without ripples. A few people on board are still waving, but their faces are already changing as they wave; they no longer see exactly who they are waving to and their feelings revolve round the present, which at first is simply empty, openly, easily, somewhat bewilderingly empty. Now the black tugs have hooted too, they unhitch the brown hawsers, drop them in the water and turn away, and now we are travelling under our own power, slowly but punctually. The last mole, black with seaweed and whitened by gulls, glides past with a lighthouse; spray flies up from the breakwaters, then we are free – for seven days – our train of waves, always the same, is lost in morning and afternoon and evening. . .

I am sitting on deck.

Boredom with my eyes on the sea, a blissful boredom: not to be dead and not to have to live. . .

I try to read.

Has anyone ever been able to work on board ship?

An idle stroll to the bar –

I'm feeling in good spirits, as I have said, not in very good spirits but with a pleasant indifference; I don't try to get into conversation, no so-called encounter; it's merely that as I strolled into the bar I recognized the blue headscarf, took note of her face – a good face, perhaps in her early thirties, but worried, shy, a face that looks round at the people on board but doesn't want to be seen itself. I'm not going to speak to her, she's mistaken, we have merely recognized each other, two people who didn't wave in Naples. And I stay in the bar and read my paperback.

The sea is blue, drably smooth.

I look round:

A lot of Italians and some Americans –

I read on.

She is sitting at the bar with her back to me. Without a headscarf now; blonde, as Italian women can be blonde, with dark eyes. I see her face, which she veils with cigarette smoke, in a mirror. Beautiful. She knows it and tries not to be noticed; but she attracts attention because, no matter how motionless and bored she acts, she is on edge. Like a person in flight. She has (I could imagine) reached some decision in a mood of despair, the mood has gone, not the despair, the decision has to be carried out for reasons of self-esteem; she drinks –

First lunch:
I find myself at a table with a young couple, everyone rather stiff, the fourth chair at our round table remains empty –
The weather is getting better.
Afternoon on deck.

Palermo:
We are just sitting at dinner, the young couple and I, and I am letting myself be informed about economic prospects in Canada and nodding, when, guided by the steward, the lady with the blue headscarf sits down at our table, now in a black evening dress and naturally without a headscarf. She is disappointed, it seems, about the table-lot she has drawn; we can't help it. She is wearing a pearl necklace of the sort I have in the past given as a present, her hair now on top of her head, and with all this a pair of sunglasses so that one cannot read in her eyes. Her hand (I see it as she holds the big menu) is wearing a wedding ring. In order not to go on looking, I act as though my fish were full of bones. Her Italian with the waiter: excellent, but not her mother tongue. Her hair (I see it as I turn round to beckon the wine waiter) is not blond, but perhaps that is the effect of the lighting in this room. Outside, Palermo in the dusk, we are still lying at anchor. My eyes on my fish, working like a surgeon, I don't even look up as the wine waiter shows me the label, entirely occupied with bones that are not to be found, I see only her hand that is breaking and crumbling grissini, and her elbow; her age. Then the young couple talk to each other. Thank God; somebody has to talk. And after the waiter has taken away my plate, I look straight ahead. She must be beautiful; I read it from the faces at the next table. Do we mind if she smokes already, she asks, and then I chat again with the young couple whose future is so assured. She eats almost nothing. She leaves us before the dessert, whereupon we nod again, but she forgets her handbag; the young husband gives it to her, a gentleman. Her teeth when she smiles, the nape of her neck, her walk across the room – peeling an apple, I follow her with my eyes. . .
That's how Lila might be.

(Lila from outside.)

As she enters, the men in the bar make themselves slim so that she can pass almost without bodily contact, and since all the red stools are occupied I rise. Without speaking to her. And she sits down without nodding. I understand her contempt for men and go on deck to view the night. . .

Gibraltar:

We anchor in the bay for hours with a view of the well-known rock, encircled by a mass of swaying boats, hawkers offer Moroccan carpets, shout, throw up ropes and all you have to do is to pull and then put your dollars in the basket, wind, but everyone is on deck, so are we, the lady with the blue headscarf and I, hands in my trouser pockets, I don't even know how we got into conversation – without beating about the bush, I believe, without such questions as: Is this the first time you've crossed the Atlantic? . . . Lila (assuming that it is Lila) doesn't buy any mementoes either, but merely watches the trading, her hands in the pockets of her suède jacket; she is gay, it seems, as light as a gull.

"Yes," I say, "no one else will be coming aboard now."

We are talking German.

"These gulls," I say. "I should like to know if they are still the same ones that have been circling round us since Naples."

She seems to have other worries.

"The young man at our table," I say, in order to stop the conversation from drying up, "claims that the same gulls will keep us company all the way to America." Pause, because I can't think of anything else to say about the gulls, and I knock out my pipe –

So much for our conversation!

With my feet resting on the trembling rail, the Atlantic between my shoes, I am sitting in my deck-chair again; I can't even read a paperback in this wake of blue idleness that stretches for hours – and I don't want to go to the bar now, because she is probably in the bar. . .

We have nothing to say to each other.

Unfortunately she doesn't play chess.

268

As soon as I imagine this woman is Lila, or even merely ask myself whether Lila might look like this woman, a strange thing happens: I have no idea who she is, and I know that I have no idea, and nevertheless I begin to interpret what she keeps to herself –

A lovable woman.

I'm certain:

A woman with such a face doesn't smash whisky glasses, but does what Svoboda, when the situation is reversed, can't do: she makes things easy for him, and since she doesn't show it when she has been weeping all night he doesn't even know to whom he owes his happiness. She isn't offended like a man. And she doesn't gossip around; no one seeing her during months like this would guess anything. Was a man ever capable of such a thing? She fulfils what the other woman leaves to her, the demands of every-day married life, becomes a bit ugly; but this too makes things easy for him. She doesn't reckon with the disintegration of all love; she believes in miracles; she doesn't threaten that he will lose her; she practises playing the minor rôle. Her magnanimity is not blackmail. She respects him. She doesn't sit in judgment on the other woman simply because he loves her. And she doesn't start digging around for causes, doesn't talk things to pieces. She doesn't strangle his gaiety, when he has the courage to be gay, and when he tells her about his work she listens as though they were talking about the thing that really matters. She makes it possible for him to be kind; only she doesn't show herself in the bath, not naked. She knows that there is another woman and doesn't want to know what doesn't concern her in detail; she finds combs that don't belong to her and gets rid of them without a word. They appear in public à trois. She isn't miserly. She talks to the other woman as to a more fortunate sister whom she admires –

A magnificent woman.

Doesn't Svoboda know that?

The way he puts it:

The natural difference between man and woman, which no equality of rights can do away with, lies in the fact that it is always

the man who acts during lovemaking. He remains himself, and the
woman knows that; she knows him. She doesn't want to know
what she can guess anyway. On the other hand, the man doesn't
know at all what a woman, when she goes away, is like in the
embrace of another man; he can't guess at all. The woman is
monstrous in her almost limitless adaptability, and when she comes
from another man she is not the same; this, when it continues for
some time, goes so far as to involve her intellectual interests and
her opinions and her judgments. Because the woman, when she
goes away, goes further away than the man, she has to dissemble
when she comes back, even when they are discussing the most
everyday topics; therefore he wants to know things that don't
concern him; the woman of taste will never reveal these things to
him, whereas the man, when the situation is reversed, so much likes
boring her by telling her things. As though he could ever be very
different when making love! This is the basis of the magnanimity
of the clever woman, her unbearable magnanimity that reminds us
of our limitations.

Thus Svoboda.

"Look," I say, "we've already got to here!" I show her the little
red flags that are stuck into the big chart of the Atlantic every
morning, our position in the blue void with meridians. "We're
making headway."

"Is it Thursday already today?"

"Yes," I say.

"Yes," says the young man who swears by Canada, "it's a pity,
we'll be there the day after tomorrow."

I leave the two of them alone.

In my deck chair, my feet resting on the ever-trembling rail, I
am just reading through my sunglasses a paperback that she would
like, the story of a man without atavism; I have just come to the
chapter in which this man, who loves a woman and has been informed
in two hundred and thirty pages that she has spent the night
with another man, serves breakfast, a breakfast à trois, appetizing
not only in respect of the food and drink, there is ham and eggs,

I read, all sorts of cheese, black bread, fruit, all very appetizingly described, but appetizing also as regards the conversation *à trois,* witty without any compulsive need to argue things out, without secrecy, without reference to the situation, which thus appears quite natural – and I'm eager to see what happens next. . .

Unfortunately the sea is very rough.

Last lunch but one:

our young couple have less to say to each other every day, above all the young man seems no longer to be reckoning with his young wife, whom he is transplanting to Canada, having any-thing to say –

Afternoon:

I read what happens next in my paperback, skipping a few pages every now and then, impatient, I don't know for what, I look to see if the gulls are still keeping us company, the same ones, I'm a bad reader: my thoughts like gulls behind a moving ship, suddenly they curve down and out onto the open sea, but come back again, fly on ahead, always the same ones, remain behind as my thoughts remain behind the story that ploughs on tirelessly full steam ahead.

Once, I see, they play ping-pong.

It seems there is still no paint that stands up to sea air; three sailors have been painting the ever-trembling rail from Naples to New York and then back again, everything white seems to have smallpox, incurably, the cranes and the winches and the ladders, the whistling ventilation tubes, everything white is as if scarred, they paint over the scars, but again and again yellowish and brown leaves of rust begin to reappear. . .

Last evening but one:

they are dancing, the lady who could be Lila and the young engineer. Her face over his shoulder – which I try in vain to describe: a lowering of her eyelids is enough, a change in her gaze as she focuses on something near or far away, a hand that strokes her hair back behind her ear in profile, and then again her laughter seen full-face, a change of light, a twist, a change from laughter to silence, a wrinkling of the forehead is enough to make all the adjectives I have collected simply fall down from her face. . .

I go to bed.

Last afternoon:

have finished my paperback and otherwise have done nothing during these long short days; hardly a conversation; with no ideas regarding myself, without a story, without plans; I observe that for half a day on end I think of no one, not even of myself, and I enjoy sitting there with my feet resting on the trembling rail, now without reading but awake, I just see the young wife who is looking for her engineer husband; have I seen him, yes, in the swimming pool, but he isn't there any more; I don't suppose the two of them have fallen overboard, perhaps they're looking at the engine-room, since he is an engineer, a ship is a maze –

Last evening:

she doesn't come to the table.

I converse at great length (really in order not to emphasize the absence of our table companion by silence, and because the engineer's young wife stares ahead of her in silence as if turned to stone), at greater length than my interest goes, with the young engineer, who did not go overboard, about the ever-trembling rail, the problem of vibration which, as I have already guessed, has still not been solved –

Midnight on deck, stars, wind.

I converse with an American clergyman from stern to bow and bow to stern and walk along beside his black flapping overcoat, nod, as the two of them feel themselves discovered on deck –

Last morning:

a pilot comes aboard, loudspeakers ask all the passengers in three languages and so on, unrest in the corridor, the ship is seething like a disturbed ant hill, passengers in overcoats, cases piled up, crew, the bed-clothes are stripped off, tips distributed, USA officers are suddenly sitting in the lounge and checking passports with an irritable matter-of-factness, more than merely passports, even X-ray photographs, inoculation certificates in my case, this takes time, all passengers are asked for the last time, bundles of blankets in the corridor. . . I think: I hope her cases and bags are packed! – perhaps she is sitting in her cabin combing her hair, before tying the blue headscarf round it again. (What does it matter to me as I stand in the queue, passport and inoculation certificate in my hand, glad that this time I don't have to bother about anyone). . .

She could be Lila.

I never saw her again.

Lila from outside:

her face in the mirror as she combs out her hair with her head on one side, and when she adjusts the mirror the nape of her neck and her naked ear, now as she holds it up her loose hair, then she lets it fall, her loose hair, too much like a waterfall, she shakes it behind her shoulders, hears the loudspeaker out in the corridor and runs the fingers of both hands over her cheekbones and temples, then under her dry hair behind her warm ears, cream on her fingers, she feels her feeling skin, the cheeks soft and yielding, then the chin, then again up to her temples, where it is hard, then her stiff-tender nose with its ridge, her nostrils, creaming, while outside above the nearby water she sees in the distance the coast – Fire Island probably – and then again her face in the mirror, she stops: you can't look into both your eyes at the same time: stops in front of her eyes that don't remain behind the glass, everything else remains behind the glass, her forehead and her pale lips and the lashes she is brushing, this takes time, the skin below her eyes shimmers transparent like tissue paper, gleaming, friable, bluish-brown like damp autumn leaves, she powders her face, that takes time, then she combs her hair, the shore comes closer as she combs her hair, a hair-grip between her teeth, a low shore with gliding trees and huts, every now and then a buoy, the combing takes time too, the loudspeakers in the corridor have stopped asking, she takes the hair-grip out of her mouth and paints her lips, which she protrudes above the mother-of-pearl whiteness of her teeth, her soft and full and gently powerful lips, which she tenses, she pouts them or presses them close together to paint the line, the

273

fine line between outside skin and inside skin, mouth, she bends forward towards the mirror to see better, mouth, damp like the flesh of an apricot that has been broken open, then she rolls her lips against each other to distribute the colour better, and screws up the lipstick, a look at her mouth in the mirror, she leaves it open but mute, it's time, the rattle of anchor chains, time for the blue headscarf, in case it's windy outside, the ship doesn't seem to be gliding along any more, she doesn't forget anything, since she is alone, and looks round, her body in the mirror: the way a man sees it, her body from outside, she doesn't think of him as she puts the blue headscarf round her combed hair, her body has already forgotten him, she ties the blue headscarf under her chin, ready to be received in a quarter of an hour on the pier with unsuspecting hands and eyes and kisses –

Is it like that?

The one who sees it like that is Svoboda.

I stand by the rail, hands in my trouser pockets, while the hawsers are thrown out, more or less the last on deck, everyone is thronging to the gangplank, arrival fever, it is a cool morning, skyline in the haze.

Am I Svoboda?

There is no end to Gantenbein's trials:

– I am shuffling around in water, alone in the flat, water that reflects, that splashes, little waves at every step, that gurgles, water all the way along our long corridor, I can hear it, and it's no use playing blind, it splashes and gurgles wherever I go in the living-room too, water from room to room, reflecting the brightness of the windows, lukewarm. . . It's not the first time that Lila, in a hurry because she is late, has forgotten to turn off the shower; but for the first time Gantenbein hasn't noticed in time. . . So I shuffle round in the water, while Lila is on the stage. I understand: she was thinking of her lines. I keep my fingers crossed for her. Or better: I turn off the shower. Gantenbein has often done this. Without ever saying a word. But this time Gantenbein has come too late.

274

This time Lila will notice who turned off the shower for her, and I shall give myself away. What am I to do? In my coat and hat, alone, I stand helpless in the watered flat. That comes of Gantenbein, in order to maintain his rôle, never saying a word. Or shall I let the shower go on spraying, sit down in the rocking-chair with my feet on the little table to make it look credible that Gantenbein, blind as he is, didn't notice the flood? A costly solution; the parquet will swell. It will be midnight before Lila comes home and the tenants of the flat below will complain. Or should Gantenbein simply go out? The water can't rise higher than the threshold of the balcony. It seems to me there is no other solution than to turn the shower on again and hang it in such a way that it rains half over the edge of the bath, and to go out. What prevents me from carrying out this plan is its pedagogic element. And, already ready to go out, I see the moody tongues of water slowly but surely approaching the books and gramophone records, which certainly ought not to be on the floor, but that's where they are, and I can't bring myself to let it reach them: I save the books and records, her satin shoes, the curtains that have already started osmosis. How can a blind man act like that? That he turned off the shower can be explained: even Gantenbein can feel when his feet get wet and hear where the water is running. But saving the books and records? So now I stand here, after bringing the books and records to safety, barefoot, in the knowledge that I shall also have to get rid of the water so that it doesn't give me away, and at once, so that the floors are really dry by the time Lila comes home. Swearing doesn't help, it can only be done with a bath towel, which I lay on the floor carefully, so as not to cause waves and thus extend the Flood, and allow it to saturate itself with water and then wring it out in the bath, each time half a pint, no more, and go on like this to and fro, barefoot, there and back and there again, at first without seeing any effects, it still reflects and gurgles. In an hour and a half it's done. I smoke my first cigarette, look at my watch: now Lila is in the third act. I cross my fingers. But what about the carpets? In my panic I never thought of them, of the soaking wet carpets, I sweat helplessly. I can't avoid dealing with them, even if only out of anger with Gantenbein, so I kneel down and roll the carpets till I get cramp in my hands, and squeeze them. And Patsch thinks it's fun; I only see the murky water that I squeeze out of the carpets, and not his paw marks all over the flat, not yet. After another hour the carpets don't produce any more water. Of course they aren't dry yet, but I leave the rest to the draught; I open all the windows there are. Then a glass of beer. Another hour till midnight! Then in the rocking-chair, rather exhausted, I ask myself whether I have really done the right thing. But I don't get a chance to think; now I see the dirty paw marks that Patsch has meanwhile made all over the flat, and this calls for a second round with the bath towel, then the bath has to be cleaned. Fortunately Lila doesn't come home when she said she would, and there is time for the carpets to dry; no doubt she has met somebody who rightly admires her, and this may take till three o'clock, I hope. Now it is midnight; I put my hand on the carpets. I can only hope that they go on to Siebenhagen's; then it will be four o'clock. The carpets won't be dry, but I shall immediately take Lila on my lap, so that her feet shan't touch the floor. She will ask me what I've been doing all evening.

"Oh," I shall say, "– working."

She'll be pleased.

I shall smile.

But next morning (this only occurs to me now!) the parquet floor: grey, pale, patchy, and I don't know how Gantenbein is going to explain it. . . Once again I am at a loss what to do. The floor will give me away. Nothing is any use. There's only one thing to do: – I put on my tie again, first a clean shirt, then my tie, then I turn on the shower, leaving it in such a way that it rains out over the bath, I put the books and records down again, after the flood has begun, then I take my jacket and the little black stick and go out.

What happens?

Lila can't believe that she forgot to turn off the shower, in spite of the flood. It must have been me. Nothing like that

276

has ever happened to her with the shower. Gantenbein can't contradict.

Is Gantenbein a fool?

Gantenbein as a father:
When the ward sister leads him to the white cot she cannot see, on the one hand, why the blind man wants this, but on the other she finds it poignant that a father will never be able to recognize his child, never, and when, on the strict condition that he won't touch or actually kiss the baby, she finally raises the curtain which is white like the cot, Gantenbein has no need to dissemble: he really doesn't see anything unique. A great moment, undoubtedly, but not for the eyes. A historical moment. What he sees: a baby. What the ward sister tells him about it, Gantenbein cannot see. A baby like a thousand others. As expected; he didn't expect anything else. He says nothing; Gantenbein has no need to dissemble; this is a good first meeting. He is glad Lila has survived it. Her screams were horrible. Now she lies there, pale with her hair sticking to her forehead, but smiling, and Gantenbein holds her damp hand.
Let's say it's a girl.
Later, alone in the street with his little black stick that he makes tap, and accompanied by Patsch, who knows nothing about the great event, then in a public park, where he sits down, he feels the first paternal worry: that when they wash and weigh and swaddle the baby they might mix it up with another baby. He himself, as we know, wouldn't be able to see it. Seized with disquiet, he goes back to the hospital. To see the baby. He refuses to be put off, no matter what the regulations are, he must see the baby, and strange as this desire seems, when he is wearing a blind man's yellow armband, he can't be talked out of it. Lila is asleep. And they have to walk on tiptoe. And the ward sister, when she sees Herr Gantenbein, a blind father, stand for at least ten minutes beside the white cot, is really moved. Naturally he doesn't ask if this is really his child; the question would be misunderstood. In the corridor outside,

which is positively seething with babies, the ward sister takes him by the elbow; he feels really blind. As never before. His worry has by no means been dissipated when Gantenbein is walking in the street again, led by Patsch, and shortly afterwards stands in a bar to knock back a kirsch. To come to his senses. And sense consists in simply believing; in now going into a printer's, not without first removing his dark glasses and his yellow armband; because the lettering, the typography are not matters of indifference to him, and he wants to see the examples clearly before he has the happy announcement printed:

BEATRICE

A beautiful name. . .

Beatrice Gantenbein, as it will be later, sounds less beautiful, but that can't be altered, there's no choice; you have a father and that's the end of it, whatever his name is.

I imagine:

Some, when they read the happy announcement, haven't the slightest doubt that the child is really Gantenbein's; others wonder, without talking about it, of course. After all, it's none of their business. They admire Lila, they like Gantenbein, they congratulate both of them, there is no lack of flowers. They assure Gantenbein how like him she is. He can't see for himself. The very spit of her father! someone thinks, and Lila is pleased when the people beside the bassinet say this, for the sake of something to say; she thinks so too.

I imagine:

Gantenbein, when the time has come for him to go out with his little daughter, hand-in-hand, and one doesn't know who is actually leading whom, the main thing is that they shouldn't get run over by a lorry, the two of them, the child with the blind father and Gantenbein, who is leading Lila's child or letting himself be led by her, Gantenbein buys her an ice and shows her the clumsy bears in the zoo who beg with their forepaws and dance on their hind legs until you throw them the turnips. And Gantenbein, the blind man, is better at throwing the turnips (as a Daddy ought to be) –

278

I imagine:

His worry that the child might one day see through him and irrevocably give the game away to the adults, whom it suits the way it is, will grow as Beatrice grows –

How long does a child believe?

I once knew a child belonging to friends, who used to grab the grown-up's glasses and pull them off the moment you took it on your knee, a mania that nothing could touch, neither threats and even punishment, nor humour; the child, then four years old, scarcely spoke; in the middle of a jolly story, which it seemed to be listening to attentively, it would grab at the glasses and hang on to them, not because it wanted them, but simply for the sake of grabbing them.

I imagine:

Gantenbein, when he sees her drawings, and these child's drawings are of such exciting beauty that one can't help believing her a genius, but Gantenbein mustn't praise her, he has to hide his astonishment, asking what Beatrice has drawn, but she can't put it into words, she can only draw with crayons, and Gantenbein sees what it is: that's Daddy, the man with the armband, and everything has been drawn that he showed and told her about on their walk, everything in bright colours, the circus, the ship with the waterwheel, the witch, the flags and the flash of lightning in the violet-coloured sky and the umbrella that got blown inside out, and everything, the mountains, the drum that makes the thunder, the fat fireman with the hose on the ladder, Beatrice and Daddy with his yellow armband and the little stick with which he points, and everything and everything, and now he doesn't even recognize it.

It's going to be difficult.

Later her first lies –

Beatrice has been at the pantry, and he can see it on her chaste lips that deny it, and on her apron, jam, but Gantenbein can't prove her guilty, he can only say nothing and smile, Beatrice cries. It seems you can't take things from the pantry without Daddy knowing. How does he know? He knows everything. Or Beatrice has wedged the bread, which she doesn't like, under the table top and has been doing so for weeks, and Gantenbein hasn't noticed, but one morning all those dry crusts are lying on the table, and although her blind Daddy doesn't punish her even with words, because he can't see what's happened, she blushes none the less. Everything comes to light. You can't lie, God and Daddy are one – for a time . . . Then Beatrice notices that where Gantenbein doesn't go, for instance into the woods, where she does things with the boys, God doesn't go either.

You can lie.

Daddy doesn't know everything.

He doesn't even know what Herr Siebenhagen looks like, who sometimes plays tennis with Lila, and what colour his fine car is; he would like to know, but that is something God doesn't tell him – Gantenbein only sees it in her drawings: the white Mummy and the white ball over the net and Herr Siebenhagen, who evidently has a little black beard, has white legs and takes long steps. . .

I imagine:

Although Lila, now back at work again, understandably has very little time after her rehearsals and performances (not to mention her guest appearances), her love for the child is absolutely boundless, her understanding when Beatrice just does as she likes. What Gantenbein understands by education is to her an abomination that makes her fall silent with her eyes on the child. She is one with the child. And naturally it looks like a reprimand when Gantenbein, without reprimanding, demands of the child what her beautiful mother does not demand of herself. Suddenly it looks as though he were trying to educate Lila. How can the child be taught not to throw her little coat down on the floor (as if she had come home tired from a rehearsal like Lila)? Then it is Lila who, when this happens, picks up her coat and hangs it in its place. What more does Gantenbein want? Her patience towards the child is inexhaustible, and what comes of it? A child who gobbles up all the guests' salted almonds, a beautiful child, and after all the guests

280

didn't come for the sake of the salted almonds, Lila is right. Besides, guests always have a sense of humour. When things go too far, for example when little Beatrice, understandably, because she is bored by the grown-ups' conversation, crumbles up a guest's Havana cigar while he is fascinated by Lila, there is still time for blind Gantenbein to intervene:

"Stop that!"

Naturally the guest, since it is not his child, but only his cigar that is involved, has more sense of humour than Gantenbein; all the same, as he discovers, it was his last Havana, and he can't remember at once what they were talking about. Pause. Well, what were they talking about? Lila goes on strike, offended as a mother; hence the consoling look she gives the child, who, after all, is a child –

"Daddy isn't nice."

That will come.

"I want another Daddy."

This, on the other hand, Lila herself thinks is going too far, although the remark does more than anything to revive the guests' sense of humour. Now it is Lila who reprimands the child and even threatens punishment. Beatrice mustn't say that. That she wants another Daddy. This costs her the dessert. Over this point Lila is very strict. And Gantenbein peels his banana in silence – the child isn't really so wrong: perhaps this man blindly peeling his banana really isn't her father. . . But however that may be, they were talking about television, television as an instrument of the industry that moulds consciousness and in general about art in a technological age, particularly television, everyone has something to say on that subject, except for Gantenbein with his mouth full of banana.

I imagine:

In other respects everything is going fine with Lila and Gantenbein now that they have a child; they go for excursions and the child is a child, and Gantenbein and Lila take her by her little arms, so that she can swing to and fro, and Lila holds the full spoon and

281

tells the story of the haycart that wants to go into the barn, and
when she is tired Gantenbein takes her on his shoulders and gallops
along hoppity-hoppity-hop, and when this time is past there are
other games, once she has whooping cough, and it is the turn of
children's books, and they go bathing in summer and tobogganing
in winter, everything in its season, and Lila buys her little skirts
with taste, Gantenbein tells her the story of the Flood and the Ark,
they laugh over her childish sayings, and when Lila is on tour
she rings up to chat with Beatrice, and Beatrice sitting on a pony
is unforgettable, and the time for playing the recorder comes,
and so on, and Lila and Gantenbein don't need to talk to each
other all that much, the child is almost always there, and when
Beatrice wants to know where babies come from they tell her
more or less. . .

I imagine:

The anecdote of their first meeting in the dressing-room, Gantenbein as the enthusiastic blind man with roses, is almost true
to the facts, but not quite – no anecdote is. . . Lila was naturally not
living without a companion at that time, which, however, in no
way concerned Gantenbein. To this extent it is right for the anecdote, which Lila is always so glad to tell, not to mention him;
Gantenbein really didn't see this Lila-companion, who was sitting
in the dressing-room at the time. And yet this man was sitting
there (if not in the anecdote, at least in reality) the whole time,
not by her dressing-table it's true, but still visibly enough in the
one and only comfortable armchair, mute, leafing through a newspaper, his hat on his head, his legs spread out and quite sure
that he is present. That was how he sat there. Like a piece of
furniture. A man in his prime, once very much in love with Lila,
now at the stage of mature love, prepared to marry but not impatient, his hat on his head. And while Gantenbein performed his
very helpless rose number, which became convincing only when it
became an anecdote, he didn't even listen, this man with his hat
on his head, who seemed to know her need for blind homage.
He would have merely had to cough in order to scare the blind ad-

mirer. Without looking up from his paper, he later asked casually: Who was that queer fish? He said queer fish, which slightly offended Lila. After all, he was an enthusiastic admirer. Without a hat on his head. She remained silent. In Gantenbein's favour. He had really seen only Lila on that occasion. A clearer proof that he was blind he could not have feigned. . . Later, of course, he learnt that Lila wasn't living alone; but then it was too late to look round: there wasn't anyone sitting in her dressing-room any more. Only the armchair in which he was supposed to have sat was there. And now Gantenbein was sitting in it. And outside on the stage Lila was still playing the same part. To leaf through a newspaper till the applause burst outside was something Gantenbein couldn't allow himself to do, since Lila believed in his blindness; she loved him for his blindness. He saw the telegrams stuck round her mirror, good wishes, some of them yellow with age; he saw himself in the mirror: a man in love waiting for the roar of applause outside. It was like this every evening, till Lila suddenly came: a woman in disguise and with false hair, a doll in part, beautiful but painted for spotlights, beautiful at a distance, eyebrows blue and eyelids green and yellow cheeks, her face so coarsened, so coarsened by beautification, even her eyes were enlarged; secretly, Gantenbein started with dismay every time. As though seeing a bird. The dressing-room was too small; Lila still with the wings of her part, but without the words. How was the performance? he asked, in order to hear her voice. Only the voice was Lila. Then she had to go on stage again; they were still clapping. Demonstratively. As though to let the blind Gantenbein know how beautiful the woman he loves is. It was like that every evening. He was proud, of course, and meanwhile opened the little bottle of champagne. Proud of what? At the same time, he felt superfluous. Gantenbein couldn't clap; he had been deprived of his homage. He filled her glass, that was all he could do. All applause finally peters out, and then Lila was glad of his love, she drank her champagne, Lila at the make-up table, while Gantenbein sat in the one and only comfortable armchair, equipped with his dark glasses. He saw her clean herself with cottonwool, Lila in a silk dressing-gown, Gantenbein with his little black stick. Thus he sat in her dressing-room, blind but present. Lila as always after a performance: relaxed, excited, absent-minded. She didn't hear the knock, and the gentleman who walked in, without waiting long for an answer, seemed to know that Gantenbein was blind; he didn't even nod. As though Gantenbein were not in the dressing-room, were not present. He might have been the theatre director, this gentleman who considered himself above good manners. A gentleman at the end of the prime of life. Since Lila didn't see him, because she had just closed her eyes to wipe the greasepaint from her lids, Gantenbein said: I think there was a knock at the door. But Lila didn't hear any knocking and the gentleman, convinced that Gantenbein couldn't see him, stood still, while Lila threw the greasy cottonwool into the wastepaper basket, more and more prepared for a conversation with Gantenbein. Busy with her fingers, which she wiped on a little cloth, she asked where they were going to eat and simply didn't notice that there was another man present in the dressing-room. What had he, Gantenbein, been doing during the day? One might have thought the other man had come to take a revolver out of his pocket and fire at Lila, an emotionally unbalanced man, mute, as though his silence rendered him invisible to Gantenbein; perhaps he only wanted to talk to Lila. Just the two of them. He was pale, unshaven, haggard. Gantenbein still had no idea where they could eat and silently stroked the dog; Patsch was restless, alert. All this didn't take a minute, nevertheless it was endless. Only when Lila leaned forward to the mirror, examining her temples, did she start in dismay, and her thin fingers, which were about to rub her temples, went rigid at the sight of the man in the mirror. She recognized him. Lila too didn't utter a word, in order to leave him invisible. Her face, which Gantenbein saw, left no doubt: so this was the man whom on that occasion Gantenbein didn't see. Now he had no hat on his head. And to show now that he isn't blind and understands the situation would have been perfidious. So he stroked the dog. Silence on his part too would have given him away; he now made

284

suggestions as to where they should eat, Gantenbein the only one talking. When Lila turned round the man had left not merely the mirror, but also the dressing-room. Without a word. His entry, comical at the time, seemed afterwards rather sinister. Gantenbein couldn't ask: Who was that? Moreover, he knew, and Lila seemed also to know the meaning of this visit. He felt sorry for her; she was pale with fear. But Gantenbein couldn't think of anything to say; after all, he had also had a fright of his own, which he had to conceal. What this man, the other man, wanted was pretty clear: he wanted his Lila back. His! That was what made him look so grim, only that wordless claim in his eyes, so that one was prepared for a revolver and hence as bewildered as the man himself. Certainly Lila had never seen him like that before. She now stood up, still pale with fright, and locked her dressing-room door, whereupon Gantenbein, to distract her, told her about another escapade of Patsch's, a new one, just as much of an invention as all the others, which didn't prevent Patsch from wagging his tail with pride; but in vain, Lila grew more and more rigid, probably at the thought that the man might be waiting for her at the stage door, hidden in the dark back yard. It was possible. And yet he certainly hadn't a revolver; he only looked as if he had; he hadn't come to shoot her but to marry her. Too late. When there was a knock at the door, Lila wouldn't unlock it; Gantenbein had to do it. And he did it too, welcoming the opportunity to prove himself a man. It was only the dresser; she handed over a note, which Lila immediately tore open and read, but then did not stick it into the frame of her mirror. When her false hair had finally been removed, she observed Gantenbein, as though for the first time doubting his blindness, uncertain whether he had really seen nothing, now in her own hair and beautiful, manifestly moved by the note, released from the fear that somebody was lying in wait for her in the back yard. And later they went to dine, Lila and Gantenbein, who took her trout apart for her as always. And later they went home. Unmolested. And when Gantenbein enquired casually whether she had ever heard again from her former friend, she said frankly that he had come back, yes, he was in the town. She had seen him but not spoken to him. Her answer sounded as unimportant as his question, and what Lila concealed, her confusion, he saw. . .

I understand:

The time comes to leave someone, a decision is a decision and unshakeable, but this doesn't mean that the parting has been carried out; one would like to carry it out with dignity, but the dignity prevents it from being carried out at all; one of the two partners can't take the situation in so long as dignity is maintained, and loves as never before; one evening he is standing there again; a parting cannot be carried out by post – when finally there was no way of avoiding it, Gantenbein was full of silent understanding for their need to see each other again. . .

That was February.

Lila at the make-up table (this time before the performance) made her disclosure almost jokingly, without turning round, waiting alert but relaxed for the bell to summon her onto the stage, not jumpy, only no longer capable of embarking on a conversation, not absent-minded, on the contrary, ready for her entry, a casual disclosure as she put the last dab of powder on her nose, in short without turning round, without looking to see who happened to be sitting in the one and only comfortable armchair now, jokingly: there was no need to grow solemn or get scared on that account, her periods were often irregular. – Then the bell rang. . . Lila was thirty-one at the time, no inexperienced girl, nor was Gantenbein a boy who finds himself for the first time confronted by certain questions. But eventually they would have to discuss it, he thought, thoroughly. But after that performance, after Gantenbein had been for his walk with Patsch, and also on the following day, Lila seemed not to give the matter another thought. Why should Gantenbein give it a thought? But he did, not in dismay and for instants almost cheerful as he wondered what sort of mother Lila would be, and he was surprised that for three days she didn't say a word about it, for four days. Her unconcern was captivating, but not catching. A thought, thought in a flash recently in the dressing-room, had

286

till now allowed itself to be repressed, a calendar thought, and in the event of all thoughts proving pointless, Gantenbein wished that he had never thought this particular thought. Lila remained unconcerned, he could see that, she was blissfully happy in the expectation of the unique rôle next autumn. When Gantenbein once asked the date on a pretext (rent), it was March; Lila was dismayed because the rent was due, and altogether: how time flies. This was in a restaurant, Lila in décolleté with candlelight and pearls, laughing: What would you say if we really had a child? The restaurant was naturally not the place to believe in it; the head waiter was pressing, even if at a polite distance, for the order. There followed a silent nibbling of rolls. The suspicion that she wanted to bring a child into the world without ever telling Gantenbein was of course nonsense; in the fifth month even a blind man would notice it. The restaurant was simply not the place to talk about it. Even his suggestion that Lila should go to the doctor was felt to be improper, and the atmosphere became tense in spite of the glimmer of candles.

From then on Gantenbein was silent too.

Among their friends she had once said that if ever she wanted a child she wouldn't care who the father was! – as a retort to a race fanatic and as such understandable, at that moment quite right; people say so many things that are right at the moment – Gantenbein didn't want to think any more about it. . . Lila made the announcement at a moment when he really wasn't thinking about it, three minutes before the guests were due:

"We're going to have a child."

Gantenbein was silent with amazement.

"I went to see the doctor –"

The bell rang as though on a cue. The guests! And a miracle happened: the calendar thought, of which Gantenbein was ashamed, really didn't fit, Gantenbein blindly rejoiced as he greeted guests who naturally imagined that they were the cause of his exuberant mood; not all of them had met Herr Gantenbein before, he saw their embarrassment at being introduced to a blind man. . . This was the occasion on which she first related the wonderful story of how Gantenbein came into her dressing-room with roses. . . Next morning, woken as though his skull had been split with an axe, Gantenbein no longer remembered the evening, only the news about the child, and it was fortunate that Lila had rehearsals at the time and had just gone out; otherwise he might have asked whether she had slept with the other man in February. What then? Perhaps she would have said: Yes. Without hesitating, simply: Yes. Or hesitated and after a silence, when the silliness of his question had penetrated him, as she lit a cigarette: Why do you ask? Even then it might be Gantenbein's child; the question is simply whether, after this question, Lila would still want him as the father of her child; perhaps she would never again say: our child. It would remain her child. . . So Gantenbein lay there, woken as though his skull had been split with an axe, and since he was alone in the house the question remained unasked. . . Perhaps she might have said: No. Not without hesitation, but then simply: No. And for the future it would have been hardly better, a relief at the moment, but his relief would have been repulsive to her, she wouldn't want to kiss the father of her child after such a disappointment, perhaps after this the child would not have come into the world. . . So it was lucky. . . There is just one thing: Gantenbein assumes that the child, her child, is not by him, but never shows that he assumes this, in the hope that it will become his child.

I imagine:

Lila would now deny ever having uttered her understandable retort to the race fanatic on that occasion.

I imagine:

Beatrice in the bath, six years old, Gantenbein as Daddy who is soaping her, her little body, her chaste skin, above all this skin, curls full of soap foam, her Daddy can't see where Beatrice is now hiding her foot, but then he catches them after all, her tickly toes and soaps them too, Gantenbein in shirtsleeves, which he also has to roll up, of course it's never Beatrice who splashes the water about, but Krisimisi who splishes and sploshes about in the bath, it's Krisimisi who tickles Daddy and hides the soap, invisible to Daddy, Krisimisi is the witch's husband, and Krisimisi only obeys when Beatrice talks to him, then the splashing stops, then Gantenbein can soap her childish back and her childish bottom, even her ears, her armpits, only she must never give away to a blind man what Krisimisi looks like, then again Beatrice would like her Daddy to see her terrible gash, and Gantenbein does see it, the tiny scratch on her knee, keeps the soap away from it and will powder and bandage it with reverence, only he can't see the Krisimisi, even when he takes off his glasses because of the steam, and because Gantenbein can't see him the Krisimisi isn't frightened when he scolds or issues warnings, and there is no end to the splishing and sploshing, till finally Gantenbein lets out the water in order to give her a shower, her curls full of soap foam, her little arms and thighs gleaming with soap, her little body altogether, no, that isn't going to be a sailor, oh no, that's definitely going to be a girl, Beatrice, quite definitely, wearing braces and putting her hands in her trousers pockets and thrusting her elbows forward won't help, nor will acrobatic feats on the edge of the bath, now she jumps down onto the mat, Daddy should have seen that, and as she lets herself be rubbed dry by his strong hand, wrapped up in the white bath towel and quite still for a while in order to enjoy it to the full, she suddenly asks: Is it true, Daddy, that you can't see anything at all? And presently, to test it out, her assertion: I can fly! which Daddy, blind as he is, cannot doubt, so he has to believe it and let go of her so that Beatrice can say: Can't you see me flying? And after he has thought for the space of a glance that perhaps Beatrice really isn't his child, and as he lifts her up with arms outstretched, her jubilant cry: You see! Her jubilant cry: Can't you see me? Her jubilant cry –

I imagine:

Beatrice, ten years old, falls off her bicycle, brain haemorrhage, a whole night long the fear that she might die, the shared fear of mother and father, this fear with open eyes that weep –

I imagine:

Gantenbein isn't a bad father, once he has begun increasingly to abandon his urge to educate the child – compelled to abandon it by his rôle as a blind man. . . When Beatrice simply doesn't do what she just doesn't feel like doing, hoping that Gantenbein can't see, for example whether her clothes have been hung on a hanger or are still lying around, and if Gantenbein, less concerned about the clothes than about the child, who in his opinion must eventually learn to do what she doesn't feel like doing just at the moment, asks in the evening if she has hung up her clothes, unfortunately seeing that she hasn't, well, what then? If Lila, as the mother, then likewise plays blind and says nothing, in order at all costs to be on the side of the child and to prevent any disciplinary measures – it takes years before Gantenbein sees that it is impossible to educate a child if the mother doesn't want it to be educated, and until he has mastered his part as a blind man in relation to the child as well and allowed himself to be deceived over a thousand trifles, so as to be a nice Daddy, free from all desire to educate and ready to come to Beatrice's aid when life itself disciplines her.

That happens.

That happens and is forgotten between one occasion and the next, when his help succeeds, yes, but a father is not a magician; a slight paralysis of the eyelids resulting from disobedient behaviour during measles remains incurable; a case of missed discipline, a slight case of guilt, one of many, but guilt creates fatherly love, and Gantenbein can no longer imagine life without a child –

Beatrice is not an anecdote.

The time of child's drawings is past and fatherly love can no longer be demonstrated by hoppity-hop piggy-backs. This was over and done with long ago. Beatrice is struggling with Latin, accusative and infinitive, love finds itself confronted by tasks that are an effort for Gantenbein too. All the things that are demanded of our children and of their fathers! In order to be able to act as though he knew blindly everything he had once learnt at school, he has to go to school again in secret, while Beatrice herself is at school and not paying attention. And algebra! A mature man would have thought he could extract roots, yet would you believe it, he has to learn all over again, a man with grey temples faced with an equation with one unknown, with two unknowns, with three unknowns and so on.

I imagine:

One day, a particularly fine and very blue day they are coming back from an outing, Lila at the wheel, on edge, a stream of traffic, and Lila has to be at the airport at seven to meet someone, someone, Gantenbein doesn't ask questions, someone who is coming alone and might be disappointed if there is no one to meet him at the airport, the more so as he is coming specially to see Lila about a professional matter, something to do with a film presumably, so it's her private affair, Gantenbein understands, Gantenbein with his dark glasses, so that he can't have seen the open telegram (yesterday), knows who is going to land at seven twenty, so he doesn't ask, and now it's six o'clock already, but a stream of traffic is a stream of traffic, Lila is in despair, time, it's always time, there won't be time to take Gantenbein and the child home and then drive out to the airport, it's impossible, poor Lila at the wheel, someone will be very disappointed, especially as Lila has invited him, a catastrophe. Gantenbein suggests a crafty short cut, that's to say not home, but straight out to the airport, Lila goes silent, no, that's impossible, why impossible, that would mean that Lila wouldn't be waiting at the airport alone, but a Lila with husband and child, family style, someone would be bound to be disappointed, and if Gantenbein doesn't understand this, no, but Gantenbein does understand, Gantenbein insists on the short cut, Gantenbein meanly cheerful with his pipe in his mouth, and Lila stops before the short cut. That's impossible, she says, I can't do that! – as though she doubts that Gantenbein is blind, and Gantenbein takes the child and gets out, if you please, in the middle of the road, someone behind hoots –

As regards Siebenhagen:

291

Who knows whether he too sleeps with Lila or used to sleep with her when he still had a little beard, friends may know, but they don't gossip, perhaps they've all slept with her at some time or other, with the exception of Burri, who knows? And what if they have! Gantenbein shrugs his shoulders. He's sick of the question where Lila sleeps and where she doesn't, of the question as such. And what if they have! All deference to her secrets, but it makes no odds whether Herr Siebenhagen has too or not. He may have, but not necessarily. And who really knows, not Gantenbein anyhow, friends perhaps, but perhaps they're all mistaken.

What's certain is the child.

BEATRICE.

Later (but perhaps it will never come to that now) they are sitting in a café, father and daughter, who is now a young lady and in trouble; it's no great disaster that has to be discussed, failure at school, a bit of bad luck, they must think over other possible schools, bad luck with pastries, while Gantenbein smokes, not without pride that he is in the world through this glorious creature who has done badly at school and needs his help and is eating pastries as she waits for it. Who hasn't failed at some time in his life? Gantenbein with his dark glasses: he sees his old hand on the table as in close-up, while he hears himself talking as a father who would also like to be understood, who is begging for comradeship while Beatrice is enjoying herself with cream, she whom he thinks he has to console by telling her of his own shipwrecks, which only bores the child. She is a child, seventeen, that's to say in full possession of her intelligence but at the same time free from experience, consequently silent with her pastry; only the involuntary twitching of the corners of her mouth and sometimes the flickering of her eyes betrays her impatience at hearing all these things that one takes for granted, for example that a woman needs to train for a profession in order to be independent, all sorts of things one takes for granted. Why these involved examples? We are never interested in other people's shipwrecks; Beatrice doesn't need reassurance, she needs his signature and the money for a better school; her demand is clear and simple, not a demand for comradeship and there is no point in a father, in order to win friendship, talking about his own life and his serious mistakes; the child sees them anyhow, smiling as she looks out at the park. What is he after? His signature and pastries, that's all she wants from him. How could it ever occur to a child, however kind-hearted, that its father also has his misery? That's his affair. Like everyone whose turn it still is, he belongs to the past, and the present is not the father with the daughter, but the daughter. A nice thing that would be, a father who didn't help! He talks much too much after giving his signature. Beatrice is right, he sees that through the smoke of his pipe or cigar, her smile light and cool, her blush over her father who needs friendship – at last Gantenbein calls the waiter and pays; out in the park waits her boy friend who takes her arm. . .

Oh my child.

She will go her own way. . .

Our child!

Late one evening (what were they talking about that rendered this superfluous information unavoidable?) Burri says someone told him Siebenhagen said Lila said a woman always knows who the real father of her child is, she herself knew quite definitely, Lila according to Siebenhagen, according to someone whom Siebenhagen told –

Gossip!

For a moment, I could imagine, Gantenbein feels this is the end; to be sure, he has always assumed that it is so, but he didn't expect that she would lay bare the mystery surrounding Beatrice, which she has maintained in front of him and which he too has maintained, to a third person (Siebenhagen) – for a moment, then he doesn't say a word.

He has none to say.

("Betrayal"?)

Her face the same as ever. . .

See her face!

Her face knows nothing. . .

Gossip!

Perhaps Burri too is a gossip.

What next?

Gantenbein at the airport: one might imagine that this happens every day, once every week at least, Gantenbein at the airport and always in this same hall, leaning on his black stick waiting to meet Lila with his dark glasses; and yet it doesn't happen once every week, Gantenbein knows, it just seems like it, seems as if he had spent all his life standing as he is standing now, all his life at the airport and in this hall and at exactly this spot, waiting to meet Lila all his life long. . . as today, as always: Gantenbein at the kiosk until it is time for the dark glasses, and then he goes onto the terrace to follow the landing of all sorts of planes from other places, and then: delayed because of fog in Hamburg, Gantenbein hears the announcement long before the loudspeakers crackle and splutter and then reverberate, and afterwards, when the announcement in three languages has been drowned in its own echo and re-echo, Gantenbein suddenly doesn't know: was it today, this announcement about fog, or was it the last time? And he has to enquire at the information desk whether the deafening loudspeakers he has just heard were real, or merely the loudspeakers of his memory – which really makes no difference to his waiting. . . Waiting is easier for Patsch, the dog; he doesn't wait, he is a dog with ears pricked up, he sniffs around, the present in front of him all the way from his nose to his tail, a dog without time, a dog all the time, he goes up to a greyhound bitch who is far too big for him, whom he forgets as soon as his master attaches him to the lead required by the regulations, forgets and stretches himself on the floor, without being bored.

A dog is lucky.

Bored by his thoughts, which he knows like the jerking of the hand of the clock, Gantenbein wanders to and fro, glad of the pattern on the floor that divides up the time, eager not for Lila, but eager to see whether he can always strike the grooves between the squares of the flooring with his little black stick; wandering as slowly as possible, because the faster he wanders the slower time passes, and according to the information desk it will be at least another forty minutes before he will see Lila, Lila with her bags and magazines as always, all his life. What is time? A pattern in the flooring, an idea: the faster Gantenbein walks, the slower the plane will fly, and he starts with fright; as everyone knows, aeroplanes need a minimum speed in order not to fall out of the clouds; what is carrying Lila is his patience, the strength of a man who waits slowly, wanders slowly, slowly, step by step, slowly to, slowly fro, waits slowly all his life like the hands of the clock.

(Must I also invent Siebenhagen now?)

Lila has landed, and lo and behold Lila is alone, loaded with coat and handbag and magazines, absolutely alone.

What has happened?

No gentleman helps her through customs –

What need is there now for the blind marriage?

No gentleman walks past Gantenbein without greeting him – I mean, everyone walks past Gantenbein, but there is no one among them who exploits the husband's blindness. . . Gantenbein very nearly waves. When Lila comes through the barrier, her kiss as always. Then arm-in-arm as always. Only Gantenbein is different, silent, while Lila acts as though everything were the same as always. What confuses him: no change in her face. He takes her heavy coat and the bags. As always. But without speaking. There is nothing about her face to show that she isn't lying, that she isn't keeping anything secret. Her face is as open as always. In the car, as he still doesn't say anything, she asks with concern what is the matter with Gantenbein. For her part she tells him the things she always tells him in the way she always tells them; except that now it is the plain truth. Doesn't he believe her? He carries her luggage as always. And when they are sitting facing each other: her joy as always, her joy at being home again. Isn't Gantenbein glad? He is astonished. For years Gantenbein has pretended to believe in her joy at being home again, and only now does he see how perfect her acting was, exactly like the present reality. That is perhaps what renders him speechless. She sits on his knee as always. For the first time he doesn't stroke her hair, although it is the same as always; instead Gantenbein gets up on the pretext of being thirsty. It's impossible. How can he be thirsty now, and even if he were! There he stands drinking water.

Lila isn't deceiving him.

For these circumstances he has no rôle.

"Lila," he says –

"What's the matter?" she asks.

And when Gantenbein takes off his glasses – he doesn't do so violently, as he has done in the past, nor does he do it so as to rub his eyeballs with the balls of his thumbs and afterwards put the glasses back on again, but differently from ever before: he is doing it for the last time – he smiles or thinks he smiles; yet he merely has no face any more.

"What's the matter?" she asks.

"Lila," he says –

"Say something," she says, "please, I don't know what's the matter, I really don't know."

I imagine:

When the scene is suddenly there, which Gantenbein has imagined a thousand times and in all sorts of different ways, the reality takes him by surprise at first by its utter emptiness. At first he shakes his head. But of course Lila wants to know what he is concealing. And when Gantenbein, although he has no urge to speak, slowly puts into words what he has been concealing for years, it is really nothing. He actually has to rack his brains; he doesn't throw away the glasses which henceforth he won't need, nor does he put them in his pocket, but holds them and looks at them like a left-over, a souvenir, and when he remembers things that upset him on this occasion or that, they're all trifles, really not worth mentioning. . . Well, really it is a declaration of love, he thinks, that he is uttering tranquilly and gaily: that he has seen and so on and probably doesn't know everything that has been going on for years, but quite a lot, though nothing precise, and now he

296

doesn't want to know anything precise any more, and that he has been acting too. . .

The end:

(brief, out of proportion)

Go! she says, taking a cigarette and then lighting it, while I ask what in heaven's name has happened. All these years! she says and smokes. What have I said? Previously she was sobbing, now she merely says, Go! smoking. What does she mean, I've been deceiving her? People talk about someone's hair standing on end. But that really happens, I can see it, her hair is standing on end. Did Lila really believe I was blind? So this is the end. Why actually? In vain I ask forgiveness for having seen various things. All these years! she says. You never loved me, now I know and now I want you to go, go away!, smoking, then yelling: Go away!

The awakening (as though all this had never happened) proves to be a deception; something has always happened, but differently.

One day I shall be interrogated.

"Well then," says someone whom it doesn't concern, and there are just the two of us, "what actually happened in your life that is coming to an end?"

I say nothing.

"A man loves a woman," he says. "This woman loves another man," he says. "The first man loves another woman, who in turn is loved by another man," he says and comes to the conclusion: "a very ordinary story that breaks up in all directions —"

I nod.

"Why don't you say fairly and squarely," he asks with his last remnant of patience, "which of the two men you are yourself?"

I shrug my shoulders.

"The investigation has revealed," he says, not without a threatening undertone, "that there is no person by the name of Camilla Huber, for example, any more than there is a gentleman named Gantenbein —"

"I know."

"What you are telling us is a lot of inventions."

"What I experience is a lot of inventions."

"True," he says, "but what really happened in this time and at the places where you have been?"

I close my eyes.

"Why don't you answer?"

I remain silent.

"You forget, my friend, that there are witnesses."

Thereupon he opens the door, I hear it, and when I hear the tip-tap of pointed heels I open my eyes again to see what is going on —

I see:

Remains of burgundy in a bottle, I know what that's like, little islands of mould on the red wine, also remains of bread as hard as brick, in the refrigerator dried-up ham is curling, in a bowl floats the murky residue of stewed fruit, apricot mud, viaticum for a mummy, I know, I sit there in coat and hat, the place smells of camphor, dust, floor polish, the carpets are rolled up and I am sitting on the back of an easy chair playing with a corkscrew, don't know what has happened, all the easy chairs are covered with white cloths, I know what that's like, shutters closed, all doors open, there is no need for me to get up, I know what it's like —

I'm blind. I don't always know it, but sometimes I do. Then I begin to doubt again and wonder whether the stories I can imagine aren't my life after all. I don't think so. I can't believe that what I see is the way of the world.

A story for Camilla:

(after the canton policeman has been)

"There must be law and order," I say. "Years ago they had a case that made them very jumpy. Here in the town. Suddenly there was a man who didn't even want to leave a name behind, let alone a story. All that was known about this individual was that he must have lived, this was proved by his corpse which they found one morning in the Limmat — one very beautiful morning, I remember,

I was just crossing the Helmhausbrücke to feed the swans there. At the time there was a big willow growing there, perhaps it's still there, a weeping willow in the enclosure for ducks and swans that let its long branches trail in the green Limmat, leaves in rustling garlands, an idyll with ducklings as colourful as if made of glazed paper, and also the white dignity of the swans, above it the Grossmünster, Charlemagne with seagulls on his crown, the eleven o'clock chimes. . . well, that's where he had got caught up. They wouldn't have found him for ages, perhaps never, if the floats supporting the duck grating hadn't rusted with the years. A matter for the Waterworks Department, or the Gardens Department, anyhow the rusty floats under the swan house had to be replaced. When they pulled up the rotten planks to get at the silted-up floats, and saw the silted-up corpse, they immediately stopped work and informed the police, who soon afterwards rowed up with a green skiff during the eleven o'clock chimes that last ten minutes – they're among my earliest memories, these chimes; they sound best, I find, when you're strolling over the Helmhausbrücke, then all the towers across the river join in. . . Perhaps that was why the corpse had got caught up just there. Of course I wasn't the only one who now wanted to see what was going on. The two policemen in their green skiff with the municipal coat of arms, one plying the sweep, the other armed with a long pole, both in uniform and helmets as though about to make an arrest, seemed rather nervous, stared at by so many people on the bridge, and for a long time nothing happened. Eleven o'clock chimes. Know-alls up above at the balustrade said the corpse could be fished out with one hearty heave, because everyone knew now that it was a corpse and the public, it seemed, had a right to know who this corpse was. But the corpse was wedged between the rusty floats. The less happened the more exciting it became, meanwhile the eleven o'clock chimes had died away and something simply had to happen, even if not for the sake of the corpse, to which hours no longer made any difference. Obviously there was no other way of setting about it: the policeman with the pole, advised by the other one, who had his work cut out to keep the boat steady against the current by working his long oar, poked about between the rusted and silted-up floats, not bearing in mind that the corpse, once released from the position in which it had been wedged for years, would immediately float off downstream. This was what happened, and the spectators on the bridge were the losers by it. Something, a corpse, drifted along, slowly, but as if it still had a will of its own, in fact a very resolute will: to escape. By the time the skiff had been swung round with skilful strokes of the sweep and was able to take up the chase, it had a start of several yards. Face downwards, motionless naturally, not helping itself along with its arms, it swam as though this was what it had been waiting for all the time, downstream, now accompanied by the skiff with the municipal arms that rocked precariously under the vigorous strokes of the oar. And yet it was obvious to any native of the city that the pursuit could continue only as far as the Urania-Brücke; no skiff can pass under that. A few spectators ran off along the Limmat, didn't run actually, but walked as fast as they possibly could. Most of them, however, in order to preserve the dignity of the city, didn't do this but went on their way as though nothing had happened, dignified like the swans that had spread their wings and now folded them again, nonchalantly swimming. Meanwhile the corpse did not get far. When it reached the Gemüse-Brücke, with its many piers, it got caught up again and the current turned it over, face uppermost. It was a man. A few flower-sellers, who have their stalls here, saw the putrefied face; the police, who happen to have a station just there, were on the spot immediately and in sufficient numbers to divert pedestrians, and at least on the bridge they were masters of the situation, not without attracting attention, naturally, the people here didn't know what was going on, and questions were not answered, and it looked as though it was something to do with the flower stalls. But there was nothing noticeably wrong with the flower stalls. It looked as though it was suddenly illegal to buy flowers in Zürich. And again nothing happened for a long time. A police inspector soon appeared to take charge of further action, but the order he gave after examining the position took time to carry out. He smoked a Rössli-Stumpen, waiting, in plain clothes. The corpse was in such a condition that if they had dragged it by the limbs it would scarcely have surrendered itself in one piece. By now it was midday, rush-hour, only the corpse was in no hurry; face uppermost, deaf to the noise of the traffic, it let the Limmat flow past its beards of mud forming little gurgling whirlpools, and it seemed to have abandoned all thought of flight. But the police inspector, a careful man, nevertheless had a guard put on it, while he chewed rather than smoked his *stumpen*; the skiff was now tied up to an iron pier, likewise encircled by the gurgling whirlpools of the current, a pole's length from the entangled corpse, and the policeman was keeping an official eye on it. It was a warm midday, August. The corpse was wearing a winter coat, gloves, but no hat. Once the policeman took off his helmet, wiped out the sweat and put it back on again, always prepared. More than anything, it seemed, the corpse would have liked simply to sink, but only the head succeeded in doing so. At this point the black car drove up with a coffin. Now there was something for the curious to see in spite of the cordon: a coffin, raw pine wood. When the moment came to attach ropes to this coffin, the police inspector himself took a hand. The plan became clear: to introduce the corpse into the coffin underwater. The corpse must be terribly putrefied, terribly slimy, and the two policemen with the municipal cockade in their helmets, who were to bail it out with the coffin so to speak, had an unenviable task. It took a long time after the coffin had been lowered on four ropes, and the curious, held in check, only saw the police inspector giving his instructions from the bridge, as though there were nothing to it, matter-of-fact, at first without excitement, later shaking his head; the corpse seemed not to be obeying his instructions. When the curious, some of them already irritated because the mute policemen still refused to answer questions, finally heard a cry, a brief cry, no one knew what had happened; some might have laughed. The police inspector merely shook his head without a word, and shortly afterwards they saw an empty helmet floating off down the green Limmat, followed by the

301

coffin with the corpse in it, followed by the skiff with the sturdy oarsman alone, while the other policeman, who had fallen into the water in uniform and boots, was swimming across to the landing-stage, taking no further part in the proceedings. The skiff could achieve nothing more either; the escort which it gave the slowly drifting coffin ended at the Urania-Brücke, as anticipated. After that the coffin floated alone, sometimes feet first, sometimes head first, as though trying out which was more comfortable for a long voyage. At the same time it drifted over to the right, so that presently it knocked into the river-wall, several times in fact, and threatened to overturn; this happened near the Bahnhofbrücke, where no one noticed it at first. Not everyone looks down over the railings, if he doesn't see any policemen. While the cordon, although super-fluous, was still being maintained on the Gemüse-Brücke, here there were no police whatever, and the corpse had a rest, especially as the river-wall is rather high at this point; they could see it rocking in the coffin but couldn't get at it. After banging into the wall several times, the coffin began to list; one arm was hanging out. A traffic policeman, who had been called down from his stand, could do nothing about it; he took off his white gloves, manifestly waiting eagerly himself to see what he would do after that, and in fact he did nothing. A lot of people turned away. It seems that it was above all the hand that horrified them, because it moved in the water, even if only slightly and every now and then, but it did move. Only the traffic policeman, his white gloves in his fist, didn't turn away, as though he owed it to his uniform to stand firm. His deci-sion to ring the main police station and make a report was the only sensible one; the corpse itself seemed to be waiting for this. But no sooner had the traffic policeman gone to make a call from a public telephone, than a swirl in the current was enough to set the coffin in motion again. Without overturning. In a gentle curve it found the opening under the station and came out on the other side of this bridge without a hitch and head first; now it was head first all the time; it had stopped turning round, it looked resolute and seemed, here by the government buildings, to increase its speed, as though determined to reach the sea this very day. Whether anyone in the government buildings happened to be looking out of the window, I don't know. It brushed up against a pier of the new Walche-Brücke, but this didn't hold it up for long; it merely turned round once, without heeling over, and floated on past the summer-green park of the Swiss National Museum, now listing to the opposite side and once more feet first, rocking from side to side but irresistibly, and it really looked as though Zürich were not going to be able to hold it – Zürich, which returned to the order of the day: the swans nonchalantly white under the weeping willow by the Helmhaus, high above, the gulls on Charlemagne's crown, instead of the eleven o'clock chimes the time signal now echoed from Beromünster, the cordon on the Gemüse-Brücke was removed, the skiff chained to its buoy, the traffic policeman on his stand was once more beckoning with white gloves. . . It was a mother with a pram who later reported it, under pressure from her husband, who thought it had to be reported; she found him by the so-called Draht-Schmiedli, the wire-smithy, where there is a weir that must have surprised him: the open coffin was standing pretty well vertical out of the gurgling water with the corpse leaning back in it."

Camilla made an oooh face.

"Yes," I say, "that's how it was."

"Horrible!"

"And yet he nearly did it," I say, glancing at my finger nails which are once more in order, "almost –"

"Did what?"

"Floated away without a story."

Everything as if it had never happened. . . It is a day in September, and when we come up into the light again out of the gloomy and not at all cool tombs, we blink, so bright is the day; I see the red clods of the ploughed field above the tombs, far-off and dark the autumn sea, midday, everything is the present, wind in the dusty thistles, I hear the notes of a flute, those are not Etruscan

303

flutes in the tombs, however, but wind in the wires, under the flickering shade of an olive tree stands my car grey with dust and burning hot, snake-heat in spite of the wind, but once more September: but the present, and we sit at a table in the shade and eat bread, until the fish has been grilled, I reach out with my hand for the bottle, to test whether the wine (Verdicchio) is also cold, thirst, then hunger, life appeals to me –